SOMEONE ELSE'S GARDEN

Someone Else's Garden

DIPIKA RAI

Harper
Press

Harper*Press*
An imprint of HarperCollins*Publishers*
77–85 Fulham Palace Road
Hammersmith, London W6 8JB
www.harpercollins.co.uk

Visit our authors' blog: www.fifthestate.co.uk
Love this book? www.bookarmy.com

First published by Harper*Press* in 2011

A catalogue record for this book
is available from the British Library

This novel is entirely a work of fiction. The names, characters and incidents portrayed
in it are the work of the author's imagination. Any resemblance to actual persons,
living or dead, events or localities is entirely coincidental.

ISBN 978-0-00-735509-9

Typeset in Minion by Palimpsest Book Production Limited,
Falkirk, Stirlingshire

Printed and bound in Great Britain by
Clays Ltd, St Ives plc

Mixed Sources
Product group from well-managed
forests and other controlled sources
www.fsc.org Cert no. SW-COC-001806
© 1996 Forest Stewardship Council

FSC is a non-profit international organisation established to promote the responsible
management of the world's forests. Products carrying the FSC label are independently
certified to assure consumers that they come from forests that are managed to meet
the social, economic and ecological needs of present or future generations.

Find out more about HarperCollins and the environment at
www.harpercollins.co.uk/green

For Indira so she might remember
&
Shaan and Tara so they might know

The Sky is for Dreaming

1

People are defined by what they love and what they hate.

Lata Bai loves the sound of a cycle's bell. She loves the rain. She hates having yet another baby.

She neither knows nor cares that somewhere the world has celebrated a new millennium, she only knows that another baby will make it seven in all. This time, after the first three weeks, she'll give it to Sneha, her youngest daughter to look after. It really should be Mamta's turn, but, with her getting married soon, her mind should be on other things. Mamta's father was too hasty with her. He is determined to marry her off soon after the baby is born: as soon as Lata Bai can look after the marriage preparations, is how he puts it. Almost twenty, so old and still unmarried, Mamta's very presence serves as a reminder of his failure.

Lata Bai's face contorts with the first birth pains. After six children, she can tell exactly when it starts and when it will finish. Only her first had taken her by surprise, but she was strong then at fifteen, and had managed just fine, cutting the cord with her husband's betel-leaf knife. She'd even cooked his meal that very evening.

'When?' Mamta is excited, almost too excited about her impending wedding; her world consists almost entirely of *whens*. She helps her mother change into her oldest sari, one she can cut into rags for the forty-day bleeds.

'Soon,' says Lata Bai, taking off her only bangle, more precious than

anything else she owns, and hiding it in the pot of ash she saves both for her bath and her utensils. 'Shsh,' she says, 'tell no one. Just in case I die, my spirit will know where to look for it. And don't you dare pinch it!'

Lata Bai extracts her daughter's wedding sari from the tin trunk. Luckily Seeta Ram bought it last week, and she can deliver the baby on its crisp, clean wrapping. She peels the noisy brown paper away carefully. Mamta tries to rub her hand over the precious material but her mother slaps it away and returns the sari to the tin trunk.

'Shall I come?' asks Mamta.

'No, I must do this alone,' she says. Mamta watches her mother from the doorway cautiously. She knows what is to come – another baby. 'This is what will happen to you once you're married,' says Lata Bai, using the opportunity to impart a lesson.

The thought of babies makes Mamta smile.

The same thought of babies makes Lata Bai grimace. Most women have the widow Kamla helping them, but not her. After doing her first, then second, and third all the way to the sixth herself, why waste money on an expensive midwife now? The paper rustling in her hand, she rushes to her mustard field and into the misty grey cloud that has slipped from the sky to settle close to the earth where the sun has forgotten to fall. *Oh, Devi, give me a boy.* She prays to the goddess of her clan – Devi, universal female energy, absolute divinity.

She knows her destination. With distance in her eyes she lurches away from her house towards her lucky patch of ground (the same place where she found her golden bangle, the one she's hidden in the ash). The baby's water is running down her legs. *It won't be long now.*

Careful not to crush the paper, she lies down, the furrow her pillow. *Devi, give me a boy.* She prays aloud: *Jai ho Devi, Devi jai ho.* No one hears her.

It was always a different colour.

With her first it was the green of young wheat. Green everywhere.

With her second it was yellow. Then there was another green, one gold, one white, one purple, and now again yellow.

All she can see is yellow. Dancing above her head, in her mouth, in her hair. Yellow in her ears, her toes, and, with her sari pushed up all the way to her waist, yellow on her big swollen belly. Even yellow in her navel and all the way inside her. All the way to the baby.

She knows this field intimately, suddenly in flower with the first rain. *Jai ho Devi, Devi jai ho.* She's worked it for how long? Much longer than twenty years. So long she doesn't remember. She has laughed in it and cried in it. Hidden in it and rejoiced in it. She's had all her babies in it and played with all her babies in it. It is her history. The field has watched her through her life. It watches her now. Its soul reaches out to her and its arms protect her. She feels the field's love pour over her. It sinks in through her pores and mixes with her blood, feeding every atavistic part of her with its generosity. Her field. She'd die without it.

She feels another pang.

At first she is like a cricket on its back, her arms and legs waving to the clouds above. Then she forces herself to be still. She knows she has to open like a flower. The more she holds, the more it'll hurt. But the baby doesn't come. Each time her body asks, she pushes, yet the baby doesn't come. She thinks of the bangle in the ash. Why won't the baby come? Should she shout for help? Who will hear her? Her life is pouring out of her. Great big rushes of blood. Every drop of blood that comes out of her dredges up another memory from her deepest being.

How was it? With her first, green, soon-to-be-married Mamta?

How green Mamta had hurt her coming out with a fat blob of blood. Mamta, her first born, who loves running in the wind. She loves to lie alone on the hay and hates the red birthmark over her eye.

With her second, yellow, Jivkant, it was over even before she knew it had started. Jivkant, already a man, disappeared on a train some-where. Jivkant the cruel one. How he loved the power he had over his sisters, especially Mamta. How he hated the love his father showed for Mohit, his youngest brother.

With green Prem it was again over quickly. Slow plodding Prem, sent to work in the Big House to pay off his father's debt, bringing home pats of butter each day. Being born was the quickest thing he'd ever done in his life. Prem loves the river. He loves flying his kite. He hates working the fields.

With gold Ragini there was some pain, and it took a long time, but that was the only trouble she ever gave her mother. Lucky gold Ragini with more marriage offers than any other Gopalpur girl. Ragini, hardly a woman, already married. She loves steaming her hair. She loved running her hands through her trousseau. She hates her brother-in-law accidentally brushing up against her.

White Sneha. She can't remember Sneha's birth . . . It's all a haze now. Sneha with the beautiful eyes. She loves flowers . . . wading in the river . . . but beyond that what else?

Purple Mohit. What about Mohit? . . . Nothing. She remembers nothing. He's her last born, still she doesn't remember . . . and doesn't remember. Only pain. Was it this painful with him too? All her births merge into one. Was it this one or the last one that hurt so bad? It's odd that it should be so yellow . . .

'Hey Devi, help me. Help me . . .' Prayer is her only option. It is a plea, not just for her life, but for the outcome of her pain. Devi, the mother goddess, she is a finicky one; say her prayer all wrong and you could earn her wrath for eternity. 'Hey Devi, accept your daughter. Hey Devi, save me.'

Devi knows all about suffering. Wasn't Devi herself forced to hide in the Himalayas for ten days and nine nights to escape her pursuers, living off plants and seeds, but no grain? Come those same ten days and nine nights, Lata Bai and her daughters fast diligently, living off wild berries and water. By the third the mind starts to wander among forests of fruit, mountains of crisp twisted yellow jalebis oozing syrup, and rivers of sweet creamy lassi. The fourth night is probably the worst, when the mind returns and the stomach burns. An internal fire without any fuel. How is that possible? From then on, the girls feel little. Their desires leached from them like precious salt in desert soil.

She recites her childhood prayer. It is the one memory that hasn't

4

failed her. She'll do well to placate the mother goddess. Everything lies in her eternal womb as seed. This day Lata Bai interprets the word seed literally. For herself, she asks that her seed might be pure. Uncorrupted. Whole. Male. For all those years of fasting, Devi must listen.

A long screech of pain. And then another. Another fifteen minutes and the pain becomes a slab, more blood and a huge slab of pain.

'Devi, my mother, help me.'

Was it ever this bad? The clouds float over her head. She feels herself being pulled right into them. Floating away from her colourful children; and the yellow becomes white. She is dying and that's why everything is so slow. Now the pain has gone into the clouds. It is floating away. Let me float in your arms forever, she prays.

Devi answers. Instead of taking her away somewhere peaceful, the clouds send a small, cold, stinging rain. Get up. Get up.

There is no other way.

She must stand.

She bunches her hands round the mustard plants. They come up with their roots. She would never have pulled out mustard plants by their roots on any other day. She turns to one side, her knees pressed into her chest. She vomits. A bit of grey slime trickles into her ear. She turns her head. The trickle climbs out of her ear and runs into her field. There is no white now, only pain. She is on one knee, then the other. She sits back on her heels, her bulbous belly slung low over her thighs. She can see it quiver. She takes her lumpy belly in her hands. She can feel her baby struggling to live inside.

'Hey Devi. There is nothing but you. Keep and protect your daughter.'

In that moment her pain and prayer merge to become a conduit for Devi's emotive love. She feels waves of energy flow and ebb through her like an open sea. The goddess's manifestations unfold before her: Kali, eternity, governess of all cosmic destructive power; Varahi, the perfect cycle of life, digesting the whole universe without discrimination; Aindri, pure perception, the ticket holder to heaven; Vaishnavi, preserving, sustaining, maker of the cycle of birth and death: Maheshvari, bound by none, but compassionate to all;

5

Kumari, the mother of valour; Lakshmi, benevolent, giving grace; Ishvari, pure reflection, holding authority over all universal wisdom; and Brahmi, governess of divine communication. Yes, she sees the energies, all-encompassing, governing what the eye can and cannot see. She knows why Devi must be all things to everyone. Is she herself not manifested in various forms: mother to her children, wife to her husband, friend to friend, sister to sister, daughter-in-law, worker . . . if she cannot simply be Lata Bai in her tiny world, then how can one form of the formless Devi satisfy all the longing in the universe?

Another pang, and then another. The flickering memory of a prayer learned falls into the pain and dies. She compromises, whispering the words into the earth. 'Hey Devi, there is nothing but you. Wherever I look I see only you. Pick me up, give me your strength. Jai ho Devi, Devi jai ho.' She can feel the baby's head now. It is smooth and slippery like skinned fish. She pulls and then the baby pops right out on the wedding sari wrapping.

The baby's head is filled with wet black hair, a full head of hair like a grown-up's. Its skin is slippery smooth with whitish birth cream. A baby girl waves at the clouds, at the sky, at heaven. At Devi.

Another girl. With so much blood and pain, what did she get? Another girl, her girl parts swollen just to mock the mother. The baby's body screams, Look at me, I am a girl.

The wind has started to pick up. The clouds are moving away, higher and higher. She can see the tip of a deformed electric pole miles away on the flat. They had promised electricity to Gopalpur years ago, that's when they put in the garland of poles. But it was a broken promise, producing a broken garland, stopping miles short. What the villagers haven't chipped away for firewood is going into the bellies of white ants. The last time she looked, the poles seemed to have been abandoned by the white ants too. It is a garland that won't fulfil anyone's dreams, not the insects and certainly not the humans. She can hear whimpering. The baby is alive.

How long has it been? The clouds have moved quite a distance and the wind is getting harsh. Soon there will be dust. Her body has

started to shake with cold and fatigue. She links her fingers together, trying to still their shaking.

'Devi, help me.'

Having asked for Devi's help, it is now Lata Bai's duty to show that she deserves it. What better way to show she deserves it than in receiving it? She must be renewed. She gropes for her husband's knife. Her blind hand flicks this way and that above her head. At last, the feel of metal.

She looks at the knife. It is sharp. Sharp enough to cut the cord that unites mother and baby. Certainly sharp enough to kill. When does a female baby become a human being? At conception? At birth? At five? At puberty? At marriage? Never? When her parents can offer her a life?

The baby isn't anything yet. Just blue and red and white. The white birth cream she should save. Take it off this girl and give it to the one who is getting married. It makes the skin soft. She holds the knife tight in her hand. She shifts, sending the baby rolling down the furrow, trailing cord. Grains of mud stick to the girl baby like black sesame seeds on a stick of caramel. She is on her elbows. The baby is crying – an open-mouthed full-throated cry, producing less than a trembling bleat. She can see right down the pink of her throat. What do they say about human babies? They are the most helpless creatures in the world. Calves walk within seconds of their birth. Turtle babies manage to rush to the sea and never forget where they were born. Snake babies fight with their siblings for survival. Bee babies eat their way out of their prisons. And human babies? What about howling helpless human babies? Useless-helpless-howling-human girl babies? She rolls after it, bringing the knife down swiftly and sharply.

For the rest of the world it may be the new millennium, but in Gopalpur time is static. Here the land lives quietly under the hills that rise from its dust, suddenly at ease with the sky, but shying away from the earth. The hills snare the rain that feeds the Chambal River that runs through the plains like a molten braid of silver.

It is impossible to piece together the story of these people's lives

from what the eye can see. There is nothing personal in the surroundings, except soil squares in different colours which announce the farmers' crop choices for the season. Gopalpur belongs to a shifting land of mud and dust. The villagers must rebuild their homes of reed and packed dung each time the wind has finished toying with them. The most permanent material here is wood, saved for ploughs, their most important need.

Why do they continue to live in this hostile land of hardship and starvation? Where would they go? To leave somewhere there has to be a contemplation of a different life, an image of different scenery. None of them has ever sensed such a thing. That is the obvious explanation. But the truth is, offered a better life they wouldn't move. It is because Gopalpur defines them as people. It makes sense of their existence and strengthens it with a homogenous experience. There is velocity in such experience, it is that which metamorphoses the present into the future. None of these people is chasing time, their future is not moving away from them, their future is moving closer. Towards them. Here time is not a force, it is a flow, not always benevolent, but nevertheless a flow.

The shadows lie low and long. They reach over the pale outline of the mountains like birds of prey and search out the woman who walks with difficulty, clutching her belly with one hand and a bundle of what looks like mustard plants in the other.

Lata Bai is grateful for the shadows. Her body is still cold, and there is no respite from the sandpaper wind.

The shame of a female birth has propelled her in the wrong direction, away from her house. How long has she been walking? A row of renegade bitter mustard, breaking away from some field to find a life on sandy soil of unploughed land, is her only guide.

She limps past the Red Ruins, planted on land too rocky for crops. The sandstone wall blushes like a shy bride beneath the veil of leaves and vines etched into stone like delicate embroidery on muslin. Superstition has been its saviour. There is the legend of the ghost shimmering in the lone window. No one dares take away one stone from the Red Ruins. *If I had a house like this I would return from the dead to look after it too.* Lata Bai can see the faint outline of dark

brown fingerprints plastered all over the wall, even enough to form a pattern. Everyone knows they are the hand marks of the bandit girls, abducted from their families and raped, only to fall in love with their captors. They say they come to this wall at night to break their bangles in a secret ritual when their husbands die, leaving bloody fingerprints as proof of their grief. An offering lovingly placed at the base of the wall withers accusingly under Lata Bai's careless feet.

She feels a cramp which pushes her into the ground. *Oh, Devi, all this for a girl.* The wind urges her forward. It knows its destination, having returned once again just before winter like a diligent relative on a family visit. Where it comes from no one asks, it just appears on the far mountains, rolling down the sides like a conquering horde bringing with it dust. It is said that the dust of Gopalpur can drive people mad. Like darkness, it creeps into everything – every dip, every iron-crease, every eye, under every nail, in stiff broom hair, everything.

It is now blowing with that familiar abandon that will become a storm in no time. She must get home before the storm breaks. She turns around to face the wind. Then lowers her head as if in obeisance.

Lata Bai is careful not to crush another's plants. She employs the sure tread of a peasant, and negotiates the furrows as lightly as her children play hopscotch – up, down, up, down – through the furrows, in between colours, yellows, golds and greens, thinking only of the next step.

Another cramp. She must get home. She pulls her sari low over her face. Her eyes become one with her bare feet. The gloating storm has no part of her. Her pain has distilled the untidy thoughts in her head into a single mission: keep walking.

No one sees her approach the hut. She can sense the lacy cracks that are about to spread decoratively on its packed mud walls. She must ask the girls to speed up the dung collection, it won't be long before they will have to start plastering again. She cannot see the earthenware pots, but she knows they are there, melding with their surroundings. Outside there is no sign of her family, a father and

four children, within. The children have been using the rope to skip again. It isn't coiled in its usual place, but lies discarded by the brambles like a snake's first skin. There is no smoke rising from her roof. Her daughters aren't home. She is disappointed and then angry.

Her breasts are already aching with milk. She puts the mustard plants down and washes with yesterday's well water before anyone sees her. She's pleased to see two extra pots, at least the girls remembered to bring the water from the well. Before forty days, she really should be washing away from the house, taking her impurity with her. The dust has started to swirl in manic curtains of grittiness. She enters her hut. The storm keeps pace with her thoughts, raging outside as an equally nervous storm builds inside her body. Home at last she can experience her pain at leisure.

Another girl.

Seeta Ram, the father, loves picking his teeth. He loves polished shoes. He hates delayed meals. Today the meal is delayed. With one wife and four children still at home why is the meal delayed?

'Lata, Lata. Food,' he shouts, sitting cross-legged and placing his turban carefully on the floor beside him. He's come home early to escape the storm.

'Coming,' she shouts back, annoyed that her daughters aren't home.

Lata Bai claims her bangle from the ashes. For a minute she is frightened that someone else has found it first. But it's the ash that's the thief. Reluctant to part with its treasure, it has slipped the bangle a little deeper into the pot.

She still has difficulty walking. *You give me a girl and all this pain too.* She looks at the picture of Devi, incarnated as Lakshmi the goddess of wealth, hanging above the fire, her lower lip pouting, her chin crinkling like a piece of paper. The picture swings in the wind. Back and forth, back and forth, ticking her life away. It pleases her to see the edges of the frame already black with soot. *Not all pink and gold with all four of your palms leaking money, standing coyly on your pure lotus, are you? What do you know about our lives?* She's angry. She doles out the daal, laying out the chapattis in a fan

10

alongside. She looks at the picture of the goddess again. *You'll get no lamp today.* She places a defiant dot of butter on each chapatti. The same butter that Prem has brought home from the Big House wrapped in ficus leaves. She's dedicated each of her baby girls to the goddess. The boys need no such dedication. Suddenly reluctant to offend the goddess, she offers up a token apology, 'Sorry,' she says to Lakshmi, 'today I need the butter more than you.'

She puts the tray at his feet. He doesn't look up at his wife. Her eyes don't leave the back of his head for one second.

'The talk is that Daku Manmohan is going to surrender.' What an unusual piece of information to give his wife: talk of bandits is exclusively for the men.

There are few written words in Gopalpur, and without written words, talk is all important. Thus far, the monsoon rains have had a monopoly on their words, ever present: an extra mouth at dinner, an impartial listener at the gambling tents, a secret bed-fellow at the Red Bazaar, a deep inhaler of the communal hookah . . . But rumours of the bandit chief Daku Manmohan's surrender have changed all that. It is giving the people of Gopalpur a chance to participate in someone else's life for the first time. This is a big change.

'Daku Manmohan,' says Seeta Ram, opening and closing his raised fist, flashing the invisible words in the air. 'It was always Daku Manmohan . . . Daku Manmohan. That killer! And now they say he's surrendering.'

'Nathu's daughter Sunita said that Singh Sahib's second son, Lokend Bhai, is going to bring him in. I suppose we should be thankful. This will end the raids.' For as long as they can remember, the bandits have been lodged in the river ravines more solidly than the most stubborn piece of stringy meat in a set of old teeth.

He is irritated that his wife has heard already and not from him. He still hasn't looked at her and seen the wincing pain flicker on and off her face as sudden as a streak of lightning. If she's heard, he's not going to talk any more. Let her hear everything at the well.

'Let's call her Shanti,' sticky with fear, the reluctant words drop slowly from her lips. She has to shout the name over the wind.

'Shanti!' Shanti is sleeping silently in her corner, though the wind tries its best to draw her out of her unconscious world.

Shanti! She has run out of love words. That's how she wanted to name all her children, with love words. Mamta, soft-comforting-selfless-melting mother's love. The kind of love that has staying power. The kind of love needed by her daughter, stained above the eye with a virulent birthmark. She had consulted the pundit and he'd produced the letter M for green Mamta. Jivkant, she'd had a difficult time naming him. There were no love words starting with J, and the priest wouldn't change the letter even though Lata Bai offered him twenty rupees to do so. So she had to settle for Jivkant, beloved of the world, not a true love word, but close enough. After Jivkant there were no more priests. Prem she named all by herself. Prem, kindly love that outlasts all passion, it is the best love between husband and wife. Then came Ragini, love, attachment, an apsara. A beautiful name for her beautiful daughter who fulfilled every dream she'd dreamt up for her. After Ragini it was Sneha, another girl. Sneha, tenderness, mutual attraction, gentle, warm, flowing, congenial love. Ordinary Sneha, to whom it seems as if the entire beauty quota has been appropriated by her elder sister Ragini. And finally, Mohit. Eight-year-old Mohit, falsely destined to be the last of her children. How could she have named Mohit anything else? Mohit, deep love, the kind that makes you want to cling on forever. The kind that drives you mad.

'Fix Mamta's date for next week. We will be ready then,' she adds, quickly changing the conversation to one that deals with getting rid of a daughter instead of adding one to their household.

He is not beguiled. 'Not another girl,' he says.

'We must accept what God gives us.'

You can't say that Seeta Ram hates talking about God, but it's somewhere up there with delayed meals. He looks at his wife. 'Don't talk to me about God,' he says. The hut is pummelled by more wind just as thunder takes over their world, proof that the gods immediately recognise irreverence.

Her children run in giggling and laughing. For them the storm has become a source of fun. Sneha and Mohit will go shower in the

rain. No one asks after the baby. A birth of a child is a natural event, like the wind; they will be told the important details – boy or girl – by and by.

'It's coming down now,' Mamta shouts, pulling her wet chunni round her head even tighter. Her new modesty is endearing. She is very conscious of her upcoming wedding, and behaves as if her future husband is already in the room.

'Don't you have any work? Your wedding isn't for another seven days.' Her father is angry.

'Mamta, Mohit, go tie down the hay,' commands Lata Bai. 'Sneha, watch Shanti.' The name out of her mouth, the reality of the baby is sealed. They have a little sister. They all know what that means. Another girl. Another burden.

'Your children, they do no work until they are told.' He accuses her of producing foul offspring.

This time she drops her eyes . . . *You are my husband of over twenty years. I have lived with you more than I have with my own parents. Except two hundred days, we have slept on the same bed every day all these years. Tonight we will sleep apart, and we should remain apart for the next forty days till I am once again pure. But on the twelfth day, you will take me back to your bed. Then you will climb over me that very night. We will pull the cloth over our heads and, healed or not, in pain or not, bleeding or not, you will pour your seed into me.*

For forty days at least she won't have to worry about another baby. But still, she does worry. She hates the nightly sex in full view of the children. Mostly Mamta gets up and goes outside to look at the sky as Seeta Ram goes up and down over Lata Bai. The boys just giggle. Then it's over. No other man would think of coupling with his wife during the first forty days, but not Seeta Ram. He'll roll off, leaving blood stains on the hay, and then she'll put her aching legs together. That's how it has been. Every time.

A baby and then another. That's where the life is going to pour out of me when I die. From between my legs and not from my nose like other people.

'I will be going to see him for myself. These men are tricky, they say one thing and they do another.'

13

'Who?' She's still with her children, but her husband has returned to the more important matter at hand.

'Daku Manmohan. He's only doing it because Lokend Bhai has guaranteed his family's safety. Why the police don't just kill him, I'll never know,' he says, eating, quietly watched by his children. Mohit joins his father, also sitting cross-legged on the floor. Lata Bai calculates the meals precisely. Today she will publicly give Mamta an extra half chapatti. Seeta Ram will say nothing, but only because she is to be married in a few days and leaving for good. Every other day he would say, 'Let her eat the leftovers. Why water someone else's garden?'

'I have explained their roles to them. You will remember when the time comes, won't you?' Lata Bai asks her children from her corner. She will eat with the girls after Seeta Ram has finished.

Seeta Ram refuses to be dragged into marriage talk. 'Daku Manmohan, surrendering. That's really something! The government is offering him and his gang limited freedom,' he says, cautiously prodding a sleeping memory of looting and slaughter. 'Pah! Limited freedom! We all know what that translates to. A jail cell more comfortable than the best hotel, with hot tea on tap, a game of cards with the guards and food cooked by their wives who will be given pukka brick houses,' he says, spitting on the floor. 'That murdering motherfucker, how many has he killed? How many has he maimed?'

'None from our family. Thank God. And only because Amma's brother is in the gang,' says Mamta, giggling. During the harvest, more than twenty years ago, when the farmers scaled down their rations and looked for new places to hide their precious grain, Lata Bai's brother disappeared. The whole family searched for his dead body, but not her father. No one knows for sure what happened to the boy, but Lata Bai's father cut and threshed his wheat with impunity that very day, while other farmers left their crops standing to rot in their fields. Blood money. That's what Lata Bai suspected it was. Blood money. A boy in exchange for protection. A boy who would one day become a man. 'Imagine, my uncle in the gang.' Her almost-wed status has made Mamta bold.

14

'Mamta!' Both father and mother censure her in unison. It isn't a subject to be discussed, as it separates the family from the rest of Gopalpur's inhabitants.

'Well, it's true.'

'Mamta, leave things that don't concern you alone,' says Lata Bai. To this day she feels guilty that her hut wasn't burned down with the rest.

'You had better shut her up,' Seeta Ram adds, slicing his palm through air in a smacking motion.

Shanti starts to cry. Lata Bai lets her cry. It will be a while before she will pick her up. That's how she's trained all her daughters into silence. The boys are picked up at once.

Mamta brings the baby to her mother. 'Tch,' the mother shakes her head at her eldest, and then she says proudly, 'See, she'll make a good mother,' because as far as Lata Bai is concerned daughters are born to be good mothers first, before anything else.

'She's just playing,' replies Seeta Ram with remarkable perspicacity. 'If she didn't have Shanti, she'd be teasing those boys from across the river. Still, she'd better make a good wife.' As far as Seeta Ram is concerned, daughters are born to be good wives first, before anything else.

Mamta will satisfy both her parents and make a good wife and mother. Loving Mamta. Patient Mamta.

'I am going out,' says Seeta Ram suddenly, unable to stand being in the house with the women any longer.

'In this weather? Where will you go?'

'To hell,' he says, charging out of the hut. He won't give her more information than is necessary.

'Take this for the rain –' She follows him out into the wet darkness, holding a spreading jute bag over his head.

As soon as Seeta Ram leaves the hut, Mamta starts with her questions. She has been dogging her mother for days, it seems she can never have enough answers. 'Tell me how it was for you,' she asks. Her giddiness irritates Lata Bai.

'You should be concentrating on your work: go collect the dung, go finish the washing, go pick the berries, collect the spinach . . . do

something useful instead of following me around! You are going to be a wife and mother soon, stop wasting your time.'

'Come on, Amma, I have only a week left, then I'll be gone and I . . . I might never come back, just like Ragini.'

'Your sister married up. It's not easy for her to come back.'

'So will I have a pukka house too?'

'Oho, stop dreaming dreams, they will get you nowhere. Now go gather the dung.' Lata Bai knows all about dreaming dreams. She had her own dreams before she was married to Seeta Ram at eight.

'Okay, okay. I'll do it. Amma, but first tell me, what was it like?'

Lata Bai looks into Mamta's eyes ringed with lashes, two bright big moons of excitement. *What should I say? It was frightening . . . painful . . . it snatched my childhood from me.*

'You got married after the drought, and then . . .' Mamta starts her mother's story for her, but she is fishing in muddy waters, there is no bite. Lata Bai looks away, remembering . . .

'What, Amma? Tell me . . .' Mamta puts her arms around her mother's waist.

'No more of this hugging baby business,' says Lata Bai in exactly the same tone her own mother had used on her, unlocking her arms and making distance between them. 'You are a woman now. Soon you will have your own children to look after, you won't be able to keep running home to me.'

'My own children? Will they be just like my Ladli dolly?' Mamta had made Ladli dolly herself when she was seven, with rags and tree cotton, embroidering her eyes, nose, mouth, and covering her head with bright red string hair.

'Oh, grow up, you'll be sorry if you don't.' But in fact it is Lata Bai who is sorry as soon as those words leave her lips. At once she pulls Mamta's arms round her again and says, 'Yes, yes, they'll be just like your Ladli dolly.'

The thought of children makes Mamta so happy and so scared. She knows children come only after jiggery. And jiggery hurts like anything. She's seen dogs do it, cows do it, cats do it, and it looks awful. How will she ever do it?

'Do you like Bapu?' she asks her mother.

'What sort of a question is that? I am a wife and a mother.'

'No, I mean do you like Bapu like the heroes like the heroines in the films?'

'So when have you seen a film?'

'Oh, Amma, you know what I mean. Do you think he will be as handsome as Guru Dutt?'

'Maybe.' Lata Bai hasn't met the prospective groom. The marriage was arranged exclusively by Seeta Ram. *I hope he checked on the family. Hai, Mamta, I hope your fate is better than mine.*

'Amma, what will I have to do? How did you do it?' This is the first time Mamta has asked her mother questions about babies and sex.

'Do what?'

'You know, have all of us.'

Lata Bai sees a disconcerting calm in her daughter's face, an acceptance that she never had a chance to own as a young bride. 'Mamta, you'll get to know all about it by and by.' That's what her own mother had said to her, hadn't she? You'll get to know all about it by and by. And she was right. She did get to know all about it by and by . . .

When Lata Bai turned twelve, Seeta Ram came with the tongawala to collect his bride. They rode back to her husband's house bouncing in a bullock cart all the way. Her father-in-law was so kind to her that first day. He dandled her on his knee all day and gave her sweets to eat. That night her father-in-law got on top of her, opened her legs to the ceiling and brought his fat body all the way inside her, till she thought she would choke on it. She'd screamed with the blood and pain. But only once. Her mother-in-law shouted, 'Quiet! Do you want to wake the dead?' from behind the curtain.

Her eyes were red from sorrow and shame the next day. 'Sorry,' her husband said to her, 'he gets the first taste. That's our custom.'

The first taste of a twelve-year-old girl. That was the last time her husband ever said sorry to her.

After that, every night her father-in-law tried to climb on her again. Every night he was stopped by her mother-in-law. 'Enough,' she said. 'You're only entitled to the first taste. She belongs to Seeta Ram now.'

His father was dying to get inside her, but her husband wasn't sure how to do it. Her father-in-law took care of that too. He took Seeta Ram to the gambling tents and bought him his own prostitute for one whole hour. It was jiggery from then on. Every night . . .

'The girls say the first time is the hardest . . . that there's blood . . . Amma, is that true?' Mamta speaks through the modest security of her chunni pinched between her teeth.

Lata Bai squeezes Mamta to her breast. 'The best day of my marriage was when I became pregnant with you . . . I remember it exactly . . . it happened when your bapu's mother went back to her own village to meet her sister and secretly sell her gold bangles to buy a transistor radio she'd had her eye on for some time . . .'

Lata Bai went to bathe at the river when her husband and mother-in-law left for the tonga stand. She'd calculated everything perfectly. Forty minutes there and forty minutes back, half an hour maximum for chit-chat, that added up to one hour and fifty minutes. Just to be on the safe side she would come back after two and a half hours, her husband would surely be home by then. The cicadas almost always started their song around five thirty in the evening. That's when she would lazily wander home, after the insects sang their first movement.

It was the last tonga fare that had decided Lata Bai's fate. The tongawala refused to start the journey without his complement of ten. The cost of feeding those bulls alone would amount to four passenger fares. Then there were two fares for emergencies, one fare for his food and a visit to his favourite prostitute. That left him with three fares of profit. That added up to one fare each for his sons and one for his wife and daughter. Less than that and it wasn't worth his while.

Seeta Ram and his mother were still sweating buckets under their banyan, waiting for the tenth passenger when Lata Bai meandered back home, humming a little, still hot and damp under her ghaghra with water dripping off her hair, leaving a wet patch in the centre of her back. All this time, her father-in-law searched the house for her. He looked in the fields: 'Come out, little mouse. Come out, little mouse. I'm going to get you,' he said softly.

She didn't see him, still holding on to her song and happiness. It was only when he stepped up behind her and lifted her off her feet that she knew she'd been caught in a trap from which she wouldn't get out till the hunter was well and truly done with her.

That time she said nothing, she didn't scream, just turned her head away and closed her eyes tight enough to see bright green dots behind her lids so she wouldn't have to look at her father-in-law's distorted features lurking above her own. He'd raped her twice, or was it thrice? Like he would never have enough of her teenage body. Her body, with its newly sprouted breasts as small as plums, a tiny waist and a bottom as hard as a teenage boy. After he was done, he'd stuffed a piece of brown sugar into her mouth. She'd spat it out on her mother-in-law's pillow.

He'd filled her body with his semen and one of those sperms made its way to her awakening ovaries. That's how Mamta came to be.

Then Seeta Ram came back. The whole world was still in order. The house was exactly as he'd left it. His wife was peeling potatoes from their field. There was washing hanging out to dry, and drips from the oil lamp staining the altar. It really was just another day. The kind of day he'd got used to.

He wasn't disappointed with his wife. She's a good woman, he thought, looking at her working with her chunni pulled low over her head. Then he saw the wet patch on the back of her blouse and felt something rush up from inside and grab his throat. Her knife flicked little potato peels on the floor. Her bangles jangled. Her feet stuck out under her ghaghra. She'd wiggled her toes, a spot of sparkle played on her toe ring. He was by her side in a second. He took the knife out of her hand. Caught her by the wrist and led her to the cow shed. She followed, a little like a tethered cow herself. 'I have to show her the new calf, it looked sickly this morning,' he'd said to his father over his shoulder.

His father smiled. 'Of course you do.'

Seeta Ram bedded his wife in the cow shed, his seed mixing with his father's inside her. That time too, Lata Bai said nothing, just shut her eyes to see those little green spots again.

Her father-in-law managed to rape her five more times. At first Lata Bai just stared at her mother-in-law with intense eyes as deep as drought wells, but the older woman refused to understand. So she didn't keep quiet during the sixth rape, but screamed and screamed so that the world might hear her. The world didn't hear her, but the person she most wanted to did . . .

'Your bapu's mother didn't buy the transistor radio. Instead she got your bapu his own field, and that's how we came upriver to live here in Gopalpur.' At least that last rape hadn't been in vain.

Lata Bai holds on to her daughter's eyes for a long time. 'My life changed for the better after I moved here with your bapu . . . we made this house ourselves,' she says, falsely recalling her own early months as wedded bliss. 'Remember, the first months are the best, enjoy them. You build so much together, lay a foundation for yourself and your children,' she says convincingly. In truth it wasn't until months after Mamta was born that they'd gathered enough clay from the riverbed and wood from the forest and begged a stack of hay from their neighbour's field to build their hut. The hut hasn't changed much, it is still just one large room where the family cooks, sleeps and dreams.

'But you will also have to work hard,' she needlessly warns her industrious daughter, 'maybe even harder than you do here. There will be only two of you there, here we are five . . . But I know you will do whatever you have to. You have never shirked work. And believe me, you will be rewarded, just as I was . . .

'Our first wheat was marvellous, each stalk fat with grain without a single telltale black powdery ear that could ruin the whole crop. It was such a good time to bring a baby into the world, Mamta. Fat wheat dancing over my head, a hut to live in, and not a rupee in debt. And then you appeared, just before the wheat turned golden. A beautiful plump baby girl.'

Lata Bai looks away, she can remember it as clearly as if it were yesterday. She'd rushed home with her new baby. 'Can you hear me?' she'd cried. 'Can you hear me? Our baby's come. Our baby's here,' she'd shouted again and again. Seeta Ram came running from the latrine, washing his hands quickly in the ditch. Lata Bai had held

the baby out to him. Even wrinkled up and bruised from birth, she thought Mamta was a beauty. 'She's beautiful, no?'

Seeta Ram had jerked back from his wife as if he'd been stung. 'You called me this loud for a girl? Do you want us to celebrate and tell the whole world of this baby girl? God, did you have to give me a girl?' he'd said, and walked out of the house leaving Lata Bai standing holding Mamta out to him as if she was a temple offering.

Girl or otherwise, that's when Seeta Ram became 'Mamta's father'. That's right, from that day to this, Seeta Ram has been called Mamta's father and nothing else by his wife. 'Arey-oh, Mamta's father, lunch is ready,' she shouts at noon, and then again, 'Arey-oh, Mamta's father, dinner.' Every day it's Mamta's father this and Mamta's father that. Each time his wife calls him Mamta's father, Seeta Ram thinks she is deliberately punishing him for Mamta's sake; he never blames custom that ordains the link between the father's name and his first-born's.

That evening the hijras came. They saw the baby was a girl and blessed it for free. They hadn't the heart to ask the new mother of a daughter for money. 'Devi has blessed you,' said the eunuchs, looking back at Lata Bai, sharing in her sorrow as only other women could. 'She will be lucky. She has the mark.' Of course the mark had to be a blessing, just like accidental bird droppings on one's finest clothes. Yes, Lata Bai had seen it too, a red birthmark tucked away in her daughter's hair.

'At least we can be thankful that the hijras won't come today. They know we have nothing,' says the mother.

'Yes, and probably they won't show up at my wedding either,' says Mamta ruefully. 'At last Bapu can be glad, he won't have to look at my ugly face much longer,' she adds.

'Uffo,' Lata Bai replies in half-agreement. Ugly-face-talk before the wedding is fitting, because any kind of praise is inauspicious. There is always someone listening, people willing to spoil your plans. She places a dot of lampblack behind Mamta's ear to take the 'perfect' out of her beauty, more as a courtesy to her daughter than anything else. They both know Mamta's beauty isn't perfect,

the red birthmark dangles above her eyebrow like a sign of dis-approval from God.

'I shall put the henna leaves to dry as soon as the rain stops,' says Mamta. 'Just imagine, beautiful red henna patterns all the way to my shoulders and up to my knees . . . hai,' she sighs.

Her mother shakes her head, but says nothing. She is going to be married after all. Another six days and she'll be gone. *Thank you, Devi.* That should put an end to the village sniggers: 'Arey, Lata Bai, how is it that you got your younger daughter married before your elder one?' . . . 'Arey, Lata Bai, have you had an offer for Mamta yet?' Even those guised as concern: 'Arey, Lata Bai, what can a mother do but love her daughter, good, bad, beautiful or ugly?' And the pitying, this-is-destiny ones: 'Don't worry, someone will come for her. You just wait and see. After all, girls are someone else's gardens. We mothers only borrow them for a time.'

Lata Bai has woken Mamta and Sneha early and ushered them out of the hut. They must be quick today, bringing the water from the well, cooking two days' food that won't spoil with keeping, repairing the roof and collecting the dung pats. At last, mid-morning she packs some dried chapattis and spicy baked potato skins in some ficus leaves for their journey. They will travel light, the only thing of value they carry is a bottle of homemade chilli pickle for her father.

'Okay, we are ready,' says Lata Bai to Seeta Ram when he comes home for lunch. 'I am taking Mamta and Shanti,' she adds, quickly placing his tray at his feet. Her husband winces, the name Shanti is too new, too disappointing, too female.

'So what about Sneha?' he says, pulling Prem and Mohit to one side of the hut, separating the females from the males as if in some fiercely competitive game. 'Take the girls, the boys are staying with me.'

Lata Bai cradles Shanti and leaves without looking back at the house. The women walk towards the tonga stand under a flowing ficus tree, an hour away. She hides the baby deeper inside her pallav to spare her the sunlight that can crisp skin faster than an open

flame. It beats down on them like a pounding stick, knocking all the energy out of their stride. The Red Ruins glimmer in the distance. Two girls are praying at the shrine. Lata Bai walks faster, lifting her hand in acknowledgement, but not her head.

'Who are they?'

'Must be some girls from the village, come to pray for sons.'

'When I'm married, I will come here to pray for sons too. I wish I was a boy. Bapu says to wait and see, my husband will sort me out well and good. I think he's waiting for that.' In Seeta Ram's eyes Mamta has no right to exist at all, but since she does, she has to prove herself day after day, working harder than the boys, eating nothing that might be noticed, and being silently present. Like the extra baby section in an orange, not missed if it isn't there, but swallowed whole if it is, without releasing any of its flavour into the mouth.

'I won't let my husband rule over me. Husbands aren't kings, you know.'

'Look here, Mamta,' Lata Bai takes hold of her daughter's shoulders tight and hard, 'you will not survive a day with that attitude. For now, work sincerely at home and stay out of your bapu's way. That's the best and safest thing for you to do. Pray to Devi every night that your husband is kind to you . . .'

'. . . and that he won't beat you or send you back to us in disgrace,' adds Sneha, who has learned the lesson of womanhood much faster and better than her elder sister.

'Huh. Small mouth, big talk,' says Mamta.

Under the appointed tree, Lata Bai opens her blouse to suckle Shanti. 'Sneha, you better go home. Nani hasn't room for us all. You can visit her any time, let Mamta have her attention, she is going away for good. I promise I'll take you next winter.'

'Next winter! But Nani might be dead next winter!'

'Sneha, back to the house! If you start walking now, you'll be there before sunset,' says Lata Bai, brushing aside Sneha's tears.

'Stay out of Bapu's way and he won't even notice you are back,' says Mamta viciously.

* * *

23

They arrive early in the morning, to the smell of home fires.

'Arey, Lata, what's happened to this girl of yours? Look at her hair, it is orange,' says the grandmother, tugging at Mamta's oily plait.

'Oho, what am I to do, he won't give her food. Each time I say give her food he says, "Am I made of money? Do you think we live in the Big House? Throw some more oil into her hair, it'll get black in no time at all." Then he says, "Look at her huge belly, is that the belly of a starving child?"' Of course they all know that a distended belly means starvation. How many children have they seen die holding their ball-bellies in their hands? But Mamta's father creates his own mirage, an image that suits his ends. He neither minds nor cares if she lives or dies.

'Come. Come here. Now you will have more to eat. You need meat on your bones, good body fat before you are married. We don't want your husband thinking we cheated him, do we?' says Mamta's grandmother, putting their hands in red clay and plastering their handprints on the mud walls of her house. 'In case I never see you again, your hands will hold me as I ride Yamraj's bull to my next life.'

'I won't let Yamraj take you any time soon, Nani. You can't go before you've told us all the stories.'

'Look at this girl of yours, Lata, to be married soon, and still she wants to hear only stories.'

'Why do you think I brought her here, Amma?' laughs Lata Bai. 'For your stories . . . and your food, of course. Hai, I am exhausted, her ears are never satisfied.'

'Come, see your bapu, Lata. Not that he'll know you.'

The women enter the hut. Lata Bai touches her father's feet. He is lying on the charpoy, loosely tied to the rope bed with strips of sari material.

'Namaste, Bapu.'

'Who?' The man's eyes seem to float in their sockets, moving from his daughter to his granddaughter's face. Lata Bai kneels by his side and runs her fingers over his feet.

'It's Lata, I'm here,' she says.

24

'Who?' He asks no one in particular.

The grandmother replies. Her frustration reaches into her gullet and pulls her voice out of her throat, catapulting it to a high pitch: 'Your daughter is here!'

'Sh, sh, Amma, sh, he's not deaf. Bapu, it's Lata.' The husband and father lies on the charpoy, useless to the two women who depend on him. 'You remember me, don't you? It's Lata.' An unconscious thought flashes through her mind which makes complete sense of the situation. Men, you can't count on them, even if your life depends on it, and still, she looks on with eyes full of love for her father.

'Bapu, we're here now. Don't worry. You can come out to greet us whenever you are ready.' Of course by the 'you' Lata Bai means his inner self, for her mother has no intention of freeing her senile husband to wander off and leave her a virtual widow. Her mother takes him to the outhouse herself and walks him round and round the yard like a cow threshing wheat. Some evenings, she oils his hair, or massages his feet, or clips his toenails, whatever is dictated by her mental calendar built up over six years of care and feeding.

'Leave it, Lata, he can't change. Not even though you are here.'

'So what's wrong with him, Nani?'

'Oh, he's been like that for years; I just hope he has a few more left in him. I don't want to survive your grandfather. At least he's given me a good life. Now just look at him . . . doesn't know who I am. I'm afraid one day he'll wander away and then the villagers will think him dead. And then your mother's brothers will come to take this land away from me.'

'Why? You saved them in the drought.'

'Yes, I did. I confused Death into thinking my boys were girls by making them wear their dead sisters' clothes. I painted their eyes with kohl and put bangles on their wrists, so Yamraj spared their lives. I did my duty, child, but no one cares for the past, least of all sons. Just look at that Pavan, threw his mother out of the hut the instant she became a widow and when she refused to leave, he dragged her out by her hair. When you are rejected by your own blood, what will other people do but shun you as well.'

'Oh, Nani, no one will throw you out. You can come live with Amma if they do.'

Her grandmother just smiles at the naïveté of the offer given with love. Of course she could never go to Lata Bai's house. Not even to visit, let alone to live. That would be the one thing that would disgrace her daughter like no other. Since Lata Bai has been married her mother has only been to see her once, and that time she stayed in the back of Saraswati Stores with the stinking fertiliser that burned her eyes and gave her headaches. She met her daughter at the well, and refused all her presents and food during her stay so she would not be a burden to her.

'Nani, story. Tell us about the dry season, when all my aunts died.' Mamta has always been a long-story girl; in that department, she was born mature.

'Just listen to my granddaughter. Cooing like a pigeon. All the time she wants to hear only that story. I try and tell her about our gods, but she only wants to hear about us humans.'

'Mamta, you cannot know the world by peeping through a keyhole. Always the same old stories,' says Lata Bai.

'Okay, Nani, then tell me about Aunt Lucky Sister and how she sent her husband packing, or about Amma's brother who was stolen by the bandits.'

'Ha, ha Lucky Sister . . . Go on, Lata, you tell your daughter about that sister of yours. All I can say is that you have to be prepared for anything after marriage . . . it can be heaven, it can be hell . . .'

'Amma, let's not talk about that now. Mamta will have a fine marriage,' says Lata Bai cautiously.

But the grandmother hasn't had company in a long time, and like a starving child who gorges itself to sickness, she can't stay away from saying too much, from giving away painful memories lightly, no matter how heartsick it might make the three of them. 'I married my daughters, your amma's sisters, just before the drought. That was lucky, because after that, no one would have come to claim them. You remember the drought, Lata. It was so bad that the earth cracked and split like chapped skin.

'Hai, I wasn't lucky with my daughters. My eldest simply

disappeared after her wedding day. We suspected she was dead, because there was never any news. My second, who moved five miles away, came home three times with a huge gash on her head. Each time I gave her a paste of turmeric and sacred basil to bind on her wound and sent her back. After the third time, she stopped coming home too. My third daughter, Lucky Sister, married an engine driver. Everyone said lucky girl. She came home every other year with saris for everyone . . .' The grandmother stops, even she can't say the words. It was through well-side gossip that they learned the true story behind the saris and Lucky Sister's happy marriage to a rich engine driver. Her rich engine driver husband put his own wife out to work, setting her up in a little hut behind the station. First it was just her husband's friends who came to spend an hour or two with her, but later, she slept with anyone. Once she became established, she threw her pimping husband out of her house. Now she has six other girls working for her. No one in Lata Bai's family speaks of Lucky Sister any more.

'So what about my fourth auntie?'

'Your fourth auntie was married at eight, like your amma.'

'Yes, and like me, she too had to wait for her period to arrive before her husband claimed her,' says Lata Bai.

'Hai, so young. Imagine if . . .' says Mamta, eyes wide.

'Oho, it was a different time, that's all,' replies the grandmother.

'A different time?' Lata Bai laughs bitterly. 'I suppose you could say that it was a different time.'

'So? What? Do you blame me, Lata? Do you think I had any choice? Don't you remember that damned drought? I can still remember the tiniest details . . . the sky a constant blue; the moon on its back, surrounded by a dance of stars, so still, so lifeless on scorching, murderous nights; the cicadas stopping mid-chirp and falling to the ground like dead leaves; the well water turning bitter; your bapu praying for rain; giving all our food to the priest who promised us rain; the rains not coming for six months; the crops drying up . . .'

'Even so, you should have checked up on the family, on their customs . . .'

'Yes, yes, we should have. I suppose you believe we could have. There were no marriage offers for you girls . . . Oh, Mamta, you should have seen it: all round us, girls were dying of hunger. Lata, how can you forget the pickled pea plants so easily?'

'Yes, yes, the pickled pea plants . . .' Lata Bai's voice is flat, emotionless. 'I haven't forgotten. Amma pickled all the withering plants she could find, just pickled them right down to a soup in salt. That's what we lived on: pickled pea plants. There were always heaped spoonfuls of green pickled soup for Bapu with a wheat dumpling or two . . . all three meals. Bapu reached a point when he couldn't swallow any more salt. Just the sight of pickled pea shoots made him want to run outside and look for a drink of water. Salt goes with water. But there was no water . . .' She can still remember the time her father threw his plate in her mother's face, splattering her clothes with green pickle stains, blaming her for the drought, the salt and no water. Her mother scraped the stains off her clothes and put them back in the pickle jar again. Nothing was wasted. She stayed in those stained clothes till the end of the drought.

'That's when my sisters started to die . . . one by one.'

'But not your amma, she was a survivor. Lata found food in anything . . .'

'I would walk up and down the riverbank collecting anything I could eat. A fallen bird, a sparrow's nest, lotus seeds, reeds, anything. Sometimes I'd come back with the last rotting wild potatoes of the season, sometimes with dried berries still hanging on brittle stems. The lotus seeds I ate alone, in the shade of a dune. Those I never took home. Perhaps that's how I survived, on a handful of lotus seeds . . . But, Amma, I never told you about the rotting cow. You remember Radha, my friend who got sick and died? She ate cow meat . . .' says Lata Bai still afraid to tell the whole truth. It wasn't just Radha who ate the cow, she did too. Neither of them told. The villagers would have killed her before the drought did for eating the cow. Lata Bai ate only the hooves. Threw them into a grass fire which she kept going for five hours. The hoofs melted and as soon as they started to drip, she caught the drip on a stick, blew on it and popped

it into her mouth. Radha wanted the meat. That's why the day after Radha was dead and she wasn't.

'Yes, and you ate the hooves. I knew about those,' says Lata Bai's mother.

'You did?'

'Oh, forget it, Lata. We've all done worse things in our lives.' It is clear this is the first time Lata Bai and her mother have spoken honestly of those days.

'If you knew about the hooves, why did you give me my sisters' food? That's why they died, because I ate their food . . .'

She physically bites down into those old images, clamping her jaw shut. Lata Bai remembers her youngest sister: two big-moons-in-the-water eyes looking around at the world. First lively, looking for anything that might help her live, a game, a laugh, a touch. Then looking around more slowly, for something to ease the pain. Lata Bai cut her sari in two, the only one she owned, and made a sling for her sister. Each time before she left to look for food by the river, she'd give her sister a huge swing. Her other sisters didn't expire quite so quietly. They screamed their terrible screams and fought with her to the end, biting and kicking, opening her mouth to snatch their food back from inside her throat. When she woke, there was a bit of vomit beside her head where her sisters had managed to drag their food out of her body. Even after they died, they continued to visit her in her dreams and pull food from deep inside her gullet every night.

'Because you were the strong one. You are still the strong one. I made that choice, and it was a good one.'

'Nani, did you eat cow hooves as well?'

'Ha, ha . . . no. I licked the dregs off the plates instead of washing them. At first the taste of the pickled soup was less bitter than the taste of shame. Later the taste of shame became less bitter than the taste of despair. Finally, the taste of despair disappeared and it was just the taste of pickled soup again.'

'Hai, Mamta, I hope you never have to witness such days,' says Lata Bai. 'Three of my friends died, and one became sick with a disease that curled her legs right into her hips. As for the other

two . . .' It was around the time of her wedding that she heard about two others who had survived. They'd been sent to the city with one of their uncles where there was food to be had. They all knew what happened to the girls who went to the city. They eventually became prostitutes and turned up in the Red Bazaar.

'Finally, the drought ended, and two months later your amma was married to your bapu.

'You remember, that Seeta Ram of yours turned up with his elder brother. His face was covered with a red cloth that shivered slightly at the mouth every time he breathed. I lifted the groom's veil just to check if it was really Seeta Ram beneath it. Those days there was a lot of switching of grooms, men who changed their minds often paid someone else to pick up their brides. His brother said your amma was too frail and sunken to be a good wife. But I said no, she is strong as a plough. And to prove it, I made her balance all our earthenware pots filled with water on her head . . . all six of them. Do you remember that?'

'Yes, I remember how you hit me on the head, and pulled my veil lower over my eyes, and pushed my head down so that my eyes pointed to the floor, all the time smiling at Mamta's father and his brother. Hai, I was so scared that I thought I would drop the pots on their toes. Ha, ha, ha . . .' Lata Bai laughs with that special relief that comes with the memory of averted disaster.

'I remember we ate one sweet semolina ball cut into eight. That was my wedding.'

'But yours will be different, Mamta, yours will be very different. Now, enough of stories, go make some the tea,' says the grand-mother. 'What about Mamta's dowry? What have you given her? Is it more than what we gave you?' Both mother and grandmother regard the bride-to-be, who smiles at them from the stove out of earshot. 'Her dowry better be enough. I mean, look at her. That ungodly birthmark has snatched away her beauty. You'd better give her a decent dowry, otherwise she might come back to you charred,' hisses the grandmother.

'Mamta's father has taken a loan from the Big House for her dowry,' the mother drops her voice too, 'we had to, otherwise we

would never have managed to get a proposal for her. We thought Singh Sahib would be kind to us, because of how much he loved his own wife Bibiji, and because we took the loan for a marriage . . . you could say to . . . to sanctify the act of love . . . but not a chance. Singh Sahib is sick. He can't be bothered with us. It's his son Ram Singh or his pet dog Babulal who come for the interest every month. Now Prem goes there to work every day, paying it off. Slavery is what it is.' Her voice is thick with disappointment. 'We took a loan and managed to buy nothing. No gold. No cows or goats either, just a bicycle, some pans, and a few clothes . . . I gave her Lucky Sister's gold earrings, they were the only jewellery I had.' Days before her own wedding, Lucky Sister had sent her a pair of earrings. They had arrived secretly at night in the hands of one of her customers, the person Lucky Sister most trusted.

'Now we are like the rest of Mamta's father's hookah-sucking friends – all debtors of the Big House. But there is some glamour in it, I suppose. They invite you that one and only time to the Big House veranda and give you tea. They said they would come for the wedding. I think that's really what made Mamta's father do it. You know how he is, he loves show.

'Remember when Ragini got married,' Lata Bai drops her voice even lower to spare Mamta the anguish of her ensuing words, 'how excited he was? How much show we put on. He gave Ragini enough dowry for three girls. How rich they were. We nearly passed out when the groom arrived on a horse. Hai, for this wedding we will be paying for the rest of our lives. Better to have been robbed by bandits.'

'It's the same anyway, robbed by bandits or the Big House. It's just the same,' says the old woman. 'I don't envy you. After Mamta and Sneha, you will still have another one to marry off,' she says, looking at the baby in Lata Bai's arms. Then she plucks a betel-leaf off her vine, quickly slaps some lime on it and carefully places half in the corner of her mouth. She pops the other half into her husband's.

'And now those damned bandits are surrendering.'

* * *

31

Showing remarkable prescience, Lata Bai has saved last season's daal for the wedding, trimming her family's rations by one spoon each day. Daal and chapattis, that's what she'll serve, and mustard greens. She will steal some mustard greens from her own field. Why steal? Because, except for a few plants, minutely calculated as sustenance for the family, the crop belongs to Singh Sahib, and the labour of her son too. That was the deal. He gave them money for Mamta's dowry, they are to give him all their produce in return. All their produce, even the vegetables they grow, go with Prem to the Big House. *Why are girls born at all? All they do is get us in debt.*

How should she cook the daal? Chillies, of course. The more chillies she uses the less people will eat. She'll make it go round with enough chillies from her own bush. She opens the earthenware pot and looks inside at the hoarded daal.

It's almost gone . . . Almost gone? Yes, almost gone. Into the bellies of weevils. They look like seeds themselves. Fat on her grain, they wiggle slowly along the edge of the pot.

Her heart beats in her mouth. The next thing, her ears go deaf to her body's sounds. She looks around. Her eyes see nothing. She remembers nothing. Not the daal or the weevils that caused all this. Her whole life can be summed up in weevils. The clouds move lazily overhead. The mustard says shrk, shrk. What should she do? She can hear everything clearly. Serve the weevils. That's what. Grind them into a paste with the daal and serve the weevils. Weevils on her daughter's wedding.

It is the good time of year, after the visiting dust vanishes into its permanent home somewhere in the mountains. Luckily, this time the storm didn't take their roof, so the girls don't have to gather too many reeds from the riverbank, and there's little work in the fields. Mamta is still with Shanti, masking the holes in her coverlet with dainty embroidered peacocks, and popping pumpkin seeds into her mouth that her mother has slyly hidden for her fittingly behind the picture of the all-giving goddess Lakshmi. Mamta really should be checking the mustard leaf by leaf for aphids. They can destroy the whole crop in a matter of weeks.

'I'm watching you,' says Seeta Ram from the door. Her father has returned unexpectedly. 'What are you doing at home? Get out there to work. And take that . . . that baby with you,' he smacks her on the back of her head, a safe place for hidden bruising. 'I'm watching you, just you remember that. I can still send you to the Red Bazaar if that husband of yours doesn't turn up.'

Seeta Ram had always disliked his eldest daughter with something bordering on revulsion. The revulsion turned to hatred the night Mamta tried to beat him off her mother crying, 'Don't touch her, don't you kill her . . .' That was when he cut her rations down to a single meal a day of nothing but a dry chapatti.

Mamta looks at her father, blaming him for her whole life. *I am glad I'm leaving you, and I won't have to meet you again.* What Mamta sees is a dictatorial, loveless, cruel man. What she doesn't see is that Seeta Ram is a man without choices, a typical Gopalpur inhabitant, shaped by the destiny of the village. A powerless, brooding man, who has never hankered after things he didn't deserve. No alternatives ever appeared on his horizon, or in his impermanent world of grass reeds and mud. His world is governed by the force of Gopalpur's dusty winds and monsoon rains, and the amount of money he owes the Big House, a force he considers on par with an act of God.

She quickly drops Shanti in her tiny hammock and rushes outside.

She swishes through the mustard. Its flowers are high, they leave little pollen dabs all across her clothes like dainty block prints. The mustard says, shrk, shrk, dropping little yellow flowers at her feet. A butterfly snags in her billowing pallav. She removes the creature as gently as she can; still, the wings come off, leaving her holding the wriggling body that looks so much like a worm. For some reason, the death of the butterfly gives her a lump in her throat, and she has to blink hard to keep the tears from running down her face. She looks into the wind, dreaming of her husband-to-be. She judges the intensity of the storm, dallying a little longer, dancing uncharacteristically, her skirt tickling her ankles. Her younger sister Sneha, a little distance away, does her job much more diligently, lifting each leaf carefully. The bride-to-be feels a pang of guilt for work-abandoned moments.

Very secretly she harbours tremulous dreams of marrying someone who loves her. But what does she know of love? Can there be such a thing between a man and a woman? She has only heard of the legend of Singh Sahib and Bibiji, but to her it is more a myth. In her experience men are so far above women that she can't conceive of a man showing anything more than kindness, bordering on pity, for his wife. Yes, for her kindness is love. Above all, she wants a kind husband.

'I bet he has a quiff like Guru Dutt in *Pyaasa!*'

'Guru Dutt, Didi, really?' She can always count on Sneha's unquestioning gullibility.

'Yes, just like him . . .' No one in the village has seen a film, but Lala Ram, the owner of Saraswati Stores, put up his favourite movie poster over thirty years ago as a community service. After that, the antique poster became the standard for good looks in Gopalpur. With his brooding cowlick towering over his sideburns, his streaky moustache, and his soft-focus sentimentality, Guru Dutt has sidled into every female heart upon teary jerks of breath.

'Hai, Didi, how lucky. With such a handsome husband you can really tell that Ramu off when he teases you.'

'Mamta! Sneha!' warns Lata Bai. 'You leave those boys from across the river alone, you never know what they might do.'

'Amma, that Ramu comes over each day to my dung patch to take the sweet out of my sugar. He says my husband won't be like Guru Dutt at all.' Mamta squeezes her eyes closed, she's not a child but Ramu's words have the power to hurt her – '*Look at you, black as dirty oil. Do you think your mother could have got you married to a Guru Dutt?*' – *Damn that motherfucker.* Each day she runs to the river, makes a pool with her hands, fills it with water and searches it for her reflection. Ramu is right, she is black as dirty oil, but not dirty enough to hide her wretched birthmark.

'You mustn't listen, Mamta,' says Lata Bai feebly, unwilling to waste time on simple lessons which she thinks her daughter should have learned a long time ago.

But Mamta can't let go. Just yesterday Ramu's friends tried to teach her a thing or two. Prem wanted to defend her, but she'd said,

'They want me, let them talk to me.' No one talked to Mamta. She could pitch a stone from a catapult better than any of them, and when she hitched up the skirt of her ghaghra and ran, there was no catching up. 'Motherfuckers,' she laughed, and tossed curses over her shoulders, 'Catch me if you can.' When they couldn't, they'd started taunting her:

> *Marked Mamta's getting married,*
> *Marked Mamta's getting married,*
> *To an old, old man,*
> *He'll come on an old horse to get her,*
> *He'll give her an old sari to wear,*
> *They'll jiggery all night together,*
> *They'll jiggery all night together.*

> *Marked Mamta's getting married,*
> *Marked Mamta's getting married,*
> *To an old, old man,*
> *He'll beat her black and blue,*
> *Her belly will be swollen in no time,*
> *They'll jiggery that night too,*
> *They'll jiggery that night too.*

She catches herself humming the ditty, feeling betrayed. 'He tried to tease me again today, but I chucked a stone at his head. Oh, what fun that was! How he ran!' says Mamta, putting her arms around her mother's neck.

Lata Bai undoes her daughter's arms saying, 'Careful he doesn't catch you one day, Mamta.'

'Huh, what if he does? He can do nothing to me now. I will belong to someone else soon. My husband will protect me.'

'Don't start with the dreams. Marriage can be anything. Pray you have a good husband.'

'You mean a good husband, just like Bapu?' Mamta says sarcastically. 'Amma, I don't know why . . . why you bother with him.' Her boldness takes her by surprise.

'You watch out. That kind of talk will get you a beating from your husband.'

'A beating from my husband . . . I don't think so. We will be in love as much as . . . as our own zamindar Singh Sahib and Bibiji.'

'Mamta!' Lata Bai cups her daughter's mouth violently with her hand. It is such a bad omen to say something so lofty about your future husband so close to your wedding date.

'What a love that was,' says Mamta with a sparkle in her eyes. Singh Sahib's great love for his wife Bibiji is legendary. He is Gopalpur's own home-grown Romeo. Gopalpur loves all of them – Romeo–Juliet, Laila–Majnu, Hir–Ranja . . . and of course Singh Sahib–Bibiji . . . all star-crossed, desperate couples dying for love. Love stories form the substratum of Gopalpur's daydreams. A man like Singh Sahib who is willing to love in the glorious tradition of daydreams is naturally a legend. Secretly all Gopalpur's men aspire to Singh Sahib's love-standard, and some even think they love their women with the same honourable hopelessness, but they don't. Their passion is nothing but a tremor in their collective imagination, a swindle by their egos.

'Love stories will get you nowhere,' says her mother.

'Yes, hai, what if he *is* old and beats you?' Sneha verbalises her sister's worst fears. Sneha's unquestioning gullibility isn't the only thing Mamta can count on.

Once again the ditty takes hold of her . . .

> *Marked Mamta's getting married,*
> *Marked Mamta's getting married,*
> *To an old, old man,*
> *He'll come on an old horse to get her,*
> *He'll give her an old sari to wear,*
> *They'll jiggery all night together,*
> *They'll jiggery all night together.*
>
> *Marked Mamta's getting married,*
> *Marked Mamta's getting married,*
> *To an old, old man,*

He'll beat her black and blue,
Her belly will be swollen in no time,
They'll jiggery that night too,
They'll jiggery that night too.

'Amma, that Ramu said Bapu would sell me to the bandits if no one turns up to marry me,' says Sneha. The taunting has left her nervous too.

'Well, you can just tell him that there won't be any bandits left by next planting season. Singh Sahib's youngest son is bringing them all in and locking them in jail,' says Mamta. 'Amma, tell us again about the bandits,' she says, moving away from the sordid world of taunting boys.

'Yes, Amma, tell us, what did the bandits do?'

'Where do these questions come from? All the time stories, stories, as if you girls have no work to do . . . as if *I* have no work to do. We can't fritter our lives away on stories,' says Lata Bai.

'C'mon, Amma, tell us about Daku Manmohan,' says Mamta. She knows she has to plead but a little for her mother to capitulate. It was Lata Bai who gave her a taste for stories in the first place. Bending the boundaries of time and place, she would weave together threads as separate as Kashmiri silk and Bengali cotton into one gargantuan tale of bravery, epic love and histrionic honour, leaping into the arena of myth with alacrity from a very lofty height.

'Yes, come on, Amma, Mamta Didi will be leaving soon. There will be no one to beg you for stories after she goes,' says Sneha, pulling a face.

Lata Bai smiles. Her children are still children. She suckles Shanti. 'Stories, stories, that's all you care for,' she says mock-angry. 'What about the cooking? What about the washing? What about the weeding and tying the vines back against the walls? What about the spices? The well water? Kneading the clay for a new pot; collecting the resin and the wild mangoes. So who will do all that then? Your father?' The children look at her, their cheeks chubby with smiles. Of course she isn't serious, they know that.

'Come on, Amma . . .'

'Okay, okay. But only for five minutes. What a time that was . . .' Lata Bai's eyes glass over. The children come closer to her, not to miss a word. They've heard this story many times before, but it is always slightly different, always exciting. 'The surprise of the bandit raid was more traumatic than the bloodiness of it.

'I remember it was evening. Earthy clouds heralded their arrival minutes before the rhythmic hoofbeats. They looked magnificent with their turban tails flowing behind them and their oiled moustaches gleaming in the sun . . .' The romanticism of the gang's appearance was shattered all too soon. Not one bandit had to dismount from his horse. Gopalpur simply capitulated, offered herself up spread-eagled, naked, defenceless, to the plunderer for his taking. All night the moans of the dead and dying glided through the fields. It wasn't a night for heroism. People hid in the hay, in ditches and in sugarcane fields. In the morning they walked out to greet a pitiless sun that showed up the destruction in its unaccountable manifestations.

'Of course they spared the landlords, the Singh family ensconced in the Big House. Some said the Big House paid the bandits to stay away . . .'

'But Prem says that isn't true. He says Singh Sahib is a man of honour, and his honour wouldn't have allowed it. He says Singh Sahib hates his son because of this surrender and if he wasn't so sick, Singh Sahib would gladly hunt down Daku Manmohan . . . right this minute,' interjects Mamta, filling in for her absent favourite brother.

'Maybe, maybe. But what do we know of Singh Sahib, the zamindar of Gopalpur living in his Big House, out of our sight? We only know how much he charges for his loans and that damned son of his, Ram Singh, is like a vulture, usurping lands left, right and centre, just like Daku Manmohan. One son adds to the bandit numbers, while the other tries to cull them . . .

'Those damned gangs. They came sweeping in from the direction of the dusty Gopalpur wind where the famines were so awful that it was said that people had begun to eat cow meat and sometimes even human flesh. At first, they took whatever their horses

could carry, mostly sacks of wheat and washing left to dry unguarded on clothes lines. But we weren't under any illusions. We knew that once the bandits attacked, they returned.

'Each night, we had to find a different place to sleep. Under the ridge, by the riverbank, or hidden in the roots of the banyan trees . . .' (never at the Red Ruins or the dry well, that's where the bandits raped the girls) '. . . in the mornings we dragged ourselves back to our huts. As the gangs became stronger, they became bolder, and started looting everything . . . including children. That's when my brother went missing. Others lost family too. Shyam Lal lost a son and Moti a son and a daughter. Nutan Bai thought the bandits had taken her daughter Kanno, but she found her hiding in a haystack, her leg poked through with the point of one of their knives.'

'Even now, after all this time, Kanno doesn't speak. We used to think her tongue was cut off, but she stuck it out at me just last week. I wonder why she doesn't speak.' Sneha is most concerned for the fate of dumb Kanno.

Lata Bai continues: 'Gope's teashop also vanished with the bandits. Gope's tea was famous. He could pour the liquid from a great height, pulling it into brown rainbows a metre long. Each time the bandits came, they stopped at Gope's for a cup of tea, tossing him not one rupee coins, but five rupee notes for his frothy drinks.

'Of course, it couldn't last. Gope was making money off the bandits, while Gopalpur was paying in sacks of grain. So the farmers managed to convince Gope to lace his tea with rat poison.

'The bandits burned down his teashop, killed his son, and, and . . . they had their way with Gope's daughter-in-law.'

'Amma means raped,' says Mamta.

'. . . and left her to die.'

'But you know what I heard from Sunita only yesterday? She said that Daku Manmohan is a hero to the girls in the village. She said he saved her sister from rape by that, that, that . . . Babulal. And Prem says he's only surrendering because Lokend Bhai asked him to.'

'I don't know about the rape, all I know is that he never shied from killing. I remember them systematically burning everything in

the village and cutting off the hands of those who dared to fight back. They left the handless and Gope alive as a lesson to others who might think of defying them. These creatures hang around by the Lakshmi temple begging for scraps . . .'

The last raid took place almost two years ago. Since then Gopalpur has managed to pull itself together. People are prosperous enough to get in debt again. And now the bandits, offered government amnesty, are surrendering all over India, and with Lokend's persuasion in Gopalpur as well. All those years of looting didn't earn Gopalpur a mention in the city papers, but news of the surrender has. From now on, Gopalpur's fate will be to teeter on the edge of infamy, written up far too often in the daily papers.

Evening has come to Gopalpur and with it some lone cowherd's flute cries out to them. Its lilting voice melts into their pores, stirring up a sympathetic pathos. Such is the nature of this trained wind, to bring equal parts sorrow and joy to the listener.

2

Ram Singh enjoys the crisp feel of the razor blade against his cheek. He needn't bother shaving for the wedding, but he does. He shoos off the flies dancing around his face with his free hand.

'Looks respectful,' he says to Babulal his overseer who comes over with steaming tea. 'When they see me all shaved and dressed up, they will know I care about them. You can't let slaves know they are slaves, they might become discontent. All you need to do is throw these people a bone or two and like starving dogs they will stop barking and lick your hand.' His words are carefully chosen for maximum effect. 'You've put Seeta Ram down in the book, haven't you?' Babulal nods, taking a warming sip of tea. 'My father always made the time to attend both weddings and funerals in the lands, and I will be damned if I'm the one to break with tradition.'

'Ram Bhaia, Ram Bhaia!' Lokend comes running to his elder brother, grinning from ear to ear. His teeth, big like shelled peanuts, burst out of his face. 'Ram Bhaia, I believe Seeta Ram's daughter is getting married. Take this box of sweets to her, will you. I would take it myself, but those damn policewalas have made a hash of Daku Manmohan's case and now he says he won't surrender unless I am there to guarantee the safety of his family. As if I could guarantee anyone's safety. They only listen to me because I am Singh Sahib's son. Anyway, if Bapu's position can be used to help someone, then why not.'

41

Ram Singh arranges his stance for a fight. 'What should I tell you? What could I tell you that you don't already know? The evidence is before you. You know what the villagers say? They say they will find peace only in their graves. They say that once again the bandits will rule this land, and do you know why? Because of your ridiculous surrender scheme. Every four years a politician passes through this place with a stack of promises, a bunch of gundas and a pack of chaiwalas. All standard issue from Delhi, but they have done nothing for our village. We shouldn't let those bandits surrender; we should hunt them down like rabbits.'

'Bhaia, guns will bring more guns. You hit a man with a rock, he'll come back at you with a stick. You hit a man with a stick, he'll come back at you with a sword. You attack him with a sword, he'll retaliate with a gun. Surrender *is* the only answer. Non-violence *is* the only lasting weapon. To *that* there can be no retaliation.' It's easy to mistake the younger for the elder.

'This may be the land of Gandhi, non-violence may have worked against the British, but against these motherfuckers we need guns.'

'Guns can never be the answer; violence is a primitive tool, the antithesis of civilisation.'

'You are a dreamer,' says Ram Singh. 'All your effort won't move one grain of the future.'

'Yes, in a way you are right, but even so, you only make your enemies stronger by fighting them. It's a misguided man who'll fight without the backing of his people. It's a foolish man who'll fight without the backing of his god . . .' He laughs. 'We must all be foolish men then.'

Ram Singh feels himself pulled into his younger brother's eyes. He shivers with irritation and says, 'I have to go, I will be late.'

'Don't forget the sweets, and give Prem a ride too. I don't think he's ever sat in a jeep before,' Lokend shouts before running off, his white dhoti flapping in the breeze.

At first glance he is a hunchback, with none of the awkwardness of the deformed, but at a second it is easy to see the deformity for what it is – a pet mongoose.

'I wish he'd get rid of that damn thing. It gives me the creeps. He says he keeps it to remind him that sometimes kindness can

defeat cruelty, just like a mongoose can tear the head off a snake. Why is the mongoose "kind" and the snake "cruel", I ask you? I think he says that to make an impression on me. As if I care. Our great-great-great-grandfather was a zamindar. Should we stop now just because my younger brother doesn't have the taste for it?'

The overseer knows better than to reply to Ram Singh's rhetoric-al questions. His brother's presence induces self-doubt. Nothing a little rum won't cure. Babulal takes a bottle out of his kurta pocket.

'No, not before the wedding,' says Ram Singh. This time Lokend's presence has an unusually long-lasting effect on him. 'I am going to see Bapu,' he says, without moving his reluctant feet. 'I better go see Bapu . . .' He looks back at the Big House. Anxious beads of perspiration have sprouted on his face. 'I must go see Bapu now or I'll be late.' Managing to convince himself in stages, he moves swiftly towards the house.

The Big House shimmers in the distance with an inner light that shrieks at the onlooker. Its gleaming whitewash puts a glare in the eye. It has been that way since it was built more than one hundred years ago. It has stood gleaming through every summer, every monsoon and every addition. Its glow comes not just from the true-ness of the whitewash, but also from the belief in its power. It stands apart and above the brown plane, a jewel of prosperity and control.

Many families living in Gopalpur owe their existence to the Big House. Most of their forefathers worked on it during the great drought. Singh Sahib's great-great-great-grandfather, the then king, kept extending the building as a means of paying the villagers in grain. The construction stopped only when the rains arrived, and it was at its completion that Gopalpur got its name.

In the old days this land of ravines was a malingering nomadic expanse, visited mostly by cattle. They would arrive from nowhere and everywhere to leave great heaps of dung pats for the wandering tribes to collect. The tribes' people named the place Gobarpur: *gobar* – cow dung, *pur* – site. Cow dung site. But Gobarpur didn't sound elegant enough to support the shining Big House, so Singh Sahib's great-great-great-grandfather changed the name to Gopalpur – the

abode of Gopal, the flute-playing, blue-skinned god of love. And to firmly establish Gopalpur as the true eponymous land of the love god, the great-great-grandfather planted a virtual forest of mango trees brought all the way from Vrindavan, from the very same legendary orchards in which the young Gopal was believed to have seduced throngs of milkmaids with a lot more than just his flute-wielding prowess. Few trees survive today, but their fruits are blessed with extraordinary sweetness. Come dusk, there is at least one flute to be heard in Gopalpur, perpetuating its name.

The Singhs didn't remain kings much longer after Gobarpur became Gopalpur. They were forced to give up the throne and their privy purses when the country achieved independence from British rule.

Gobarpur or Gopalpur, king or zamindar, the people still look to the Big House for sustenance.

Ram Singh strides to his father's room, a man with a purpose. The slaps of his sandals echo so loudly in the corridor that he has to turn and look to make sure he is alone. Asmara Didi is standing outside Singh Sahib's room, waiting as it were for Ram Singh's appearance. He is annoyed.

They enter the room together.

Singh Sahib, the widowed father of the two boys, is in bed. An untidy chess game is spread before him like an unfinished meal. From his vantage point Ram Singh can see that the black king is in a snare he can't get out of. He feels in much the same snare himself.

'You are white, I hope?' He mocks his father. 'Which one of his pet dogs did he get to play with him today?' Ram Singh asks Asmara Didi. She has no intention of replying. In days long past father and son might have played a game of chess together, but that is no longer the case.

Singh Sahib looks at Asmara Didi and lifts his left hand slightly. That one tiny movement serves as a swath of communication between them. Her knees are stiff and both crack mutinously at different times as she kneels to touch his purple gout-infected toes with her forehead.

'Oh sht . . . op.' Singh Sahib absolved Asmara Didi from touching his feet months after she cured his wife Bibiji of her mysterious illness and made her strong enough in the 'female department' to bear him a child. But Asmara Didi has neither acknowledged her status in the Big House nor her employer's wishes.

Still kneeling, she removes Singh Sahib's quilt with one flick, a little like a magician revealing the finale to a most complicated trick, and places his turban on his head in an unpunctuated movement. Singh Sahib, standing six feet five inches, the biggest man in the region, at his heaviest one hundred and ten kilos, was never a fat man. Now, uncovered and turbaned, his immense frame takes over the room.

Singh Sahib's right arm dangles like a curtain pull by his side. Asmara Didi places the limp limb in his lap, palm facing upwards. It falls to the ground. Once again she places it with great care in his lap. Again, it slips. She has to discipline the unruly curled hand a few times before it will stay still.

Ram Singh moves closer to his paralysed father, allowing the dead limb no dignity in his scrutiny. Asmara Didi wrinkles her brows and throws her head quickly forward and back a few times like an old mare. Move back, she says silently. Move back or else.

Even now, five years since his father's illness, Ram Singh feels uncomfortable standing taller than him. He bends his knees and straightens. Sitting, head higher than Singh Sahib's, is unthinkable. Technically, standing is disrespectful too, but standing is more deferential than sitting.

The son looks from the shining buckles on his sandals to his father's feet. He stopped touching them long ago. He still remembers the day that his father spitefully kept pulling them out of reach till Ram Singh was almost chasing those elusive toes on his hands and knees like a dog.

Singh Sahib makes an initial attempt to speak from the mobile side of his mouth. He only manages to leak spit like a dripping tap. Asmara Didi wipes his spit with a towel. It is clear the old man puts up with the woman's fussing with a degree of annoyance. But he has grown used to her. He installed her in the Big House years ago

45

to keep his fading wife company. He has a lot to thank her for, including his own two boys. She was clever with her potions even then.

'How'sh . . . brother? Come . . . closher.' Singh Sahib's words are like river stones bounced by young boys across rushing water, leaping along, with great gaps in between.

Asmara Didi and Ram Singh move forward together in the single movement of a cast net. Again the turbaned man signals to the woman with a look; this time she leaves the room. Her eyes linger long and hard on Ram Singh's back where the whitewash from the wall has left powder marks on his indigo Nehru jacket.

Ram Singh feels an old welt open up again, and he says, 'Fine, I imagine,' with practised nonchalance.

'Whe . . . ll . . . you sheen him?' Wheeze in. Wheeze out.

'Yes.' Monosyllabic answers convey more than full sentences.

'. . . jealoushy . . . no . . . n,' the old man says out of the working side of his mouth.

The son looks into his father's face without a trace of emotion. His father is forbidden to him. Singh Sahib's long morning in bed has not dulled the glow of his pristine crackly starched embroidered white muslin kurta with precisely thirty-seven deliberate creases in each sleeve. Asmara Didi takes great care of Singh Sahib's clothes and puts the creases in herself each morning with a heavy brass iron studded with little arched windows along both sides through which she blows at the hot coals.

The sun is high outside. The light perfectly illuminates the picture of the elephant-headed Ganesha flanked by peacocks painted by Bibiji on the back wall of the room. There are bars on the window. Rectangles of sunlight dance just above Singh Sahib's head, falling in and out of his eyes.

The old man lies prone, mentally shading his eyes. As it is, he can't use his good hand for fear of falling over. The thought of falling over makes Singh Sahib's mouth flicker with the hint of a smile. He can clearly recall how Bibiji had fallen over in the backseat of their jeep when he'd brought her back as his new bride. How embarrassed it had made her and how prettily she'd blushed. How that

blush had reached out to him and grabbed his heart from inside his chest, never to let go.

What does he have to smile about? Ram Singh has learned to read the nuances of his father's face but not his thoughts. The old man closes both eyes as the sunlight catches him mid-thought. He thinks of his wife a lot. That's one thing he can still do with his crippled body.

'Ask Asmara Didi to put in curtains,' says Ram Singh, his voice packed with irritation, starting to pace the room, placing one diffident foot slowly in front of the other, thinking each step carefully through. He knows his father doesn't like pacing. He has to calculate exactly when to stop, just before Singh Sahib's irritation burbles over into a spurt of reprimand. He wants to bring up the issue of the property again, but doesn't. He already knows the answer, from years of having this conversation, way before his father's face got twisted. 'Want me to die, do you? I am not dying yet, my brain is still as sharp as a new lemon. Forget about things that don't concern you. You will get what you deserve when you deserve it.' His father always spoke as if he was talking about Fate, but of course he was talking about his own plans for his son. Today he would want to say the same things through his paralysed mouth. Why bother? The son already knows the words.

Ram Singh has to grind his teeth together to stop himself from speaking. His father's unsaid words make him prickly. *Forget about things that don't concern me, indeed. The property does concern me, all seven hundred hectares of it.* And if Babulal is to be believed, the additional four hundred and sixty-seven hectares virtually owned by them in everything but name.

'Lokend . . . Daku?' Always talk of Lokend, his younger brother. What has Lokend got that he hasn't? The sun drops. The rectangles slip with finality into the old man's eyes. A trail of ants marches through the scene of pastoral delight and frolicking gods behind Singh Sahib's head. *Silent rebellion will get you nowhere, my friend. As long as you divide the land fairly, half and half. After all, there are no smaller halves. Or are there? In your realm anything is possible.*

'Can we talk about the lands? There are two problems.'

The father keeps his eyes closed, forbidding him the consideration of sight.

'Well, you have left me in charge, haven't you? Do you want me to quit? Would you like to handle the lands yourself?' It is the continuation of the same argument they have been having since before the stroke. Ram Singh's words have become progressively more cruel. His father doesn't attempt to reply.

'Then if *you* can't handle the lands, let me do the work. I am the only one who has kept this place together. Why can't you see that?' The son speaks for both of them, aloud for himself and silently for his father. He knows his father's mind, and there is no approval in it. *You wish I was more like Lokend. But he is the least like you. Look at me. Can you not see yourself in me?* There is more than a vestige of the old man in his son's finely carved features, the straight nose and the strong moustache.

Singh Sahib has that twitch in his lip that tells his son the interview is over.

But the son won't be brushed away this easily. Physically he has the upper hand. Trapped in his inactive body, his father can do nothing. Ram Singh squats close to the old man's ear. 'We have to act soon. More and more people are talking about taking loans from that Lala Ram. We have to stop that. I have a plan,' he whispers harshly.

Lala Ram tried to hide the tin signs collecting in a growing heap in one corner of his shop, even so, they have popped up all over Gopalpur: *Hypothecated to the Bank of India*, written in curly-wurly yellow paint on black.

'We are losing ground. There is talk of opening a branch here soon, right in that Saraswati Stores. Then we can forget about getting any interest payments at all.'

'Huh,' says the father, who isn't at all worried about the Bank of India grabbing his share of the loan business. After all, who in Gopalpur is going to fill out a litany of papers asking impossible questions requiring complicated answers? Date of birth? Repayment terms? Security? And on and on. With him, they just have to plant their thumbprints in the lower right corner, place the paper bonding them – sometimes for life, sometimes for generations – in

their rafters away from mice and, if they are lucky, termites, and forget about it for eternity.

'You just give me the word, and I make sure Lala forgets about the banking business.'

Singh Sahib finally opens his eyes. He still has one weapon left: The Look. Ram Singh hasn't seen that look in his father's eyes for years now. The last time he had seen it was when he and Lokend fought and he had broken his younger brother's jaw. His father had lashed him in full view of the servants, continuing the thrashing till the belt broke. Ram Singh still has the scars on his back. After a particularly bad day, he likes to look at them.

'Lea . . . ve!'

'Times are changing. You will have to do it sooner or later if you are to survive as Gopalpur's zamindar. After all, it is my future too. I will not be the one to break with family tradition because of you. You yourself say that tradition and honour are everything . . .'

'. . . do . . . hnt! Honour! It ish . . . n't . . . you!'

The ruthlessness of the insult shoves Ram Singh to the wall. Defeated but not crushed he bounces back: 'I know what you think. You think I have no honour. Do you really think you would do things differently? Say what you like, I am more like you than you know. Honour before Life.' He shouts out his father's motto before leaving the room.

Singh Sahib does nothing to curb the hatred that lodges in his throat making it difficult for him to breathe.

'You leave him alone!' Asmara Didi accosts Ram Singh outside the door. 'Remember, I brought you into this world.'

'Yes, you keep telling me so . . . So damned what, do you think you can take me out of it too?'

'It would have been better if she'd never had you!' says Asmara Didi, surprised at her brutality. 'Your father loves you, I wish you could see that.'

'Yes, he loves me so much that he never wants to see my face.'

'That's not true! Don't you remember how the two of you used to eat dinner together every night? It was always Lokend who didn't have his attention.'

'Lokend may not have had his attention then, but he certainly has his love now.'

'Give him a chance, won't you . . .' she says, visibly softening. 'He is in a bad way. When your amma died, he stopped living too . . .'

'He better have, it was he who killed her. She was too good for him.'

'Ram Singh! Your father loved Bibiji more than life itself,' she says. 'A love like that is fraught with danger, it can be very fragile . . . but you wouldn't understand . . .'

'He went with other women till she died of a broken heart.'

'No . . . she was weakened by her breathing sickness,' she says, shaking her head. 'She was very weak, she couldn't handle the strain of bearing a second child,' she reiterates, trying to convince herself as much as Ram Singh. In her opinion it was misguided jealousy that killed Bibiji, not childbirth.

It was a cruel trick of providence that had placed Bibiji at the window the day Singh Sahib put his hands on the shoulders of a village woman waiting under the spreading mango tree. The woman, one of his numerous bachelor dalliances, had come to ask for money to go to the city. Singh Sahib had grabbed her shoulders to impress upon her never to come to his home again. The woman may have been no one to him, but for Bibiji she was her nemesis, sent by the gods to quell her laughter and teach her the one universal truth: Nothing is Permanent.

That day an alien loneliness, thus far held at bay by her husband's love, rushed up and grabbed Bibiji by the throat. All her loneliness and desolation attacked her, and for the first time since she had arrived at the Big House she regretted her superior marriage that made her unfit to return home. After that, she lived in constant fear, her stomach balled up so tight that she was unable to eat. Day after day, the situation received sustenance from the placenta of her imagination. Her love became desperate. In his absence she found herself cleaning all her husband's things in a frenzy, just to be close to him. She lay alert and unsleeping night after night thinking her self-cruelty would give her resilience, but it only intensified the pain. More and more, she spent long hours at her open window

gazing into the fields, closing it only on the days when the maddened dust came to visit Gopalpur, accepting her situation, having nowhere to go and nothing to change. That's when she'd started having the midnight attacks which left her breathless and half-conscious.

'What do you know? You were only four when she died,' says Asmara Didi. 'Did you know your mother was a commoner, a mere village girl, but still he married her. He went against his whole family, this village, tradition, to bring her into this house. She didn't have children for many years, and he could have taken another wife, but he didn't.'

'Maybe he should have taken another wife, then she might be alive today . . .' Ram Singh misses his mother in that gruff way of tough men who can never acknowledge their feelings.

'Your mother was – no, is, your father's entire world. She was simply too suspicious of her good fortune, she couldn't accept her destiny. She was so lovely, so delicate, so lonely, so weak . . . Everyone has a story, Ram Singh, mark my words; each of us has our own burden.'

'Huh, each one of us, indeed, except my perfect brother, damn him, and that godawful mongoose of his.'

'You used to keep mongoose pups too, you know. After your mother died you spent all your time beside a wooden crate hidden behind the cowshed which held four abandoned mongoose pups. Their eyes just barely open, you kept them alive on a rag dipped in milk.'

'Do you really expect me to believe that?' he says, his voice wavering. Of course he remembers. He remembers vividly. It was on one of those dank days when the clouds were distended over the fields, stretched big and fat with rain, that he thought he would make the world right for his grieving widowed father. He'd brought one of his pet mongoose pups into his father's despondent room, walking heel to toe like a thief in a vaudeville act, and quickly placed the pup in his father's hands before thought could change his mind. Then he'd run to the safety of the darkest corner in the room to hide behind the curtains, believing his father would be fooled into thinking the present came from the heavens if he hid well enough.

He'd watched secretly as the pup arranged itself into a confident ball, so tiny that it was no more than a bony warm feeling in those massive palms. He had wanted to leap out from behind the curtain straight on to his father's lap, but before he could make a sound his father dropped the pup on the floor. The spell was broken and Ram Singh knew not to declare himself.

'You are free to believe what you want.'

'Amma died, but not me, I was alive, I am still alive – when will he see *me*? Honour before Life. My God, what does that man in there know about honour then?'

The chill has returned to the air. It enters Singh Sahib's good leg and spreads through his body like ink on blotting paper. Asmara Didi is back to light the fire. 'Leave h . . . it,' he says. He can't get his temperature just right with the fire going. It's comfortable for a while, then too hot to bear. Of course Singh Sahib could keep a retinue of constant servants by his side to move him around the room, if he so wished, but he doesn't. He wants to be alone, as do all the guilty. He can just about stand to be in the company of Asmara Didi, and that too for very short periods.

'Lokend has gone back to the bandits. Hai, when will he learn? After they have lopped off his obstinate head in one swift stroke? As if those scoundrels need our help now, after they've ravished our fields and raped our women . . .' Asmara Didi's chastisement contains more pride than anything else. It is a description of Lokend's foolish courage, with the emphasis on courage. 'Through and through he's your son . . .' Far from the truth, her words die on her lips. In fact, every cell in Lokend's body proclaims him as his mother's son, even though Bibiji never had a chance to hold him. She never recovered from childbirth, and when Lokend was only four weeks old, she died with a soft sigh. All joy died with her and the Big House's fate as a place of sadness and guilt was sealed.

The memory of that time still brings a shudder to Asmara Didi's frame. Overnight Singh Sahib's skin began to hang on him like baggy wet clothes two sizes too large, and prayers and incense ruled the Big House, lodging deep inside cupboards, up trees, under quilts

and in each and every vessel in the kitchen. Ram Singh and his father had their heads shaved so all the world would know of their grief.

After that, Singh Sahib never left his room and refused to see his younger son, whom he blamed for his mother's death. The little Lokend, talking in a language oiled with m's, had only Asmara Didi. When he said Am-m-ma for the first time, Asmara Didi was tempted to let the word fly free on shimmering wings right into her waiting ear to fill the child-lonely spot in her heart. But she couldn't. 'Not Amma,' she'd said, 'Didi.' There is a reason why mothers are called Amma. It was much harder for the boy to say didi, elder sister, it was a word learnt, not like amma, which sprang from his soul un-solicited. But she was more than a mother to him.

The word out of his mouth, there was never any confusion in Asmara Didi's mind as to her duty, and she aggressively grasped her role as surrogate mother and teacher. She instantly recognised a special stillness in Lokend, which she couldn't shake in spite of her attempts to draw him into her world with childish games. Sometimes she thought she didn't have to teach him anything, just jog his memory a little for ancient knowledge to pour out of his mouth in a fountain of pure speech.

She is glad she wasn't picked to be his mother. There is some-thing heart-rendingly tragic about a spiritual child because he belongs to everyone and to no one at the same time. It was her duty to formally impart the holy knowledge of scriptures to him. Luckily she knew the words of the *Bhagvat Gita* and the mantras of the Vedas. Her husband had been a bit of a dilettante with his learning, and though he never made it to the enlightened stage, he certainly knew the theory by heart. More than most, Asmara Didi and her husband had shared a closeness that rarely occurs in childless couples. It was to fulfil her role as companion that she had thrown herself equally into divine learning. But her knowledge wasn't for herself, and it was only years later, in the employ of the Big House, that Asmara Didi realised it was fated for her tiny charge.

She looks at the old man's face. It is a pleading face full of confused sorrow. He should have made peace with his son years ago. Such

torment in a father is no good. Asmara Didi has come to know the staunchest part of the zamindar. It is a part certainly worthy of respect, perhaps even love.

'Ra . . . hm Shingh's ta . . . hlking . . . Lala,' Singh Sahib's thoughts are still with his elder son.

'Why do you let him upset you like this?' It's clear the woman has no softness for the subject of their conversation.

'Look Lok . . . hend. He . . . sh so . . .'

'Different,' she completes the sentence for him like she has been doing for years. 'Some pups are born black, others white. That's just the way it happens. It's no one's fault. Do you really wish Ram Singh was more like Lokend? You don't really wish that, do you? Having a soul like Lokend's is a huge burden.'

'. . . but . . .'

'Don't you think Ram Singh wishes he was more like Lokend? Don't you think he would be if he could? Be nice to him. That's the least he deserves. He'll come around.' She knows it is no more possible to take her own advice than it is to bring back the black into her hair.

The father shakes his head, the only part of his body over which he has any real control. The zamindar may wish for Ram Singh to be more like Lokend, but he cannot accept his younger son or the path he has chosen. Singh Sahib is a temporal man. Lokend's asceticism incenses him, he feels as if he has been somehow left behind by his son. *You live vicariously through the lives of those you help. You remain detached and pure, a rock, loving everyone equally. Loving everyone equally, you love no one. But nothing I say gets to you. You are ice, freezing any water that comes to change you into a shape of yourself.*

'Is it better to spar with one or admire the other always from a distance?' Asmara Didi asks, reading his thoughts. She knows it is Singh Sahib's intransigence that keeps him deeply disappointed with both his sons. If he had his way, they would have turned out like him, with his values, playing by his rules, upholding his brand of honour.

* * *

It is that bright blue time of evening when the sky appears deep and close. The big man looks out of his window. It will be some time before the stars come out. How his wife loved this time of day. The cicadas are in full swing, and the house is rumbling with kitchen sounds. He doesn't eat like they used to, still, the cooking goes on. Asmara Didi presides. She has taken him off garlic and onions and all manner of vegetables with tiny seeds. What does it matter? His tongue is dry from talking and disappointment. It feels like a piece of cardboard in his mouth.

He lets his thoughts return to her. *Do you know what your son did today? He went to help those bandits surrender. Don't shudder, meri jaan, it's true, they will surrender and fill up the jails like cows returning home from the forests after a fat feed. He is giving away his share of the lands to them, and I can do nothing to stop him. He thinks zamindari is wrong. He said as much. In the eyes of God these lands aren't ours, is what he said.* After all these years he can still remember the parchment frailty of her body. She is as delicate as a deer's leg. He can see her blood as it travels beneath her skin. She gets that familiar colour in her cheeks for no reason at all and looks so beautiful that he has to stop breathing. He can sense the pulse beating in her neck. That single pulse, up, down, up, down, ticks in unison with his own. Tick, tick, tick. He tries to push her away, but she stays. *What can I do? I have to sit here and wait for news like a moulting bird. You are my only companion now. One of our sons gives away our lands while the other never tires of acquiring more. And they both do it in the name of honour! What do they know of real honour? Nothing. How could they, you say? I never taught them about my kind of honour. I should have brought them up after your death.*

Talk to Lokend, you say. How can I? He defies me at every turn. That is a strange way to love a father, no? He owns the words, but somewhere inside there is admiration for his boy, so secret that even he doesn't know it's there, under the frustration, anger and guilt. *Have I been a bad father? Maybe he is standing up for what he believes. I should know all about that, you say. I know what you think, my beliefs . . . my traditions, will be the death of me. You are probably right. That's what used to upset you the most, our traditions . . .*

Perhaps I should have allowed you to change some things around here, then you might have been happy. Oh, meri jaan, I miss you . . . Do you remember how we used to go hunting every winter? I know you cried inside yourself each time I bagged a deer. I'm not hungry, you would say at dinner, just so you wouldn't have to eat its flesh, my dear sweet love. You were so delicate in so many ways, but so strong when you wanted to be. I remember our chess games, you were much better than me. Don't think I didn't notice that you let me win . . .

If you could see me now. Would you pity me? Would you love me? Your boy did this to me. No sooner do the words become a coherent thought than he regrets them. But everyone knows the zamindar blames Lokend for his stroke. *I try not to think of it. But I can still smell the stink. There he was, on all fours like an animal, cleaning the shit with his hands. His hands, the hands you and I created, doing a Sudra's work. It might as well have been my hands that were polluted. We are Singhs, we are not Sudras. I have never let the shadow of a Sudra fall on my family, and there he was, cleaning shit. Bibiji, you are the lucky one, dead before your son could baffle you with his behaviour.* An angry tear struggles out of his good eye. Protected by darkness, he doesn't wipe it away.

Every time he goes to the toilet he is reminded of that other shameful day. His son on his knees, holding a piece of wood piled high with brown human waste, a stinking brown blob with no sense of decency. It was slipping off its perch, sliding to the ground like a slow drip on a spider's web. A taunting, insulting pile that his own son was handling with his pure, even loving, hands. Neither his son nor his pet mongoose was disturbed by his labour, by the stench of it or the blue flies that settled alternately on the brown mass and face unchecked because the hands that belonged to the face were too busy to wave them off. But that's not what disgusted his father into a stroke. It was the complete sense of normalcy in Lokend's bent back, as if he'd knelt to pet a favourite dog, that crippled the old man.

The first thing Asmara Didi did after the stroke was get rid of the squatting toilets. They were replaced with Parryware commodes. Grey and ageing, the commodes now support a brown ring just at the top edge. The flush has never been used. The rusty chain hangs

down from the ceiling like a noose. There are always buckets of water sitting in the bathroom to be poured into the cistern. Singh Sahib leaves a hanky hanging on the door handle if there is some big business in the toilet, otherwise, he pours a mug of water in himself to dilute the colour to a respectable, barely noticeable yellow. He is still uncomfortable on the Bakelite seat, and if he could have stood without support, he might have squatted on it. But he can't, so he sits, properly, legs falling off the edge, cringing every time his skin touches the cold hard surface. *Bibiji, in the cities everyone is using these filthy things. Can you imagine? I have to trust Asmara to clean the seat for me. You are the lucky one, dying once . . . I may be alive, but I do not live . . . I die a little every day . . .*

'Brooding isn't good for you.' She comes on silent feet. She shakes her head to herself. She can smell it in the room, that air of resignation. She tries to shun her thoughts physically by shrugging her shoulders, but they stay wrapped round her like a warm shawl. She wipes her upper lip and with a smile faces the man waiting for death. Still smiling, she lights the candles and ignores the tear.

He is tempted to tell her to go lose herself in the kitchen, but he doesn't. 'Lokend will be back tomorrow. Will you see him?' she asks.

The big man says nothing, he looks at his feet with great intent. What can he say? Yes, he would love to see his son, nothing would make him happier, but there is so much history in their desperate destinies. How does one wash away history? He is in that gully of silence between mountains of anticipated rejection. To climb up one of those mountains he would have to give up his crushingly heavy fear. He might have been able to release his burden to Bibiji for safekeeping, but he has nowhere to put it now. The gully is a safe place. *Help me. Please help me,* he asks of the dead.

It is the living that replies, 'Good, I'll tell him then. I'll make something nice for your lunch. Lokend loves puris.' Asmara Didi chuckles. 'Does he love them, or does his mongoose? What's its name again? Raja?'

Today it's just the same. The memory of holding a mongoose pup rushes over the old man unbidden. He feels the tears once again creep up under his skin, thick and strong.

'Go,' he says with desperation to the woman.

There isn't just sadness in his tears, there is also anger.

But as they fall, they become tears of regret.

Lokend jumps into the jeep. 'Let's go,' he says to the mongoose, 'let's go find those bandits.' He starts the engine. The jeep jumps into life, Ram Singh has left it in gear again. The sudden jump jogs Lokend's thoughts. 'Better not, my friend. I better take the truck. My brother is all spruced up for the wedding. He'll kill me if I take the jeep and he has to ride in the truck.' He chuckles.

Lokend started talking to Raja a long time ago. All through his lonely youth, he knew he was different from his brother who deserved and received his father's vague attention. If he was someone else he might have been jealous. But he has no time for jealousy, or for that matter sadness. If there is one regret in his life, it is that his mother died before him. He would have liked to have known her.

3

WHAT CAN SHE DO ABOUT HER BIRTHMARK? Her mother has suggested a little turmeric mixed with flour. When her father became indebted to the Big House, Ram Singh magnanimously invited him to consult with the widow Asmara Didi. She had silently begged her father to take her to the Big House and get a cure for her birthmark then, but he did not. Why? Acceptance, that's why. Her father had accepted the birthmark on his daughter's forehead as finally as he accepted the weather or the bandits.

The dew hasn't formally evaporated off the mustard leaves outside. Except for the sleeping baby, she is alone at home. Her mother gave her this much. As an excuse Lata Bai left Shanti behind for Mamta to look after. She has an hour before her mother will return from the well.

Mamta runs her hand over her wedding sari. For a minute she considers why it is already lying unwrapped, in precise folds gleaming like a treasure in her mother's tin trunk, then she remembers her mother had used the wrapping to deliver Shanti. She picks up a corner and looks through the sheerness of the fabric. Everything turns red, the red of love. Mamta smiles. It is as it should be. 'Keep my world red, oh Devi,' she prays. 'Jai ho Devi, Devi jai ho,' she recites her mother's words. Almost a married woman, she feels she has an equal right to them. The baby stirs in her cot. 'Shanti, hey, Shanti. I am to be married. I hope Amma will be proud of me,' she

says with a laugh, and then quickly makes a face and adds, 'and I hope Bapu will be pleased with me for the first and only time in his life.' Shanti gurgles. 'You should be happy, your turn will come. I will pray you get many suitors and that each one is more handsome and richer than the next!' Shanti gurgles again.

Mamta interprets her baby sister's sounds: 'Will mine be a handsome hero?' She cannot afford to indulge in self-doubt. By Gopalpur standards she is already an old woman, her younger sister was married before her. She looked after all her brothers and sisters and she's still at home. Without the borrowed money, no one would have taken her. What kind of man accepts a woman, almost in her twenties, with a birthmark? It has to be a desperate man. 'Of course he will be a handsome hero. Do you think Amma could have picked anyone else for me?'

'He'll come on a horse and then we'll ride away together . . .' *I'll make sure to cover my birthmark with my pallav.* She takes the sari over to the baby. 'Have you ever seen anything this beautiful?' She rubs it against Shanti's skin. The rough ersatz silk makes the baby cry.

Mamta scoops up the baby and starts rocking her, automatically. 'Yes, we will be in love forever like Singh Sahib and Bibiji. What a love that was! Then, when I have my own baby, I will come home and you two can play together.'

She bends her head over Shanti protectively. The baby sees the red birthmark approach. It is a comforting red, it is this patch of red that has cared for her since her birth. The patch of red and her mother's wiggly nipple, that's what Shanti knows of love.

Mamta regards her sister carefully, dressed in one of her old converted blouses, now no more than a cartography of spilt meals. She outlines each stain with her finger as she sings.

'He'll come on a horse to get me,
He'll come on a horse to get me,
He'll bring me a new sari to wear,
He'll bring me flowers for my hair . . .'

She sings into the baby's ear. It is the song that the boys from across the river use to taunt her. Delivered by Ramu, the words, sung to the same tune, are much harsher. But singing it to Shanti, she takes the bitterness out of it, much as she does with the wild cucumbers, rubbing one cut end against the other to bring out the poison, as foamy as a madman's spit.

'You are not married yet, get back in the field.' Her father has returned earlier than usual.

Mamta drops Shanti in her swing, and rushes out, forgetting to give it one push before she leaves. The abandoned baby starts to cry. But it has learned not to cry long; no one will come.

Mohit and Sneha are beating the dust out of the reed mats. Prem had hung them up in the Babul tree before he left for the Big House in the early-morning dark. He'd stopped Mamta from helping him: 'Your hands are already shredded,' he'd said, 'save them to massage oil into your husband's hair.' For an instant she feels the tips of her fingers on a strange skull of black hair, soft and light, and a timorous shyness envelops her like diaphanous silk.

'Mamta, come play,' says her sister. The word 'play' sits uncomfortably with her. She is so old that she feels no right to their game, invented to sweeten their work. There is such a gap between them. Their youth makes her feel older than she is.

'Stop it, you two. Come on. We have to finish here and then help Amma bring water from the well. We have to make lots of tea. Prem is bringing fresh milk today and he is going to try and get a big pat of butter too.'

The golden cry of the koyal calls to them. The children recede into the dust. After a while, they are barely visible from their hut.

Seeta Ram extracts the contracts from beneath his wife's green sari in the tin trunk. The paper creaks accusingly as he bends the pages open, one by one. He cannot read, but the bureaucratic text still speaks to him. Why did he do it? Because he had a brand-new baby daughter? Because he hoped the crop would be good this year? Because of destiny? Because of nothing? No, he did it to get Mamta off his hands. He can't come close to her without feeling a deep

rage. For her and what she stands for. And for what she has made him do.

He will never look at those contracts again once she leaves, he tells himself. But the sturdy thumbprint in the right-hand corner tells him another story. He knows he might have given away more than he bargained for. He thinks of Daku Manmohan. Lucky bastard. First he lives off the fat of the land, then off the fat of the government. Lucky motherfucker.

The baby whimpers uselessly in its swing while staring at the unfamiliar face. He doesn't feel any urge to pick her up. She starts whimpering again. Resentment fills his belly, then his lungs and lurches towards his throat, like rising froth on boiling milk.

'That's done,' Lata Bai comes in wiping her hands on her sari pallav. She's cooked the daal well and is satisfied. 'How many is he bringing with him?' she asks about the wedding party. 'Do you think Jivkant will come?'

Jivkant was born when Mamta was two years old. Lata Bai had prayed for a boy and Devi had answered her prayers. The birth of a son changed his mother's fate. Had he been born a girl, Seeta Ram would undoubtedly have taken a new wife, letting Lata Bai find her own way in the world. She had chosen the Red Ruins to have her second baby, far away from the house, for she'd decided that, if she produced another girl, it would be a stillborn birth. It happened very quickly. She hardly had time to smooth Mamta's freshly washed blanket under her hips as the boy appeared, bright and fat, just like a boy should be. Her heart had leaped out of her body to dance with the pale lemon clouds overhead. She'd clutched him to her breast, coaxing her nipple into his mouth. Through her watery happiness the damaged electric poles danced as they did in the heart of summer, and her whole field had shimmered and sparkled. Still aching, she'd run towards the house, shouting, 'A boy, a boy. Mamta's father, you hear? You have a boy. Mamta's father, come see your boy.'

The hijras arrived promptly. They must have plucked the news of his birth, achieved almost silently close to the Red Ruins, from the wind. This time they conducted themselves differently than the time they had come to bless Mamta. There was a lilt to their song,

and they danced for hours in front of the house, wiggling their hips still much too stiffly to be mistaken for true women. Seeta Ram had circled their heads three times with rupee notes without getting annoyed, such was the extent of his happiness. Eventually he chased them off with curses as one always has to.

Jivkant was her husband's from the start. She took no credit for the baby, it was an obligation fulfilled, a duty completed.

A distant train whistle makes the air quiver. Husband and wife look up. The wife runs to the door. It is a train whistle that'll bring her son home. She has forgotten the disquiet she feels. She is anxious to have her progeny close.

'I'm sure he can write now. The first in the family,' she says.

'What for would he learn to write?' The father cannot see a life beyond the farm for himself or his children.

'Perhaps Prem will get a chance to learn. And then Mohit.'

'From whom, the Big House?' he mocks her.

'I know the Big House gives nothing away.' She is more perspicacious than him. 'But Prem could learn from one of Lala Ram's twins after he gets home from work.' She is also more optimistic than him.

'Leave it,' he says. 'Reading and writing is not for us.'

'I wish Jivkant would come,' she says. 'The widow Kamla has arranged Mamta's henna ceremony.'

It is the women's time before the wedding; laughing, talking openly about their men and completely comfortable in each other's company.

Lata Bai undresses Mamta. Kamla helps her, pulling her clothes off her eagerly. 'Arey, Kamla, be gentle. I am not in a hurry to send my daughter off.' The mother looks into her daughter's eyes and cracks her knuckles against her temples. 'Be happy, my daughter, be happy.'

Mamta's heart is gripped by love. A stone of tears lodges in her gullet. She swallows painfully, but doesn't let the tears fall. She hugs her mother. Lata Bai doesn't undo her arms this time. 'Now remember, there will be no running home to me over the slightest

problem. You will have to learn to sort things out for yourself in your husband's house.' Practical advice, the best salve for a sentimental heart, sounds just right for a young bride but not for someone well past her prime.

'Oho, Lata Bai, of course she will. She's not a child, you know. Look at her. She's a grown woman. Surely you know all this. Right, Mamta? Right?' Kamla will not stop till she has extracted the embarrassment to the surface on the bride-to-be's face, just as she has the pigment from the henna leaves. Lata Bai looks away from her unfortunate daughter. Kamla gives the henna another determined stir. She has mixed the powder herself, equal parts leaf dust and okra mucus. She tests the consistency delicately on the back of her hand like she might unproved rice custard. The henna feels as slimy as an oiled snake. Perfect. She quickly rubs the paste off.

'Don't want to get my hands yellow like a bride's again, now, do I?'

Kamla guffaws at her own joke. Lata Bai abandons her uneasiness and joins in the laughter, encouraging Mamta to do the same. It is unthinkable that the widow Kamla's hands will ever be decorated again. She isn't entitled to any kind of adornment, having shamefully outlived her husband. Now she stays dressed in one of her two white saris, next to the outhouse on her son's farm. She makes sure her head is closely shaved and sometimes one can see her bald grey-green scalp peek out from under her sari pallav. It is because she is the only skilled midwife in these parts that she has a home at all. Cursed and thought to bring bad luck, the last three widows were chased out of town. Two went to beg at strangers' doors, one preferred to stay, and lies very still on the temple steps. She lets her hair grow and fall down her back, but no one cares. In the old days she would have flung herself on her husband's funeral pyre.

'No thank you. No more husbands for me,' Kamla says, as if she has a choice in the matter. She has let loose words that could only be said at a henna ceremony. For this one day, men are fair game. 'But for those who still need them, it's lucky we have Asmara Didi to cure the impotent ones,' she guffaws. 'Remember how she cured Lala Ram?' She directs her story at Mamta: 'Lala Ram tried his hand

with Nathu's daughter. Now you know Nathu's daughter, she would have given herself to a pig if it brought her a new bangle or pair of sandals, but even she rejected Lala Ram, though he had the shop and land . . . the everything. He brought her four silk saris. No response. Hai, did she tease him good . . . walked blouse-less up and down the street right under his nose, her boobs jiggling like horse bells, and him salivating after her like a dog. He tried, but couldn't get her to accompany him for even a minute behind the well. Finally he went to Asmara Didi for help. That concoction she whipped up really did something for him: Lala Ram couldn't get his dhoti to behave after that, stuck out in front like a raised flag. He was so proud when someone asked if he had a pound of flour under his dhoti. They tell me the village boys applied the same concoction to the stray dog that used to feed in the rubbish tip. Had him humping all the bitches in no time!' Kamla hoots with laughter, 'that was something. Hump, hump, hump, up and down the street all day long, till he burst!'

Mamta looks up with a sharp jerk of her head and disbelief in her eyes, not for the story, but for the indelicacy of it, while Lata Bai shakes her head with bemused resignation from side to side. Kamla nudges Lata Bai in the ribs: 'Your husband has taken a loan from the Big House. He is entitled to ask for her services, you know . . . if need be . . .' The two older women are tangled in a dance of words and companionship, of shared fortunes, and experiences of plain and simple womanhood.

'No need for Asmara Didi's concoction in my home . . . but really, sometimes I wish mine was impotent.' Lata Bai's hands flitter to her mouth like butterflies to cover the embarrassing words that just left her lips. She looks up and catches sight of her daughter, brows knitted in the middle of her forehead, a question forming in her inexperienced mind. 'Forget it . . . let's be serious now,' says her mother quickly.

'Did you hear the news?' Kamla asks earnestly.

'Yes, about Daku Manmohan. Mamta's father said —'

'No, not that old news, this other thing . . . they found Sharma's wife.'

'You mean the one who ran away after the last big wind?'

'Yes, what a fool, but quite a beauty, no?'

'I guess her mother should have tattooed the "ugly" dot to spoil her perfection on her face instead of the back of her ear. I heard she ran away with the circus.'

'Circus? No circus – with another man.'

'Oho, what is the world coming to?'

'It would have been better if she had run away with the circus, they never would have found her, but they did. Stripped her naked under the banyan, shaved her hair, four of Sharma's brothers raped her and then they rubbed shit on her body.'

'Hai, poor thing,' says Mamta.

'Poor thing nothing, she got what she deserved. Imagine if all the wives started running away, simply because they were unhappy,' says Lata Bai.

'Amma, how can you say that?'

'Leave it, Mamta, you won't understand. You have to be married as long as me to understand.' Lata Bai turns to Kamla. 'Why are you telling this story now, on this auspicious day?' she whispers fiercely enough for Mamta to hear.

'Okay, okay, let's leave it, but let me tell you just one more thing . . . the poor girl has to still live with Sharma, in the cowshed. Her head stays shaved, he has already taken another wife. That's it, no more talk about Sharma's wife.' She clamps a hand over her mouth. 'Okay, so who's doing the ceremony? Not that thief, Pundit Jasraj.'

'Yes. He was the cheapest,' says Lata Bai, defending her choice.

'I believe he tried to feel up the last two brides,' Kamla says, arresting her giggles.

'Really? I hadn't heard,' lies Lata Bai. 'Well, it won't be a problem this time,' she says, trying to set her daughter's mind at rest.

'Why not? Do you think me that ugly?' Mamta touches her forehead. She's heard of new brides being bathed in milk, but for her, a teaspoon of turmeric paste is what the widow Kamla prepared. Mamta rubs the turmeric off; underneath, her birthmark is a bilious caricature of its former self.

'Oh no, Mamta. That's not what I meant.' It's too late to paint

over her slight, so Lata Bai changes the subject. 'I wish Jivkant would come.'

'Maybe he will come just as we sit down with the priest.' What Mamta really means to say is, why would he bother? He was the cruellest of all to her. Fat little Jivkant. The love of his father's life. From the day that he emerged, soiling Mamta's blanket, he became the thief of his sister's future.

The first thing to go was Mamta's thali, her dented tin plate into the back of which her mother had impressed the symbol Ohm in tiny dots by hammering a nail in a pattern. It was given to Jivkant and Mamta began to share her mother's thali and food. Whereas before Seeta Ram had never objected to Lata Bai preparing a thali especially for her daughter, now he wouldn't hear of it. 'Let her eat the leftovers,' he said. 'Why should I water someone else's garden?'

'Do you remember when I made him drink kerosene? That was something!' Her mother looks at her with disappointed eyes. 'Oh, come, Amma, don't be that way. He probably has a big city job now.'

Lata Bai knew all along that Jivkant would leave; hadn't he always believed he deserved better? She can't remember a day when he was still inside his skin, yet Seeta Ram was surprised when his son took off, full of as much live powder as a late-firing cracker, following a train whistle to his destiny. He wanted to be an engine driver just like Lucky Sister's husband, the one who put his wife out to work as a prostitute.

'Perhaps he can't get leave.'

Lata Bai's eyes cloud over for a second. *Yes, gone to a good city job over a year now and not one rupee sent back to your family. What did you say before you left?* 'Amma, look for your money order at Lala Ram's shop every month.' 'Maybe he can't get leave, but what stops him from sending us money? He had one of Lala Ram's twins write down the address for him, not once, but twice, one for his pocket and a back-up for his satchel. The day he left, I put a red tilak on his brow and fanned the flames of the oil lamp towards his bowed head. Your father had tears in his eyes and Prem ran behind him all the way to the waiting tonga. But he left without looking back at us, twirling his moustache. He was so eager to go. I went to

Lala Ram's shop every month for a whole year, sometimes twice, sometimes thrice a month.'

At first Lala Ram would give her some brown sugar – for the children – he'd say. Then later, when he saw her approaching, he would go into the back, reluctant to deal with her expectation and disappointment. Finally, he started shooing her away from a distance, saying, 'Go away, he maybe lost . . . dead . . . the city swallows them up.'

I know my son isn't dead or lost. If anyone could make it in the city, it would be Jivkant. So where are those promised money orders?

Her husband has prepared his verbal offence carefully. He will let loose his tirade upon his son as soon as he sees him. There will be no 'When will you help us? After we are dead?' or 'Look at your mother, her eyes swollen from crying every night.' No, he will appeal to his intellect, because he knows, sure as the red birthmark on Mamta's forehead, that his son has learned the most useless skill of all – to read and write – and is now an educated man.

'Even if he does show up at the last minute, he won't bring any money with him. Of that I'm sure,' says the mother, still hoping she is wrong, but armouring herself against disappointment by pointing out the worst.

'Leave it. It may be a man's country, Lata Bai, but you will get joy only from the girls,' counters Kamla. 'Why, even the men see the dependability in our sex. Just see how they organise their lives so that they can be looked after by a woman. Have you seen one in our village that isn't married? Have you seen one widowed father who hasn't got a daughter or a daughter-in-law looking after him? I tell you, we were better off when our country was looked after by a woman Prime Minister. Poor thing, murdered like that, and her sons too. Just look at us now, under this big man Atal Bihari Vajpayee, bandits running wild as weeds. I might have to shave my head as a concession to the men, but it is only because our sex has the true power.' Kamla's features have long acquired that androgynous look of so many women who are forbidden from celebrating their femaleness.

'What power, Didi? They keep us pregnant from year to year. I say to Mamta's father, the country is moving into a new era. Our

children aren't dying like they used to because of the government's survival drops. I tell you, those things have magic in them. There hasn't been one curled leg in Gopalpur since the drought. Remember how bad it used to be? The legs of girls, and even boys, used to just wither and die at the slightest sign of unseasonable rain. Remember?' Sickness in the family was the most debilitating thing of all. With each waking minute accounted for, there was never any time to look after the sick, especially when it required collecting special herbs and plants and supplicating the gods. Who had the time to make poultice after poultice or check on a fever? None but the old and the discarded, who more often than not perished together with their patients. But things have changed with the city mobile clinics making sporadic forays into the villages, bringing medicines, cures and vaccinations. 'You've seen the change? Whenever those doctor-vans come from the city, I go to the Big House for my dose. To tell you the truth, I have more faith in them than in Asmara Didi, though Mamta's father will say that is blasphemy. I can tell it to you straight, their medicines work better than hers. Why can't we use those things that stop the babies from coming?'

The mobile clinics not only bring polio drops for the children but birth control pills and IUDs for the women. Though the women know not to couple in the middle of their cycle, because that is the most blessed time, no one understands the nature of pills. To take one every night to stop a baby from happening sounds too much like magic. IUDs they accept, but it is a brave woman who has an IUD inserted without the knowledge of her husband. Recently the van brought Nirodh condoms. *Nirodh, the sheath to a happy life*, that's what the advertisement says, that is what Lata Bai believes.

'My husband refuses. He says . . .' she lowers her voice and cups her hand to her mouth, pouring her words directly into the older, more experienced, woman's ears, 'he says it isn't natural that there should be something between a man and woman when they are, they are . . . you know what. It's not satisfying, like smelling the smoke from another's hookah.' She raises her voice back up again: 'He has a third ear that hears those thoughts before I have them. Look at me, a new baby only weeks old, and I am marrying off my

first daughter. My second daughter has children older than mine. Now what's the sense in that? Weren't six children enough? I think it's because we have no other form of entertainment, but to, to . . .'

'Is it that? Or is it because our religion demands it?'

'When it suits us, we follow the letter of our religion. We all aspire to emulate the myths, should we all have a hundred sons, just like the Kaurav clan then?'

'I agree with you, Lata Bai, but someone has to think about such things to want to change them. I was lucky I only had sons, three sons, and then my husband died. That Seeta Ram of yours sees his friends having one child after another. He thinks, more children . . . more hands to work the fields . . . a better crop, he doesn't see them as mouths to feed. What do you expect from that husband of yours, then?'

'Nothing, I suppose,' says Lata Bai, suddenly realising that her husband is a weak man, whose inaction will continue to cost her dearly, just as it did when she first married him and was repeatedly raped by his father. But in fact Lata Bai is wrong, Seeta Ram is not just a weak man, he is a cruel man; a cruel man whose brutality isn't deliberate, but stems from something as innocuous as an unquestioning nature. And therefore it is the worst kind of cruelty, that can't be shut off at will. Where the wind blows, Seeta Ram will follow. He will never be one to change anything.

'Still, Lata Bai, if you really look at it, seven children in twenty years is nothing. You have to consider yourself lucky that you aren't like your Seeta Ram's cousin's wife, married fifteen years with fourteen children to show for it, five of them already dead, one stupid in the head and one not able to walk. At least yours are healthy.'

'Yes, I suppose they are healthy, for the most part. Though Mamta's hair has been getting more orange these last few months, and Sneha's getting that big belly on her matchstick legs.'

'Oho, come now, now's not the time to talk of this,' says Kamla, putting an arm around her friend's despondent shoulders.

But Lata Bai is a train, off and running. 'No, she should know how to protect herself.' She shakes with humourless laughter. 'What protection can there be against a man who wants to couple? Eh,

daughter, if after sex you start itching down there, make sure you wash with lemon juice and neem tea. But if you start making pimples and fainting, then you have to find some government doctor man to help you – that's if your husband will allow you to go to one. The pimpling disease has no cure, though you can try Asmara Didi's prescription – drinking your own piss.'

Mamta listens intently while pretending not to, gelled solid by equal parts embarrassment and fear.

'Lata Bai! Does she have to know all this?'

'Yes! Yes, she does. I am her only defence. You know how it was with poor Lalita.' All the women of Gopalpur are familiar with Lalita's story, though the men hardly discuss it at all. 'Now you listen to me, Mamta: it's our place to accept, and accept . . . be demure. Don't say anything till addressed, don't make a sound, don't do anything to make him beat you, because you'll only have yourself to blame for it. If you displease him, he will beat you. And if you do something really bad, then he might hold you over the stove and start by singeing the hair from your eyebrows, and after that, it's burning to death and a hasty burial. You remember how Lalita turned up at the well, looking like a boiled egg.' Even now the memory of that day makes the two older women shudder. An impertinent wind had blown Lalita's pallav off her burned dome, and they had put their hands to their lips and laughed out loud. Lata Bai and Kamla couldn't stop even when the poor creature was far away, a tiny speck chased by laughter. She had left her pots behind, and they never thought to return them.

'Poor Lalita, her husband gave her the disease and then denied her the medicine. And finally, he burned her to death so he could have a cleaner, healthier wife,' says Kamla. 'Yes, you better listen sharp to your mother. No one will be able to interfere or help you if you get in trouble. But enough now, Lata Bai, we have shared enough secrets. Let's talk about something else. Tell me, what about that Ragini of yours? Lucky girl.'

'Yes, she is blessed,' says Lata Bai, her words heavy with pride. Lata Bai never worried about Ragini. Golden Ragini, blessed with beauty so unassailable that it was impossible not to be awed by it.

Mamta took care of Ragini like her very own child, and at fifteen Ragini was married and gone before her elder sister got even one offer of marriage.

The groom's family had approached her. He was a gentle soul, with no ambition. One look into his face and Lata Bai knew his type instantly. He would be ruled by Ragini. Seeta Ram sold the family cow for the wedding. He'd insisted on a grand wedding because Ragini's in-laws seemed so rich and refined. For years Lata Bai dreaded seeing her daughter returned to her scarred and burned because she didn't bring in enough dowry.

But Lata Bai doesn't have to worry any more. Her daughter's position in her new home is secure with the birth of her children: two sets of male twins, little darling children, with large dancing eyes like rabbits, all bright and black with kohl. Of course she would have produced only boys. Golden Ragini.

'Even the mother-in-law, who thinks she's spoilt, can't touch one hair on her head.' Lata Bai laughs silently inside. 'Bless you, Ragini,' she says, 'bless you. Live, my child, like I never did. No, I don't worry about her at all. She is loved by all those who know her.'

'I've heard that. She is loved by too many, in fact. She should be careful. Thoo, thoo, thoo, thoo,' Kamla spits into the four directions to ward off any evil spirits who might be hovering, waiting to ruin Ragini's future. 'Stop that! Running your hands through the bucket like a thief through gold! How can I pattern your hands if your whole palm is red?' says Kamla. But it is too late. It's good henna. Sneha's hands are already a strong orange. Kamla laughs and puts them on her cheeks.

'Yellow hands already, and still so young,' says Lata Bai with a tear in her voice.

The women sing. Mamta is quiet. Kamla dances, her hips strangely agile for her age and her widowhood. Lata Bai feels very much that she is losing a part of herself, something that should have been cut from her a long time ago. But she has grown so attached to her eldest that she doesn't know how she'll survive without her.

'I am the fruit on your vine, craving water from your hand.
Why do I let you go, my innocent one?
I am the dove in your cage, cooing for your attention,
Why do I let you go, my innocent one?
When your palanquin departs there will be emptiness . . .'

Kamla's feet stir up puffs of dust. Dhhub, dhhub, dhhub . . . she leaves definite footprints in the earth.

'Enough, Didi, that's enough. Let's sing something more cheerful. This song is putting a grinding stone on my chest.'

'So what's it to be?'

'The groom's song. Let's do the groom's song.'

'Come, come, my beloved
I wait here, dyed in love
Without you there is no garland,
No jasmine, no rose, no queen of the night, no blossom.
Without you there is no sense in jewellery,
No bangle, no earring, no necklace, no hair braid.
Without you there is no pleasure in adornment,
No kohl, no rouge, no powder, no henna . . .'

Kamla claps her unpainted hands, while the other three smile at the words of the deeply familiar wedding songs. The songs stir up Mamta's excitement again; she is eager to accept her new life. She chooses to ignore the example of her mother's marriage, the story of singed and burned Lalita, and Sharma's runaway wife. Her fate will be different. She will bring indomitable love to her duty and like a river bursting its dam it will be unstoppable, covering every-thing in its path, much like the dust of Gopalpur.

The green henna patterns glisten industriously. Lata Bai will wash her hands off ahead of time, in accordance with custom, else her husband will never cook his own food. It was the same for Ragini's wedding; after painting her hands with henna she'd had to wash them to cook the evening meal. Lucky for her, her hands receive colour willingly.

Mamta is careful with her pattern. Every so often she dabs her hands with lamp oil. A dark pattern means she will be loved by her mother-in-law.

A new life at last. Something to be excited about at last. Marriage at last. What is marriage? Coupling. Sex. Disease. Her mother's words have unsettled her, but then Nature calls out to her, shouting louder than her unsettled feeling. The whole universe seems to be in harmony with her being, a part of the same crescendo. Everywhere she looks she sees the signs, and in them reads the language of love: long beans entwined passionately on their vine, pumpkin flowers nuzzling each other, doves necking, weaver birds building their nests . . . She sinks luxuriously into her new womanly feeling.

She knows what is expected of her. Still this wedding is a dream. A love dream. She lies on the floor in the cool of her hut, palms up to the ceiling. Her mother lets her be, it might be the last time.

Lata Bai can see Mamta's chest rise and fall in contented breaths. In spite of her age, her daughter looks tiny, lying stretched out like that. Lata Bai crushes the urge to lie beside her. She remembers the days when she had sung her daughter songs and told her stories, correcting her notions with playful lies and filling her heart with fanciful images of pearly halos on kings' heads and mysterious forests filled with magical creatures with immense powers. Lata Bai watered the desert of her daughter's intellect with colours and bubbles, and as she grew up, she'd added an immense amount of practical knowledge, which Mamta remembers more by rote than anything else. What was the true value of her gift? Did she give her daughter mirages to accompany her on her unwary journey, or prosaic knowledge that could rescue her wandering heart from the worst dangers of ignorance and injustice? Did she solidly carve out a place in this world for her or keep her seeking in vain for what could never be found? Did she give her sadness or vision?

Lata Bai feels the anxiety burbling up into her throat. *Oh, Devi, make him a good man. Jai ho Devi, Devi jai ho.*

'Amma, what was that you and Kamla were saying about the

74

lemons and babies? Who will I ask about all that when you are not there? Amma, I'm afraid.'

'Tch, tch, you are getting married, not going to some hell.'

'Look what happened to Lalita and her sister.'

'Oho, that's not going to happen to you.' It is time to put things in perspective, so Mamta can realise that she is better off than the sisters. 'You won't be like Lalita. You will be a good wife. You won't be like her sister either, expecting a baby from God knows whom. You will be a good girl.' Lata Bai has only words, but she knows there are no guarantees. Lalita, burned for no fault of her own, but only because she became sickly, and her sister, sent to the Red Bazaar soon after her baby was born because she was unfortunate enough to get pregnant with her own father's child. Lata Bai has seen the boy, no longer a baby, at Saraswati Stores and has to drag her thoughts away from his history. He was accepted by his grandmother as one of her own to redress the deficiency of a womb that produced only girls. Had he been a girl, he wouldn't be alive today.

Her disquiet temporarily allayed, Mamta rolls on to her stomach, propping her chin up with the backs of her open hands, still careful with her hennaed palms. 'Tell me about Shakuntala. Just the short version. How she had pearls in her hair and beauty –'

'No, enough!' says Lata Bai, slightly annoyed now by her memory. Each time she'd told that story, she'd replaced the main character with her own daughter. But it is now time to acknowledge that Mamta is anything but beautiful. Fantasies are the worst thing a bride can take to her new home.

Mamta lingers all day with her hennaed hands held out to the sun like a beggar asking for alms. It is custom, and custom alone that makes this the women's day, the day they rest and beautify themselves. Seeta Ram doesn't approve, but he can't do anything about it. Today Lata Bai and Sneha will do all the cooking.

> *I am the fruit on your vine, craving water from your hand.*
> *Why do I let you go, my innocent one?*
> *I am the dove in your cage, cooing for your attention,*

Why do I let you go, my innocent one?
When your palanquin departs there will be emptiness . . .'

It is a while before Lata Bai realises she is humming Kamla's song. She switches off her internal melody; it brings her no pleasure. Today Mamta will become *paraya,* the other, and when she needs succour or solace after this day, she may not seek it from her mother because she belongs to another.

Shanti has been quiet most of the day. Lata Bai has fed her twice since the morning, but she didn't feel like sucking much. She's blown on her face at least four times for a reaction since the morning to make sure she was still alive. She would have skimmed off some of the daal water for her, but because of the weevils she thinks she might stick to breast milk today.

She looks in on the baby. She is sleeping peacefully, each eye ringed by a cluster of flies thick as smudged kohl. She shoos off the flies, wets the corner of her pallav in some water and bends over her to clean out her eyes. Then she changes her mind. Instead she opens her blouse and squeezes a bit of milk out of her wrinkled right nipple. She cleans the baby's eyes with breast milk. Shanti whimpers, but stays sleeping. Her forehead feels clammy, but Lata Bai ignores the dampness and goes about her business with gusto. If her daughter has to fall sick at all, she is determined that it will be only when the government doctor-van arrives in Gopalpur, and not a moment before.

'You know what, they are coming to the wedding. I overheard Ram Singh Sahib and Lokend Sahib talking to each other,' Prem bursts in, followed by the sweet smell of roses. 'Look what I've brought back. When I told Asmara Didi my sister was getting married today she cut all her roses and gave them to me. "Go, decorate your house like a king," she said to me.'

'I wish she'd given us something to feed the guests instead,' says Lata Bai. 'Did you get any butter? Any milk?'

'Yes, yes . . .' He pulls out a parcel of ficus leaves from his kurta pocket and a pot of milk. The leaves glisten from the grease. The smell of stale milk mingles with the roses.

76

'She'll part with fresh roses, but not fresh butter.'

Prem looks at his mother, at the unfamiliar sound of bitterness in her voice. 'Look, I got this too –' He places a lump of jaggery in her hand, the size of a grapefruit, and looks at her, his eyes saying *Happy?*

She looks away. Yes, she should be happy . . . one daughter producing only sons, one son with a good job in the railway, Prem working at the Big House and bringing back pats of butter and, after Mamta's wedding, one less female mouth to feed. What more can she ask for? What more could her heart possibly want?

'Sneha, get to work!'

'Amma, there's time yet.' Sneha wants to leave the henna on her hands a little longer.

'Sneha,' she warns, 'chapattis.'

'Yes, Amma.' She washes her hands in a cup of water. 'What about Jivkant Bhaia?'

'And *what* about your brother? A fancy job and not one rupee sent back to his family in all this time.' She speaks in the third person to disassociate herself from her offspring.

Prem says nothing, but his eyes give him away. Jivkant is who Prem aspires to be, except for the not-one-rupee-sent-back-to-his-family part. Perhaps one day he too will leave to find his place on a train going somewhere. He can hear the faintest whistle blow across the fields, and when it does, he lifts his head suddenly like a watchdog and looks over to see if there is any smoke, proof that the whistle isn't just a fibrillation of his desire. He doesn't know what Jivkant has made of his life, but he's meant to be coming back for Mamta's wedding. That much he knows. Prem had taken his brother's letter to the Big House to be read, and it said that Jivkant was coming back. Prem had wondered if Jivkant had written the letter himself and for a moment he'd felt the high fever of jealousy ride up under his skin and bring a flush to his face.

'Even Lucky Sister sent us something. She didn't just fritter the money away on herself, and she had more reason to . . . the way we all shunned her,' says Lata Bai. In spite of her anger she can see that comparing her son's railway job to her sister's prostitution is unfair.

'Still, there's time. Perhaps he will show up for the wedding tonight, after all. Well, you might as well put the roses out. Keep a few nice ones for your sisters' hair,' she says, softening.

Lata Bai pulls the sari tight round her daughter's waist. At her age, Mamta still can't get the pleats right. Sneha is more accomplished at tying a sari.

'Stand up straight!' The mother tugs at the five-metre cloth, dragging her daughter with it like a piece of driftwood on a sea of red. 'Can't you stand still?' Mamta goes rigid to obey her mother's command, but the moment is spoilt.

The widow Kamla left straight after lunch, so there are no outsiders at the house now. Though Prem has been sent home early by Asmara Didi to help with the wedding preparations, he works the fields with his father and brother. Why waste labour? Almost a man, his back is bent over exactly like Seeta Ram's. He is most like his father physically, but he has his mother's softness. Mohit never turned out quite as robust. He has the delicate frame of a girl, long wiry legs and a skinny chest with two sunken nipples defiling the even brown terrain.

'We're off.' The mother is dressed in her green sari. The one she wears on every special occasion. It looks new. Her oiled hair makes a huge knot at the nape of her neck. She has no need for pins. The man and boys look up in unison.

They briefly see a flash of green, one of pale orange and another of red. Seeta Ram recognises the red sari as the one he bought for Mamta for her wedding with borrowed money last week. He shakes his head, trying to rid himself of the memory of the incarcerating thumbprint.

The women walk purposefully away, Lata Bai carrying a thali with a bit of jaggery, sindhoor and rose petals. Sneha holds Shanti; and Mamta, the bride-to-be, walks unfettered. The flute plays on.

The evenings here are long and languid, it is well before sunset.

The mother sets the pace, slow, sure, deferential. The flame has gone out of the sunshine. Still the stones cling to their heat and poke the women's bare feet. At this time of day the land is feminine. It is full of colour, both divine and human.

A waterline meandering home from the well intersects their path. Sneha lifts her hand, filtering the sun through her pallav. There is no pantone for that particular orange, diluted with sunshine, distilled through the muslin, alive, organic, elemental, yet changing as soon as the mind grasps its tone. It is truly a colour created from the earth. Here the women prepare their own dyes from leaves and tubers. It takes three seasons to extract an unyielding indigo blue, and even longer for a hectic yellow that doesn't fade. But what is time to them? They have learned that degree of patience that favours minute industry, recherché dyeing techniques, intricate patterns, tiny stitches, weaving something out of nothing. And yet, they take their colours for granted and don't recognise the certain alchemy of the turquoise green as deep as a bountiful pond; or the freedom of the yellow as weighty as a sunflower dial; or the self-indulgence of the saffron as loquacious as a cloudy sunset. The women go quietly about their business, unaware of the psychedelic circus that endures without their attendance.

At this hour, the men can be found under the banyan smoking a hookah and listening to the news on Lala Ram's transistor radio. The power of this innocuous activity cannot be overstated. Talk, and implicit belief in the common wisdom of the peer group is what unites them. There is only one type of man under the banyan in this place of tight traditions and few choices, cut from a die which fashions uncomplicated puzzle shapes that link easily together to form a larger picture. Each time someone wants to break free, he is reminded of Kalu, the untouchable Sudra who dared to bring water from the village well a mile away instead of the river four miles off. He had every bone in his Sudra body broken and his wife had her nose cut off. Such popular justice is the staunchest protector of tradition, and deviation, even the slightest one, is unimaginable.

Seeta Ram hurries to the banyan to catch the tail end of the news on the communal transistor. The news is slow today, so the men twiddle the knobs till they hear the scratchy sound of Hindi movie music. These days they strain to listen for word about the bandit surrender, but it doesn't come.

The Red Ruins are waiting for the women, pink with anticipation

in the buttery light. Mamta clasps her pallav closer. This is the place she did most of her growing up, picking wild spinach and berries. Lata Bai walks to the east-facing wall. Her daughters follow close behind. They pray together. The praying is reserved for females on the bride's side.

What does Lata Bai really know of Mamta's husband and his family? Not much. She doesn't even know that he has two children from a previous marriage. She knows nothing of his nature and yet she is bequeathing her daughter to him in good, bad or indifferent faith. Why? Because Mamta is someone else's garden, a female burden to be rid of. Even her second daughter, lucky Ragini, had to pickle her lemons right until she produced her male twins.

The chants leave Lata Bai's lips on an anonymous journey. She has the drought to thank for the purity of her knowledge and the discipline of her ritual. That's the time her family had turned to rigorous prayer. Only Lata Bai knows the true meaning of the words, whereas her daughters know their essence, the stories they tell, and the superstitions they embrace.

Lata Bai circles the air with the thali, dispersing more incense smoke as the flame cavorts in the breeze but doesn't go out. It is a robust oily flame, culminating in strong, creamy smoke. She looks over her shoulder, Mamta steps forward to take the thali from her mother's hands. She continues to sing her mother's song, but she does so very softly. She's afraid to make an audible mistake. Finally it's Sneha's turn. She hands Shanti to her mother and starts with her own smoke circles.

'Ohm, Ohm, Ohm . . .' the beginning of the universe. First there was nothing and then there was the cosmic sound Ohm, which manifested Nothing into Everything. Its residue resides in all nature, the sound of the wind, the warmth of sunshine, the blue of the sea, in every heart, in every thought. It is the link to eternity, it will transcend everything, never ending, once sounded always enduring. The mother sings the Gayatri Mantra, the girls join in. The energy is transferred back and forth between the women and they know exactly when to stop together . . . Just like that, there's silence.

'This prayer is very important for you, Mamta. Devi is your everything. She will fulfil you and protect you.' Her mother's tone is sombre.

'Let's see if there are any fingerprints.'

'Sneha, your head is filled with hay,' says her mother, but she walks them to the other side of the wall to fulfil their curiosity.

'Aiee.' Sneha drops to the ground. Not only are there prints, there are also broken bangles, hundreds of them, lying on the ground. Sneha picks the glass out of her foot. She licks her finger to seal the bleeding wound. Lata Bai sits on a rock to feed Shanti, saying, 'We should be getting back soon. Your bapu will be wondering.'

'Amma, so many bangles. Did all their husbands die?' Soon to join their ranks, Mamta is worried for the fate of all the married women in the world.

'Must be this Daku business. Some in his gang maybe didn't want to surrender and went out looting instead. This is the result.' Lata Bai scours the ground for offerings, picking out discarded spices from far richer plates than hers. She ties the cinnamon, jaggery, cardamom and fennel seed in a ball at the end of her pallav.

'What will the widows do?'

The mother shrugs.

The women start walking back to the hut. The green and red are upright, the orange bobs up and down all the way, like the float on a fishing line, bouncing unevenly on a wounded foot.

Mamta's nervousness is a runaway horse. It gathers speed as her mother and sister knead the dough for the chapattis and boil the last of the tea leaves. The mother flavours the tea with offerings from the Red Ruins. 'Thank you, Devi. Jai ho Devi, Devi jai ho,' she whispers each time she tosses in a spice.

Mamta needs something to do. She's twisted the end of her pallav into permanent creases which radiate out to the rest of her sari from the damaged corner like a fan. 'So what is the first thing I'll have to do?'

Her mother and sister don't look up from their work. Sneha has already started on the chillies for the chutney and her hands have

started to burn. 'You'll get to know by and by.' Usually her mother loves to talk while cooking, but today is different. Today the weevils are worrying her almost as much as the fact that Jivkant and Ragini haven't arrived.

'They will be arriving soon.' Seeta Ram struggles out of his kurta and puts on a fresh one. The boys stay as they are. They have nothing to change into.

Lata Bai gives Lucky Sister's gold earrings to Mamta. 'Put these on.'

Mamta approaches the mirror hanging from the tin door with a length of wire, the family's only piece of vanity. She can't see her whole face in it at once any more. The last big wind blew it off the door and left a huge horizontal crack in it. Luckily it didn't break completely. Her face is divided along the crack, and the two halves don't match up.

She looks at her lips first. They are her best feature. She turns away from her birthmark sulking like a child might from a disappointing present. The yellowed skin crinkles as she looks closer. She bares her teeth, trying to look even uglier to satisfy some desire to hurt inside. She has started to despair. She replaces the sacred basil sticks in her earlobes with the gold earrings.

'Now what are you looking at? Haven't you seen yourself hundreds of times before? Spending all day at the mirror as if you were a great beauty or something!'

'Stop it, she's only putting on her earrings. On this one day . . .'

Seeta Ram doesn't let her finish: 'Every day is "this one day" where Mamta is concerned. Yours is precisely the kind of useless "love" that spoils girls. See how Sharma's wife turned out; I bet her mother also gave her some funny ideas. Running away like that. Serves her right. Serves her right, you hear?' he shouts towards Mamta, pulling the inalienable rules from under the banyan tree into the room. 'You listen to your man, you hear.' Next he attacks the mother: 'What will her husband think? That we've sent him someone vain and lazy and old?'

'Namaste. Namaste.'

Seeta Ram rushes out when he hears his son's voice greet the guests.

Lata Bai pulls the pallav low over Mamta's head, covering her whole face and neck. 'Don't worry, people have been getting married for thousands of years, it will be fine. Just don't run away,' she says half joking, bending beneath Mamta's veil to smile into her daughter's eyes.

The women stay indoors. It's men's business outside. Mamta's dowry is piled up on the family's hay mattress in the centre of the newly flattened courtyard. The dishes reflect a lusty sunset.

She hears her father say, 'Come, come, my friends,' hesitating at the word friends, and shouting loudly, 'Lata, tea!' with singular authority.

'They've come,' whispers her mother under her breath, as if it's a huge surprise that anyone's turned up at all to partake in her careful preparations. She carries the tea out in tin mugs that the widow Kamla kindly lent her. Her husband doesn't introduce her and once the hands have grabbed the mugs, she retires inside to be with her daughters.

'There are four of them. Your husband looks very handsome in his turban. Mamta, you are a lucky girl,' she says, pulling her daughter towards her. In actual fact, she didn't look up from serving the tea so she doesn't know what the groom looks like. Not that she could have seen his face anyway beneath the curtain of slightly bruised jasmine garlands that hung down from his forehead to chin like so many plumb lines. She hopes her lie will ease the pain of separation. Mamta has started to sweat and quiver. Finally the almost-twenty-year-old realises that she might never see her mother and siblings again. Up till now, the wedding has been a game.

'What's keeping that damn priest? I gave him the advance he asked for.' She would never have dared to say this about some other priest, but Pundit Jasraj-feeler-up-of-brides-to-be is undeserving of her reverence. Her mother's fretting fuels Mamta's agitation.

Finally Prem brings the message Mamta dreads: 'The priest is here.' She hugs her favourite brother for a long time. His presence comforts her.

'I . . . I . . .'

'I'll be there, don't worry,' he says. She pulls up her veil and looks

into her brother's eyes, still filled with childlike luminescence. Prem, the boy she looked after when she was only five years old. He would always stop crying for her, and she took him on her hip wherever she went. But today, it is he who is the stronger, easing her nervousness.

Just three steps to a new life, through the door of her hut. Mamta puts one foot in front of the other. She stops in front of the door. Lata Bai kicks it open and pulls her daughter through by her arm. It's as awkward as being born. The two women pull in different directions. The mother wins. Did the mother pull her daughter through on the day of her birth as well?

Lata Bai pushes Sneha back. 'Stay here, don't you go outside, and look after Shanti. Give her some water if she cries.' She wants no comparisons made between the two sisters, one young enough to make the other look even older than she is.

Just out of the door, Mamta hears an engine running at full capacity. She feels the dusty breeze on her face and up her nose before the engine stops with an angry cat screech. She stands forgotten, all eyes except hers are on the jeep. Hers stay looking on the ground.

'Not too late, I hope. Not too late.'

'Sahib, you are our mother and father, how can *you* ever be too late. We would repeat the wedding for you. You grace our home with your presence. The gods have smiled on us today,' there is a cringing awe in her father's voice.

For Ram Singh, coming or not was a matter of casual choice, but for Seeta Ram and his family, Ram Singh's appearance is nothing short of a miracle. This is the classic social seesaw that isn't going anywhere. Ram Singh is so far above Mamta's family that he has no conscious notion of what impact his attendance at the wedding makes. The stage set is instantly different, the players are totally reshuffled, someone new now has top billing.

Brown sandals alight from the jeep. They are adorned with large decorative shiny brass buckles. The sandals are followed by oversized sturdy black leather shoes, with an air hole for the big toe to breathe. Ram Singh doesn't go anywhere without Babulal his bodyguard.

Mamta can see her father's blue rubber Hawaii slippers walk up to the brown sandals. The buckles flash decisively in the fading light. The buckled sandals make her nervous. She can see her father's feet fidget. Just like a new bride, she thinks, and almost giggles.

'You've done well. I can see that you haven't wasted your loan.' At the sound of the word loan, her father's Hawaii slippers do a small dance. Her mother's bare feet walk to the dancing slippers. The slippers are still.

'Tea, please.' Her father's voice is pleading.

There are four more sets of matching new shoes, the smart polished city kind, with laces. The kind her father loves and will for sure envy. Mamta doesn't know it, but her dowry has paid for them all. The laced shoes fill her with pride. Her new in-laws have taken the time to dress well. Just like Guru Dutt in *Pyaasa*, she thinks. The four pairs are in a circle. A cloud of murmured conversation rises like smoke from the huddle.

'Meet our new in-laws.'

The shoes fan out to form a straight line so the buckled sandals can make the acquaintance of their owners face to face.

'Namaste.'

'Namaste.'

'From where?'

'Barigaon.'

'Ah, Barigaon, do you know Rattan Das? He's a family friend.'

'Not our zamindar, Rattan Das?'

'Yes, exactly.'

The buckles have successfully set the stage for conquest. Suddenly the owners of the city shoes realise who Ram Singh is. It's the turn of the city shoes to dance.

'Please, sit. Come, come, why are we standing round?' The shoes squash together on the rope charpoy, jostling to get a place next to the buckles. They sit, leaving a wide gap on either side of them. Mamta can see more of the men now. She can see the hems of the dhotis, hanging limp above the shoes.

'My daughter, the bride,' Seeta Ram introduces Mamta from a distance like he might the Red Ruins to a visitor. Mamta's blouse is

wet with sweat. First she was hot, now the wetness has left her cold, a little later, she will be shivering. Her mother stands next to her.

Sneha is still in the house, all decked up with no one to look at her. Her sister almost married, she is dreaming her own dreams. She peeks outside, rocking Shanti violently. She hopes to see one suitable face she can place in her daydream, but all the men seem too old to her. Guru Dutt has raided her thoughts too, and one of Lala Ram's boys. She let him feel her up behind the temple last week. She thinks Pundit Jasraj might have seen them. She wasn't careful. The searing hot blood in her veins and liquid feeling between her thighs had made her crazy.

Lata Bai seizes the moment to push Mamta towards the shoes. Mamta knows exactly what she has to do. She goes from sandal to shoe to shoe, bending low to touch each big toe.

The buckles give her their blessing, from the oversized black shoes there's nothing. Then again from three of the city shoes there are more blessings, each one brushing the top of her bowed clothed head with a hot heavy palm. She presumes the city shoes that didn't give their blessings belong to her groom, still too shy to touch the top of her head with his palm in the company of strangers. She is both pleased and eased by her deduction. Not to leave her father out, Mamta touches the toes in the Hawaii slippers also.

Lata Bai pulls Mamta towards the charpoy. Three city shoes rearrange themselves to give the bride room to squeeze in next to her future husband. Only the buckles stay where they are, surrounded by a moat of space.

Then the white apparition that is Pundit Jasraj-feeler-up-of-brides-to-be appears, and deposits itself on the floor. Instinctively Mamta pulls her bare toes away, like a cat retracting its claws. The train whistle sounds in the distance. There is only one word on Lata Bai's mind: Jivkant. She looks up, showing her face to her guests. Mohit and Sneha poke their heads out of the hut as the whistle goes off.

It is up to the priest to create a miniature replica of the cosmic world on the earth between him and the couple. He deftly places a small pot with sacred fire at his feet and surrounds it with geometric symbols.

Pundit Jasraj-feeler-up-of-brides-to-be may not be wholly holy, but he knows the philosophy of enlightenment well and is able to impart it with authority. He starts by propitiating the prodigious pantheon of over three million gods, demi-gods and avatars. His hymn is an ancient secret code revealed to the sages during their deepest meditation in a language long dead. It celebrates the universe in its myriad and infinite forms, thereby proving that the universe must be formless; and acknowledges the multiple opportunities that exist concurrently embodied by cause and effect, thereby proving the connectivity of creation.

But the priest's erudite hymn fails to ignite. The empirical world has the singers in its grasping hand. And though it is only in the human form that beings are able to realise their true self as one with Singularity, it is also only in this form that they are able to enjoy the pleasure that exists in the duality of the senses, not because it serves some higher genetic or divine purpose, but for the sake of the experience alone. Lata Bai, engrossed in samsara, the bonded world, can only think of what all this costs and how they will pay for it.

The buckled sandals start shaking with impatient energy. The wedding goes on in the lee of the violently noisy bed. The priest starts chanting, faster and faster and faster. The buckles stop shuffling at last when they judge the tempo fast enough for a speedy ceremony, their impatience satisfied.

'Please, feed the flames each time I say Swa . . . ha.' Pundit Jasraj points to the swastika radiating from the floor, its arms symbolic of the four directions. Poised for movement, it is also symbolic of all motion, including time.

It is all fitting in for Mamta. It might be her wedding, but it has to be conducted according to the rules of the Big House. All this time, she'd felt important. The widow Kamla had painted *her* hands with care, her mother had tied *her* sari with precision, her sister had prayed for *her* happiness . . . But now? When did she lose her importance? Her wedding has become a ceremony to be performed, hurriedly, while she stands like a bystander at an accident site, jostling for a better look at the centre of attention.

The chanting done, the priest pulls the bride and groom to standing. They must circle the fire seven times. Each circumambulation defines a bond for the bride, her role in the partnership. The priest tries to explain: 'For the first three circles the bride walks ahead, for the last four the groom . . .' The buckles start pacing. 'Go,' the priest commands, also mentally pacing.

At the conclusion of the revolutions her love, obedience, succour, industry and allegiance belong wholly and solely to her husband. Never again may another man enter her realm and ask anything of her.

The circling done, once again Prem, the eldest brother present, has a part to play. He slips a silver ring round Mamta's second toe, and holds out a patch of sindhoor in his palm to his new brother-in-law. The groom takes a pinch between thumb and forefinger. The mother folds back her pallav slowly, neatly, to expose Mamta's middle parting.

The man pours the vermillion dust on to the naked skin in Mamta's hair. His hand seems to waver as it comes close to her birthmark, but none watching can say for sure.

Mamta, tied to her husband, is turned around to head away from her hut. Lata Bai hugs her daughter roughly. She can feel Mamta's bones through the sari. A bony bride . . . it is not a good sign. She wishes she'd had the means to fatten her up before the wedding to make her more desirable to her husband. She presses a piece of paper into her hand, saying, 'My daughter . . .' Her voice cracks. It wants to release all those motherly words that will help the new bride in her future.

'What about her slippers?' Lata Bai whispers harshly to Mohit.

'Slippers? Slippers?'

'Go on,' Lata Bai gives Mohit a push towards the hut.

'Slippers? Bapu didn't buy any slippers.'

Prem takes off his own rubber slippers. Mamta stops, she hitches up her sari so he can place his slippers on her feet. A vehicle drives up the instant Prem's slippers become hers.

She hears the machine even as she sees leather slippers hop out from the truck and run towards her. She wants to take a step back,

but she's tangled in the knot that keeps her close to her husband. 'Here, here, take this.' The leather slippers hand her a box of sweets, then they make their way to the buckles.

'Lokend, you came.'

'I told you not to forget the sweets.'

She looks at the box, a picture of Devi looks up at her. The goddess too is decked in a red wedding sari just like Mamta with a huge nose ring dangling down her cheek. The sweets have left a grease stain on the cardboard box. She doesn't recognise the insouciant smell of saffron. Her father's Hawaii slippers approach. He takes the box from her hands. 'Sweeten your mouths,' he says, passing the sweets around to other hands.

'Oh no, I gave them to the bride to take to her new home. We can have sweets any time.' The leather slippers bring the box back to Mamta, much lighter. 'Be happy,' he says.

Tears sting the back of her eyelids. *I wonder if he knows about my birthmark.* It's not the city shoes she's thinking of. She falls to the ground and touches the leather slippers, her fingers linger on the tips of the toes. Warm hands round her shoulders bring her back to standing.

Lata Bai brings her hands to her mouth, arresting her serrated tear-filled breath. 'Amma! Amma!' Mamta clings to her like she did in front of strangers as a little girl. The groom tugs at his bride, claiming what is his. For both mother and daughter it is more the end of something than the start of something new.

'Go,' says Lata Bai, knowing that this might be the final time they will see each other. She takes her daughter's face in her palms, and wipes the tears from Mamta's eyes, so her world will cease to tremble. Over her mother's shoulder the new bride sees an unknown man with an unforgettable face, and eyes that lock with her own. All the peace of the world is instantly transferred in that quiet look. Her soul is confused yet comforted, and she is strangely calmed.

4

LOKEND COULD NEVER HAVE DONE IT ALONE. He has convinced Daku Manmohan to surrender, even though the police have instructions from Delhi to pre-empt it with a capture and an execution.

All the secret meetings have been arranged with the help of one of his father's indentured cowhands, Prem. The bandit chief, Daku Manmohan, recommended the boy for the job by name. He said that if anyone could help them it was Prem, Lata Bai's son.

The boy works at the Big House because his father, Seeta Ram, has borrowed money from Singh Sahib. Each week he arrives with vegetables from his farm to add to the overflowing produce baskets in the Big House's kitchen. At the end of the day he forages through the kitchen waste and gathers the discarded cauliflower stubs and potato peelings to take home to his mother.

Though Prem's working at the Big House is a form of slavery, ironically he doesn't have to work as hard as he would have at home. It is confounding how soft his life has become. Out in the farmlands, he had to use his faculties more in the space of an hour than most people at the Big House have to in their entire lives. He believes the zamindar's fields stretch out to the limits of every horizon, all golden in the sun, more fertile and less weedy than his own.

All the jobs are neatly assigned to the others who, like him, have lost their liberty because of a family debt. When a job is done, it is done, and after that one can lounge, smoke a bidi, or go wait in the

back of the kitchen for scraps. His training at home has made him quick. There he did every job: weeding, fencing, digging, planting, mending . . . when you have nothing it seems like all the labour in the world won't help you get ahead. Only once has he seen men here work as solidly as he did in his father's fields: when putting out a wildfire in the granary – without any instruction – just for the sake of survival.

Lokend had to do very little to convince Prem to accept the cause. For Prem, Lokend is an avatar, a man made of glory, a true representation of what a saintly being should be. He would go to hell and back if *his* Lokend Bhai asked him to. But still, the boy has to rationalise his conduct every day, because he knows that by some yardstick he has betrayed the village. He has heard the stories: rivers of blood, maiming, slaughter and rape. And he has seen the scars on men and women, now more than twice his age: a jagged piece of bone jutting out where the elbow should have been, eyes gouged out, tongues struck dumb, legless beggars at the temple steps . . . He has nightmares filled with writhing, shrieking bodies, blood mixing with blood of every caste, thrown on a pile higher than his head. And still he helps the bandits, those same demons who have terrorised his village since before he was born. All for his mentor Lokend Bhai.

Setting conviction aside, the boy's situation becomes more tenuous every day.

'You just have to say the word and I'll find someone else,' says Lokend. 'Don't think you must do this job just because Manmohan asked for you.' Lokend is the only man in all Gopalpur who says the bandit's name sans the condemning prefix *daku*, bandit. Daku, more than a label, is a part of the dreaded man's name: Daku Manmohan, the words go together like chillies and chapattis.

The boy looks into Lokend's face, unsure. No one has ever given him options before. He doesn't know how to react. This man means more to him than his own father, but he dare not show his devotion. Why, Lokend Bhai probably has hundreds of people equally committed to him. Prem squirms, his bare toes biting into the damp soil of Asmara Didi's rose bed.

91

'Think about it.' Lokend does not explain how dangerous the boy's job is, that it might get him killed. For months the wily chap has managed to pass missives, rolled in leaves, in perishable chalk code under special rocks and milk pails, back and forth, back and forth between Lokend and the bandit. 'By the way, that was a nice ceremony . . . Your sister's marriage . . .' he explains as the boy looks askance at him.

'Oh, yes. The best part of it was that you came. My father liked that. I think she liked the sweets you brought.'

'Yes, the sweets . . .' Lokend suddenly realises that she has lingered with him. 'I hope she will be happy. Do you know anything of her husband?'

'No, Bapu accepted the first offer that came his way,' he says cautiously. 'My sister was too old for marriage. They said we had to be grateful. The dowry . . . the dowry . . .'

'You needn't be embarrassed; I know why you work here. She has a good marriage because of you. You must know that.'

'I wish she could have had a different destiny. Found someone different.'

'Found someone different?'

'Yes, someone kind and gentle, someone like you maybe.'

The man and boy smile at each other.

'Think about it,' says Lokend again, 'don't tell me now. But you only have to hint . . .'

The last thing Prem will do is think over the one job he is so proud to have. He is relieved when the conversation is over. He turns back to the roses, weeding, pruning, grafting, coaxing them into flower.

At least Lokend has the weight of the Big House behind him, but Prem, he has nothing. If the police knew of his involvement in the whole affair, they would throw him in jail without filing any appropriate paperwork, that's if the villagers didn't lynch him first. The rage against the bandits is so high that the slightest hint of suspicion would be enough to dispatch the boy's dismembered body to the dunghill the very next day.

Lokend cautiously tucks a roll of paper wrapped in a betel-leaf in Prem's palm. The boy clutches it tight. Lokend is glad this whole

business is coming to an end. A few more missives and then it'll be done. The police and their jeeps will have to give up, throwing up their hands in the face of a job well finished. The boy hides the leaf in a secret pocket. Now that Mamta has gone, he has to give it to Sneha to leave under the rock by the well tonight. She won't ask any questions. How many times has he been tempted to hide by that rock and wait and see who comes to claim the message for Daku Manmohan, but he dare not. Lokend has warned him, 'The less information you have, the safer you will be.'

Tonight's message might be the most important. It is the one that tells Daku Manmohan where the surrender will take place – in exactly twelve days in front of Lala Ram's shop.

A senior officer and a city boy are there at the appointed cross-road to guide Lokend to the jail meant for the bandit. For good measure, the city boy puts a blinking light on top of the jeep. Not that there is anyone to take note of it. The senior officer shows his displeasure by riding out in silence.

'We Indians find the worst possible uses for our beautiful old buildings, turning them into prisons, post offices or municipal ware-houses,' says Lokend as they come round the bend face to face with the prison tucked in the lee of the Red Ruins.

Almost complete, pigeons are already roosting in all three of its rooms. It is farcical, standing comically against the Red Ruins whose stones have been appropriated for its retaining wall.

'This is the cell and these two rooms are for the guards. One will double as an office. They forgot to put in the door to the cell, but it will be in this week . . .' The senior officer explains the details with the uninspired pomposity of a man in uniform. The cell is tiny, any prisoner would have difficulty standing erect in it.

'This is it?' Lokend's intonation saturates his words with dis-belief.

'He's a bandit, or have you forgotten? Some say you have thrown in your lot with these men. Some say you are one of them.' The insinuation isn't lost on Lokend, the senior officer is accusing him of taking bribes.

'Boss . . .' the city boy restrains his superior from saying another undignified word. He is spellbound by Lokend's gnostic calm. For him Lokend represents all those amorphous beings of his childhood stories who tackled adversity with fortitude. He sees a miracle in Lokend, whereas his superior does not.

Lokend holds up his hand to the city boy and smiles. There is no anger or embarrassment in his face. 'No, I am not one of them,' he explains to the senior officer calmly.

'Then how can you go against your father, against the village, and help these murderers? How have they won you over?' The senior officer sees the situation very clearly in the context of his value system. It has to be a bribe.

'Do you think something as worthless as a bribe made him do this?' asks the city boy, suddenly unafraid for himself.

'Leave it, my friend. We all suffer from the blindness of proximity. The closer something is to us, the less we are able to see it, like the lashes round our eyes.' Lokend is willing to part only with riddles at this stage. He has had these conversations before. People will believe what they will.

The senior officer recovers his bureaucratic poise and prepares to deliver his own speech. But before he can do so, Lokend explains, 'Don't forget, Daku Manmohan is surrendering of his own accord. He doesn't have to. He is doing it because I asked.' From someone else's lips the words might have sounded arrogant, but the delivery leaves no room for mistake: it is merely a statement of fact. The exposed sincerity in Lokend's face sends a shiver of shame through his accuser's frame. There aren't many who can withstand the force of Lokend's gentleness.

The senior officer debates the case internally. After a while he says, 'What can we do about it now?' Slowly he is crossing over to Lokend's camp. 'It is too late to build something else, and the daku insists on being jailed here.'

'If this jail cell holds him in, it will be only because he has given me his word that he won't try to escape. Build the door. We will keep him here for a few months and when the frenzy dies down, we will transfer him to New Delhi. That's where he belongs anyway.'

'The surrender will be difficult. You cannot rely on the police,' the senior officer warns Lokend. 'After all, it will be a crowd . . . a crowd of the wronged.'

'We will face it.'

'But why didn't you do it somewhere else, in secret? Or in a place like New Delhi, where we could have put the collective shoulder of the police force behind you?' Both men know this is just talk.

'I tried, but Manmohan wouldn't hear of it. He said he didn't want to cheat his victims any longer. It was agreed in our final meeting. Anyway, he'll be paraded by politicians in every important city, right up to New Delhi. Why start sooner than we have to?' he says to the policemen.

'That's if he survives. Does no one read the papers? Gopalpur is described as Daku Manmohan's playground. Delhi doesn't understand that this event needs at least two hundred policemen to see it through safely. And how many are we getting? Thirty, if we are lucky. I just hope it won't be the innocent who will die,' the senior officer adds earnestly. 'The safety of Daku Manmohan and his gang rests with you. You shouldn't depend on police guns. Your speech will have to be convincing.'

All this time Lokend has managed to dodge the reporters, but not today. Today they will find him, which is just as well. They are his best armour. If their photographs will be in the papers the next day, the villagers wouldn't dare harm Lokend or take down any unarmed bandits for fear of reprisals.

'Lokend Sahib?'

'Yes.' Lokend has returned to the Big House, the appointed meeting place for the interview.

'Rajiv, from the *Times of India*.' The reporter is glad for this assignment. It was either the dusty back of beyond or answering more irate reader letters about the Rajasthan nuclear weapon tests. 'So, sir, tell me what attracted you to the bandit's cause?' Lokend has been judged a soft shell. He will be an easy one to interview, even manipulate.

'Well, let's see. Ever since I was a boy the talk was always of bandits

in our lands. When I became a man, the talk was still of bandits in our lands. I think I'd like to grow old and not have to listen to the same stale talk of bandits in our lands.'

'Ha, ha, well put. But why Daku Manmohan? Do you think you are serving the cause of justice? I mean, if he were tried and convicted in a court of law, wouldn't that be more fitting than this surrender? After all, there is a death penalty hanging over his head.'

'You know my friend, I believe in connections.' The reporter purses his lips. 'Yes, you never know when and under what circumstances you might meet someone again. Always keep that in mind before you toss anyone in the rubbish dump.'

'You mean give them a second chance?'

'I mean keep an open mind. Action and reaction, that's what it's all about. Killing will only spawn more killing. We have to let the life out of this movement.'

'There is talk about a following among the women here. Has he really protected them from rape? Bandits are notorious rapists, but in this case it seems he is their saviour.'

'He is an extraordinary man. If you met him under any other circumstances, you would put your faith in him. He lives by a strict code of conduct. Often stricter than our community's. I can't tell you if he has or hasn't protected girls from rape, but that is just the kind of thing he would do.'

'And what about you? Why have you given away your lands? What do you stand for?' Might as well cover two stories in one go.

'This is not about me. It is about Daku Manmohan.' Lokend will not be lured into saying more than he has to.

'So where is the surrender?'

'At Lala Ram's shop. In twelve days. Be there.'

'I still think that he should be judged in a court. He should not be allowed to surrender here after what he's done to these people.'

'You mean we should be like the priest who bars a man from praying at the temple because he isn't worthy of God?' Lokend laughs loudly.

Something awakens in the reporter's memory, 'I know you . . . Do I not know you from somewhere?'

'We've never met before.'

The reporter shakes his head to loosen the garrotte of disquieting thought. He recognises Lokend, he's sure of it. And then he isn't as sure. His mother would have immediately explained it as a karmic connection, a meeting in a past life.

'We are building a cell here, just for him. He wants it to become a place of pilgrimage where people might come to relinquish their hate.'

'Yes, and there is so much to hate.'

'When the world is done and gone there will still be hate. People think that not hating is a conscious decision, whereas hating is spontaneous. But I tell you, to love is just as easy as to hate . . .'

'I wish you spoke for the whole village, Lokend Sahib, but unfortunately you don't. The bones and cuts may have healed, but their hearts still bear raw wounds.'

'Depends on how far away you stand . . . in time, I mean. Look at events from the distance of time and hatred becomes benign. They may hate tomorrow, may hate even for five, ten years, or a hundred . . . a thousand, even two thousand . . . What then?'

'What are you two huddled over? Here, drink some tea.' Asmara Didi carries the tray herself.

'So, Mataji, as a resident of Gopalpur and so close to Lokend Sahib, what do you think about the whole affair?' The difference in their ages is much too vast for him to think of addressing her as Didi.

Of course Asmara Didi is against the whole project, but she will never say so. She assiduously avoids the issue, except when she has to defend Lokend against Singh Sahib. Would he do the same for her? No, he wouldn't. Love and loyalty would never alter his plans. He is that sort of man, a soul that can only live in the realm of Truth, somewhere on a lofty ascetic plane, unattached; and to some, pitiless, even callous.

But Lokend is neither pitiless nor callous. He isn't sapped by some internal fight, or spent by someone else's code of ethics. He is one of those so unconcerned with the outcome of his action that he can participate in it fully.

'What does it matter what I think? I am old. I have lived with this bandit business for most of my life.' Asmara Didi puts down the tea. 'I just hope and pray that peace is in our destiny.'

'I don't believe in destiny. For me, destiny is one's private plan, it is much too narrow-minded, it is personal, egoistic . . .' says Rajiv of the *Times*. 'Give me a divine plan for samsara any day.'

'I don't care if there is or there isn't a divine plan,' says Asmara Didi. 'All I know is that this man might die for what he is doing. The surrender will not be accepted by the village. There has been too much blood spilt. But who can tell him to stop?' She turns from Rajiv of the *Times of India* to Lokend. 'Now give this old woman a hug,' she commands, 'and remember I still want grandchildren!' The mongoose safely out of the way, Asmara Didi opens her arms to embrace her surrogate son.

Instead, Lokend takes her by the shoulders and says, 'You are like a mother to me. You can be sure of that.'

Suddenly, blocks of clouds and shafts of filtered sunshine crowd the sky. A rainbow commands consideration, each of its colours well defined, supported by another equally distinct arc as companion. Her life has been filled with omens, with every quirk and twitch of Nature remembered and each detail treasured for its clairvoyance. But today all the luck embodied in the rainbow is tossed aside for the dread in her heart.

'Lokend, your father, your brother, the village, the police, the . . .' she lists his adversaries in order of importance. She is agitated, all the scriptures she learned by heart as a young wife are inaccessible to her. She is unable to think clearly.

'Asmara Didi, you worry too much. See, even the gods send their blessings,' he laughs and waves to the rainbow as if it were his personal possession.

'You will be careful, won't you? If not for your sake, then for mine?'

'Yes, Asmara Didi, I will. You know I will.' The sincerity in his voice disarms her, and makes her instantly afraid. She turns to go.

'She worries needlessly,' he says to the reporter.

'Yes, it will be a great day, I'm sure.' The reporter has his own story.

It grows by the second in his mind, swirls of valour laced with mutilation, death, glory and grand deeds. Oh, what a picture. He will change people with his words. A book, perhaps even a sequel. He sees a TV serial in his future.

'At Lala Ram's then?'

The reporter nods.

Twelve days later Lokend knows exactly what he will say to both the bandits and the villagers. He will publicly give the bandit a second chance, and ask the whole village to do the same. Daku Manmohan has killed many, but it isn't the number of dead that's the problem, it's the number of living that the bandit's left behind, broken and wretched, in some cases incapable of eking out any kind of existence at all.

All those loyal to him are in place. They will be thickly scattered through the crowd. Their only function, to talk, to convince, to cajole, to debate and turn as many to their way of thinking as they can. They are all, without exception, people who have benefited in the form of donated land from Lokend, their saviour, their friend.

They have been lucky for the rain. The musky smell of wet mud is around him. The breeze is cool, there is little dust. The rumble reaches Lokend over the sound of the truck's engine, deep from the belly of the earth. The crowd is larger than he expected.

He spots his trusted messenger, and as their eyes meet Prem's chest fills with pride for his secret part in the affair. Lokend gets out of the truck and moves towards Lala Ram's shop.

The crowd has gathered at Gopalpur's centre that comprises one short street flanked by Lala Ram's establishment Saraswati Stores on the sunrise side and on the other by Topaz Suppliers, a most useful business opened by Babulal, Ram Singh's chief henchman. Lala Ram has worn socks and shoes, and put up streamers to mark the occasion. The tinsel rotates in the breeze, catching the sunlight in its loops. It is very important to declare one's wealth at the right time when such information might make the most impact. A sepia Guru Dutt leans across the *Pyaasa* poster. They may not have seen the film, but Lala Ram has told them all the story many times over.

The hero's pathos is evident even to the most hardened heart. A man betrayed by his love and by society. A man who refused to be enslaved by the era and chose to give up a life of luxury and fame for the obscurity and peace of a village – a village much like theirs. They look to the poster for answers and would not be surprised if Guru Dutt broke into song to explain away this astounding gathering.

Hypothecated to the Bank of India: ten such signs are stacked against the walls like wainscoting. Lala Ram is leaving nothing to chance. The Bank has promised to open a branch in this village once this bandit business is concluded.

The senior police officer was right, there are too few policemen. Lokend can count the uniforms, outnumbered more than a hundred to one. They patrol the perimeter listlessly. Every once in a while they spread out their arms, and the crowd shrinks back upon itself from the living rope.

Lokend walks towards Saraswati Stores skirting the edge of the crowd; nothing must disturb such a compact mass of people. Many recognise him, the zamindar's son, famous for giving up his lands. Two plainclothes policemen immediately fall in step with Lokend. Their senior officer had been categorical about this. 'If it comes to saving one man, save this man –' he'd said, pointing to Lokend.

The reporter has already managed to find his way to the veranda of Saraswati Stores, using his camera as a weapon. The crowd recognises him and parts for him. He has taken hundreds of pictures of the villagers and given many away. Ram Singh, Prem, Lata Bai and Mamta have been among his subjects.

Lokend climbs on to the veranda-stage. Rajiv locks arms with him, each one's hand gripping the other's wrist, and helps him up.

The crowd leans back in one giant wave when it hears the jeeps arrive. The men turn together like the hundred heads of Ravana and look towards the sound. It is exactly as Lokend imagined. The jeeps stop a long way away. The crowd starts to murmur. Click . . .

Three men jump out of the jeep dressed in police uniforms,

complete with pistols in shoulder holsters, no doubt the advance party. They wade through the people swirling round them. It was Lokend's idea to have the bandits dress as policemen so they could safely get through to the podium. Click . . .

The three men climb on to the stage, they don't need any help. Click . . .

Lokend knocks the mic with his forefinger. Tak, tak, tak. It is a call to order and attention. The living rope of policemen becomes instantaneously active and vigilant.

Simultaneously, the hissing starts and becomes a chant. 'Daku Manmohan murdabad, murdabad, Daku Manmohan murdabad, murdab . . .' The crowd demands blood. It's then that the mutilated slowly start gravitating towards the centre, as if they have been waiting in the wings to take a bow all this time. These battered members of humanity, some of whom have been begging at the temple and others who have been in hiding in the forest or lying discarded in the back of their family's outhouse for years, are finally ready to show themselves. They display their wounds as advertise-ments for the bandit's death. They know that their malefactors are getting a chance to give themselves up. The bandits have hurt too many to be allowed to surrender just like that. They will not forgive. The memories are still vivid: a heap of severed limbs, young girls pulled out from behind the well by their hair and raped, the blood tainting the well water for weeks, the wounded lying beneath the banyan without medicines or help, mothers beating their heads on the floor, fathers shaving their heads . . . The stench of blood got so bad it attracted the wild animals from the forest, and for weeks after, people had more reason to fear the leopards and hyenas than the bandits. Finally, the carrion eaters clouded the sky so thickly that they blotted out the sun. Oh no, they won't allow these men to get away lightly.

'Killed my son, raped my daughter, took my family, burned my shop . . .' on and on they shout. But there is danger in en masse tragedy. Like too much of anything, too much misfortune closes the mind and leaches it of pity. The sight of the cripples is overwhelming for the spectators. They are numbly detached from the scene.

They have sanitised its brutality by considering it usual for that time and place. Every mind is made up in that crowd. This is our destiny, they say, and yet they plead and watch for something better.

Lokend's heart shifts in his chest. He is a man stranded by his philosophy. For him it is a fresh tragedy, requiring an urgent solution. For the moment, Daku Manmohan is not the one on his mind. For the moment, Lokend is one with the cripples before him, crawling forward, stripped of all dignity and humanity. He can feel his emotion unchecked for the first time in many years. 'My God,' he says. It isn't a phrase, he is genuinely appealing to the higher power to make the present sensible. He squeezes his thumbs into the corners of eyes painful with tears.

The crowd has already apportioned blame where it thinks it is due. It is that blame that absolves each man standing before the stage of his responsibility. But not Lokend. He alone eschews the luxury of blame. The cripples are his personal responsibility.

Then Daku Manmohan declares himself, standing a little taller on the podium. 'Daku Manmohan murdabad, murdabad, Daku Manmohan murdabad, murdabad . . .' chants the crowd: *Death to the bandit.* More gang members start breaking away from the crowd to jump on stage with their leader. The crowd is losing control – the screaming gets worse and stones start flying. The bandits hide their heads in their hands, but not Daku Manmohan. He stands erect, refusing to be judged by the rabble – both able-bodied and crippled.

Then a foot emerges from the police jeep in the distance, followed by a body. The body is clad in policeman's khaki. It makes its way to the edge of the crowd. The chant collapses on itself in a low rumble like music from a fading transistor radio when it recognises that the body is female. The woman walks through the sea of men to her mate. The men put their cupped hands to their mouths to whisper a history for her into a neighbour's ear. This time they won't be fooled by the uniform. The crowd draws in a single breath. It is one organism, one giant enraged organism, unable to make sense of the situation and the strangely unrecognisable apparition of a woman dressed in man's clothing. Click, click, click . . .

This woman has always made Daku Manmohan proud. The camera records their private thoughts, clearly visible on their faces. A stone whizzes through the air and opens a red gash just above his right eye, the woman's hand reaches up to her own eyebrow to stem the blood. He is hurt, but she feels the pain.

The spot of silence gives Lokend his chance to take charge. 'Brothers and sisters,' he shouts into the mic. The mic emits a cackle. The crowd hears nothing, stilled, stunned into a stupor by the woman who stands before them every bit as deliberately as Daku Manmohan himself.

Lala Ram abandons his prized position to go check on the mic together with Rajiv from the *Times*. The reporter stands well behind Lokend even as he fiddles with the mic. The stones are coming from all directions; impartial, they will land equally on his head if he dares to step forward on the stage. He has been writing furiously. The words jumble on the page: . . . *four thousand strong . . . stones and a riot waiting to break . . . surrender . . . justice denied . . . rebuilding . . . cripples . . . loot . . . murder . . .* Impressions that will make good copy.

Not more than three minutes have elapsed since the appearance of the woman. 'Brothers and sisters,' Lokend shouts again. This time the mic releases the words and then goes dead. He couldn't have planned it better. He has their attention now. He will be able to say brothers and sisters four more times before the crowd will become fed up with the novelty of the words and the loudspeaker. Right now, they are waiting for his speech, held back by the capricious mic, a high bone to an untrained dog. Lokend resumes his speech.

'Harsh times demand brave actions from us. I know you find it hard to make peace in your hearts with this man and the things he has done. But I ask you not to judge him on his past. I ask you to look to the future. A future of peace and prosperity.' Lokend indulges the crowd's false sense of power. The surrender will go through with or without its approval. If need be, he will stand in front of Daku Manmohan and take the bullet meant for the bandit in his chest.

The woman steps closer to her gang members. Now it is her proximity to them that makes the crowd notice them. There are

about twenty in all, but the crowd can pick out the three chiefs easily. All three of them have very impressive black moustaches. Their sunken eyes, crowned by shadows, give nothing away.

'Are you prepared to become murderers yourselves because of this man? We can only survive if we put an end to this war. Otherwise, your children and your children's children will be haunted by raids.'

'Not if we kill the motherfuckers now!'

'Kill them!' The crowd draws back its head and spits out the words in a single, united voice: 'Kill them, kill them, kill them . . .'

The woman grabs the mic right out of Lokend's hand and shouts into it. 'Stop! Stop!' The mic retaliates with unsympathetic static. Lokend pulls the mic a little away from her mouth and gives her a nod. She speaks into it again. This time she is heard. 'What purpose will that serve? There will be others who will rise up to take our places. That is the curse of injustice.

'I used to be one of you,' she says. 'This man –' she clings to the subject of her speech with a long look '– this man, this bandit man, kidnapped me and took me from my family when I was only nine years old. Since that day, this man has been my family, my husband, my all. You say kill them, but you know nothing of our history. You say kill them, but you know nothing of our honour. You say kill them, but you don't know what would have happened to me had I not been rescued by this man. Look at you, standing there, judging us as if you had the right to do so. Some among you have sent their daughters to certain death by marrying them into a family looking only for dowry. Some of you have sold your sons to the Big House for a few rupees. Some of you have drowned a female baby in a bucket of river water. Some of you have burned a daughter-in-law or thrown a widowed mother out of your house to die in the street like a dog. And some of you have made an appointment for your wife with Yamraj, so you could be free to take another wife. *Tell me, who among you is innocent!*'

The silence is big, as big as the sky. 'If you cannot bring me such a man,' she says, her voice soft, 'then you cannot judge us. We are here to surrender, yes, but only because Lokend Bhai has asked us to. This slaughter has to stop, he says. And he is right. I am a mother now.

I want my child to outlive me . . . I want all children to outlive their mothers.'

It is lucky she still has the heart of her audience beating in her hands, otherwise it might have relapsed into another confrontation. A lone rose, flung by an unseen admirer, lands at her feet. Lokend looks up just in time to see Prem's outstretched arm return quickly to his side. Clever boy, he thinks, and smiles. Her value is once again secured by this display of infatuation. As most crowds, these people have now been told what to think. The rose is quickly transferred into the heart of every man present. A spontaneous murmur escapes into the air like evaporating dew on a spring morning. It's now or never.

Lokend holds up Daku Manmohan's arms to the crowd. The crowd roars. The real policemen take the bandits' weapons and symbolically lay three rifles and three revolvers on the ground, emptied of cartridges.

The bandit holds out his hands, his two chiefs repeat his actions with the precision of dancers. The senior officer cuffs the leader while his junior officer fumbles with the cuffs of the other two men. Eventually, with the help of Lokend, all three are cuffed and led away. The junior officer tucks the revolvers into his belt and carries the three rifles awkwardly on his shoulder. The woman leads them off the stage in single file. The audience parts for her, individually smitten, yet collectively uneasy. It is only as the men drive off that the crowd recognises its alien uneasiness for what it is: irony, at being led this far by a woman.

Daku Manmohan is immediately separated from the rest of his gang members, who are all sent to New Delhi. He is incarcerated, as promised, in the tiny cell by the Red Ruins. The woman who spoke so valiantly on his behalf lives three hours away with her son and the wives and children of the other two chiefs. They will not meet again. That would be too much for the villagers to bear. Already there is talk of evicting her and her companions from their huts built on the land donated by Lokend. Every day Lokend must fight someone else on their behalf so they are safe.

Each time Lokend sees the woman he says the same thing: 'Sister,

be patient. People will forget about you in time. Don't you remember a time when you were happy? Well? This too will pass. Believe me.'

The woman has withdrawn into herself. Away from her mate, she feels nothing. She avoids all mention of her beloved Manmohan, and never asks after his fate.

And what of the bandit's fate? It is the fate of an active man with suddenly too much time on his hands, the worst kind of fate to bestow on someone who has something to repent. Intermittently his thoughts turn from visions of looting and slaughter to images of his wife and son. He thinks he will go mad. He is only kept sane by the heckling of the villagers who come to taunt him and throw things at him daily. The guards, his protectors, allow the villagers their petty revenge, turning away when one shows up with excrement or stones. Daku Manmohan tries not to show them that he needs their hatred to survive, to pass the time in his cell where he cannot even stand upright. The muscles in his legs have started to soften and shrink. All this time he kept himself robust and healthy; agile for a quick escape and strong for an unexpected fight. But now, if he had to run from a pursuer, he would have to use more than just his legs to escape.

He thinks of death. He is not afraid of it. He is afraid only of its aftermath. It would be seen as an act of cowardice. He could never leave such a legacy for his son. Whether or not people recognise the reason why he chose this life of pillage and plunder, it wasn't because he is a coward.

Lokend has managed to get away to visit him today. He is un-prepared to see the bandit dressed in the heavy blue-and-white stripes of a formal prison uniform, the result of the jailer's personal initiative. The guards continue their game of cards, smoking a com-munal bidi in silence. They barely acknowledge the familiar visitor with a look.

The building reeks of damp and the pungent smell of urine, its walls are already green with mould and fungus. As Lokend reaches through the bars to take Daku Manmohan's shoulder, he realises that in the few weeks that he has been in jail, the prisoner has become older than his years, with a laboured walk and stiffness in his bones.

'You don't need this battalion to protect me. One man will do,' says the bandit. 'You know I won't try to escape.'

'I know,' Lokend replies. 'These men aren't here to keep you in. They're here to keep those who wish to harm you out. Besides, I think they enjoy the company.'

The bandit laughs. 'Don't think I don't know that your job is harder than mine. You've made many enemies because of my surrender. How many fights have you fought on my behalf? With the village, the politicians, your own father. And for what? Why do you do this?'

'To fulfil my desire. Does one need a reason for that too?' Lokend smiles. 'Because I think it is the right thing. Look, Manmohan, we have to have peace here. New Delhi cannot give it to us, much as it wants to. New Delhi is just too far away. This is the only way.'

'What of my family? My son will have my name linked with his till he dies. What kind of a life is that for my boy? Sometimes I think we would have been better off hiding in the ravines and living off raids.' He's almost disappointed in himself for surrendering, for finding Lokend's motivation too compelling to decline.

'Don't worry about the boy. You have my word on this. I'll not let anything harm him. I am trying to get work for the wives. Sewing. I know it's different from what they did before, but there is money enough in it for them to live with dignity. Your wife will convince the other two.'

'My wife?'

'Yes, your wife.' She'd jumped at Lokend's offer, knowing it was her one chance to pass time and remain sane.

'Is she all right?'

'Yes, yes. She doesn't believe it, but she is.'

'Does she ask after me?' He had to ask. Daku Manmohan has made no pact to spare himself the pain of a family lost. He comes back to it again and again, like picking at canker sores.

'Leave the asking to those who will,' says Lokend, patting the man on his shoulder. He retrieves his hand from within the bars.

'I must know,' the bandit insists. 'How can you understand? You've never been in love.'

A deep longing takes Lokend completely by surprise. 'I'll be back,' he says, leaving.

The bandit doesn't look up to see his friend walk away. Too many farewells have touched his life.

'I don't believe it.'

'Believe what you like, he's gone. Escaped. At night. I found my men tied with their socks stuffed in their mouths. Luckily, no one was beaten. I tell you, not all of them surrendered. There are still some on the outside. Those were the ones who freed him.' The same police officer who first took Lokend to see the jail is back to handle the embarrassing escape. 'You said you didn't need so many guards to protect him. Huh, not so many guards indeed! If I'd listened to you, he would have got out much sooner,' the police officer says, trying to pin the responsibility and blame on Lokend. 'Now what do we do?'

'He gave me his word.' Lokend is genuinely mystified by Daku Manmohan's disappearance.

The irritation percolates through the police officer's voice. He clicks his tongue. 'I am not a fool,' he says, silently urging Lokend to stop being one. 'A man can no more change his nature than a tiger can stop eating meat. A bandit will always remain a bandit,' he explains very slowly, as if talking to a child.

Lokend speaks with conviction: 'It wasn't his doing. Someone else had a hand in it. Keep it quiet. I don't want a word of it leaked to the papers, do you hear? If the villagers hear of this, the blood will start running again. You don't want that on your conscience, do you?'

'No, sir.' The man stands upright, honouring the new, forceful Lokend. 'Yes, sir.'

It is Ram Singh who puts an end to his brother's search. 'Our father wants to see you urgently.'

There is little eagerness in the younger man's gait as he walks to his brother's jeep. His head is heavy with thoughts. The elder brother looks at the younger, walking, head bowed, to the jeep. *Why does he prefer him over me?* Again the same question.

'Hurry up! He said *urgently*. He can't wait to see you! I've never seen him this agitated before, not even when he heard the news of the surrender. You should've seen him! Even Asmara Didi wasn't safe in the room that day. I have never seen him that angry.' Ram Singh cannot resist twisting the knife.

'I know. He has been against the surrender from the start. He thinks it was the most dishonourable thing a man could do. You know how Bapu is fixed on honour.'

'Yes, he keeps reminding us that it's more important than life!'

'Honour before Life,' both men say their father's motto. There is conviction in Lokend's voice, but only sarcasm in Ram Singh's. 'Zamindars are landowners, nothing more. He's no king. He seems to forget that quite conveniently. Always resolving petty differences and conducting weddings. Always curing the incurable and acting like a god. He behaves as if he owns people.'

'Yes, Bapu does have the royal touch, doesn't he? Maybe it's in his blood,' says Lokend, smiling. 'It is so easy to be lost in Maya . . .'

'You and your spiritual bullshit! Just because you've opted out of life doesn't mean we all should. I have to do my duty as the future zamindar. Look at you! Running after anyone who poses as a victim long enough to get your attention.'

Asmara Didi waves Ram Singh off. 'He asked for Lokend to come alone.'

The elder brother has to squeeze his eyes shut to stop himself from exploding. Why does his father reject him at every turn?

'Come on, no sense in wasting time. Let's get it over with,' she says, pushing Lokend into the room. Clearly she knows what's on his father's mind.

The reclining man regards his son with his good eye. It is a long, slow look, the same kind of look he used in his hunting days.

The old man has become a sort of indistinct version of his former self. Almost unable to speak and all bone.

'He'sh . . . here.'

Lokend stands motionless, needing no explanation.

Singh Sahib twitches his hand at Asmara Didi. She stands up from kneeling and starts talking on his behalf.

'Daku Manmohan is here. Your father, Singh Sahib has put him in jail. You know the old outhouse . . .'

At this point the father locks eyes with his son, willing him back to the day of his stroke. The very day he discovered – no: caught – Lokend cleaning the outhouse like a low-caste servant.

'Yes, I know the old outhouse. Is that where he is now?'

'And . . . wi . . . ll shta . . . ay!' Singh Sahib releases the words like bullets.

'Singh Sahib, too much excitement isn't good for you,' she says loudly, then drops her voice. 'We have to keep him calm,' she says to Lokend, her co-conspirator. 'What could he do?' she pleads with Lokend on behalf of his father. 'It was like the old days. Villagers were coming to him every day asking him to do something about Daku Manmohan. Lokend, you have no idea how this event has stirred up the people. They feel betrayed. That too by you, their saviour, their mentor. They've always had the utmost love for you. You know that. But this surrender has made them question every-thing. You, this family, Singh Sahib, the zamindari, everything. Your father had no choice but to step in. The village and your father reached a compromise. They begged Singh Sahib to take charge. They wanted Daku Manmohan to be jailed on your land, where they could be sure he won't be treated like royalty,' she finishes in a single breath, waiting for a response.

'Say something. For God's sake! Can't you see your father needs it?' Asmara Didi gruffly whispers to Lokend. Then she notices some-thing in Singh Sahib's face that hasn't been there in a long time: the will to live again.

Lokend stands silent and still as his father's rage boils round him.

'What harm can it do? Jailed here or just outside Singh Sahib's lands, surely it is the same thing?' She drops her voice once more so the zamindar can't hear her succeeding words: 'If something should happen to him, even you would not be able to forgive your-self.' They both know that she is not talking of the bandit.

The thought of destroying his father for a second time never entered his mind. He takes his father's hand. Infinite love pours

through his fingers. 'You keep him,' he says. 'I'll let the police chief know. They are out of their minds with suspicion.'

It is the last thing the old man expected. He had resolved to fight for the bandit, he had commanded Asmara Didi, his mouthpiece, not to back down, no matter what Lokend said and how much it hurt him. He is annoyed by his son's acquiescence. *Does nothing move you? Fight like a man.* 'You keep him. Here or there, it doesn't matter,' says the son, his words mock his father more than he knows.

'What did he want?' Ram Singh crowds his younger brother outside the room, trapping him between his large frame and the wall.

'He's got Daku Manmohan.'

'What? Where?'

'In the old outhouse.'

'What for?'

'Bapu is going to be his jailer from now on. The villagers asked him to do it. He says it's his duty.'

'Duty. As if! It's just to relive the old days,' he says, shaking with anger.

'He has that old look in his eyes,' says Asmara Didi, joining the brothers. 'He's alive again, Ram Singh, how can you deny him that? It is wonderful to see your father so eager and enthusiastic once again.'

'Yes,' Ram Singh stretches out the word, leaving no doubt that he doesn't share the woman's elation.

'Bhaia, don't be angry.' Lokend puts a hand on his brother's shoulder. This time Ram Singh doesn't shake it off. 'We all want the same things from life.'

'You make me sick with your spiritual nonsense! You know you have our father's love and his attention. You can afford your equanimity, I can't. To use language you understand, conflict *is* my lot.'

'Use it then! Use your struggle! Use your conflict! Use it to understand the Truth.' Lokend stops his brother and faces him square. Ram Singh, a whole head taller than Lokend, has to stoop to look into his younger brother's eyes.

'Truth?'

'It's the same for all of us. It's the same for me, too. Every day I have to struggle against myself, to keep my eye on the Truth.'

'What Truth?'

'Immortality. That Truth.'

'Don't be ridiculous!'

'Impermeable, fixed, permanent, unconcerned with Death. Eternity. That's what I am talking about.' Now the younger bull-dozes the elder brother.

'Don't talk to me as if I were a child.'

'We – you, me, Bapu, Asmara Didi – all conscious beings seek it. But we think it doesn't exist, so we distract ourselves with other things. Don't settle for anything else, Bhaia, all else will disappoint.'

'All else will disappoint.' He repeats his brother's words with a whine in his voice. 'Really, will it? Meat to a vegetarian. That's what your words are to me: meat to a vegetarian. Useless!' He turns to go. Lokend turns with him.

'You will drown in your wishing well.'

'I always wanted our father's love. But not any more. Now I want only what is rightfully mine. My share of the lands. He shouldn't squander my inheritance on you. On you who will give it away. I will be the next zamindar, and Bapu knows that. He must give me my rights, and by virtue of the life you have chosen, all this will be mine. Mine. All mine. Every last grain of soil. Mine!'

'Agree or disagree, none of it will bring you peace. How much more will be enough? How much better can you eat? How much better can you dress? How much better can you travel? How much more power can you wield? Will adding another field to your lands really change your life? Will another vassal make you any happier?' Lokend isn't asking rhetorical questions. He takes nothing for granted, and gives his elder brother enough time between questions for answers, continuing to the next question only when certain that one isn't forthcoming.

'Do you know why even the richest, most successful man is an unsatisfied man? Because personal strife is a condition of life. The only way to rid oneself of strife is to be dead. The strife of ordinary folk encompasses things like where will I get my next meal? Where

will my family sleep in the time of the next flood? How will I get a job for my eldest son? . . . a dowry for my daughter? But the rich have no such simple strife. They have to find stronger, bigger, better means to satisfy the craving of their souls. How many times have you heard someone say, But why did he kill himself, he had everything?'

'You mean to tell me that the poor are happy?'

'No, I mean to tell you that those who don't want as much need a lot *less* to be happy. Ironically, having everything means you have a much higher level of personal strife to satisfy. The easiest way to staying happy is by borrowing someone else's simple strife.' Lokend's eyes seek the horizon. 'If so much in life is axiomatic, and has been done by others before, why isn't it all tried and tested to perfection?' he asks of no one, walking away from his brother without a goodbye.

What are words anyway? Just whores that pass from person to person, thinks the forgotten sibling.

Monsoon Darkness

5

THE ONLY DREAM MAMTA HAS OF love between a man and a woman, the kind she wants for herself, comes from the one faded movie poster in Lala Ram's shop. The darkly brooding actor and his true love, the actress who stands one step behind, buffeted by his shadow, with icicle tears running down her cheeks, are the standard-bearers of her brand of romance. What she doesn't know is the tragic end to the movie, which turned out to be a tale of unrequited love and destroyed lives. She lives with this dream in her head and her heart in her mouth, and each day she takes little bites out of her heart. And as her heart becomes smaller, her dream starts to dissolve, flowing out of her like water through her fingers. It takes all her faculties to survive as a wife.

In her brown sari she blends into the sombre mud walls of her husband's house, so much a part of her surroundings that her existence is defined by them. Sometimes her husband comes home and doesn't notice her sewing silently, watching him from under her eyelids, doing nothing to give herself away. When he does notice her, he sometimes walks over to hit her.

In return, she taunts her stepdaughter. Her teasing and bullying aren't just meanness but an acknowledgement of the younger girl's place as a confirmed ally. The two girls are co-conspirators, a push-me-pull-you couple who feel safe in each other's company because their destinies aren't all that different. Strangely enough, each taunt

serves to bring the two girls closer. With the stepson, Mamta has a totally different relationship. She avoids him, yet she does as much for him as she can. The boy in turn is completely indifferent to both the girls. They are dust under his feet. He knows he can command them with the flick of his impetuous hand. One damaging word from his lips would be enough for his father.

She has been at her new house for six months now and she still doesn't know her husband at all. If she had to put it into words, her strongest emotion is fear. Fear to live in a house in which she has no place. Still, she cleans it and cooks in it daily. And every night lies down on the straw to sleep. In her mother's house it was different. There wasn't such fear; she knew where she stood, certain if she kept out of her father's way she would have a good day. Here, her fear has turned her tongue bitter and put her stomach on the boil. She quivers in the knees if she doesn't sit down, and every day thinks up new excuses, explanations and reasons that she might have to use to rationalise her existence should the need arise. If for a moment her husband judges her to be redundant, then that could be the end of it all.

At first glance her husband might seem cruel. But he has his own history that has brought him to this place. He inherited his indentured life from his great-grandfather. Each generation of men in his family has been pushed round by landowners, uprooted and sent off to other lands that needed tilling. Mamta's husband himself was moved to Barigaon, the village closest to Gopalpur, when his son wasn't even six months old. His first wife was a physically weak woman. Her delicate bones irritated him to such an extent that he loaded her up with the family bedding for the journey. The last few miles she made on her knees, too frightened to complain to her husband who walked on ahead straight, strong and proud. And that's how he's remained: straight, strong and proud in front of his family. It is only by making them fear him that he feels a sense of power in his senseless life.

'Lower your pallav!' He snatches the end of Mamta's sari and jerks it down. She should be thankful for the dignity it brings her. She clamps the end between her teeth to stop it from blowing away.

An unruly veil might get her a broken arm. She picks up the broom. She's dreamed so often of sweeping her own veranda, but now her gait is old with dread. Her husband looks at her from afar. He is used to her birthmark. He remarked on it constantly, and it irritated him when she started to cry. The thought of drink and prostitutes is never far from his mind, but he has no money for either. What is a man to do with two little children but take another wife? He should never have let their mother die, he thinks; the replacement is far inferior. But in truth, he could have done nothing to save his first wife.

The goddess is scuffed and oil-stained, but each of her imperfections only serves to make her dearer to the girl with the birthmark. The lingering smell of saffron, a soft memory from a different life, is her escape. She has looked into the box almost every night since she came here, and each time she opens it, she is overwhelmed with images of an unknown man and warm hands round her shoulders.

The sweets were quickly gone, into the bellies of her husband and stepson. The son she didn't mind so much, because he didn't eat quite as decisively as his father and she was able to gather the crumbs that dropped from his mouth into the dirt and stuff them into her own.

The empty box of sweets has become her memory box. In it she has a dried garland of jasmine flowers from her wedding, a photograph of her and her mother taken by Rajiv of the *Times of India*, and a lock of Shanti's hair (it used to hold Lucky Sister's gold earrings, but her husband asked for them the day he brought her home). Her mother had pressed that photo into her hand just as she was about to get into the tonga. It was such an act of sacrifice. No one else would have simply given their picture away to their daughter to take to another's home. They would have hung their photo on their door together with the mirror, or put it under their pillow like her bapu did his.

'Amma.' She jumps. The little girl looks directly into her own eyes. How can she get used to being called Amma when nothing has ever grown in her womb?

'What is it?' Her voice has the same bullying tone as her husband's.

'Am . . . ma . . .' the girl is not sure of their relationship '. . . can you help?' She holds out a ribbon. It is an old ribbon. It might have been red once, but it is now brown.

'You stole it?' It is merely a question to establish context, not to accord blame. Mamta's morals do not recognise stealing as wrong.

'No.' Even the child knows the ribbon isn't worth stealing. 'I found it in the dung.'

'Uh.' Mamta takes the ribbon and starts braiding it into her fingers. 'I'm not your mother.'

'But Bapu says that you are our new mother and that we have to listen carefully to what you say, because you will live with us till you die.'

'So what do you want me to do?'

'Can you put it in my hair?'

'This ribbon that's rotted in the cow's stomach for God knows how long, and you want me to put it in your hair?' Suddenly Mamta starts to laugh. 'This ribbon from a cow's stomach . . . ha, ha.' Her laughter fills the house. It has no care who hears it. Like incense it races through her mouth and out of the door. It takes on new tones and lilts, it wafts and wanders, runs and hides, shines through and declares itself. The child looks on in amazement.

> 'Make a chapatti, bake a chapatti,
> Give one to your father, give one to your mother,
> One for your sister and one for your brother,
> Then what's left? One burned and dry,
> Give it to the little girl to make her cry.'

Nonsense words of a nursery rhyme filled with sense. Rhymes such as these have served generations of children, reconciling them to their place in the world. Mamta aims to hurt, but she might in fact be doing her stepdaughter a service. The girl sees nothing sinister in the words. She smiles. The rhythm has play to it.

'You are older than my amma.'

'Older than your mother, am I? Well, I am not your mother,' she says, pressing a tiny shell into the clay above the fireplace. The Tree

of Life – the most commonly used pattern in these parts, is emerging quite nicely. This place may fill her with dread, but an unconscious part accepts it as the only home she will ever know. There is nothing odd in her impulse to decorate the walls of her hut, a place that has so far brought her no joy. She is one of those people with boundless patience and it is these people who can coax beauty from nothing.

The girl comes to help with her own ideas, carefully placing a twig in the border of wet clay. Mamta slaps her wrist. She will not be helped. 'Do something else.' The child stays, back to the wall, slowly sliding into a squat. Watching.

Mamta presses in another shell. Then she looks back over her shoulder. The child is still there, back to the wall. After the third shell, her annoyance gives way to indifference. Let her watch if she wants; why should she care?

'Amma . . .' Each time the stepdaughter tries conversation, Mamta's hand goes still. It's a signal for the little girl to stop talking.

'Bring in the clothes,' snaps Mamta. It has started raining.

When it rains, Mamta has to press her husband's legs because his bones ache with the damp. If she doesn't do it just right, he kicks her with the top of his foot, which causes him even greater discomfort, so he kicks her again, this time with the heel. She doesn't mind the kicking too much, but she hates it when he grabs her arm and gets on top of her. Her mind makes comforting patterns: a saffron-scented world, leather slippers outside her hut, laughing into quiet eyes . . . but it can't make the leap to warm hands on her shoulders. It takes her husband forever to finish and roll off. Immediately he is disgusted by her and tells her to get out of the hut. Now she leaves of her own accord when he finishes. The lemons she brought from her mother's home are brittle and dry on the outside, but they still have some juice left and she washes herself after each intercourse to prevent the itching she's sure will follow.

She watches the rain.

Helpful rain. Life-giving rain. Beautiful rain. Bountiful rain. *Thank you, Devi. Jai ho Devi, Devi jai ho.* The rain is her ally. It is her time of stillness. She prays daily to Devi to send her rain, not so much

for the crops, but for herself, so she might sit outside in safe solitude and dream a destiny. In her dreams she is leaving on a tonga with red in her middle parting and a ring on her second toe, clasping the hand of her husband, but it is a different hand, and she sees leather slippers walking in time with her own.

Concealing rain. Peaceful rain.

The soiled clouds unfurl overhead. The girl drags in the washing. Mamta checks it, crushing each piece into a rosette. She is a good washer, able to remove the most stubborn stain. Goat droppings mixed with lime will get any stain out of white clothes when rinsed in running water. She folds each article carefully, and puts her husband's startlingly white kurta on the blue shelf above the straw mattress. They work quietly, their combined industry pushes them closer.

'*Babooji namaste, chole khao saste, pani peo thanda, sir mein maro danda.*' The girl shares a nursery rhyme of her own.

Mamta's husband is a farmer who tills another's lands. She has yet to meet the owners. They will come at the end of the year like they've done so for the last eight years to collect their dues. In the meanwhile, he answers to a bunch of white-kurta-clad moustached men who arrive in a tonga with sticks. So far Mamta has seen them only once. The men stood outside her door the whole time and watched the family drag out four sacks of wheat. That was the first time she'd seen her husband afraid, cowering in a corner like a wet cat, emerging from the hut only when called. One of the men had poked a sack with an iron spike and caught the cascading grain in his palm. He'd blown into it to check that there was no chaff mixed in, then the men loaded the wheat into the tonga and left. It was after one such meeting, during which the men had found chaff in the wheat, that Mamta's husband had knocked his first wife to the ground so hard that she'd never quite recovered. She had a lingering stomach infection, which he had caused to bleed earlier than it would have on its own accord. She would have died from it anyway; it's not something you can pin on Mamta's husband.

'Amma.' The girl won't let Mamta out of her sight. She refuses to be satisfied with nursery rhymes, historic words; she demands

something more personal from her. With the same glee with which a child might tease an animal, Mamta retrieves her memory box from under the bedding, takes out the garland and presses it to the girl's nose, and then immediately pulls it away, leaving her gasping for more.

'Show me. Show me!' She jumps to grasp the brown garland of jasmine, smelling equally of damp and perfume. Mamta pulls it so far out of reach that it is a jump the girl cannot make. She gives up and sits, her back to the wall. Staring.

'Do you know this flower's story?' Mamta's engaged. 'It used to be a girl. A girl who prayed so faithfully to Shiva that he made her into a flower and gave her the boon of perfume, fresh or dry.' Mamta injects her mother's intonations into a story she's heard many times. 'That's why it smells so strong. My mother told me that.' The young girl looks on with disbelief.

'Why would a god want to make a girl a flower?'

'Why not?' There is a big difference between the two girls. It doesn't occur to the younger one that the gods would ever waste their time fulfilling a girl's wishes, whereas the older one, whose mother allowed her to experience a little of girlhood, owns the hidden gift of a powerful imagination. An imagination that may have lost its sauce and become not much more than a hazy palimpsest beneath her new fearful portrait, but it is one she can resurrect with the gentlest attention.

The stepdaughter reaches out, caressing the long-dead jasmine blossoms dangling from Mamta's fingers.

'Give it here.' Mamta snatches the garland from the girl's hand and puts it back in the memory box. 'Don't go getting any ideas. This box is mine. Don't you go near it! Touch it and I'll break your arm. And don't call me Amma, I'm not your mother.'

'Show me that other thing.'

'This? This is a photo,' she says. 'Of me and my amma.'

'Can I see?' The girl has no idea what it might be.

'No!' Mamta peers at the photo. Her face, tucked just below her mother's right ear, looks back at her. By some gift of light, her birthmark came through as a shadow in the portrait. She certainly looks presentable, almost beautiful. She changes her mind, and hands the photo to the girl.

'Aeee, what a picture. Who painted it?'

'You stupid girl, it isn't painted by someone, it is painted by a machine.'

'A machine? Can I have one too?'

Mamta snatches the picture back from the little hand. She looks at the photo again, satisfied by the even colour on her forehead. 'It was taken before my wedding. It was grand. Sahibji L-lokend . . .' she trips at the name '. . . from the Big House brought so many sweets that we couldn't even finish them.' She sinks into a familiar pleasurable aching memory.

'Really?'

'Re . . . ally,' she mimics her stepdaughter's high pitch. 'Do you think I'm lying?'

'And that, what's that?' The younger girl pokes the hair with a diffident finger.

'My sister's hair.' Mamta's thoughts shift to her old home longingly, each of her senses replete with its memory. Her mother's touch, Shanti's smell, Mohit and Sneha's voices screaming at each other, Prem's stolen butter pats from the Big House, but nothing of her father.

'It's so soft. Just like mine.'

Mamta packs the box and puts it away under the bedding. 'If I catch you touching it, I will thrash you. Remember that.'

Most people's lives are measured and marked by some major happening: the loss of a fortune, the birth of a child, winning a lottery. But here, in Barigaon, where the slow plodding tedium of trying to stay unnoticed is Mamta's main preoccupation, life happens in the small things. In small innocent things which might happen to harbour a tiny bacterium of deviation.

'Why n-no lamp today?'

'There's no oil.'

'So what happen-ned to it?' She can smell the alcohol on his breath. The sharp astringent smell hasn't gone stale yet. It is a different smell in the morning. The evening's smell is better, almost clean.

'There's been only a drip for a week.'

'How dare you c-c-criticise me! On-nly a drip of oil in-ndeed. I'll sh-sh-show you a drip of oil.' The drink makes him stutter.

The slap damages her eardrum and sends her spinning to the other end of the hut. The blow takes her by complete surprise. Almost as much surprise as the rumours of eviction had taken her husband. The zamindar wants his land back, they said. In return for the land, the landlord would release people like him from bondage, they said. But a man in bondage is sometimes a secure man. He is a man who curses his luck and attacks his fate, but when fate sets him free he is paralysed by the insecurity of leaving the only life he knows. Mamta's husband is this type of man.

There are others like him. Other terrified men who might also have to give up their lands and indentured lives. But why now? It is uncertain, but they've heard that each village has to set up a shelter for the families of surrendering bandits. It is a terrific scheme that has been engineered by Gopalpur's zamindar's youngest son named Loken, Lekhen, Lokend or something like that. Mamta's husband has no idea that his wife will recognise the name Lokend Bhai. In fact it is a name she will never forget. It belongs to those leather slippers who brought permanent sweetness into her life in a gold and red box. She can trace every detail of his face when she thinks of him. The name isn't mentioned in Mamta's presence and that one quirk of circumstance will change her whole life.

She picks herself up. Her stepdaughter and son are hiding outside. The son has very little interest in what his father does to his new bride, but the daughter is, for the first time in her life, afraid for another person. She didn't feel this much for her real mother.

'N-n-no oil, n-n-no land. You un-nlucky, evil woman. It's because of you. Brought you in—n-nto my house and n-n-now look what's happened. They s-s-said don't take the witch with the mark, but I did-n't listen. I was s-s-so s-s-sad for my little children. They n-n-need a mother I s-s-said. They n-n-need a mother! And n-n-now you've done it. What they s-s-said was true. N-n-no wonder God marked you from the s-s-start. I should have s-s-seen it right away.' Each word is accompanied by a blow. It is a dance, he hits

125

her to a beat. Word – blow, word – blow, word – blow . . . Fretful spit is spraying from his mouth. The stepson is now in the hut. He too surveys his surroundings. Mamta is still in a huddle on the floor and the stepdaughter is outside, just behind the door, trembling. It's her turn next. She knows where she stands in the family hierarchy. When her father is done with his wife, almost a perfect stranger to him, he will start on his daughter.

The fear is thick as smoke, and then just as suddenly it's gone, gone with the man who stumbles out of his house without a backward look, dragging an indistinct trail of drunken curses behind him.

Mamta's mouth is bleeding. One of her teeth has come loose. She hasn't said a word, she is still, she has forgotten to breathe. If she lets go, her pee will run down her legs in an uncontrollable river of fright. Her birthmark is glowing red, engorged.

The words are lurking on her stepdaughter's tongue, but she hasn't the courage to spit them out, instead she puts out her hand. Mamta turns her head away sharply, expecting another slap from human contact. The stepson walks round his stepmother as if she were a dirty thing to be avoided. He believes she is unlucky.

Mamta runs her tongue along the inside of her mouth, and spits out a piece of broken tooth. Her eyelid is torn. The stepdaughter pokes it with a tender finger. She takes Mamta's head and puts it against her bony chest, blowing every so often on her damaged eye. Bruised and battered, Mamta is sure that her husband will kill her the next time. She too is starting to believe that she is an evil unclean thing, a thing to be despised. She tries to think of something soft, but she cannot recall the softness of her mother's touch. She tries to think of something kind, but she cannot recall that unknown face. This time, the moment is too real to tolerate her dreams. At last, her battered eye releases a tear. Her stepdaughter wipes it away with her hand, leaving a streak of black. The kindness is even more painful than the beating, and Mamta wraps herself up in her sari, leaving not a chink for a peephole.

'*Babooji namaste, chole khao saste, pani peo thanda, sir mein maro danda, Babooji namaste, chole khao saste, pani peo thanda, sir mein*

maro danda, Babooji namaste . . .' the girl sings of a city gentleman eating cheap chickpeas, drinking cold water and being hit on the head with a stick. Her nursery rhyme makes about as much sense as the beating her stepmother just received. She rocks Mamta back and forth to the lisping tempo, and Mamta sinks into a quiet memory of unknown eyes.

The evening has turned cold. A thick fog starts to accumulate.

Her husband returns the next afternoon calmer than before. He smells of stale vomit. A little drink puts him in a bad mood, but a lot makes him mellow. The drink of last night is still with him. His eyes are red as chillies and burning every bit as much. He has put his fight aside for the sake of his sickened body.

He'd passed out in the field of makeshift tents where the men mingle after sunset in the glow of a single lightbulb burning with electricity purloined from electric poles with bits of wire joined together in innumerable places. The men often don't talk amongst themselves. For so many people, the field of tents is curiously silent – until the betting begins.

Wives have a vague idea of that place; only two dared to follow their husbands there, but they are old now and never speak of what happened. As for the rest of the wives, they pretend the tents don't exist, and the new ones like Mamta truly know nothing of the place. The only women who hang about the edges of the tents are the ones that work there. Prostitutes, young and old.

Last night the tents were thronging with others like him. He didn't bet, but uncharacteristically bought a whole bottle. The bootlegger opened his book to a fresh page lined neatly in blue. In the left-most column he wrote Mamta's husband's name and in the far most column a number. There would be no dispute over the number and date written in the book. He would have to come up with the money on the appointed day.

He doesn't look Mamta in the eye or touch the tea or salted cha-pattis she's made. The mother and stepdaughter had spent all early morning picking wild bitter spinach for the man. He doesn't taste the vegetable. The daughter slyly eats most of it before the son can

get to it. Mamta unrolls his bedding, leads him to it and he sinks into the turned straw, a deadweight.

She douses the fire, which has started to smoke. Her newly patterned wall glimmers through the miasma in and out of her vision. Her ribs hurt from the evening before and she winces when she lifts her arm. The two girls literally dragged the water pot from the well that morning. They managed to bring only one instead of the usual two. More than half of it they've hidden in a bush behind the house for the man.

'Some guests are on their way.'

Mamta takes it to mean that she must make more tea. Still the man doesn't look at her. What should she be feeling? Hatred in every aching pore? Vengeance in each battered limb? Fear in her solidly plundered body?

If she thought about her thoughts, they would surprise her. She feels no hatred, vengeance or fear. She can see each tea leaf fall with finality into the bubbling water, and knows she can count the leaves accurately. She admires the tips of her fingers. How well they release the leaves in a smooth stream, an aesthetic, even beautiful, stream of brown powder. The tea leaves live in a red Brooke Bond tin, slightly rusted round the edges. The tin has lost a hinge. Every two weeks her husband brings the tea leaves wrapped in newspaper. She pours them into the tin, then she boils the newspaper to repossess every last bit of essence from it for her own brew. The tin has precisely ten and a half pinchfuls left in it. She can tell by the weight.

They don't often have guests. The last time there were guests she and the daughter had to go out and look for fallen mangoes. The man had wanted mangoes for his friends, and mangoes he got. *Oh, why doesn't he send me out to look for mangoes this time? It is winter, silly woman, where would you find mangoes?* A rueful smile rushes to her lips, filling them with blood. She wants to be on her own, with her swollen eye and broken tooth, to heal in the embrace of some unknown tree like an animal, free in her solitude and feeling like a live thing. Here she feels dead. She has that detached quality that tells her she may have strayed into another's nightmare.

'They've come,' says a girl's voice.

Mamta tilts her head and looks into the fresh eyes of a child. They give her a melting softness on the inside, like the feel of warm hands bringing her back to standing a long time ago. *Where have I seen those eyes before? Whose face is this? These hands? What place is this? What state is this?* A hand grasps her fingers.

'Amma!'

My daughter. Of course.

She can hear the men talking outside. The smell of tobacco enters the hut looking for a place to sleep. There are four, maybe five. The night is too thick to penetrate. But even if she could see their faces, she wouldn't recognise them as the city-shoe-wearers from her wedding. The men sit in a circle covered by blankets as if afraid of wolves. This is the first time she's seen her husband gather the sticks from behind the house and pile them up into a nice and tidy cone ready for burning. The fire is sickly, it goes out three times before he is able to keep it alive by blowing into its heart.

Yes, go on blow. One puff. Now from the side. Lower! Almost there. One more puff and you'll have it. She shouts silent instructions to her awkward spouse. With the fire going, the men turn to the matters at hand.

The husband sends his son to call Mamta.

'They're waiting,' the boy announces from the door. Her step-daughter lets go of her hand. Mamta grabs it again. She will be lost without this child. This child gives sense to her life, purpose to her sense. The girl uncurls her stepmother's fingers with her spare hand, one by one. Even at her age, she knows this is a matter for Mamta alone.

The night air bites into her wounds, immediately stiffening them. Under her pallav her face tests its limits, winking, crinkling, hurting, blinking, hurting, hurting.

'So this is her.' She can't tell which one has spoken. They are so tightly huddled against the cold.

'Is she all right?' That voice she knows. It is her husband's and he is not asking after her health.

'She should do. When?'

'As soon as possible.'

129

'We've already spoken, as soon as possible, could even be tomorrow.'

'Tomorrow then.'

Her husband waves her back into the hut.

'Tell her nothing, no need to make her nervous,' says the first voice.

What could he do to me now to make me nervous?

The men stay well into the night, smoking. She has to make tea three times before they will leave. Each time it is a different snatch of conversation that she hears.

'. . . come with you then . . .'

'No, we'll go alone. I'll take my son.'

And the next time.

'. . . by the river, that's the best kind.'

'You'll need much more for that kind.'

And finally.

'. . . no she won't. No one has died before. Why should *your* wife?'

'She might, just to make trouble for me.' The men laugh. 'I don't want any trouble.'

How will she recall that night she awoke in the white-lit air-conditioned van? The night her husband and another man carried her to the bullock cart, bouncing back to her hut, placed under the gunny sack to wait for morning? Will she recall that night? Or is it one of those too horrible times that her brain, taking pity on her soul, will choose to wipe from the memory? She *will* recall that night, but not in terms that you might think. When she realises what happened, she will recall it as the night she did her duty for her family, with no sense of shame or lingering fear. She will be matter-of-fact about it, resigned and, therefore, resilient.

6

Singh Sahib looks out of his new room at the ancient trees, barren with age, yet standing tall. He breathes deep of the mustiness round him and twists what he can of his face into a smile. The animals smile back at him. They are all in a state of readiness with bared teeth, upright tails, exposed claws and a listening gaze. He is well matched here, amongst the animals he killed himself. He is proud to point out that none were killed in cold blood, some wounded him in return and several got away before finally ending up in his sights. Surrounded by so much death, the zamindar is curiously alive.

Asmara Didi has raised Singh Sahib's bed just high enough for him to get a view of the outhouse from the new window she's had put in for precisely this purpose. Each day he looks out through the trees to the grisly building beyond, the very building responsible for his own downfall. Each day he watches someone new approach to shout a filthy curse or throw something at Daku Manmohan. The bandit never retaliates. His silence rings loud.

Day by day the zamindar observes his prisoner. Day by day he finds his life returned to him in the plans he makes for the bandit's torture and prolonged death.

The songs start as soon as Asmara Didi approaches. Daku Manmohan knows that singing gets to her the most.

Oh innocent heart, oh innocent heart,
What is your desire, what is your destiny?
In this material world,
You are a lost soul,
Oh ignorant heart, oh ignorant heart,
What is your desire, what is your destiny?

It is upon a fractured wind that the bandit's ghazals, songs of desperate love, yearning and loss, reach Singh Sahib's ear. The words take the zamindar on a personal journey, forcing him to relive each of life's disappointments over and over again.

'Arey-oh, Daku! Can't you leave the singing to others? Have you ever thought that you have no right to defile such beautiful words with your filthy tongue. Beast! You know only of killing. How many have you killed?' Asmara Didi shakes her head at him in rage. For all her early spiritual learning, she is still an agitated soul.

'Many more than you people say, you old crone. Ha, ha. Come here to torment me, have you? Better people than you have tried, old woman, and where has that got them? Come a little closer if you dare, I'll smash your head in with my bare hands.' He speaks strongly, but there is no real fight in him.

'Then Singh Sahib will chop off your hands. It's because of Lokend that you are still alive. Thank your lucky stars.'

Singh Sahib is used to the sparring between Asmara Didi and Daku Manmohan. She is the only one he ever graces with a reply. He thinks it is more out of respect for the old woman than anything else.

Each day the battle gets fiercer.

'How long do we have to keep him here? All day long he sits and stares, looking at us with those killer's eyes. Can't you find something for him to do? Yesterday Gope and his friends threw a beehive into his cell. He was covered with stings the size of lemons. He thrashed around like a landed fish. But did you hear a word out of him? No. It's unnatural, I tell you, downright unnatural. The day before it was excrement, last week it was snakes. It's too degrading. He doesn't care what we do. Just sits and looks, and sings his mournful songs. That's become his life's work.'

'It'sss . . . my word.'

'Oh yes, you've given your word, all right. There are too many of your kind who have. Giving your word as freely as chaff riding wind,' she says under her breath. 'What about the group that came to see you yesterday? Surely you are not going to give them free access to the temple so they can exhibit their cripples in front of his cell like seasonal melons.'

'The gulsss . . .' He puckers his lips into a smile, a private joke; he doesn't take the woman's fretting seriously.

'Huh, the girls. Don't tell me about the girls,' she says, throwing her hands up in the air. 'Singh Sahib, girls will be girls. Oh, I know what they say. He is an avatar, their saviour. If rumours are to be believed, he has saved the whole virgin population of Gopalpur from rape. It is idle talk, just idle talk. Uneducated people are easily fooled, they need to treat someone as God, you know that. Plus he is handsome.'

Singh Sahib looks at her in questioning surprise.

'Oh no, I'm way beyond noticing a man for his looks. But girls . . . give them something different and they are infatuated right away. Maybe he saved some of them from rape. So what? He's committed his own heinous crimes.'

Singh Sahib chuckles.

'Laugh all you will, but that man can't be kept like this.'

Singh Sahib moves his head slightly. She knows what it means. Daku Manmohan's proximity has put her in bad humour and made her irreverent. 'At least give him something to do. How about the corner field? Let him plough that,' she barks with exasperation.

He nods. Anything to stop her yapping. He has come to a point where he enjoys his thoughts, rolls them around in his mind like a hard-boiled sweet . . .

'This incarceration is making you unnaturally happy. Don't think I don't see it, Zamindar Sahib. Hai! I wish Bibiji was alive, what would she have said to all this?' Asmara Didi thinks that by bringing Bibiji into the room she can force the zamindar to acknowledge the absurdity of his ways. But Singh Sahib is not biting.

'Hiss . . . sss . . . inging . . . ha, ha.' This time he laughs aloud. It

133

is a huge effort of will for him. His prisoner has made him fierce, focused, not even talk of his wife can lure him away. The bandit has been in captivity for six months now, and Singh Sahib has recorded the moments of his life in the minutest detail. That remains his biggest occupation. Nothing else seems to concern him.

She tries another tack. 'Lokend has got some NGO from Delhi to give him money to complete the building. The well is already dug. I'm told Gope and Kanno will move into the new ashram soon.'

Lokend has done it virtually unaided. He has built an ashram for the victims of the bandit raids, the same cripples that he saw on the day of the surrender, on the same piece of land he had intended for Daku Manmohan's prison, exactly behind Babulal's Topaz Suppliers, purveyors of farming equipment.

'I thought that having the bandit this close would force Lokend to come home. But he is too busy fulfilling other people's dreams.' Asmara Didi's sarcasm bites like a red ant. 'He *has* come to see you, hasn't he?' she asks, knowing full well what the answer is. It is now her turn to bait the old man.

'Huh.' It hurts Singh Sahib that Lokend meets only Asmara Didi each time he comes to visit the bandit.

Asmara Didi wipes her forehead and looks at the ceiling. Summer is returning with gusto. Overhead the cloth fan attempts to drag the still air from side to side in the musty room. She made it operational just this morning. Now one of the servants sits outside the window pulling on the rope tied to his toe to move the giant cloth frill. She chose yellow for the colour of the fan to inject some light into the room, but one can see that it makes little difference, hanging too far above their heads to provide either air or colour.

'There is Ram Singh,' she says, hearing footfalls in the corridor. 'Must be time for his daily visit,' she growls.

Each day Ram Singh makes sure to pass the bandit's cell on his way to his father's room, as usual firing barbs along the way. 'How goes your life today? Everything to your satisfaction? Not too hot, is it? How about the food? Too spicy? Not enough meat?' He spits on the floor. 'Filthy man. Filthy, filthy man, not fit to be called human. Ruined our poor village.' As usual, Daku Manmohan just

stares at him. As usual, this unnerves Ram Singh. 'I'll break your face if you stare at me like that. How dare you look at *me* like that?'

He enters his father's room. 'Can't you get more light in here? Why do you sit in darkness all day? Your prisoner has a better room than you.' The father bristles internally. Ram Singh is the person he least wants to see.

He approaches his father. 'Get rid of him, Bapu. That man is a disgrace to us all. Let's hang him from a tree. Then the village will know what we've done for them.' His words are laden with zeal. Like the bandit, the father too keeps silent. 'But no, you can't do that, of course. You have given your word, and we all know your word is more precious than your life. Good God! Bapu, for once listen to me. He should be cut into bits and fed to the dogs for what he's done to the people here.'

'I hate to agree, but this once I think Ram Singh is right.'

Ram Singh looks from his father to Asmara Didi. Her agreement makes him suspicious.

'Do it, Singh Sahib. Do it. Or get someone else to,' she urges.

'Yes, you won't even have to associate yourself with the deed,' says Ram Singh. 'Just give me the word, Bapu . . . I'll have it done.'

This time it's the old woman who looks from father to son, her nose and mouth quivering with revulsion. 'He'll have it done,' she says. '*He* has the people for the job.' No one is deceived. She isn't complimenting Ram Singh on his competence.

There are so many words lodged in the old man's throat. Has it all come to this? An ignominious murder by an anonymous hand in the middle of the night. Is that to be his brand of justice?

Only one word flies from his mouth. 'Nnno!' It's the most important word anyway. What use are explanations? What purpose will they serve? Maybe it's best that God robbed him of his speech, he couldn't change his son's mind even if he tried. Or Asmara Didi's, for that matter. It would be easier to fill a lake with a perforated spoon than change their minds.

Singh Sahib resolves to put more guards round the cell to keep would-be assassins away. He needs someone he can trust. Lokend would be the first choice, but he is away so much. Who

then? Prem. That's right. Prem, the indentured farmer's son who is devoted to Lokend, that's who he'll send for.

With great reluctance, Asmara Didi, the mouthpiece of Singh Sahib, explained the job to Prem. 'It is now your duty to look after the prisoner. I don't mean really *look after*, I mean just be an extra set of eyes. Report anything strange directly to me. Here, take this drum, beat it if anything suspicious happens, but don't beat it needlessly, otherwise I will beat you myself. Remember, you are doing this for Lokend Bhai, only Lokend Bhai,' she told him.

The boy examines the cell hesitatingly. The bandit catches his look. Why have they brought out the damn boy? He reminds him of his own son. The prisoner waves the boy away. The boy stands his ground. He has been instructed to keep watch by Lokend Bhai himself. He feels that manly feeling filling his chest. It is more than duty that stops him from walking away.

Asmara Didi approaches, kicking a path through the offerings of flowers and fruits left by grateful village girls. 'What has the world come to? People will idolise almost anyone, no matter how evil. Why we should have to employ someone to take care of this murderer is something I will never understand,' says Asmara Didi. She takes Prem by the arm and sets him to one side like a piece of discarded furniture. 'Murderer,' she shouts at the prisoner. 'Murderer! Don't think you will be able to lounge in your cushy cell for the rest of your days. Today you start ploughing Singh Sahib's fields. I have arranged the most stony, barren, virgin field of all for you. You know a lot about ravaging, right? Let's see if you know as much about building something of value.'

'Eh, old woman, there isn't a field you can give me to work which I won't be able to tame.'

'Yes, you have a lot of experience with taming, haven't you? Your brand of taming is rape. Rapist!'

Red creeps into Daku Manmohan's eyes. 'I may be many things, but I am not a rapist,' he shouts at Asmara Didi. 'You want to see a rapist? You don't have to look far. Your zamindar's eldest son, he is the rapist.'

Singh Sahib listens keenly to the conversation from his distant window. It was as recently as yesterday that he'd seen two young girls, just in their teens, hand a plate of food and a garland through the bars to the bandit. They'd bent down as if to touch his feet, but the bandit had waved them off. The two girls claimed that Daku Manmohan himself had saved them from gang rape by members of the Big House.

The lovesick adoration of village girls has made the incarceration far more interesting than he'd hoped. Mixed up the truth, made a muddle of morality, a cocktail of good and evil, blurred the boundaries, made everything grey, just like life. What would Lokend's *Bhagvat Gita* say about all this? *By the delusion of the pairs of opposites sprung from attraction and repulsion, all beings walk this universe wholly deluded.*

He can hear the bandit's denial clearly. 'I am a man of honour. I am a family man. I have a wife. I have never raped a girl,' he shouts, but Asmara Didi is already halfway to the house, too far away to hear him.

7

WHEN HER HUSBAND POKES HER WITH his toe, it always seems to connect with the scar that runs across her left side. *A little deeper and you could have cut me in two.* She knows so little of the workings of her body that she thinks they've fixed her up. For what? Possibly no children, but she doesn't really know.

It is one of the men from the night huddle who helps to put things straight. Again he arrives smoking a bidi. This time during the day.

'So how is she?'

'Good. The same.'

'No problems then?'

'No, not really. In the beginning she complained of pain in her back, but that was for a few days only. I stopped her going to the well. That's the only thing she really couldn't do. "The children are grown," I said, "let them bring the well water."'

Mamta doesn't remember that conversation. Let the children bring the well water? Maybe they did. Maybe they didn't. With her insides on fire, what did she know or care? Her stepdaughter gave her white pills every day. Her husband came home and counted the pills and demanded his son's corroboration before he was satisfied. If you miss a single pill she'll die, he'd told his daughter, using the doctor's words.

'So how much did you get?'

138

'As you said, enough to buy another piece of land, but not enough to move by the river. Still, it's good. I trust nobody, I got the money in cash. He offered me some papers to sign, said, "Keep the money with me, it will grow in value," but I said no. Took me for a fool, I think. I said, "No, give me the cash in advance." So they gave me everything but twenty-five thousand, which they gave me after the operation. That too they tried to cheat from me, but I threatened them. I had taken my knife and stick. I said I would report them to the police for having cut the flesh out of her. Ha, ha, there was nothing they could do!' He is proud of his victory over a far stronger foe.

'Now you have the money, and we don't have to move. We never had to, it was just a rumour. That man, Lekhen or whatever his name is, is giving his own lands to the bandit families.'

The men laugh, their bodies relax, relieved by the news. Then he's angry for the injustice of it all. 'Why did they tell us that we had to move?'

'Look at it this way, if you hadn't heard the rumour, you wouldn't have got all this money for nothing.'

Again he relaxes, happy in the thought that things have at last gone in his favour.

'I'm going to have my wife done too.'

Now Mamta's husband is the one with all the information. They all look to him for advice.

'Don't go after three in the morning. I met two people there whose wives were done after three . . .' He shakes his head, and not with sorrow. 'The best time is twelve to two. The doctor is still fresh.'

'If you are sure everything is okay, then I will arrange it soon.'

'Make sure there is someone at home to give her the pills. You know these women, they won't take their medicines if you tell them to, just to spite us I think. I don't know what gets into their heads. After all, we don't want to be responsible for a death.'

And that's how Mamta knew that her scar had somehow bought her family a piece of unneeded land.

Her stepdaughter touches it often.

'It's so long. Lucky they stopped. Hai, Amma, you might have

died otherwise.' The girl can state the ghoulish obvious without the slightest hesitation or embarrassment. She still hasn't learned the tact of grown-ups; for her, such a strange thing cannot go unmentioned.

'Yes, they could have.' Mamta says the words but feels no fight. She's alive, what more does she need? Nothing that leaves you alive can be all that bad. She doesn't shake off her stepdaughter's hand, and endures the tickling sensation which conceals a friendship. What did they take out of her that was worth money? She has no one to ask, no one to tell.

She's seen the notes and doesn't know what to make of them. She thinks the bigger ones are worth more. Each morning her husband counts the notes, then he shoos them all out of the hut and hides them in a different place. He trusts no one. With so few bonds he thinks his own family might rob him blind.

The boy has been pestering his father to buy him a kite. For the past few weeks he's been flying the one rescued from a nearby tamarind tree. Actually there is nothing quite like the thrill of finding an abandoned kite, like luck itself, a gift from God. The kite was riddled, but Mamta patched up the holes in an obsequious bid to buy the boy's kindness. For a few days after, the boy and the step-mother were cautiously aware of each other, even friendly to one another. But that friendliness was dispelled with her husband's next slap. The boy knew not to align himself with the lowest-ranking family member.

Mamta sees that money has changed her husband. The money has made him unpredictable. Sometimes he is ebullient, and comes home singing the latest Hindi movie song, at other times he is brooding and sulky. He goes more and more to the tents, but he doesn't have to put his name in the book any more. In fact, he has taken his name out of every book, paying his debts in full. His only tangible purchase so far has been a little transistor radio which only he can turn on. To make sure of this, he takes the batteries with him in his kurta pocket when he leaves the hut.

She allows herself an hour to search for the money after the males leave. An hour is a long time. Most days she is able to find it, then the girls have a little satisfied giggling session and go on with their

chores. She can tell by the thickness of the wad how much her husband is spending on transitory improvements in the quality of his life including five bottles of good booze (the kind guaranteed not to make you blind), a few hookahs with the other men, three visits to the prostitute and a game of cards. He is a lucky man, the game of cards has allowed him to fatten his wad and even get his son the longed-for kite. Money for free, he has thought of buying the prostitute a nose pin and new straw for his mattress. But it is a dangerous game he's playing. Now, not just winning and losing but playing or not playing are decisions out of his control.

His new status is such that twice a week men come to his veranda to gamble. Yes, they shun the tented city, where there is a levy on every win, to play on their friend's land.

He has acquired many new friends since the last time Mamta served them. She pulls her pallav low over her eyes, and brings out the tea. The tea has improved with the money, it is thick and sweet. With each sip they notice its spicy rich flavour.

They talk of her as if she's not around.

'Lucky woman, no, to have a husband with so much money. Have you seen the land?'

'Yes, but I am going to wait to make enough to go by the river. Once and for all, I will move to a fertile field. Not to this place or another like it, where we have to till and till until our backs break, and depend on the rain. My son works Kanti Nath's plot. I will pull him back and have him work for me instead.'

The reluctant moonlight lights up their faces in turn so they become partly visible to the woman serving them. They hold their cards close to their chests. It's not just from the voices that she knows who is missing but also from the prizes her husband brings home: a recognisable ghaghra choli or a pair of sandals. Sometimes it's sacks of grain or cooking pots. Her kitchen has filled up in the past few months with other people's possessions lost to her husband in a game of cards.

Mamta's husband has begun to contemplate a novel future. He is no longer paralysed by the insecurity of freedom. As a rich man he will certainly get a new wife. He will either beat Mamta and send

her back to her parents or arrange a cooking accident for her. The prostitute has got under his skin. He would like to marry the woman with the hefty cleavage and delicious, well-fed thick hips. The songs she hums under her breath make him dizzy. His transistor is no comparison for her voice.

How she hands him the end of her sari as soon as he arrives, and hides behind the red gauze. How she allows her sari to unravel, spinning like a top. How her little bleats for release from such brutish torture make him mad for her. How he takes her naked on his knee. How she is shy and not shy at the same time. Oh, how, how, how!

His prostitute is no novice. There are many moths addicted to her flame. She's had offers of marriage before and knows precisely how to tune her men. She knows that her love-struck suitor will no doubt offer her a home and married life. She has no intention of trading her thriving business for life at a sooty fire, but she gives the man no hint of this. Let him bring her expensive gifts.

Unravelling his favourite pink sari and seeing his desire spin before his eyes, he pictures her in his hut, handing out tea to his friends. He imagines keeping her just for himself, totally covered in front of other men. He can see her eyes, black liner drawing them out into almond shapes and swishing lashes marking her cheeks with shadows. The anything-but-gentle swell of her breasts. The lock of her thighs.

'W-when will you say yes?' He is breathless, his mind has taken him where his body has not.

'W-when?' She is playing the question game. The game which invariably ends in victory for her. Answer question with question. Eventually they think up the answers they want to hear and she's free.

'Why not next summer?'

'Why not?' Oh she is an expert. No one can confuse her words for true answers, and yet, one can see the possibility, the plausibility in her responses. He is no match for her.

'Come on, meri jaan, say yes. I will buy you anything you want.'

'Anything?'

'In a few months I will be twice as rich.' An idea has come to him. Another operation. Why not do it again? Twice the money. Sell the other kidney out of Mamta. She won't survive long as it is. With the other kidney, at least he will have sufficient reserve.

'Twice as rich?'

'Yes, you wait and see. I will be so rich, we will have our own land by the river and a pukka house.'

'A pukka house?'

'You just wait and see.'

All the way home he smiles at the memory of the naked prostitute, the yielding mountain of pink gauze lying by the bed and rolling . . . off and on, off and on. He thinks of the prostitute and then of the operation. But how? Even he knows another operation is as decisive as death. He must ask the men.

This time the men come especially to discuss the second operation. So confident are they in their venture that they don't bother looking for a place away from the hut to hatch their murder plan.

Again, Mamta comes with the tea. This time each one gives her a long lingering look, so long that she is persuaded to look down at her own chest. Has a breast come inadvertently bare? Has her sari come loose? She pulls the pallav lower over her eyes, a hood.

But now the men must talk. Seriously talk. The man can't bring himself to discuss the operation in front of his wife. For the second round, he asks for the boy to serve the tea. Why the boy? The daughter is jealous. Why didn't he ask for her? It is an irrational emotion, she can't wait to be free of her father and the stony fear he brings to their hut. Still, she wants his approval, especially now that he's asked the boy to bring the tea. She refuses to be passed over, left where she is like the polite last morsel on a dinner plate. She nudges the boy roughly out of the way while Mamta blocks the door with her body. Allied the two are strong. The stepdaughter takes the tea outside.

'She will die if you cut her again.'

The girl hears the *Die* word. What a captivating word it is. She waits in the shadows. No one seems to miss the tea. Mamta's body

is still blocking the boy's path. She will pay for it later, when he has his father's ear, he will make his father beat her for this infraction.

'Yes, you won't find one who will do it easily. There aren't many who will take the responsibility for someone's death.'

'It's not allowed. If they catch you, it's the jail,' says a second voice.

'You have to be clever. You must make out that she died of some other illness. The doctor will sign the papers, don't worry about that,' says the first voice.

The stepdaughter pours the tea out on the ground. She leans over, making sure it sinks silently into the mud and brings the empty glasses back inside.

She looks at Mamta with a secret in her eye. Of course all girls know what such looks mean. The boy is too angry to notice.

'They liked it. They are leaving,' says the girl. 'Bapu is going with them.'

The boy runs out after his father, but the men are covered by darkness. The moment's passed, he will not be able to get even this time.

'The man told Bapu that he had to find someone very special to do it because it was not allowed and there aren't many who will take the responsibility for someone's death,' she remembers the words perfectly as only one who doesn't understand them can. 'What does that mean, "take the responsibility for someone's death"?'

'It means they are planning to cut me right in half this time, much more than before. It means he is planning to kill me.'

'You mean kill you dead?'

'That's right, kill me dead.'

'Maybe they have to kill you because of my new amma. I don't want another amma. I never want to be separated from you.' The girl has guessed about the prostitute. Her father brings home little girlish mementoes. A wilted rose, a book he cannot read, a perfumed handkerchief. She puts her arms round Mamta. 'I don't want another amma.' This time Mamta doesn't undo them. She twists the girl round and places her in her lap.

'Don't worry, we will never be separated. I won't let it happen. We are going away. We will run away. If he hears, he will kill us

144

both, so keep your mouth shut.' Her fear is irrationally tinged with excitement. No matter how dangerous the running away, staying will kill her. The adrenalin is roaring in her ears.

'Run away . . .' The little girl's eyes are glassy with excitement.

'Not one word . . . if you don't want your head shaved and shit smeared over your body, you just be ready when I wake you at night. Just be ready.'

'Tonight?'

'Maybe, maybe not. Depends.'

'On what?'

'On something, on many things, on . . . I don't know yet.'

What is courage but another name for desperation? It is a brave soul who can be courageous without being desperate. Mamta is not such a soul. She knows the consequences. If she runs away she will never be able to return to Barigaon or Gopalpur. Not ever. A married runaway, just like Sharma's wife. A rule breaker, a tradition killer.

The right time comes three nights later.

The man comes into the house, he counts the money and puts it under his pillow. He is so close to spending the bundle that he doesn't bother hiding it safely. Another hundred rupees is missing. He's been to the prostitute. He is in a good mood. He's found a doctor. The demand for the doctor's services is so high that he will have to wait a whole week before he can take Mamta for her operation. He is drowsy with satisfaction.

He goes to sleep dreaming about the money and doesn't think it odd that his wife is sitting outside, her back to the mud wall, looking into a moonless sky. She's seen him put the money under his pillow. Without the money she doesn't have a chance.

Mamta is the only one who will not sleep. Whenever her brain wanders to how it will be once she runs away, she pulls it back like a disobedient dog on a leash. In her life, there has never been any time to think, only time to act. And this time too, she can't spoil it by thinking.

She adjusts the covers on her stepdaughter, pushing the child as far away from her father as possible. Her stepson is sleeping with

his arms and legs flung out wide. He will be a hard one to avoid. He is a noisy sleeper, a small disturbance could set in motion a series of whines, whimpers and clicks that could wake her husband. She takes her memory box from the shelf and places it by her step-daughter's head. Then she lies down beside her husband, adjusting her petticoat so that it flares away from her, taking the small kitchen knife sewn into its hem with it. Mamta must wait for the right time, but not too late, because her only chance is to escape with darkness left over to spare.

She sidles closer to her husband. She can see his nose hairs sway. In, out, in, out. She'd fed them all a heavy meal, even her husband had remarked on the generous dollop of butter. The fat meal lies comfortably in his stomach, spreading a contented warmth through his body. Her husband is a dead weight, relaxed in sleep, a peaceful, even handsome man. She looks into the face and records its every nuance. She never wants to forget that face. The face that will for her become the template of cruelty, the one against which she'll judge all other males in the future.

He moves, rolls over. The pillow is free. Quickly, she slips her hand under it and pulls out the wad. She clutches it tight between her thighs, lying as frozen as a long-dead body. She doesn't move for hours, or is it minutes? Her husband's breath is even. Her stepson's breath is even. She slowly ties the money in a knot at the end of her pallav. Her stepdaughter is lying in a good position away from the men. Mamta gets up, holding her memory box close to her chest, and moves along the darkest edge of the hut. Here she will have a chance in case her husband wakes. She pads on silent light feet towards her stepdaughter. She's gone over the whole scenario so many times that her motion is automatic. Luckily her stepdaughter is light, with delicate bones. She'll place her left hand over her mouth, and drag her from the hut before the child makes an involuntary sound.

Her stepdaughter moves in her sleep. *Stop that.* The child obeys. Mamta takes a step closer. She can feel the kitchen knife drag on the floor. *I hope it doesn't cut through the cloth.* She bends over her step-daughter. At that precise moment, the girl rolls over again. That single

roll takes her right into the centre of the room. The boy starts to whine, whimper and click. The girl's roll makes Mamta stop, stock still. She is stunned. It's gone all wrong . . . It doesn't fit in her plan . . . *How could it have gone this wrong? One move? . . . why? . . . Why that one move?* She is by the door.

She looks at her feet, her heels are just outside the door, she's still bent over, ready to pick up her stepdaughter and run. The girl's head should have been by her feet, but it's by her brother's head instead. The whines and clicks grow deeper. Her husband moves. He takes the pillow in his sleeping hands. There is much too much time between thoughts, she thinks. She knows she has to think faster. Act faster. Think faster. Act.

She steps backwards and almost falls over her husband's slippers left carelessly in the doorway. Even in her fearful state it annoys her to see the slippers. He purposely leaves them there every night for her to pick up. This night she does pick them up. She takes a step back from the door. Then another. And another. Before she knows it she is far away. Far away from her stridently sleeping family.

Later she won't remember leaving her memory box, her ultimate sacrifice, in the warm dip of her stepdaughter's bed. She has left the sleeping girl her happiest memories, her connection with her mother, Shanti, the leather slippers and her benign childhood. Even deep in her conscience, where unconscious thoughts lie, she knows she will never be able to forgive herself for this night, but with a sacrifice so grave perhaps the judging universe will be able to forgive her.

Intuitively she runs away from the well, as she has no way of knowing how many hours there are to sunrise when it will be in full use. No matter how early she gets to the well, someone is always there before her. At best she hopes to find a ravine or a mound where she can hide till she finds a bullock cart going somewhere . . . *perhaps to Gopalpur.* Of course she has no place in Gopalpur, but she is desperate and thinking irrationally. She is already making up her stories. A story for the bullock cart driver who will get her to Gopalpur and a story for her father who will most certainly want to send her back.

And, if her story doesn't work, then she has money enough to buy her freedom within her own family.

Ignoring the cool night air, the sweat leaks from her pores like resin from a gum tree. She still hasn't realised the flaw in her plan. She may be clutching a wad of money, but hasn't thought to pack anything to eat. How many days will she have to stay in hiding? Perhaps someone will find her skeleton pecked clean by vultures and long polished by the sun. Perhaps someone will shed a tear or two for her, but most likely she will die unnoticed and unmourned.

She divides the wad of notes into different piles. One goes between her breasts, the other she ties in the end of her pallav that's tucked in, and the third she rolls into the band of her petticoat. She releases her knife from bondage and tucks that too into the band of her petticoat.

She thinks of the bandits and their hideouts, but the river ravines are miles away. She thinks of the wolves, silent on dead moon nights, feasting on her tired flesh. *Wolves mate for life. Where would one find such loyalty these days but in animals? If wolves can mate for life, why can't humans?*

Her eyes have got used to the starlight, but she has no reference point to guide her. She has now come way beyond her hut, beyond where most men from her village have been. Then she sees them, her personal guardians, darker than the night.

The electric poles are almost the end of her. She feels she's safe, and in that very instant becomes aware of her body. Her thirst is dire. Her shivering is real. Her thoughts are cacophonous. Why did she leave her behind?

She is on the cusp of an epiphany, but she won't loosen her grip. She must leave her past behind if she is to survive and conquer it, only the enlightened can withstand its heat and in the blue flame of communion conquer its lust. Her immediate reality must become her only valid reason for survival.

Thirst rakes the back of her throat. She pulls her hands out from between her thighs. She is alive, that has to be enough for now. She realises the flaw in her plan. Why didn't she think to bring some food? Her thoughts send her to her knees, but she won't allow them

to take over again. She shuts her eyes. At least now she doesn't have to make those elemental decisions, turn right or left? She must now just stick to the poles and walk. That's all. She walks on, towards the electric poles. The same electric poles she's seen back home in Gopalpur, the white-ant-eaten electric poles that will bring her home.

But suddenly she is unsure, almost certain the promise is a trap, a looming betrayal. She is still on the sine curve of uncertainty; it will make many zigzags before she will be able to rely on herself. Her battered body must rest. She lies down in the furrow of someone else's field, consciously renewing her resources. It is a poorly planted field, the crop not even inches high. It won't yield much. Even on such a night she knows that the seedlings have been planted late and that the worms will get to them in warm weather. She thanks Devi it isn't her field that's planted late, and suddenly she is afraid in a different way, more than of being raped, even more than of dying under some stranger's knife. She is leaving behind the only life she knows. She can't lie still any longer. Her feet have started to blister. She slips on her husband's slippers. They flap like useless chapattis in the sandy soil. She cuts off the ends and ties them to her feet with strips of sari material taken from the inside pleats, a place no one will notice.

Unconsciously pacing herself, she walks on, but she knows that soon the dawn will come. The sunrise, her true enemy, will appear as unexpectedly as a surprise.

Eventually she finds a straggly bush to serve as her daytime nest. She is exhausted, the sunshine may turn the colour behind her lids to blood, but still she sleeps in dreamless comfort, a gift from her exhausted body.

The tinkle of cowbells sends her into military readiness. She digs deeper under the bush into the earth. Watching. The cowherd, oblivious to his audience of one, pulls out his flute, places it side-ways against his lips and blows out a sweet sad sound. He is only a boy, his clumsily tied turban an untidy tangle on his head. She is tempted to ask where she is, but then she pictures her dirty face, her birthmark, the scar along her body . . . and decides to stay hidden.

She thinks of her stepson, but sees her stepdaughter's face instead. Her thoughts censure her. Why did she leave her behind? How could she leave her behind?

Do you know what I did? I condemned a young girl to death.

She wants to scream.

Mamta is afraid she is going mad. She tries to think of the direction in which Jivkant left. He took a train. Where would she have to go to catch a train? She is helpless, hopeless, held prisoner by a sweet sad song.

The cowherd moves on. Mamta moves with him, from bush to bush. He must be from a nearby village. She must find something to eat, or a roaming cow to milk. It isn't easy to milk a cow, especially one that doesn't know you, but Mamta has always had a way with animals. The cowherd sets aside his flute, sits down with his back to a tree, tilts his turban over his eyes and goes to sleep. He will awake just as it is time to go home. The cows always come back to him.

Mamta moves slowly, crouched low. She can hear the deep sounds of wooden cow bells, followed by the tinny sound of a calf's bell. A calf means milk. She runs towards the sound. She sees the mother, white, gentle, elegant, with deflated udders. She has been recently milked. Nevertheless Mamta approaches her, unthreatening, staying as far from her calf as possible.

Mamta smells of earth and grass, of nature. The cow recognises a creature just like herself, a vulnerable animal. She lets her come close. Mamta kneels, and squeezes a teat, gripping it between her forefinger and thumb, coaxing the milk out. The cow moves away. She goes after it, first on her knees, then her feet. It continues to distance itself. Bent over with pain, Mamta gives up the chase. The cow stops.

This time Mamta is gentler and manages to squeeze out just enough milk for a few gulps. She drinks directly from the teat, completely unconcerned now with hiding herself.

When she picks herself up, wiping the back of her hand across her lips, she sees something so familiar in the distance that she is disoriented. The gleam of the Big House. There is no one in sight,

because of the time of day; afternoons are time to hide from the sun.

She walks, runs, trying to stay hidden, towards the house. Why? Because people naturally gravitate towards other people. It is a rare soul who is a true pioneer, making his home in uninhabited lands. Even such a pioneer almost never does it alone; if he can, he takes his group with him. No matter what cruelty man wreaks on another – the human race is always one to seek itself out. At best Mamta had hoped to find a ravine or a mound where she could hide till she could find a bullock cart going to Gopalpur, but she's done far, far better than that.

She runs straight towards the old outhouse, the new jail for Daku Manmohan.

8

In Prem's dreams he is already a hero, the only one in the village with first-hand knowledge of Daku Manmohan. The thought makes him smile smugly. He sits, looking into the distance enjoying his newfound status. The boys will want to know if the prisoner has scars or a hidden gun, the girls will want to know the precise details of his appearance down to the exact length of his moustache and the great love he bears his wife. He can almost taste the sweet-sour tamarinds soaked in jaggery on his tongue. How many will he demand per answer? Not too many, just enough to keep the questions affordable. After all, the responsibility of the myth now lies with him.

Like the other village girls, Prem's sister Sneha too has a crush, sight unseen, on Daku Manmohan, and sends little mementoes with her brother to his cell every day: folded betel-leaves, a weaver bird's discarded nest, a dried-up blue butterfly pressed carefully between two ficus leaves, and perfumed half-fermented mauwa fruit, almost ready to become an alcoholic drink. What's fit for consumption Prem eats en route, the rest he throws away.

'Boy!' The summons is a gunshot. Prem drops to the ground his ear touching mud. 'Ha, ha. So much fear for a chained man. What is the world coming to?'

He is instantly on his feet, embarrassed.

'I won't bite. Promise. Come. Closer . . . Closer still. Closer, I said. I wish to see your face. What's your name?'

'What's it to you?'

'You're fascinated by me, aren't you, boy?'

'What makes you think that?' Prem speaks nonchalantly.

'Look at you. A young man, with a young man's dreams, but soon you will be an old man; an old man with a young man's dreams. You have nowhere to go. What can you do with yourself in such a place? Your father has sold the family into bondage. What is left for you but to work another man's fields or become a bandit like me?' Daku Manmohan ensnares him with the expertise of one well practised in the art of persuasion.

'I will never be like you. I will die first, Daku. I will kill myself rather than become like you,' Prem counters with the idealism of youth.

'Then why are you here, hanging round my cell every day like a pet dog?'

'For Lokend Bhai. Don't think I would ever protect you if Asmara Didi hadn't asked me to.'

'Protect me? You protect me? From what? I know why you are here. What else do you have to do? Now you've met me you will become the big boy in your gang. I'm right, aren't I? All the boys will ask about the dangerous Daku and you'll tell them, won't you?'

The boy is confused by how easily the bandit can see through him. 'No! I'm here because Lokend Bhai asked me to be.'

'That's what you think, but you are really here because my life seems so exciting to you. You are here because you wish you could be more like me.'

'More like you? You? If they let me, I would cut off your head.'

'No one's stopping you – cut it off then. It would be a blessing for me. I won't harm you, I promise. You know where the knife is? You'll find one on the roof of the shed; the guards keep it there to pare betel-nuts.' The boy stands still. 'Don't believe me? Go see for yourself.' The boy runs off.

From her hiding place, Mamta has heard the conversation, and

now she sees someone approach. Prem! Is she mad? *Thank you, Devi. Jai ho Devi, Devi jai ho.* She is saved. He was always her favourite, the most humane of them all. She takes a step forward and then stops, scared. Will he force her to go back? *Oh, my brother, please . . .* She thinks back to the younger Prem, the one she carried on her hip. *Surely for all the times I gave you my food, picked you up, patched your wounds, played with you . . . you will be on my side.* Then she is unsure. *I am unclean, useless, untrustworthy . . . I left her behind. I am nothing.* She drops down in the mud, from where she is she can see the shed quite clearly. Prem jumps up, trying to reach something on the roof. She can see the guard resting inside. Prem cannot reach the top of the shed with his hand. He takes a stick from the tamarind tree and sweeps it along the edge. A knife clatters to the floor. She sees her brother hesitate, confused. He knows he is trapped. What should he do with the knife? He can't kill the bandit, but he can't take the knife and then not kill the bandit without being judged a coward. So he leaves it in the dust and walks back to the cell, out of Mamta's sight once more. She listens for conversation.

Prem returns empty-handed. 'It wasn't there. You lied,' he says it viciously enough to give credence to his words.

'You see, at your age it's easy to fill your belly with brave words and dreams.' They both know the truth.

'What do you know about bravery then? It is braver to earn an honest dry crust of bread than to steal a cake.'

'My, don't you sound grand! A day will come when you will find that even a dry crust of bread won't be forthcoming. I can see that you have been spending too much time with our mutual friend Lokend.'

That name. Those leather slippers . . . that quiet look. Wherever Mamta goes, he is with her.

'You aren't fit to mention his name, let alone call him your friend,' the boy jealously claims his mentor exclusively for himself. 'If it wasn't for him, you wouldn't be here. Without the protection of the Big House you would be dead!'

These are his lands, he has walked here, lived here, slept in that mansion over there. Mamta knows she is crazy.

154

'Yes, you would think that. Boy, you know nothing of my life. You cannot judge me.'

'I *can* judge you. I *will* judge you. Each and every time I meet you, I will judge you. There is nothing you can say about your life that will justify what you've done to other people. Do you realise how many you've ruined?'

'Yes, I do! Don't you think I think about that every day? Every day since choosing this life I have prayed for forgiveness. I am like the goddess Kali who needs human blood to purify her soul. I too have my bloody destiny.'

At last Mamta realises the man is Daku Manmohan. The bandit, the destroyer, the dream breaker; the saviour, the dream maker. *Oh, Prem, there are crueller men than this bandit of yours, and I have met them all in one man.*

'Destiny, pah! I spit on your destiny. If you were a man you would kill yourself rather than accept your destiny like an unmarried girl. Give me the word and I'll bring you a rope to hang yourself or a knife to cut your veins,' says Prem, realising he can never carry out his threat. But the bandit doesn't need to know that.

'Do it then! But don't dare judge me, for as sure as there is sight in my eye, I will cut out your tongue.'

'From in there? You'll cut out my tongue from in there, will you?' Prem laughs and moves closer to the bars.

Careful, my brother. Step back. Mamta retreats into the bushes. If she's caught they will report her to the village, a runaway wife.

'You are Lata Bai's boy, aren't you?' Their mother's name puts both siblings on guard. Mamta takes a step forward, ready to defend Prem.

Caution enters the boy's frame and he is instantly still, waiting. He looks at the bandit. 'What's it to you?' he asks.

'Did you never wonder why your family was spared?'

How can he answer such a question? Yes he did, but he was grateful to his gods.

'Didn't reach for the truth then, did you? What difference would it have made if we had looted you? Your fate would have been no

different, you would still be working for the Big House. Think about that, my friend.'

'You are a dog. The worst kind. You sneer at the Big House, without thinking that your friend Lokend Bhai is from the Big House. Each time you say something against the Big House you say something against Lokend Bhai.'

Again that name. *Oh Devi, give me some rest.*

'The Big House saves me today, but it was the Big House that made me a bandit years ago . . .'

'Hello, my friends, I see you are getting to know each other,' says Lokend.

Mamta recognises the third voice. She recalls his eyes, that look that has calmed her most frantic thoughts and kept her connected to life.

'Lokend Bhai, don't worry, I will keep an eye on this bandit. He won't escape while I'm on watch,' says Prem, the big man in front of his mentor.

'I know, I know you will. Manmohan, your fields seem to be doing well. The harvest will be good.'

'Yes, perhaps it will. I was never a farmer, you see.' Daku Manmohan smiles wryly, the world outside has little impact on him. It passes over his head like a cloud in fast flight. All he knows is that, come shower or shine, he will till.

'As the crops come in you'll see that time passes quickly,' says Lokend, leading him into the future.

When will time pass quickly for me? I have been running all my life. And now you are here. Perhaps this is God's answer. Lokend Bhai. His name is too heavy for her thoughts.

'Stay away from him, Lokend Bhai,' says Prem. 'He is deceitful. He would kill you if he had a chance, he would kill us all.'

'Oho, Prem, let down your heavy load, my boy, lead a lighter life. Don't worry so much. I know Manmohan like I know my own brother.'

'Leave it, Lokend, the boy's right. People like me have killed his faith. Now I just want these days to be over. I am so tired of wishing my life away.'

'Remember, my friend, the Past and Future are both spoken for, only the Present remains free.'

'The present, yes, the present . . . it torments me. I took away their food, their crops, their everything, how can I ever return their future to them?' The bandit pleads for his sanity.

'We all have to resolve our strife in the best way we can. Look at it this way, your fields will one day fill the stomachs of those you wronged, so I would say that you have found a path to returning their future to them; often kings don't achieve as much in their lives.'

'Do you know what I think about most? I feed them, but I can produce nothing for my own son. What then makes me a man, if I cannot do anything for my own? Tell me now, what makes me a man?'

'Just thinking about it makes you a man, my friend; just thinking about it makes you a man.' Lokend grips Daku Manmohan's hand through the bars.

'Come, Lokend Bhai, let's go.' Prem pulls him away. 'For me he will always be a murderer and a rapist.'

Rape! Sharma's wife, shit-smeared and raped, and now Mamta, soon-to-be-shit-smeared-and-raped. Her fingers physically close her mouth to prevent any sound from escaping. *I deserve to die, I know I deserve to die, but, Devi, please keep me alive . . . Prem, help me stay alive . . .* Her heart is ready to burst out of her ribcage for all its pounding.

It isn't long before Prem returns with gunnysacks for Daku Manmohan. As he leaves the bandit's cell, Mamta approaches him from behind.

'Prem,' she whispers with dread. She thinks her brother will be able to see right into her soul. A husband-leaver, a stepdaughter-leaver.

The boy stops, shocked.

'It's me, Mamta.'

He turns to face his sister.

'What, what? How? Why? Mamta? What are you doing here?'

157

'Just tell me which way I should go to get to the city. Tell me. Quickly, tell me the way! Do you remember the road Jivkant Bhai took? You do remember it, don't you? Thank God I've found you. I am not going back.'

'Not going back? To where?'

'To Barigaon. To him.'

'You mean your husband?' he whispers with disbelief. 'You aren't going back to your husband?' He looks round anxiously.

'No, he will kill me. Please just help me, tell me which way. Don't tell Amma, don't tell Bapu, don't tell anyone. I will be like Sharma's wife. I don't want to be like Sharma's wife.' Mamta is babbling, she stumbles, falls, except for the cup of milk, she hasn't eaten for two days. 'Water, do you have water?'

'Yes, I will bring you water. Come, I know a place where you can hide.' That is the miracle of Prem, he understands quickly and acts instantly; he is a protector, it is in his character to help the underdog. 'It's Asmara Didi's old place. I'll get you something to eat and drink and then tomorrow night you can go on. There you will be safe. No one goes to her old house except bats. You aren't afraid of bats, are you?'

Prem takes Mamta's hand. His young palm is stiff with calluses from working the farm. Mamta allows herself to be pulled along by him, sinking into the safety of his clasp. He takes her to the rotting hut on the far edge of Singh Sahib's lands. He has to steady her many times during the short journey.

He sets her down against a stone near the hut. 'Wait for me, I will be back. I am going to the Big House to get you food.'

She extracts a bundle of notes from her waist, divides them in two to give Prem. 'For Amma.'

'You stole, is that why you are running away?' Prem's association with Lokend has fruited into an unambiguous moral code.

'No, I never stole.' She snatches the money out of his hands. 'It should have been mine. I worked for it . . .' *I gave my flesh for it.* 'Oh, it's too hard to explain.' She touches her scar. 'Here, take it,' she says, curling his reluctant hand round the notes.

'No, I can't. It's yours,' he says with conviction. He is much

changed. The old Prem would have grabbed the money out of her fist and calculated exactly what he could do with it before he had taken a second breath.

'You mustn't tell Amma you saw me. You mustn't tell anyone. Promise me. Promise me!' she chokes on her words. Outside the rotting hut the rain falls thick and heavy. The sky sheds warm tears in her stead and the earth offers her a mantle to wipe them away.

'I promise I won't. I promise.'

It is only when her brother leaves that Mamta realises she has asked nothing about his life. *Keep him safe, Devi, please keep him safe.*

Prem blunders back to the Big House, abandoning himself to the rain. Perhaps the kitchen will still be open and he will be able to beg for some scraps for Mamta.

He moves swiftly along the retaining wall. Mamta a runaway. He has already rehearsed his story, his sick grandmother has come to visit and he needs extra food. The extra food will no doubt be put in his ledger by some scrupulous maid and he will have to pay it off in labour hours, after all, he works at the Big House because his bapu took a loan for Mamta's dowry.

The kitchen is closed, the bulb above the door fused, the night has gobbled up the building. He tests the door, and then he remembers the doorway for the rats, the window that never shuts. Because of Daku Manmohan and Lokend he had promised himself to live a good and decent life, but today stealing food for his starving sister somehow seems the honourable thing to do.

He stuffs his kurta with the crisp ready-treats kept for unexpected guests.

'Who's there? Is there someone there?' Prem drops the treats and crouches down on all fours. 'So late. Go home, Prem.' The boy shades his eyes against the glare of the torch. 'Your mother will be worried,' says Lokend. 'Come on now,' Lokend extends his hand, 'get up, I'll take you home.'

'No, Lokend Bhai . . .' the boy is scared. He is sweating and his eyes are oscillating from side to side, not daring to linger too long on a single object as if searching for something secret. His keenest

feeling is one of shame, even more than fear. He needs to explain his deceit. He trusts that Lokend Bhai will understand, but what's to stop him from being disappointed? For the first time, the standards Prem has set for himself seem unachievable. He is trapped, the incriminating evidence rubble at his feet.

'Are you hungry?'

'Not exactly . . . I mean, I am not hungry for myself . . .' He has never asked Lokend Bhai for anything as earthly as food before.

'What is it, Prem? Let me help you.' Lokend takes Prem by the shoulder and lifts him to his feet. 'Don't be afraid. I never want you to be afraid,' he says to the boy, handing him crackling bags of food.

'Lokend Bhai . . . I know what you must think of me, but please . . . if there was some other way, any other way . . . I would . . .'

'You must let me help you, Prem.' Lokend can see the desperation in the boy's face. He has come to know the boy well, and stealing is not in his nature. He wants to give Prem the opportunity to unburden himself.

'It's her . . . she's here . . .'

'Who?'

'Bapu will kill her, they will rape her, strip her . . . my amma . . . the shame . . . I must help her. You must understand, I have to save her.' He promised not to tell anyone, but he can't contain the heavy secret from his mentor – his mentor who always preaches truth. 'Mamta Didi, my sister – you came to her wedding, gave her the sweets.'

He remembers her eyes locked with his over her mother's shoulders, saying *Some day you are going to remind me who I am.* 'C'mon, Prem, there's no time to lose.'

Mamta is asleep by the time they return. Prem has to shake her strongly to wake her. 'Eat now.'

'Mamta.' Again that voice.

'Sahibji!' She shrinks into a ball. Another man has come to take her away. And though her spirit would gladly be led by this one, her body will not.

'Mamta Didi, you must eat, you have to leave quickly before sunrise.' Prem's situation is precarious. He too could be lynched by the village for his part in helping a runaway wife.

'Prem, give her a moment.' Dishevelled, with bleeding feet and dirt-encrusted hair, the wildness of her appearance makes Lokend approach her gently. He feels an overwhelming urge to protect her. 'Let her rest today. Leave tomorrow night. Looks to me your sister won't last if she leaves in this condition.'

Shivering she shrinks from him. He puts out his hand to her. He wants to dispel her helplessness. 'Amma, Bapu . . . They can't know. They will kill me . . . Sharma's wife, she ran away, and now me . . .'

Lokend puts out his hand again, 'Don't worry, you are safe,' he says. 'I won't let anyone harm you. Don't be scared. You go to the city, where no one knows you.' Lokend has lived his life in selfless duty and sacrifice for others, but this time he feels oddly attached to the outcome. 'There you will be safe and get a good job . . .'

'. . . and make lots of money.' Prem embellishes his often re-visited dream for his sister.

'Go, Prem, go,' urges Mamta, reluctant to put her brother in further danger, 'you shouldn't be mixed up in all this. After all, I am now a runaway, an outcaste; ordinary rules don't apply to me. I am less than nothing. No one can give me shelter without reprisal. Go! Please, Sahibji, take him away. Go, leave me. I am a creature of the night now. I must stay hidden from Decency.'

'Didi, eat now and leave before daylight. We've brought you some food. No one saw you?'

'No, no one saw me, but it won't be long before he comes searching for me,' she says, thinking of the wad of bills.

'Come, Prem, let her rest.'

Prem grips Lokend's arm, defying custom. 'Lokend Bhai, please don't tell anyone,' he gulps. He has been too forceful in his instruction, he has crossed the boundary of respect. The boy releases his grip and says, 'Sorry, forgive me. Yes, Lokend Bhai, let's go.'

She is past caring, she hasn't touched the food, and a bright, clean dawn is calling. Soon she will be forced on her way again.

'Mamta.' The backlight protects her visitor's identity. She moves swiftly to the ruined wall, brick in hand. 'Put it down, Mamta, I'm not here to harm you.'

161

'Sahibji, you c-came back.' She looks around, searching for something he might have lost. 'You came back for me? Why?' Her husband's wad of bills dislodges itself from its petticoat hiding place and falls to the floor.

'Mamta!' He knows this much money couldn't have come to her without some deception.

She is defiant: 'It's mine. I worked for it, it's mine,' she pleads. 'You have to believe me, I never went back for her . . . she is just a girl . . . I left her behind. I must pay with my own life. I deserve this . . .'

He has brought fresh food for her. He dips a buttered chapatti into the rich daal. 'You must eat.'

His hands are feeding me. Her eyes are wide with confusion. 'Oh, Sahibji . . .' She recounts her tattered story. 'See, this is what I was to him –' She drags her petticoat down to reveal the scar. 'This was my value, my flesh,' she sobs, but her eyes remain dry. 'Please tell no one. They *will* find me.'

She recognises the confusion in his eyes, his obligation to duty tested beyond breaking. He places his hand against her cheek furrowed with tear tracks. Convention is their enemy, but Lokend hasn't given it any substance. As usual, his decision ignores the dictates of society. 'This is your life. Grasp it, participate in it. Whether you believe it now or not, there is unbounded kindness in destiny. Go and embrace yours.'

She will choose to believe that he will tell no one, be that one person who saw *her* once. And that must be enough.

Love is a River

9

Mamta has stowed her memories securely. She will not think of Lokend Bhai, that is her promise to herself. She needs her energies to escape. To live. To go and find that unbounded kindness in destiny.

The air is pungent with the smell of drying red chillies. She holds her pallav to her nose to stop herself from sneezing. Red chillies, burning, beautiful plump chillies. She thinks of the chillies her stepdaughter had planted in front of their hut. They had planned to bring them to the weekly barter market by the well. She imagines little hands picking chillies, a laughing face blowing on smarting fingers. *Why did I leave her behind?*

Well fed and rested, she is stronger now, with a fugitive's energies, sixth sense and night vision and doesn't feel quite as betrayed by her circumstances. Diligent in her grateful prayer, '*Ohm Bhoor Bhuwah Swaha, Tat Savitur Varenyum, Bhargo Dewas Dhimahi, Dhiyo Yo Naha Prachodaya . . .*' she recites the Gayatri Mantra learned at her mother's knee, clinging to the words as if they are her raft home. One hundred and eight is the magic number. Each recitation will ignite one of the hundred and eight energy lines converging to create her heart charka. That number will free her!

Somewhere around the seventieth recitation an owl hoots and she loses count. A hooting owl, what a bad omen. She starts over, resuming her prayer with vigour.

She can see a light shining in the distance, a constant, unwavering light. Not capricious candlelight. When her husband's card partners talked about electricity coming to their village, her husband always shrugged and said, 'Not in my lifetime,' but she had rebelliously imagined that her husband was wrong, and that one day she would find a bright bulb shining right outside her door. And here it is! She must tell her mother that the poles are working, that somewhere, where no one can see it, is a light shining for someone just like her, a girl running away from her husband, a girl running away from home, a girl running towards her future. *Amma . . . if you could see this light now. It is a miracle. Thank you, Devi. Jai ho Devi, Devi jai ho.*

In the bottomless night the light is a panacea. It doesn't occur to her that the light could be revealing, that it could lead to her capture. Blessed with a destination at last, she runs towards it. As she draws closer, she realises that the light is attached to a mechanical animal barrelling towards her, and is not a result of the electric poles which are, as her husband and mother suspect, sterile.

She has no estimation of speed, no idea of distance. On any other day she might have approached the bus with caution, gauging its character before venturing close, but today, she runs into its path. She knows all the important things about buses. They take you places. Faraway places. Places where no one can find you. If she jumps on this bus no one will be able to find her. She rushes towards the bus, her nemesis . . . her saviour . . . her nemesis . . . her saviour. She has no reason to live. She will catch the bus, even if it kills her. It brushes past her. She falls. Her nemesis . . . her saviour . . .

'Did we hit something?' 'Hai hai . . .' 'Stop!' 'Don't stop' 'Go!' 'Go!' 'Go!' 'Stop' 'Go on.' The bus is a mess of tangled opinions. It stops with a shudder.

The shouting switches off with the engine. The driver jumps down from the door, eager to get it over with. It's the victim's fault, he knows. He has a bus full of witnesses who'll testify in his favour. Mamta looks up, arms outstretched.

'Mad, are you? Want me to run you over like a stray dog? This is no way to stop a public bus,' he shouts into the night, shading his eyes against the headlights with his hand.

'Take me. Please, please, take . . . me . . . take me . . .' she sobs, lying prone in the dust, 'I am here,' she calls to the driver, afraid that he might not see her in the frugal light.

'Get in before I change my mind. These people just come out of the village and think they'll get a ride on any old bus going to the city. They all want to go to the city. What's there in the city? Mad, all of them. Mad, all of you. Totally mad.' His words are blustering, but in fact he's relieved she's still alive. A death would have meant a hot night spent here on this wretched stretch of road where they would have had to wait hours to get word to the police.

She's cheated death yet again. Twice now! An uncontrollable giggle rises up her throat threatening to explode. A bus, she's on a bus. A bus to the city. *Oh, Prem, buses do exist and they run exactly where you imagine them to. Thank you, my brother. Thank you, Devi. Jai ho Devi, Devi jai ho.*

'You have money?'

She nods. He isn't convinced.

'I'll not hesitate to throw you out.'

She hands him a note.

'A hundred,' he says, admiration mixed with mistrust.

If there is one thing Mamta has learned to do it is read eyes. Before he can say another word, she plucks the note out of his hands and gives him another, hoping it is the right one. It's a smaller one.

The man pockets it.

'Where to?'

'How far does this bus go?'

'Begumpet.'

'Yes.'

'Yes, what?'

'All right.'

'All right what? All right Begumpet, or all right Ranakpur, Sonpur, Seeta Gaon, Rajunagar . . .' the conductor reels off names of towns en route from memory.

An irritated voice shouts, 'Give her the bloody ticket. We are all trying to sleep. She's from the village. None of them has heard of the city. You know that.'

'Begumpet then,' she says.

Her ticket sits tight and secure in her hand.

Now that the danger's past and the other passengers see what it brought in their midst, a pitiful thing like Mamta, they quickly fall back to sleep. Some with their heads thrown back and their mouths gaping to the ceiling, others with their children stuffed in laps.

Mamta is lucky to have been nearly run over by this particular public bus. Babu, the driver, is an ex-army officer who had to take early retirement because of an injury. He follows the All India Bus Permit Rules, and will take as many passengers as can sit on the seats and thirty-one standees only. No one sits on the luggage carrier overhead. His sister's son had fallen from one such luggage carrier and died on the spot.

The blue nightlight glows eerily, illuminating the faces of her companions in fits and starts. For the most part, the other passengers are just conical shapes, covered in their blankets more against wind rushing in from the windows than for privacy. Like most villagers who live in hot places, they think stirred-up air of any kind a health hazard.

The only one awake is the conductor, the man who sold her the ticket. He lounges on the bus stairs, perfectly comfortable to be standing, bouncing violently, holding on to the rail loosely with two fingers of his right hand.

He looks into the night, taking in each flashy new milestone along the road. He knows they aren't actually milestones, but kilometre stones, as the whole country has moved into the metric system. But he'll stick to miles, as it isn't easy to explain to his passengers that the distance in miles or kilometres between any two places is the same.

'No vomiting, you hear,' he shouts over the engine, 'want to vomit, stick your head out of the window.'

Vomiting. Window. Why would she vomit? And there isn't a window next to her. The lack of a window sends her into a new kind of panic. Her breath comes in short bursts and suddenly she has a pain in her chest.

'Forget it, he says that to everyone. I haven't seen anyone vomit in years.' The fat woman rolls over and goes to sleep after discharging

this important and untrue piece of information. For the rest of the night, she burps and lets off noxious fumes in Mamta's direction – the remnants of her lunch.

In the morning Mamta will see the yellow streaks all along the outer side of the bus, proof of the perilous nature of the journey. But for now she is content just to be. Enough time has passed for the real threat of rape and shit-smearing to give way to sadness.

Unexpectedly, the tears start running down her face. She has no control over them. Embarrassed, she hides herself in her pallav. The conductor has seen many tears. He can almost time them. Half an hour into the journey, and the girls start crying. He never asks why or looks into their faces when they do. None of his business, he thinks; why get wrapped up in other people's affairs? Conducting is what he does. He is one of those rare few who enjoys his travelling job, and passes the time by acknowledging each landmark along the way, a friend revisited.

The driver Babu, on the other hand, is distressed by the tears. In the rear-view mirror he can see Mamta's face bent into her arms, shoulders shaking. There are some types of sadness that become real only when shared. There are others that are elusively niggling, like a hair in the mouth. And then there are still others that feed on themselves and engorge. The woman's sadness puzzles him. What kind of sadness is it? He would like to know Mamta's story, but he keeps his eyes on the road, attentive, adjusting the mirror so he doesn't have to look on her grief.

Lokend's kindness may have fortified Mamta's will, but it has left her tender and completely at destiny's mercy. Her sadness isn't so much for herself, but for the choice she made. The imprint of the memory box with its faded goddess raids her every thought. She deserves karmic retribution. She should have tried harder for her stepdaughter. She should have chosen another night. How could she leave her behind? Now hers is the only body that can be offered up for butchery. When everything else failed, Lokend was there for her, a wall behind her back. Why couldn't she have been a wall behind her stepdaughter's back? The one person who loved and depended on her, how could she have left her behind?

It would have been better if I'd died of starvation, because starvation is what I deserve. Now she might die of starvation or something worse. My daughter, doomed, because I left her behind. Left her behind to die. A groan escapes her lips.

Her neighbour, drifting in and out of the uneasy sleep of fat people, misreads her whimper.

'Water? This is a good bus, ask the conductor if you want water.'

'Cold drink, cold drink . . .' the sharp tinging of a bottle-opener run up and down glass bottles closes the door on her past.

She is realising something new: she can eat or sleep without asking someone else's permission. She is the one who will decide how much of the money that is scratching between her breasts should be spent on what. She pokes the wad with her finger, jamming it further down her cleavage.

'Chai, chai . . .'

'How much?' The fat lady is awake and ravenous. 'These people are highway robbers. That's why they work along the highways.' She giggles at her own joke. 'I never buy anything from them, but I ask the price anyway. Who knows, one day, the price will be fair and I might decide to buy from them.' The fat lady is travelling alone. She is a Sikhanni, as fierce as any man from her clan. Sikh women have an equal place in society as their men, so much so that boys and girls are given identical first names. This particular woman's name is Paramjit Kaur – Paramjit, supreme conqueror – a grandiosely militant title, typical of a Sikh name.

Paramjit Kaur has finagled a holiday for herself at her sister's. Her two children are grown and running the house for their father, a surprisingly effete man. Her success at home has made her magnanimous. She will do whatever she can for her fellow passengers. Even such a sorry one as Mamta.

'How long do we stop at these places?' Mamta is scared of stopping. Motion is her safety. Stopping means she has to make herself disappear again, like one of the sleeping people, under her sari. The only reason she has chosen to reveal herself this time is because of Paramjit Kaur's conversation.

'Can be minutes, can be hours. It's all up to the driver. I have been on this bus three times before. Once it took me one night to get to Begumpet, once two days. Who can tell? Don't worry, they sell food too. Get the puri bhaji. It sells fast, so it's unlikely to be rotten, and they also give you water to drink.'

The bus comes suddenly awake for the puri bhaji. 'Two . . .' 'Three in the back . . .' 'What about me? I've asked you three times for one . . .'

Orders fly. She looks from face to face, from voice to voice, from order to order and then softly says, 'One here.' No one hears her or listens.

'One here,' she says, lifting a shy arm above her head. No one notices.

Packets of puri bhaji dash past her up and down, from hand to hand, but not one for her. The smell is making her faint with hunger. The back of her mouth is already swimming in the spit of antici-pation.

'Arey-oh, puri bhajiwala. Got cotton in your ears, have you? Send one to the back right now for this woman,' Paramjit Kaur's voice booms like cannon shot over the heads of the other passengers. Mamta's shoulders hunch up to her ears, cringing at the attention the fat woman might attract. But she need not worry. Paramjit Kaur, the supreme conqueror, has won again. Her words find their mark. Miraculously, a packet of food appears in Mamta's hand.

'What are you saving it for? Eat while it's hot!' Her saviour prods her with a finger.

'Eat? But . . . but the others . . . they might . . . they might . . . What about the others?' she whispers, meaning the men on the bus.

'What about the others? You just eat up. He's going to want his money soon. It's unbelievable how he keeps track of all his customers. Never misses a payment. The water comes with your change. Arey, eat, I said. You village girls, such scaredy types,' she says. 'Let my man try and say something to me, just let him try. Why I can fire a gun better than my husband even. We are kshatriyas, all fighting types, men, women, all. You must not be a scaredy type, otherwise you will be chomped up like a rabbit.'

There is always one on every bus, the free-advice-giver.

Mamta opens the dried leaves. The smell of fried potatoes nesting in a flower of more than six perfectly round golden brown puris is almost overwhelming. *Surely it can't be all for me?* She breaks off a piece of the flat bread, wraps it around the potatoes, and stuffs it, bite after bite into her mouth. Almost at the end of her meal, she stops. 'Thank you, Devi,' she whispers, 'forgive me.' *Forgive me.* The pickle is hiding in the last morsel. The acid of raw mango sends fresh juices flowing into her mouth. She sees no one else lick the leaves and against her better judgement she doesn't lick the wrapping either, but makes sure there is nothing sticking to it, cleaning it with her thumb before tossing it out of the window like the others. 'We are not like you,' she says with regret to the free-advice-giver.

'I can see that from your clothes.' Paramjit Kaur is wearing a salwar-kurta splattered with pretty yellow flowers and a matching scarf looped round her neck. Mamta squirms in her sari, the indistinct colour of filth; she can't even remember what colour it once was.

The puri bhaji seller enters the bus to collect his money. No one asks the price, they all seem to know how much to pay. As he comes closer to Mamta she squints to see how much the others are paying. She can't tell, some pay in coins while others in notes.

'Don't you have small money?' he asks her neighbour who hands him a blue note.

Bewildered, Mamta holds her cupped hands above her head. Paramjit Kaur tugs at her pallav, pinching the tiniest piece of dirty cloth between her fingers, pulling her arms down. 'Never beg, you hear me, never beg. The worst thing you can do is beg. If you are hungry, go to the Gurdwara. They give out free food from twelve to three. I have eaten there so many times myself. My husband is so embarrassed,' she giggles. 'He says Gurdwara lunches are for the poor, but you should just taste that food, my . . . what food . . . So where are you going?'

'Money?' The puri bhaji seller saves her from giving herself away.

Mamta decides to take a chance and places the note she received in change from the conductor in the food seller's palm.

He returns a coin to her. She looks at it. A small 50 shines up at

her. The coins she knows well. That's all her husband spent on her since her marriage: 25 paisa for this, 50 paisa for that, one rupee for the other. Her husband. Her stomach starts to boil again. *He must be mad. He must be thrashing her. Forgive me.* The tears start up in her throat again. She swallows them.

'So, you will never find a Sikh begging. Oho, what's wrong with you? Be brave, my girl. Be brave. All change is opportunity, all journeys discoveries . . .' Paramjit Kaur passes out unsolicited philosophical tips in exactly the same tone she might use to discharge advice on the best way to remove stains from white clothes.

Water splashes into Mamta's palm that still bears the coin. She cups her hands and drinks. As the first wayward drop finds its way to her mouth she realises it is fresh. She isn't crying any more.

She gets off even before she is fully awake. 'Side, move!' A hand pushes her into the grime of the Begumpet Bus Terminal. It has taken her twenty-six hours to escape to this small city, almost exactly in the centre of India.

Mamta stands, it doesn't occur to her to dust her clothes.

For the first time Mamta looks at the fat lady, alighting behind her. Paramjit Kaur's skin is milky, with apple pink spots on her cheeks where broken veins have released their sweetness. Two comely black moles of the non-raised kind have been placed on her chin by nature, as a standard of comparison only, to accentuate the creaminess of her skin. The fat lady was once that stereotypical beauty described in all the matrimonial advertisements in the *Times of India*: 5 feet 2 inches tall, large eyes, wheatish complexion, medium build, long hair.

'You have to be quick in the city,' Paramjit Kaur gives her one last piece of invaluable advice, 'your village ways won't work here.' And to prove her point she pushes past her into the breaking light, sending Mamta flying to the floor.

Mamta is left alone, as alone as anyone can be in a city.

Her feet do the thinking for her. Primeval automation sends her out of the terminal and into the street safely. It is lucky for Mamta that the city is still in that state between sleep and wakefulness. Soon traffic will flood the streets, but for now, it is the occasional

rickshaw that lurches past in slow motion, that's the only reason Mamta isn't run over. She doesn't know yet that she must look both ways before crossing the street, but that will be an easy lesson for her. Her keen mind will see, record and follow.

Across the road, a municipal tap gushes water into a waiting line of pails. Taps. Mamta has only heard of them. She looks at the large group of women, rubbing sleep out of their eyes. The tap bleeds water into the street, gushing at the mouth like a fountain. In Gopalpur what wouldn't you give for so much water surging out right at your feet, enough to create a mudslide? The thick ooze puckers its grubby lip to kiss the edges of the saris of the waiting women. While she watches, the tap runs dry. Women are left holding their empty pails. They shake their fists at the tap and at others with full pails, but then wander away resigned, swallowed whole by the city. Some days the tap is generous, on others it is not.

'Kalu, if you want to sleep here you have to sweep. Get up, you lazy bastard! Do you think this is a free five-star hotel?' A man dressed in khaki shouts into the underbelly of a building in a row of three-storey flats hovering along the edge of the road.

'Chacha, I fixed your cycle chain.' A man emerges from the darkness under the stairwell dragging a cycle behind him.

'Get to work, lazy bastard.' The night watchman pushes the man called Kalu away with his stick, taking care not to soil his hands on Kalu's lower-caste body. Mamta watches through the iron grille gate that bisects the perimeter wall crowned in broken glass to shred the feet of any who might dare to climb over it. Hindi movie posters inches thick cling to the whitewashed wall, stuck on with glue so strong it is impossible to peel them off. Pasted one over the other, the hits stay on the longest, the flops get brushed over with glue before the coat beneath has had a chance to dry.

Kalu waves off the staring Mamta with the back of his hand. When she doesn't move, he sticks out his tongue at her. For the first time in days, she feels shy laughter flutter in her throat.

'Thief! Bandit! Ungrateful wretch! Give them a home and what do they do? Rob you blind, that's what! Get out! Go, I said! Don't come here ever again, I will make sure you don't get work in the

174

whole of Begumpet. Thief! It's a wonder we all haven't been murdered in our beds.' A woman beats her slipper against the head of a skinny boy who shields himself from her blows with open palms that stand out flour-white against his almost naked black body.

The boy runs doubled over, tripping, straightening and tripping again. The skinny black body summons the memory of her younger brother Prem. She is disoriented. She may have left her stepdaughter behind, but she won't allow her brother to be beaten with a slipper. Mamta takes a few fumbling steps into the building to help him up. But the boy rushes past, leaving Mamta in his wake.

'You, come for the job, have you? Where do these people come from? Made of air they are, appearing like spirits! Hardly one thief out, when another appears. Don't think I don't know all about you.'

Instantly afraid, Mamta squirms in her sari and covers her scar with her hand. How could this woman a whole night's journey away from Gopalpur know about her husband's money, her husband's slippers, her running away? The city must have eyes everywhere. She could send her back to Barigaon for her deserved punishment, or back to her family in Gopalpur for the village's crude justice. Shit-smeared and raped, the image pops up, real again.

'She's a good woman, memsahib. I know her well. She comes from the next village. They call her . . .' Kalu looks to Mamta, questioning.

'Mamta,' she says, 'Mamta.'

'Honest Mamta, that's what they call her.'

'All right, Honest Mamta. Do you know anything about cleaning bathrooms?'

Mamta's eyebrows arch into her hairline.

'Don't look at me like I'm speaking English. Can you clean bathrooms?' The woman comes closer. 'Arey, is this woman dumb? Are you a Sudra?' Each word brings a spray of saliva with it, no doubt because of the gap in the woman's front teeth.

Kalu nudges her in the ribs. 'She's also very shy, memsahib. Honest and Shy Mamta, that's what they call her. Are you a Sudra, Honest and Shy Mamta?' He nudges her again. 'Say yes to the memsahib, she's asking you a question.'

'Yes, yes, I am,' Mamta lies, admitting to a bogus lower-caste status.

In truth, she is a Vyasia, a worker bee, miles above a lowly Sudra. But Sudra is what the lady wants and Sudra is what she'll get. Things work differently in the city, in the city a lower caste can be an asset.

'Start this evening. Don't forget, I know you, I will find you. Rob me and even Jesus won't be able to save you.' The fat woman waddles up the stairs, complaining loudly, 'Hai when will the committee put in a lift?'

It's then that Mamta is distracted enough to notice that her mistress-to-be is wearing a man's grey shirt and black pants with stirrups round the arches to keep them stretched through the length of her leg. She shivers with disbelief and blinks several times. 'Mrs D'Souza. From Goa.' The man called Kalu explains of the retreating figure. 'She barks a lot, but she's not bad. She might beat her servants, but she gives them leftover food. That's the best part. And she helps poor people. Her god demands it. Charity.'

How poor do you have to be to be helped?

'You're not afraid of dogs, no?'

'Dogs?'

'She has a noisy one. Baby. A snapper, that Baby, but she's small, so don't worry.'

'She has a dog?'

'Kalu, are you going to keep chatting all day or do some work?' the man in khaki shouts from the gate.

'I have to get back to work. You better get going yourself,' hisses Kalu. When he sees that Mamta isn't about to take his advice, he hisses at her again, 'What's wrong with you? Stop acting like an idiot.'

'Yes,' says Mamta, still acting like an idiot.

'You can sleep under the stairwell with me. Get your things. Don't worry, no one will touch your Sudra belongings here, too unclean for them.' Mamta doesn't move. 'Go on. Get your things.'

'Yes, yes,' she says, turning to go. Then she stops and asks, 'Who's Jesus?'

'Mrs D'Souza's god.'

'The one who demands the help for the poor? Jesus,' she repeats. 'We didn't have him in Gopalpur,' she says, walking out of the gate.

'Be on time this evening,' says the khaki-dressed man. 'Too many

of you new ones land up late for work on your first day. Five o'clock.'

Out of the gate, Mamta realises she has nowhere to go to wait for five o'clock to arrive. It's still early, but the city is quickly adjusting to morning. The garbage dump opposite the three-storey flats is as busy as an anthill. First the humans arrive. Children all, sent out to pick through the decomposing remains of the previous day. The rubbish tip is a larder to them. The boys comb the stinking top layer, quickly eating anything they can digest, while the girls save their pickings to take home, tucking pieces of rotting vegetables and dirty paper into their chunnis. Then come the old rag pickers. They dig a little deeper, choosing their treasure from the discard of the younger masters of the heap. Sometimes there is a fight between the young and old. The young always win. They snatch the loot from weaker hands, running away much too fast for the old to catch up. After that, it's the cows, then the goats, the dogs, the rats and finally, by the evening, when the sentient beings are done, it will be the turn of the cockroaches.

Mamta looks at the rubbish tip. Will this become her sustenance too? No, she has lived like an animal for so long, she won't do it again. She walks back towards the khaki-dressed man. 'This address?'

Without thinking, he scrawls something on a piece of paper, handing it to her carefully enough not to touch her lower-caste hand. She stares at the precious address, firm writing and confident slant of the letters topped by a flat line sturdy as a roof.

What is she going to do with a written address? 'What name?' she traces the letters with her finger.

'Himalaya House,' he says, without making the connection that she cannot read. There are many types in the city, the most unlikely ones can read, he has stopped wasting time on unnecessary judgements.

She is afraid to stray far, seeking and finding again the women in the morning's waterline. Their tin and cardboard homes built on the pavement crawl with children of all ages. The smell and the sound emerging from the slum are both equally vulgar. The houses all lean to one side, tilted by the last monsoon wind. Several will

177

collapse this monsoon season. She notices with a sense of satisfaction that the slum houses are more fragile than her hut back in the village. She enters the tiny lane which meanders senselessly through the higgledy-piggledy mess.

She cranes her neck and looks into one of the houses through a hole in a rotting wall. It isn't just curiosity that drives her to look inside, but a belief that she belongs with these people, this strata of society that has nothing, this homogenous mass of destitution that calls the pavement home. But of course they won't let her belong. No slum accepts intruders easily. Over-population, not disaster, is what ruins a slum. This particular one has survived seven conflagrations and twelve evictions, each time returning to life within hours. It is a tribe that is willing to cull its extras by killing them, or by sending them out to forage a living in other slums. For people like Mamta, the slum is a dangerous place to dally.

The slum dwellers may not be house proud on the outside, but on the inside their homes are filled with treasures: plastic buckets, cupboards, shelves, lights, transistors and the most coveted prize of all: televisions. She tunes in to one particular transistor going full blast. A woman's golden voice sings to her:

> 'The lamps are dying,
> My eyes are tiring,
> Softly, softly, take me, my love
> Come to me, come to me . . .'

Softly, softly, take me, my love. The music conjures up an imaginary stage, hands grasping her shoulders. Her head resting on a yielding chest. Distracted, she admires rows of tiny cowry shells cleanly and cleverly plastered over the opening that serves as the doorway. She recognises the impulse immediately. She herself did the same, didn't she? And her husband's unhappy, sinister home looked the better for her decoration. *Softly, softly, take me, my love.*

It is such a small thing, the flick of a warning hand, but the stranger's shooing strangles her dream. Her gullet starts to fill with tears. She is worse than dirt, more lowly than an animal. The slum

dwellers would tolerate any one of the million stray city cows in their midst before they would tolerate her.

A stream of slum dwellers, marching off to work, part precisely round her like ants. She feels filthy against their spurious cleanliness. They have washed with ditch water and now appear clean and oiled, hair slicked back, and more perfumed than any bona fide shower-taker. She follows them out. The slum is not her place.

Mamta's city education has begun.

As the morning heats up, the babies fall silent, while the young children wander off in gangs to conquer the city as beggars, newspaper sellers, petty thieves and prostitutes. She sees the little girls flirting with men almost twice their age using practised gestures learned by rote. Today might be the day they will cease to be children and finally cross over into the knowing, earning land of adults. Every once in a while they forget what they are to become and revert to their childish ways, teasing, running, and playing invented games.

The mothers and older girls load the babies on their hips to go beg at the thickening traffic jam. 'I beg for my baby,' they imply, 'not for myself.' They wear their filthiness like armour, extending their stick arms to the sky, coaxing an elusive coin from strangers' hearts. On a good day one person in ten rolls down his car window to throw some money at them. The women dive after the coins, their drugged babies lolling to one side like dying flowers on long stems. They pick up the money and toss Mamta a stare over their shoulders. With no baby dangling off her arm, they do not consider her a genuine threat.

The smell of the city is overwhelming. It is the first thing that hits a newcomer like Mamta. It is the stale smell of unwashed humanity, the acrid smell of gasses emitted by rot and refuse, the noxious smell of poisons let loose indiscriminately to fly on the wind, but most of all, it is the smell of industry. It is this intoxicating smell of industry that keeps more people coming to the city every day, every hour, every minute, every second.

The morning is quickly going stale. All along the ditch, children, some bald and some hairy, sit in straight rows with piles of shit

dropping into the drain below in full view of passers-by. Most of their parents completed their ablutions in the dark pre-dawn, before the city was fully awake, but there are always a few latecomers. Mamta doesn't look at them, she too lifts her sari and squats, alongside the rejects of humanity. There is no room for shame in her action. Like the others, she too washes herself clean with water from the ditch, and rises, equally purposefully.

She thinks of Mrs D'Souza and her dog Baby and Kalu her benefactor. This evening will be better. *Thank you, Devi*, she prays for her life. *Jai ho Devi, Devi jai ho.*

The city is acquisitive, grabbing her bit by bit. It sneaks in through her pores, dragging her ever closer with each passing moment. There is so much food for sale at every turn: vegetables piled high enough on handcarts to obscure the seller; mounds of fruit – apples, oranges, grapes – spread out on sheets, enough to feed a whole army; sweet dough sizzling in hot oil, sugar-infused, making its way straight from the frying pan into a hungry mouth; fiery curries with dollops of wobbly yogurt dripping off the side of leaf plates; sweet frothy spiced tea scenting the air. Things she's never seen before, things she's never tasted, all for those who can afford to buy from the hawkers. Her saliva flows freely, and suddenly she realises she hasn't eaten a bite since the puri bhaji.

She stands back and waits for a city person to make a purchase, looking carefully at the money offered. She buys some jalebis and stuffs them into her mouth, hardly tasting the first bites. In the village she had to eat hidden, first from her father, then from her brother, later from her husband, and finally from her stepson. Here, she has spent her own money and she can eat openly, flashing her food in anyone's face. Her anonymity makes her bold. This is her chance to recreate herself.

For the first time in her life, her fear leaves her. Surrounded by strangers, she knows she is safer here than she could ever be at home. A few stare at her birthmark and leave her alone, but most don't notice her. It is better this way, not to be noticed.

Smiling politicians, painted by the movie poster makers, line the roadside. One painter swings high in his rope basket in the nostrils

of Prime Minister Atal Bihari Vajpayee, while another paints in his companion's eyebrows one hair at a time.

It is the face of Lokend!

Begumpet loves Lokend Bhai and is keen on making him one of its own. Lokend looks down on the traffic, and into Mamta's eyes. He watches her. She smiles into herself. He is still her private saint, her unintentional benefactor. She subdues her feelings with rationalisation, the most powerful one being that it is in Sahibji's nature to help the downtrodden. That's all. His tenderness towards her was effortless enough to have been something less than extraordinary. What impact could she have hoped to have on him, someone so outside his sphere?

Mamta lounges near a sweetshop to listen to the radio. It secretes music as delicious as the sweets glistening in the window. She eyes the barfi, precise squares of sweet milkcake, covered in layers of silver leaf and pistachios.

'Kanakji, a kilo of laddoo and half a kilo of gulab jamun.'

Kanakji, the owner, manager, cook and salesman sits cross-legged on top of a kind of sofa throne a whole foot above her head with his wares spread out neatly in a glass case at waist level. He works fast. His arms flash over the rows and rows of sweetmeats, deftly packing rich laddoos into red boxes here, handing out gulab jamuns in leaf plates – two to a plate – there, simultaneously shouting at his little assistant with the bare feet and dirty toenails to deliver the thick sweet tea faster.

'Kanakji, here, one plate laddoo.'

'Two plates samosa.'

Kanakji doesn't miss a beat, his arms are in constant motion over his round belly barely concealed under a sleeveless vest that has rolled up just under his pectoral muscles like a woman's brassiere.

Food flies across Mamta's line of vision and she follows it with her eyes like one of the city's stray dogs. None of the customers seem to mind the presence of this filthy, bedraggled, obviously starving woman. To them she is invisible, nothing but a karmic blip. The radio sings on . . .

'Oh queen of my dreams,
When will I see you?
You exhilarating creature,
When will I see you?
My life is ticking away,
When will I see you?'

As if in answer to the song, a horde of intoxicating, passionate girls fills up a bench in the sweet shop. These fascinating creatures are dressed in skivvies, with satchels on their shoulders and bindis on their foreheads, the curves of their breasts as distinct as mangoes. A short while later they are joined by boys who settle into another long bench. The girls look and sound so smart, matching the boys answer for answer, and laughing, a lilting free laugh, loud enough to be heard. How can it be that there are these types of girls, much younger than her? Their aura announces them as definitely not scaredy types, but makers of their own destinies. These girls would have made Paramjit Kaur, her bus companion, proud. Right then and there Mamta decides that she too will be mistress of her own destiny one day.

Kanakji leans over the glass counter which threatens to cut his belly into two, and throws a chapatti into the cupped hands of his assistant. 'For the cow,' he says.

Mamta feels a wet muzzle against her arm. Animals have always been attracted to her. She runs her fingers along its forehead. The boy looks at her and shakes his head. 'Shoo, shoo,' he says to the cow, simultaneously stuffing the chapatti into its mouth and smacking it on the rump. Having dispatched the cow to another part of the city, he immediately returns to his task of handing out endless cups of tea.

Bent over the counter, Kanakji sees Mamta. 'Go on, shoo. Don't you have anything better to do?' The same impulse that makes Kanakji give the stray cow the chapatti drives him to chase Mamta away. A holy cow fed on chapattis will improve Kanakji's karmic balance of payments, but meddling in some unfortunate human being's karma could damage it equally.

This time, the shooing brings no tears. Not because Mamta is

getting used to it, but because she is making a secret friend of belliger-ence. In time she will learn to attack adversity head-on, just like the slum dwellers.

If she wants to be mistress of her own destiny, then she must engage with the world. She gulps. 'Time?' she asks one of the girls whose wrist supports a large watch with a floral dial.

'Two thirty,' the girl replies, ice tinkling in her glass of sugarcane juice, without looking at Mamta.

Mamta holds out her hands like the beggar women at the lights. The girl shrugs her yellow-sheathed shoulders, and hands her glass to Mamta. There is an inch of juice still left in it. Mamta gulps the juice. She is startled; the ice is violently cold, it rolls inside her mouth like a tamarind sweet, but without taste. It is glorious, the most wonderful untasting thing she's ever eaten.

The assistant elbows her out of the store, snatching the glass out of her hands. 'Not allowed,' he says to the girl with the mango breasts, 'not allowed to give glass to beggars, they are Sudra, dirty,' he says, lobbing it on to the road to shatter. 'You must pay for the glass,' he says, looking from Mamta to the girl.

Mamta runs, swallowing the lump of ice. The bits of broken glass poke their way into her husband's rubber slippers.

She lingers outside Himalaya House, presenting herself to the khaki-clad watchman at precisely five o'clock. 'Third floor. And mind you don't touch the handrail,' he says without looking at her.

She enters the stairwell, keeping her hands stiffly by her side to avoid polluting both the wall and handrail.

'Ah! Shy and Honest Mamta, so you came.' Mrs D'Souza tiptoes ahead of Mamta clad only in a towel. The blue lines of her mistress's varicose veins show up and down her legs. Mamta can see Mrs D'Souza's knees quite clearly, dimpled in three places, knocking together with every step. She averts her eyes, she has never seen ample knees before.

'I would ask you about your previous employment, except that thief from this morning had worked in six houses before mine. All good homes, mind you. No, I have decided that I will keep an eye

183

on you myself.' Mrs D'Souza raises her arm to adjust the towel and place a hanky against her nose, so she can't smell her new sweeper's body odour. Mamta can see the swelling top of Mrs D'Souza's right breast. She tries to concentrate on her mistress's instructions.

'Now listen carefully, for I will only say this once. Your job is to wash the floors. You first sweep the floors, then wipe them with the wet mop from under the kitchen sink. The floors have to be washed with phenol once a week. Then the toilets . . .' She leads Mamta round to one bathroom and then the other, all the time holding her towel up with one hand tucked between her pendulous breasts. 'Don't you dare mix the toilet rags with the floor mop. You will then wash out Baby's dish. Downstairs.' Baby instantly recognises its name and comes bounding into the room. 'Oh, Baby, Baby, come, come, Baby, come,' says Mrs D'Souza, patting the surging expanse of her upper thighs, beckoning the small fluffy white dog into her arms. The towel and the hanky fall, while the dog makes no attempt to jump into its mistress's inviting cradle. Mamta rushes to pick up the towel, she can just see a shiny green nylon triangle peeking through Mrs D'Souza's gelatinous thighs.

The village allowed no reason for nudity. She can't remember a time when she saw her mother naked. Breasts, yes, they were naked all the time feeding children, but thighs and knees . . . The only time you saw a woman naked was in childbirth when she was both most and least womanlike. But the men, they were born flashers, she'd seen the male apparatus often, mostly on men other than her husband. Her husband had made her shut her eyes or turn around, and that Ramu, why he'd begun stroking himself in her presence even before her marriage was fixed.

'Turn around,' Mrs D'Souza barks, unabashed by her accidental ninety per cent disclosure in front of Mamta, her servant, a non-person. She ties her towel back on and bends to pick up her yapping pet. 'I'm glad someone still loves me,' she says. The dog's hair cascades over its glistening eyes. 'Wash Baby's dish, bathe Baby once a week and brush her hair. *I* will put the food in her dish. You just take her for her walk. See that she does her big business outside before bringing her back. Three hundred rupees. Okay?' Mrs D'Souza isn't

asking for corroboration of the pay offered, but rather wants to know if Mamta has understood all of her brisk instructions.

The truth is that Mamta does not understand her new mistress's words entirely. But she will learn, not just to understand her mistress's language, but also to anticipate her will. Offered this opportunity of a lifetime, she's not going to spoil it simply because of a language issue. The working class must learn quickly if they are to survive. If she stays long enough, she'll learn English just from hearing it spoken by Mrs D'Souza on the telephone.

Mamta looks at Baby's incredibly sharp teeth barely showing along the sides of her mouth. It's as if the dog is surreptitiously threatening her with a not quite so concealed weapon. 'Yes, memsahib.'

'Then get to work. Don't forget the order: first the floors, then bathrooms, then Baby's food and walkies. Yesh, that's right, Baby, you are going for a walk. You love that, don't you? Yesh, you do, I know you do.' Forgetting about Mamta, Mrs D'Souza's focus is completely on her dog. Mamta stares; in the village, this much attention wasn't even lavished on a child. Things are very different in the city!

'Now get to work.'

It is the most beautiful house Mamta has ever seen. Mrs D'Souza fills her life and space with family photographs and fake flowers. Everywhere she looks, she sees flowers in every imaginable hue standing in perfect bloom, even more glorious than Nature herself could conjure. Sprigs of cherry blossoms in impossible blue caress a photo frame, while a bouquet of alpine spring flowers lounges insolently on the dining table. Mrs D'Souza's collections of a lifetime are wreathed in cobwebs and streaked with old dirt, but Mamta doesn't notice the cobwebs or the dirt. She sees only the abject beauty in each delicate bud that seems to know it will never attain maturity, and the carefully scalloped edge of every perfect bloom. Her hand, awed by such irresistible perfection, has the terrible urge to touch, darting in and out of her clothes like a snake's tongue. It has to be reprimanded several times before it will stay still by her side. Mesmerised by the flowers, it is a while before she notices the family photos.

A young, slim Mrs D'Souza stares into Mamta's eyes, her frame delicate against a background of white. Mamta has heard of it: snow

that lives in mountains. The young Mrs D'Souza has on one of those woolly hats with a pom-pom. A man's arm is draped across her shoulders like a shawl. Mamta feels her own shoulders tingle with the sensation of the photo man's touch. She crosses her arms over her breasts, hugging her shoulders and swaying, for a flickering second she allows herself to luxuriate in fantasy. *Oh, Sahibji, how can it be that a man holds a woman and stands still enough for someone to take their picture?* Then she thinks of her own photo, left in Gopalpur in the warm dip of her stepdaughter's bed. *Why did I leave her behind?*

Mrs D'Souza emerges from her room changed into a skirt, not unlike a short petticoat, it is a little less astonishing to Mamta than this morning's outfit. She is as perfumed as a whole basket of temple jasmine, more to drown out her new sweeper's smell than for any love of dressing up. There is something in the new sweeper's face that brings conversation to her mistress's lips.

Dragging her buttons closed over her undulating flesh she says, 'Kufri, that was in Kufri, before Cynthia came. My husband, handsome no? It was so cold I tell you, my nose nearly fell off. The photo is badly faded now. I've lost the negative, otherwise I would make another one.' Fully dressed, Mrs D'Souza realises that she might be hindering her new servant with talk. 'Get on with your work. Look at me, chatting with you as if we both had nothing better to do with our time. Go on, get on with it,' she says, laying the photo on the table face down. Mamta's silent connection with the sepia players is broken.

She bites down on the panic that threatens to seize her soul. All this space, in her eyes already spotless, must be cleaned, swept and then mopped, all these duties . . . all reasons for mistakes. She already knows that her life belongs in the hands of the plump Mrs D'Souza and her hairy dog. She would never find a place in a slum. If they ever got to know about her, then it would be over, they would take her straight to the police, or worse, back to her village, where the only thing waiting for her is death.

Mrs D'Souza lights a flame in a glass cup. It is the first familiar sight of the day. She follows her new mistress's motion from under her lids. Mrs D'Souza's plump hands thin with memory. The hands

extend into wrists, supporting a single bangle, going round and round in front of another altar. Mistress becomes mother. A tide of memories breaks painfully against the rock that has become her heart. She looks to the floor, ceding her recollection to reality. How could she explain running away to her mother, her relatives, her village? She knows she will be judged harshly for jumping on that bus. Under-the-banyan-tree village rules are clear: she belongs with her husband, forever. She might have run away, but her courage frightens her. *Oh, Devi, help me.* Mrs D'Souza's flame is still, unwavering. It floats above the cooking oil like a miniature shining boat. She sees her mistress place it on the little ledge above the dining table, at the feet of a picture of the lady holding a baby. *Oh, Devi, help me.* The lady with the crown and the sleepy closed eyes of a saint has her head tilted towards her. Both mother and baby have halos round their heads. Mamta swallows; so this is Mrs D'Souza's Devi.

Mamta can't understand the English words that flow from Mrs D'Souza's painted lips as smooth as summer air. Her mistress chants with her eyes closed, but every now and then one flickers open to see what her new sweeper is up to. 'What are you staring at? Let me say my prayers in peace. Go finish the floors,' she says, seamlessly moving from English to a lazy kind of Hindi.

In time, Mamta will learn all about Jesus, his mother and the angels, and she will come to love the Madonna almost as much as Mrs D'Souza. Her mistress waddles off into the recesses of her dimly lit two-bedroom flat, leaving the living room and her altar to Mamta's scrutiny.

She scrubs harder. The smell of phenol makes her gag. As a sign of eagerness she started her new job with washing the floors with the chemical. She doesn't know this smell, they never had any of these bottled things in the village. The floors shine through. The terrazzo shows its shapes to her. She stares into the marble chips, into her own private kaleidoscope, it changes obligingly with the angle of her sight. What a beautiful house. *If you could see me now, working in this grand house, how proud you would be of me. Look where I have come.* She touches the scar on the side of her body to remind herself not to become too complacent.

She moves from the floors to the toilets. All familiarity ends at

the bathroom door. First of all, there is no smell to greet her. The commodes glare at her. She looks at them, not quite sure what to do, then reaches behind the toilet and pulls out the bushy plastic cleaner to brush the sparkling white ceramic. Accidentally her hand releases a tiny platinum handle to one side. Water rushes into the toilet. She is mortified. She has broken the tank. So much water gushing out needlessly. Should she tell Mrs D'Souza? *Leave it. Do you want to lose your job?* She goes back quietly to work.

Now get to the dog's dish. Baby's dish lives behind the kitchen door. For years it has prevented the door from opening fully, but Mrs D'Souza is a stickler for habit and will not have it any other way. She almost sacked two sweepers because they insisted on putting Baby's dish to one side of the door. But with this one she need not fear, Mamta will never think to disturb the dish's position.

Steel pots reflect a distorted, fatter version of Mamta's face. So many pots, all for one family! The spices, powdered to a fine miasma, rest in rows of bottles with tightly closed lids, standing tallest to the shortest like a line of diligent school children. Mamta can make out the chillies, but not the others in myriad brown hues. The quantity of food is overwhelming. With so much food, Mrs D'Souza could feed a village. She wants to ask how many people live in the house, but is afraid to talk, and even more afraid to question.

Behind the open door above the dog's dish are shelves filled with every variety of dry good possible. Mamta might never learn all their names: papadums, crisp as a winter morning in plastic wrappers sealed with a candle flame for freshness; white rice sans gravel; lentils of every colour; indeterminate mixtures smelling of cardamom and chillies enough to make the eye water; a square hunk of white wrapped in brown paper which looks vaguely like the round sweet buns that Lala Ram's wife made for her children. Shelf after shelf of food. Her sight bumps into the stove. Lifted high off the ground on a marble counter, its rings stare fiercely into her face like unfriendly monster eyes. Mrs D'Souza's kitchen doesn't force you to cling to the ground, it lifts you up and sets you free.

She drops to the floor with reverence before the stove.

'Don't give Baby any bread, it makes her sick.'

'Bread?'

'Yes, that bread –' Mrs D'Souza points to the square hunk wrapped in brown paper. 'Don't give her any.'

'Yes, memsahib.'

The kitchen is a cornucopia, all the bounty that Lakshmi could possibly bestow on anyone surely resides here. Mamta looks hard for the pitchers of water, the single most important item in her own kitchen space. But she doesn't see any. Almost as if intending to put her mind at rest, Mrs D'Souza waltzes in, pirouettes and washes her hands in the kitchen sink.

'I, I . . . I thought that was a . . .'

'Don't you dare wash your hands in this sink. It's meant for the dishes only and clean people. I don't want the muck of the floors and bathroom dragged into my kitchen. You wash hands at the floor tap in Cynthia's bathroom.'

'Yes, memsahib.' Much the same way, Mrs D'Souza waltzes out.

The ants have got to the dog food first. They get to it every day because Mrs D'Souza puts much more in the dog dish than her precious pup can possibly eat. Mamta eyes the kernels of rice still fluffy from the night before. The minced meat scattered evenly through the rice speaks to Mrs D'Souza's attention to detail. Mamta picks up the dish. The movement disturbs the ants. They immediately retreat to the outer edges of the dish. She brings the dish close to the rubbish bin and opens its plastic lid. From the contents within, she can easily piece together the daily life of the D'Souza family. The dog's food slides down the edge of the dish. A spoonful falls in the bin before Mamta catches the cascading rice and mince in her fist. For her, waste is not an option, it is a lesson learned in childhood, tattooed into her brain by impermeable hunger, never before in her life has she ever thrown out food, good, bad or rotten. Food always has another incarnation. It can always be given to one more hungry. Her mother once ate cow's hooves to survive a drought. She brings her fist to her mouth.

Now the smell of phenol is inside her. She wipes her lips with the back of her hand. She looks around. She can hear Mrs D'Souza pottering in her room somewhere, loud enough to say she is engaged. Quickly, illicitly, lovingly, Mamta opens the shining brass tap in the

forbidden sink. A trickle of water emerges like a gift from God. A trickle of clean delicious water, she has the urge to taste it. She must hurry, the trickle is tinkling now, announcing its presence. She quickly wrings her hands under it, then anoints herself with three wet fingers horizontally on her forehead, more precious than any blessing she ever got out of temple.

It is her first time with a tap.

Then she hears another sound of big water gushing. She knows this sound. Mrs D'Souza emerges from the bathroom. 'Mind you don't flush the toilet. Sometimes they cut off the water earlier than expected and then the tanks are empty. I always go in the evening. I will do the flushing. You just scrub the commodes. Okay?'

Mamta nods silently. No flushing the toilets.

'Now take Baby for her walk.'

She almost asks *Where?* A debilitating fear grabs her feet. Where would she go in this city? She only arrived this morning. 'Her chain is behind the kitchen door. Stay away from Venus building, Baby hates that black dog that hangs about at the entrance. Last time he nearly bit her leg off. Poor Baby. She had to have stitches.'

She tries to hook the chain on Baby's collar. It might as well have been a fish in her hands, the number of times it falls to the floor. At last Mrs D'Souza can't stand the fuss any longer.

'Stop that!' Mamta drops the chain, it clatters to the floor in an aggressively loud musical movement. Mrs D'Souza secures her dog and sends both Mamta and Baby out into the leering city.

The dog and its escort walk side by side, the dog the far more confident of the two.

She is lucky her first work day happens to be on the weekend, otherwise she would have experienced rush-hour human traffic, enough to lift her off her feet. To her village eyes it seems that the whole of Begumpet is on the streets, rushing, clashing, all going somewhere. But where is this somewhere? When will she have a direction? She is an island, in a swirling eddy. She puts on a smile for all those strangers. No one replies. Very quickly she will learn

that she is invisible. She reeks of diffidence and has a long and awkward journey to make before becoming a city dweller.

The village has taught her not to look at the men, but the women are fair game. Their open hair and city clothes force her to wrap her sari more tightly around herself. A woman and man walk hand in hand. Hand in hand! How? Where does such courage come from that enables them to walk like that? She has seen same-sex hands linked in friendship or camaraderie, but never hands of opposite sexes. The clasped hands make a mockery of her marriage, her beatings and her sacrifice.

Then Baby tugs at her chain. She runs after the dog. Right turn, left turn. Don't run on to the road, she pleads. Right turn, left turn . . . She looks for landmarks. Her mind is completely focused in purpose. She must be able to find her way home. She is terrified of getting lost, she is terrified of being found. Lost, found, lost, found . . . The faces change, they leer at her, all the men become her husband, all the women Lata Bai. She can hear her mother's words: 'Rules, you will understand them when you have been married as long as I have.' She is Sharma's wife, shit-smeared and raped. Baby runs. *Stop, Baby.*

She steps on the dog's chain and quickly snags it between her toes with the deftness of one who has walked barefoot all her life. Chain in hand, she looks around her at last. She sees nothing familiar. A panic as forceful as dry retching seizes her. She still has that written address tied in her pallav. She can always ask someone. But how do you stop someone in a city? She looks for a friendly face to stop, all the while letting Baby drag her where she will. Unknown to Mamta, Baby does know her way home. She is her strongest ally, her friend, her guide.

Mamta must recognise every stone and make friends with every tree along her path. She must become one with the humanity that doesn't smile back, anonymous, and confident in her anonymity. Baby squats to defecate. Immediately the stream of people, marching with purpose, parts precisely to avoid the dog's excrement. The indignity of the street creeps past automatic feet.

The end of the first day is a time to remember and forget many things. Mamta's new mistress may have made her work, but it is nothing

191

compared with what she did in the village. She still has her reserve of energy, and it is stoked and hot. Kalu finds her under the stairs all a-jitter.

'Hey, which is my side? You said I could sleep here, right? Right?' He is only one person, the overwhelming humanity of the day has made her competent against a single enemy. She is ready to fight for the promise he'd made that morning. She trusts no one and nothing.

'Yes, it's okay.'

'You said so yourself, you can sleep under the stairwell with me . . .'

'Oho, get a hold of your tongue. I know what I said. So where are your things?'

'Don't have any,' she says, quickly grabbing a spot under the stairs.

Kalu looks at his companion. Much too old for anyone to confuse her for one of his love interests, he thinks. 'So how was it today?'

'She has such a beautiful house, but the dog scares me.'

'Get used to Baby, otherwise she will give you the runaround. Don't let Mrs D'Souza ever catch you hitting Baby, okay.'

'So tell me, why did you help me out?' The question has been on her mind all day.

He shrugs. 'Maybe because my life is so good,' he laughs. 'I don't know. Maybe because you reminded me of someone. Maybe because . . .' Kalu may find all the reasons in the world to answer Mamta's question, but his answers will be bland. There is only one reason for such spontaneous action that holds the power to change the destiny of another human being – and that is soul-recognition, acknowledging that bond which connects us to all things worldly and unworldly. At such times we feel more than an exact empathy. We don't just fully understand the other, but somehow we *know* the other. Such instances aren't rare, they occur daily, but like lightning they are gone before they have a chance to be recorded or recognised as miracles.

Still jittery, her hand rushes immediately to hide her birthmark.

'No, I don't think that was it. It was something else. I know what it was, it was the way you laughed.'

'I can do it again,' she says and laughs. Her laughter surprises her. Her belligerence, the stance she's been holding on to like a life-giving

breath leaves her. Without the aggression she is infinitely tired, but she won't give up this chance to talk, her first real human connection. 'Where do those cows go?'

'Their owners let them roam free until they start producing milk. They are sacred cows. Sometimes I snag one, and drag it around the colony. You should see what people are willing to feed sacred cows. Chapattis, jaggery, even barfi. Sometimes I manage to pluck a little out of its mouth for myself. Dragging a lucky cow behind you on a rope is better than begging in person.'

'In my village all the cows have rich owners. You milk someone else's cow and you could get your hand chopped off. My younger brother used to do cow-duty for the Big House . . .' She looks up; Himalaya House, true to its name, towers like a mountain over her head. She laughs again. 'Here everything is big except the moon! The houses, the roads, the lights; even the people are big. Lucky fat city girls will never have a hard time getting married. Why, in the village fat like that would get you a string of proposals.'

'No one in my family has the lucky fat,' Kalu says wryly.

'Did you come from the village also?' she asks.

'No, I was born here.'

'So you know all the ways of the city then.' She regards him from beneath her eyebrows. Kalu looks into Mamta's eyes. She looks away, but the path is open for further conversation.

'I suppose you could say that, but it doesn't help me much. I am still a sweeper, and I'll remain under this stairwell till I die.' He spits a squat, compact, city-dweller's gob on the floor next to him.

'Any family?' Villagers always ask that question.

'Yes, nine brothers and eleven sisters, because my amma wasn't one of those who buried her girl babies alive in the ditches by the slum.'

Nine brothers and eleven sisters. *I have seven in my family, and one could be in this very city.* She doesn't presume that Kalu will be the least bit interested in her story. 'Don't you miss them?'

'What's to miss? I was the lucky one who got away. We fought over everything all the time. My father beat my mother. He beat her to death. He used to send us begging.'

193

'Boys aren't much good when it comes to begging,' she says, thinking of the girls at the lights.

'No, we aren't. But the gangs fix that.'

'Gangs?'

'Those city gangs, the begging gangs. You don't have them in the village?'

'There is no one to beg from in the village. All the extra girls get taken to the city. My father would have liked to send me to the city, but I got . . . away.' She almost says 'married'. The word sears her tongue.

'The gangs make you into beggars, cut off your hands or scar your face. I think they did that to my brother. Bapu said he was sick anyway.'

'Well, if he was sick, then it's a different story.' Strong, surviving children are an asset, but dying ones, well, some sort of use has to be found for them too, just like some sort of use was found for her. Should she tell him about her scar?

Suddenly she is afraid, the image of Sharma's wife, shit-smeared and raped jumps into her mind. She wants to share her fear with her benefactor but she doesn't fully trust him yet. 'So how did you come here?' she asks, quickly making him once again the subject of discussion.

'I helped them build it.'

'You built this building?'

'No . . . Yes . . . No. I broke the rocks for the concrete. Then when the building was complete, I just stayed on. They inherited me. Then Chacha came.' He uses the familiar Chacha to describe the khaki-clad man, no relative of his.

'Chacha wrote the address for me,' Mamta states with wonder.

'Yes, he's BA pass.'

'BA?'

'You have to study for years and years, nearly more than half your life to become a BA pass. It's hard.'

'My brother left to work in the city. His name is Jivkant. He said he wanted to read and write, but he can't study half his life. I suppose he'll never become a BA pass. I will look for him the next time I take Baby for a walk.'

'Forget it, you can never find anyone in the city. People come here to lose themselves. How much is she paying?'

'Three hundred rupees.'

'Of course you'll have to find work in another house otherwise you'll starve, even though you have a place to sleep.'

She's half tempted to tell him about the stolen money, but instead she says, 'How will I find another house?'

'Ask Mrs D'Souza to recommend you to her friends. Be very, very nice to Baby and then she'll be very nice to you. I think it's because she doesn't get on with her daughter that she's in love with that dog. Her husband died two years ago.'

'I tasted ice today. Ice.'

'Sleep with your head on your hand, otherwise rats will bite your face and worms crawl in your ears,' he says, unimpressed with her discovery of frozen water.

Mamta gulps. Kalu pulls his blanket over his head and immediately sinks into a deep sleep holding his head up with the palm of his right hand.

The night falls round her drop by drop. She is tired, her night on the bus has left her hurting in places she never knew existed. She can't switch off her thoughts. They crash in the cave of her mind, bouncing like disoriented trapped birds, gathering momentum and volume with every circuit. *Why did I leave her behind? A runaway, that's what I am now, a runaway, like Sharma's wife. What will Gopalpur say? What will Amma think? What will Sahibji think? Where will I find Jivkant?* Left alone in the night, safe for the time being, with a job in hand and a roof over her head, Mamta is simply lost.

She can just about see the edge of the sky if she cranes her neck to look beyond the stairs. It is a bluish white. The city lights have eclipsed the stars. *How is it possible that men are able to obscure the creation of God? So much light for a sleeping city. If I had but one bulb at home, what wouldn't I have done with it?*

It will be months before she will realise that the city rarely offers up a moon and never in winter when the pavement dwellers light whatever fuel they can get their hands on to keep warm, adding to

the smoggy sky with smoke from their sooty fires. It isn't the same as in the village, where she took the moon for granted.

She thinks of her stepdaughter and feels the burning prick of tears. *Why did I leave her behind?* If she'd had a companion at that moment she would have told them her whole story, about her mother, her marriage, her kidney, her stepdaughter, the money, perhaps even about Lokend. But Kalu is asleep. His open mouth dribbles spit, making a dark patch by his bent elbow. Suddenly, too tired for thoughts, she allows the deepening night to pat her to sleep.

She wakes before light. The under-surface of the staircase climbs over her like a cave. She shrinks into herself. 'Amma?' She calls to her mother to make some sense of her situation. Then she sees Kalu's bed all rolled up and tucked to one side. She knows where she is and what she must do. She climbs out from under the stairs. One side of her body is polka-dotted with mosquito bites. The morning brings new fears and new guilt . . . she left her behind. Mamta scratches her bites; her body, pricked with itching sores, brings her back to her senses. She checks between her breasts, her money is still intact. She makes her way to the waterline. The tap runs dry three women before her.

'Here, take this. You have to wake up earlier next time,' says Kalu, handing her a single clove. She bites down, savouring its nascent astringent flavour.

'Keep it till this evening. She's bound to talk to you. She loves to talk. Talk, talk, talk. That's what she does. You don't want to give her stinky answers, do you? Get yourself some neem sticks. Three roads up and to the left by the little temple is a neem tree. If you aren't afraid of heights you can pick your own, but early in the morning, otherwise buy them for fifty paisa at the grocers. Don't let him overcharge you. He'll be able to tell you're a country mouse with his one good eye.'

She returns with Kalu to the building.

'Go look for other jobs. Ask Chacha. He might have something. I have to get going.' Kalu steps out of the gate and melts into the city. Mamta stays watching him till the last possible moment. When

will she be able to simply step out of the gate and melt into the city like that?

Go look for other jobs. Ask Chacha. She'll have no luck with Chacha the Taciturn who won't give anything away, but Mrs D'Souza of the stretch pants, now that might just be a possibility. But first she must buy herself a new sari.

She wanders through the market, clutching her filthy sari pallav in her hand, her hidden money chafing her skin. There are so many customers in the shops, why would anyone attend to her? 'Come, Didi, want to buy a sari?' a little boy calls to her. He has been placed at the doorway of the shop by his blind employer to snag wavering potential customers, be they any caste or creed.

'Yes, yes,' she replies, breathless with excitement, stepping into the shop's cool interior.

'Masterji, she wants to buy a sari.'

'So what do you want? Nylon, cotton, silk, polyester . . . it is a new material, very popular . . .' The blind Masterji invites her to sit on the white sheet-covered bench. 'What colour? We have every-thing. You just tell me and I take out for you. No hurry, you see as many as you like.' Masterji's sightless eyes, jutting out like pieces of mutton fat from his pockmarked face, pierce right through to her giddy, spendthrift soul. This is the first time she has bought clothing, dyed and patterned by someone else. Suddenly she is unsure, and tries to leave the shop. 'Nothing yet, Masterji, I will be back,' she says, as he opens up a stack of saris, trapping her with their colours.

'Orange, pure silk, brocade from Benares; green one from Bombay, good wash, polyester, latest fashion . . . and this one cotton . . .' He runs his hands over the cloths, feeling for both material and colour. The blind old man knows his merchandise, and his customer. She is the type who will want a good-value sari, something she might be familiar with from the village, but nothing like one she might have been able to buy at a place like Saraswati Stores.

'I have the perfect one for you, good value cotton, very strong, here – smell it.'

She places the new fabric to her nose, it smells of wheat fields and

wet earth. That's what gets them every time, the smell of new fabric. He laughs on the inside because he has her now, she can't escape.

Mamta takes hours to decide on the sari the blind man has chosen for her, a good-value cotton of bright blue with an orange border.

Dressed in her new sari, she pops the clove in her mouth, and runs up the stairs, touching nothing.

Mrs D'Souza, in her floral pink-and-white nightdress with a tiny pink bow at the neck and black curlers in her hair, is a sight to behold. Her fat arms are bisected by the tight elastic of her sleeves. The lower halves attend to buttering bread in the kitchen. Her door is wide open to let in fresh air.

Mrs D'Souza's bright loud voice greets her. 'Cynthia,' she shouts, 'time to wake up.' She sips her tea, wincing as it burns her tongue. Mamta will never get used to the falsetto of a mother talking to her child. She's never heard it before. There's no time for childish games where she comes from. The business of living in the village does not tolerate lightheartedness.

'Memsahib . . .' Mamta faces Mrs D'Souza's pink-and-white night-dress, stretched tight across two perfectly round buttock cheeks, each a complete circle in its own right.

'Cynthia, church.' The falsetto calls to the daughter again, but it is a token demand. The daughter won't emerge from her room till the day is nice and ripe.

Mamta stands in the doorway, half in half out. That's the state of her life now, half in half out. Displaced.

'Memsahib . . .' Mamta looks with awe at the curlers in her memsahib's hair. Then she grabs the kitchen broom and starts sweeping the landing. At last she has a purpose.

Mrs D'Souza turns around, blowing at the teacup in her hands, a faint smile on her lips and a single eyebrow arched condescend-ingly. She has judged her new servant well. This sweeper will never think of saying no to extra work without extra pay, not like the thieving boy. She could never have asked him to clean the landing; he would have been standing on her head with his hand held out for a big tip if she had.

She tugs the curlers free. 'What is it?'

'N-nothing.'

'Well, if it's nothing, then come with me.' The door locks behind her with a click. Short of taking Mamta by the hand, she pulls her down the stairs with her will. 'Bloody people, call themselves civilised. Just look at these walls. That Mrs Nath, filthy woman, should be shot. Most of this is her mess. My Cynthia has to pass by this every day.' The woman waddles laboriously down the stairs.

Mamta can see nothing on the walls that might upset Mrs D'Souza. 'Paan stains, piss, and just look at what these uncouth gundas have scrawled. My God, I blush at my age.'

Mamta has seen too many betel-juice stains to be offended by them. In Gopalpur it was mostly the men who chewed betel-leaf, a woman chewing betel-leaf meant she was the boss in the family. Betel-juice stains are a good thing where she comes from. And the piss, yes, the ammonia goes up her nose too, but it isn't as delicate as her memsahib's. The smell offends Mamta too, but she may not hold her nose, that is the privilege of memsahibs. Mrs D'Souza marches Mamta downstairs. 'Give her a mop and broom. Let her clean the stairs. I will pay for it myself,' she commands Chacha. Sunday may not be a day for any good Christian to work, but a Hindu Sudra can work on any day . . . or night. Mrs D'Souza is not one to meddle in another's religion. 'Come find me when you're done,' she says, turning quickly to climb back up to where she came from.

Chacha hands Mamta a pail, mop, plastic bristle brush, coconut husk, ash. It is a desperate stairwell requiring robust cleaning.

Mamta wraps her new sari pallav across her face . . . wheat fields and wet mud. She smiles into the blue fabric and starts on the walls. Three hours later she is done. The stairwell has exacted its toll: the skin feels raw on her hands. But what does she care? She is free, clothed in fineness, she would scrub a hundred such stairwells if it kept her away from her husband.

'Cynthia, the church won't wait,' she hears her memsahib say as she comes upstairs to return the broom.

10

DAKU MANMOHAN IS TRUE TO HIS WORD. There isn't a task they can set for him that he doesn't complete with care and passion. He has turned, not just the corner plot, but the whole area round his cell into luscious fields. Asmara Didi half expects the barren mango trees overhead to start producing fruit just to be a part of the fecund cycle he seems to have put into motion. Reluctantly her admiration for the man she hates is growing.

Each day the bandit is let out of his cell. He hitches the yoke across his shoulders and with measured steps reaches his field. He has transformed that parched and stony earth into prolific greenery through sheer will. All along the edge of his field stand precise rows of marvellous roses in glorious bloom. Heads of flowers as large as cabbages – his personal undeclared gift to Asmara Didi – drop occasional petals to the turned earth below.

But the novelty of the prisoner is wearing thin, and now only the staunchest hecklers – Gope and mute Kanno – remain. Time has made them still and silent. The only one who remains keen as a ripe chilli is Singh Sahib himself. His heart still reverberates like a tuning fork in unison with the bandit's daily prayers. Subconsciously Singh Sahib knows that their entwined destinies will bear a profound fruit.

He finds himself humming one of the prisoner's tunes:

'Oh innocent heart, oh innocent heart,
What is your desire, what is your destiny?
In this material world,
You are a lost soul,
Oh ignorant heart, oh ignorant heart
What is your desire, what is your destiny? . . .'

. . . and realises that since he abducted the bandit, he hasn't once thought of his lovely late wife Bibiji. Singh Sahib has begun to take apart the thick skein of his prisoner's life and now thinks of him as a person, a family man with a history; and it is with building acceptance that he sees his son squat beside the cell to chat with him.

Each day Singh Sahib listens for their conversation, but the words elude him because they talk softly. In their loose postures he sees a familiarity that he lacks with his own son.

Ram Singh still comes to his father's room nearly every day. He smells of alcohol and his manner is accusing and brooding. He talks of nothing but getting rid of the bandit. The elder son wants his father to act through him, he wants his father's approval to kill the bandit. Singh Sahib's approval would represent a conscious choice, a choice in favour of him over Lokend.

Today Prem's thoughts are more with Mamta than with Daku Manmohan. *Where are you now? Mamta, take care of yourself. I always thought I would be next in line for the city, but it turned out to be you.* He is disappointed, but not as much as he thought he would be. Looking after Daku Manmohan seems almost better to him, much more dangerous, much more responsible, much more exciting. He turns around to face his charge.

'Come here, boy, I have a story to tell you, but first one question: do you think people are defined by their deeds?' asks Daku Manmohan.

'No,' replies Prem cautiously.

'So, could you accept me as a man, instead of judging me for what I have done?'

'I don't know.'

201

'I like your honesty. Did you know your uncle was my right-hand man for many, many years, and that's why your family was spared?'

'Yes, we suspected as much.'

'He was a good man. I trusted him with my life.' Daku Manmohan thinks back to a different time. His eyes sweep past the bars of his cell into the brightness beyond without focusing on anything. 'You remind me very much of him. He was just a little older than you when he went on his first raid.' The boy is entrapped by the story made personal for him. 'Shall I go on?'

'Yes, yes.'

'Then listen. My family used to be farmers too, just like your family. We too had debts with the Big House, just like your father does. My father was one of the farmers interested in forming a panchayat to regulate things like repayments and interest on loans. They would have got their panchayat if our crops hadn't failed that year. But because our crops failed, we weren't able to make our payments to the Big House. Singh Sahib's father sent his henchmen to destroy us. They said that because we hadn't paid what we owed them, they owned everything we had. So first they took our grain, then they burned down our hut and after that they took all my sisters away and sold them to a brothel in the city. My eldest sister was to be married one week later. She killed herself.' The bandit's eyes are red and burning.

'Go on, go on,' says the boy, unabashedly showing a morbid interest in the tragic tale.

'My mother went mad after that. You may know her. She is the one who grabs the feet of all the temple-goers.' Prem knows the woman well. She lies by the steps, breasts exposed; sometimes a passer-by will throw a rag over her. Lata Bai always put some food in her thali, cursing the bandits as she did so.

'But we thought . . .'

'Yes, everyone thinks that we did that to her. But I didn't do that to my mother. As for my father, he disappeared that night, leaving us three brothers alone. We knew they would come for us the next morning, so we ran away. We went into the mountains and ravines where more like us lived. There we learned to shoot straight and

sever a head with one blow. We learned to ride fast and hide in seconds.

'The year of the drought, that's when we hit. Hit the village as hard as we could so it would never recover. At that time, I was just a little older than you are now. After the success of that raid, there was no looking back. We raided all the villages from Gopalpur right up to Begumpet, adding to our numbers by kidnapping young boys. That's how your uncle came to us. He begged us to spare his family, and I honoured that pact.

'I became a senior in the gang three months before we looted Sonpur. The bandits always thought that Sonpur had the best-looking girls; most of our women came from there. The ones who didn't eventually stay with us of their own free will became prostitutes, traded amongst the men. That's where my wife is from, Sonpur.' Daku Manmohan, the proudest, most feared bandit in the whole of India, allows tears to form in his eyes.

'She came to me hardly nine years old. They all wanted her, but I said no! No! No!' Years later, the memory is still strong. 'I taught her to read and write. I protected her, and in time it was my good fortune that she came to love me. I married her. She is a beautiful, brave, educated woman, much too good to be a bandit's wife. I swore that no child of mine would ever have to live like me.

'Soon after I got married, Sardar Ranjit Singh, the head of the gang, asked me to take over from him. That was a shock for my elder brother. He felt betrayed by the Sardar, so he grew to hate me, the person who had stolen his birthright. He even turned our younger brother against me. They knew how I loathed gratuitous bloodshed, so just to spite me they were ruthless in their raids. For them no amount of blood was enough. The blood . . . the blood . . . Cruelty is not the biggest killer, desensitisation is.

'Though I threw them out, the reputation for cruelty stuck, and there was nothing I could do to change it. Then I had my son, Abhay, and I knew that he too would be forced to become a bandit one day. So when Lokend asked me to surrender I said yes.'

Prem's eyes glisten with unshed tears. Like a seashell that contains

the sound of the sea, people have an empathy which connects them with others. Prem's tears aren't for himself, they are for his prisoner.

'Why does Lokend Bhai do the things he does for you?'

'Lokend Bhai. He's a conundrum. He doesn't do those things because of my story. If it were up to my history, no one would do anything for me. You don't know how many I've killed, how many I've destroyed. No, for Lokend I am a concept. I am just a soul. Ask that man over there what I've done.' He points to Gope, squatting by the temple steps.

'Do you want me to hate you?' asks the boy.

'Don't hate him,' says Gope. 'I hate him enough for the both of us. I hate him enough for the whole world.'

Tenderness is a strange thing, and it is perhaps most ardent in a hard man. Somehow Daku Manmohan has allowed himself the love of Prem. In return for the boy's love, he has been teaching him to read and write.

'Hindi is a very scientific language,' he reminds his pupil daily. 'It is like learning to dance with your tongue! Take the tip of your tongue on to the roof of your mouth close to your teeth to pronounce the first consonant, K, then slide your tongue back a bit for the next one, KH, and a little further for the next, G, and so on.'

When Prem can't get his pencil round a particularly difficult curlicue, the bandit affectionately scolds the boy without any harshness in his voice.

Each day the boy arrives at the cell, books and kite in hand. He has given up the pretence of guarding his prisoner and instead avidly shares the blitheness of the season with him, making the bandit's imprisonment (he hopes) easier to bear.

'How do you know to write?'

'Do you think only village boys joined our gang? No, it was all types. There were many educated boys in my gang. One of them taught me to read. That boy died in the first Gopalpur raid.'

'Do you miss your son?' Prem asks slowly.

'Do I miss my boy? Yes. Yes, I do. He is just about your age. He

must be flying his kite too.' Daku Manmohan starts pacing his cell like the tiger he is, trapped in a small space.

'One of those in the sky might be your son's.'

'You know, each night I look at the moon and I say to myself, "Take heart, old man, take heart, you share a common moon." I may never see my family again, but we share a common moon.' He pauses; Prem offers his silence as tangibly as a clasping hand. 'I don't know how much longer I will be able to wait and watch dawn break at the appointed hour . . .' He stops pacing. 'Why won't they hang me? I have become an example, that's all. People look at me and they tell their children, "Eat your food or Daku Manmohan will come and get you." I thought I could take anything. But when I see you each morning here with your book, I think of my son . . .' The man's voice starts to thicken. Prem puts his hand in through the bars. The prisoner grips it tight. The warmth of the little hand dissipates the old hurt.

'Maybe you will see your boy again, you never know. I am sure I will see my sister again. She ran away from her husband. You know she came to me the first day I came to work here. I hid her at Asmara Didi's old place for two days and then . . . and then she went to the city. She was married hardly one year back. She said her husband would kill her if he finds her. I don't know what she did. Mamta was my best sister. Bapu borrowed money from the Big House for her dowry, you know. That's why I'm working here, to pay off Bapu's loan. I didn't want Mamta to marry that man. She was his second wife. He had two children and the boys all said he'd killed his first wife. I know he will kill Mamta if he finds her.'

'Under the circumstances, I think she is best left hidden in the city amongst thousands of people, and you have to believe she's safe. Perhaps she'll run into Lokend in the city. They say he's doing big things there. He is a good man. I wish his father could see beyond the family tradition.'

'Yes, Lokend Bhai is a great man. You know, he helped my sister too, brought her food . . . now who else would do that for us low castes? He is another Gandhi, they say.' Just the thought of his connection to Lokend Bhai makes Prem's chest swell with pride.

A guard comes over to let the bandit out of his cell. He doesn't bother putting the shackles on his ankles any more; they know the bandit won't go anywhere.

Daku Manmohan prepares to slip on his yoke, legs bent at the knees anticipating its crushing weight. The boy runs to his side to help him.

'No, I do this alone.'

He bounces the yoke up and up, on to his shoulders, staying bent double to support the weight as he starts to walk. 'Not today.' The guard walks up to him and hits him lightly on his back with a branch from the tamarind tree. 'Today you have easier work in store for you. Lucky bastard. See, he's become an animal. He takes the yoke on his back, ready for work. You donkey, don't you remember the fields have been ploughed? Don't you remember cutting the wheat? Don't you remember threshing the wheat? See what an idiot he's become.' The guard's head is wobbling frantically on his neck. Each wiggle gives credence to his question. 'In the beginning we had to beat him.' The guard rotates the bandit by his elbow, lifts up his vest and shows his back to Prem. The bandit offers no resistance.

The boy turns his head away from flesh more furrowed than one of the bandit's newly ploughed fields.

'Arey, this is nothing! I would break both his legs if Singh Sahib allowed me to. I enjoyed doing this to him. How many people has he killed? And guess what they have in store for him now? Grinding the wheat, that's what,' he says in a falsetto, then spits on the floor. 'Why don't they give him something even easier to do? Why don't they give him Asmara Didi's roses and ask him to make jam or make dough for the chapattis? Phah, for all the killing he's done, he should be hitched to that yoke for eternity!'

The watersheds in people's lives appear in the commonest of places. Daku Manmohan's intended change of job is about to try destiny's determination to the limit.

'Yes, you'd better hitch me to this yoke for eternity, for I won't grind wheat!'

'Why Daku Manmohan, what's that I hear? You won't grind the wheat. Won't you just? We'll make you do it!' The guard is excited

at last to have got a rise out of his prisoner, he is relishing the prospect of a fight, his head is all but rotating right off his neck.

'Not even God can make me do it. It is woman's work. Do what you will to me, you will never get me to grind that wheat.'

'Perhaps I will have a chance to break both your legs after all,' the guard says.

'Don't listen to him, Daku Manmohan. He's just babbling to confuse you. What's there in grinding the wheat? It will give your wounds time to heal and then it will be ploughing season again,' says the boy, displaying logic belong his years. But even to his youthful imagination, the picture of the bandit sitting over the grinding stone rotating away like he's seen his mother and sisters do seems vulgar.

'No! No one can make me grind the wheat! I've said what I have to say!' Daku Manmohan allows no glimmer of enlightenment to pass through common sense. He turns suddenly and wraps the guard's collar in his fingers. The man takes in a sharp breath, caught unawares. Slowly the danger of his situation reveals itself. An unchained killer has him by the throat. He crosses his legs to stop that urinating feeling. 'You tell your zamindar that I am of the warrior caste, a kshatriya, and our kind will never do a woman's work. Let him do his worst. He can get me to grind the wheat only when I am dead.' He flings the guard away from him, walks back into his cell and shuts the door. 'I will not do a woman's work,' he repeats, locking the cell door from the inside.

The news is with the zamindar before the bandit has locked his cell door. Singh Sahib chuckles. His disability cannot camouflage the delight that takes over his entire frame. *At last, the rules change.* He smiles with carefree zeal and meanders through rows and rows of thoughts and plans, all to do with breaking Daku Manmohan's will and his ultimate downfall.

Why does he relish this prospect of cruelty? Why is he bent upon snatching away Daku Manmohan's dignity? The reason is strange and convoluted. It is because of his sons: one a do-gooder and the other a common thug, with not an honourable bone between them. Both his boys have let him down, his fate has let him down, so now

he has declared war on Fate. He will be avenged. And what better revenge on Fate than to ruin someone else's by taking away the one thing he values above all else: his dignity.

The laughter gurgles in his stomach like a bad lunch.

Asmara Didi rushes to his side, and sets him upright, but she can't quell the strange shakes that have conquered his body. 'Calm yourself, Singh Sahib,' she says, just about ready to rush off and get one of her balms when she notices his eyes.

Since Bibiji's death, the zamindar's eyes have lacked a vigilant depth. But today she sees something extraordinary in those old and weary sockets. She sees an ancient zest in them that makes her anxious.

As for the bandit, he gave no quarter and asks for none. Without a struggle he offers his burned-out body to its torturer. And the torture is tremendous. There are days when the bandit cannot rise from the floor, still he whispers to the earth beside his mouth, 'I will not do a woman's work.' One of his legs has been dislocated at the hip and jammed back in without care. It will leave him with a limp for the rest of his life, still he says, 'I will not do a woman's work.'

Each evening Prem is there by the bandit's side, soothing his hair through the bars or bathing his eyes with a wet cloth, scurrying away like a cockroach at the sound of Asmara Didi's footfall. Even she has to turn away from the injustice of the scene. And as for Gope, he too has stopped relishing the bandit's torture. The beatings are too much, seeing the bandit dead would be much easier.

But Singh Sahib remains resolutely keen. The zamindar demands the precise details of the bandit's condition and torture every day. Slowly he is beginning to recognise the true twist of Fate, which is offering him real revenge. In the bandit's actions he recognises a budding axiom, a dedication to honour that makes Honour proud.

If you want to see a real man, look at Daku Manmohan. Him I understand. His honour is the most important thing, without it he would die, just like me. What has a man got anyway, but his honour? My prisoner knows this, but not my sons. How can I bring Lokend back to govern these lands? How can I stop Ram Singh from terrorising those

that depend on us? I wish they would learn something from that man.
What a man!

What a man. Indeed.

Though the guards beat Daku Manmohan for not grinding the wheat, Singh Sahib secretly prays that the bandit will not break under torture. And the bandit doesn't disappoint him. Each day that Daku Manmohan refuses to grind the wheat is a private victory for Singh Sahib and a public victory for Honour. It is with greater and greater reluctance that Singh Sahib orders the torture of the bandit, but he can find no reason to stop.

Until the day Lokend shows up.

'Bapu, what you are doing is criminal, it is inhumane!' says Lokend, more agitated than his father has ever seen him before. The mongoose makes an appearance out of Lokend's kurta to inspect the scene; he too has never heard this tone in his master's voice before.

So finally something gets to you.

'I agree with Bapu. Now that we have the opportunity to torture him to death, I say let's do it, for all that he's done to this village,' says Ram Singh from the doorway. Neither his brother nor his father heard him come in.

The father's lip twitches at his older son; he wishes he could speak at this moment and let loose the words needed to crush him.

'All your looking can't harm me now, you old, crippled man. All this time you have tortured me like that bandit with your pathetic talk of honour.' Ram Singh remembers every silent, torn and jagged day when he yearned, first for his father's love, then his respect, and finally his approval, but he got nothing.

'Stop it, stop it, Ram Singh!' says Asmara Didi. Compromised by her weak knees, she is unable to prevent Ram Singh from entering Singh Sahib's room and making his acrid speech. Ram Singh will not be stopped today.

'You remember how I used to follow you round like a puppy dog,' the elder son's gaze hangs on tight to his father's and takes him on a journey demanding remembrance, 'until the time you beat me

because I didn't wear the correct-coloured turban. Do you remember the time you locked me up without any food because I didn't bag enough partridges? Or the time you insulted me in front of the villagers because you didn't like my method of calculating interest payments? I could go on forever, but what's the use? You probably don't remember any of these incidents. You disguised your hatred as disapproval. That I understand now. You never liked me, and you never knew why, that was your problem. Perhaps you are worse off than me, cursed to live with me when you cannot bear the sight of me. But all through that time, I loved you. It's just as well you've lost your speech, because your words have lost their power. You old, bitter man, waiting to die. Die, I say, die! Die.'

'Ram Singh, you will get out of your father's room now.' Asmara Didi has managed to get on her feet. She clamps her hand on Ram Singh's elbow and steers him toward the door. 'Out, Get out!'

Lokend rushes to his father's side, his mongoose dives deeper into the safety of his kurta. 'You know Ram Bhaia; he's a firecracker, full of explosive words.'

'Lokend, you've no more done your duty by your father than your brother has.' Finally Asmara Didi will have her say. She too won't be stopped, she knows where her loyalties lie. She may love Lokend, but she knows that his deeds are partly responsible for the enmity between his father and his brother. 'You and your good works. How far above us are you that nothing touches you? Who is your father going to leave these lands to?'

'No one, Asmara Didi. Share these lands with those who till them. These lands don't need governing.'

'What you are suggesting will leave us with anarchy.'

'Asmara Didi, I am not suggesting a political or an economic solution, I seek a spiritual solution. Open your eyes. If Bapu goes on like this he will kill Manmohan.'

'Well, that may be in both their fates. What do you care? Isn't that what you believe in? Fate. Leave everything to Fate, let Fate take charge.'

Lokend smiles. 'Yes, yes, it is, but that's only half the story. Half will never satisfy you, my mother. Yes, Fate may be in charge, but only

when we live on its level. I am talking about a step up, a chance for Bapu to create his own fate. "As the mighty air moving is rooted in the ether, so all beings rest rooted in the Eternal,'" he quotes from the *Bhagvat Gita.* 'Bapu, listen to me. Don't do this to Manmohan. Don't give him wheat to grind, give him something more difficult to do.'

The father looks up into his son's eyes. Lokend can see a tiny reflection of himself in them. There is nothing but contentment in those still, deep, old eyes. *Finally, something gets to you.*

The torture stops, not because of what Lokend or Ram Singh have said to their father, but because Singh Sahib wants to get to know Daku Manmohan, a man he considers to be moulded from the same clay as himself.

'He's calling for you, Daku Manmohan. They are going to take you to the Big House.' Prem clings to the bandit's hand, shackled behind his back in steel for the first time in many months. 'Tell me, Daku Manmohan, why are they taking you away? Are they going to kill you?'

'Go home,' urges Daku Manmohan. 'Go home.' For him, death would be a release.

'Come closer,' Asmara Didi commands Daku Manmohan.

Singh Sahib lies almost supine on his bed. He faces his prisoner.

'Singh Sahib says you don't have to grind the wheat any more.'

'I never did grind the wheat.'

'Hold your tongue, I could have it chopped off just like that.'

'Look, big sister, I am not your performing monkey. I am a prisoner. Kill me, that I understand. Torture me, that too I understand. But talk to me and I am unimpressed.'

'Huh.' She has to admire his spirit if nothing else. The complete absence of fear makes the bandit much stronger than any weapon could. 'Sit.'

Now it's the bandit's turn to be surprised.

'Not here, there at Singh Sahib's feet.' But the zamindar pats the mattress next to him with his good arm, inviting Daku Manmohan to sit as an equal.

211

'Singh Sahib –' He lifts the same arm, silencing Asmara Didi mid-sentence, and waves her off. 'But, Singh Sahib, are you sure?' She doesn't have to spell out the danger for her employer; they both know the bandit could break the cripple's neck if he wanted, even with his hands tied behind his back.

'Release me.'

'You're mad or you think me mad. Like hell I'm going to release you.'

'I choose to stay here of my own will. Now release me.'

She feels compelled to argue. 'So you can wring Singh Sahib's neck? So you can kill us all in our beds? Huh, I may be old but I am not senile yet.'

'I give you my word.'

'What is it worth to me? The word of a bandit like you.'

'My word is my life!'

Again Singh Sahib raises his good arm and points to the bandit's hands, open like flowers behind his back.

'I will do it if you say so, Singh Sahib, but I am warning you, such a man is not to be trifled with. He could have your head off your neck in a second.'

Singh Sahib waves her off, his arm obeys much too slowly for his impatience. If he could speak he would tell her to stop her rambling. He has no fear of the bandit; Daku Manmohan's word is good enough for him.

The bandit is disoriented by the zamindar's offer of dignity. His chest feels too small for thoughts, forming close to his heart for the first time in a long time. His wounds are instantly cauterised. The bandit's memory fades in patches. He looks at his captor, unexpectedly filled with gratitude. He feels like a free man. The zamindar too finds himself dreaming his own dreams, he recalls a distant conversation in snatches, words flowing freely between himself and Bibiji, his own true love.

Both men have received a charge from being with the other.

The zamindar draws out his favourite chess game from beneath his pillow.

The bandit knows what's expected of him and he lays the board

out on the bed between them. They battle out their differences, matching move for move. Both are formidable players. The familiar room becomes a new place for the crippled man. The old and tired conversations bleeding from the fissures that have plagued the zamindar's every waking and sleeping dream are at last silenced. There are no words any more, only chess, and the soft thud of a piece sacrificed in battle to a better mind.

Today the day is over quickly. Asmara Didi kept watch outside his door the whole time Daku Manmohan was inside. She listened, but heard not a word spoken.

Singh Sahib looks forward to the evenings now as eagerly as a schoolboy looks forward to the holidays. Daku Manmohan walks slowly to the Big House every evening to sit with the old man. They play chess, drink tea and laugh. Through their chess games, the two opponents begin to regard each other with a new respect.

Daku Manmohan has resolved not to hold anything back from Singh Sahib. He sees the zamindar as his equal, his conscience, his judge, his jailer, his defender . . . Each day he talks of raids, expelling the poisonous memory from his soul. He doesn't ask for forgiveness, he doesn't even ask for understanding, but for something simpler, something more primal: he asks for companionship.

The servants of the Big House have started talking openly about how the zamindar has betrayed them by befriending the bandit. It is Asmara Didi's job to silence the voices of dissension, though she can be counted amongst them. Asmara Didi has already sacked four bearers, one of them was a fourth generation servant in the Big House. He had taken off his turban and placed it at Asmara Didi's feet, saying, 'Blood and water cannot mix. It turns both to poison,' before leaving.

Asmara Didi couldn't agree more, but she has to keep up appearances. She is the only buffer between the zamindar and the outside world. Perhaps the zamindar is insane, she thinks secretly, but she knows that not to be the case. The zamindar is more lucid than he's ever been.

* * *

The moon is out of hiding, a beam knocks against the prison bars. In silent desperation he pulls into himself. At last he has something to lose, and he experiences the alien feeling of fear.

'So who won?'

'Singh Sahib, of course. It was just one bad move that decided my fate, just like in my life. But tomorrow I get a chance to do it over. Tomorrow it's another game.' Daku Manmohan gives Prem a pat on his back, locks himself in his cell and tosses the boy the key. Singh Sahib has dismissed the bandit's guards. The bandit could go free, but he chooses to live inside his minute cell with its straw mattress and tin bucket. He cleans his own cell daily and washes out his chamber pot.

'Is that all you do? Play chess all day?'

'I do all the talking, not that there is much, and Ram Singh doesn't come in any more to annoy us. That is what I miss most, my sparring with Ram Singh. But no, we don't just play chess all day.'

'So what else do you do then?' Prem has been waiting all day for him to return with a story from the Big House.

He looks at the boy. *What can I tell one so young? We talk without speaking of grand things, of brave things, of pure and clear things, of things that make a man who he is, of unchangeable things, of permanent things.* Suddenly all the talk, all the valour seems ridiculous. He laughs. 'We talk of useless things like the old days. Singh Sahib and I see the same pictures, we dream the same dreams. But how can you understand that with the legacy that people like us have bequeathed you? You must follow your Lokend Bhai's example. He is the truly honourable man.'

'Prem, Prem,' a familiar voice calls out to him.

He turns. 'Amma, what are you doing here?'

'What am I doing here? The question should be what are you still doing here, at this time of night? Whiling your time away with this thief and murderer.'

'Amma!'

'If your father could come he would have come and not me. But your father's sick.'

'Yes, I know just how sick he is. That drunken bastard! Just look

at your arms, your shoulders . . . what does he do to you every night? Wring you like a towel or hang you from the roof.' It's true, Seeta Ram is spending more time at the tents. He doesn't waste money on prostitutes, but finds that his tongue has a way with words after half a bottle of alcohol. The words make him forget the debts, but his wife doesn't. She reminds him of each paisa when he returns, so he hits her to shut her up. Lata Bai isn't Mamta, she is never hurt badly enough to relinquish her fight.

'Shut your mouth, talking about your family in front of strangers. Have you no shame?'

'This man is not a stranger. He is like a father to me. He isn't who you think he is.'

For the first time Lata Bai allows her gaze to rest on the bandit. Daku Manmohan sees the flicker of something so familiar to him that it sends a searing pain through his lungs. He can hardly breathe. 'You look so much like him,' he says to Lata Bai. 'Your brother was my best friend. He died with honour. Each day he wanted to come to see his family. He is the one who arranged Ragini's match.' It all made sense. Lata Bai had never understood why a rich family had suddenly come out of the dusty golden yonder to ask for her second daughter's hand in marriage. 'He said we would spare their family if they took Ragini. And look how it turned out. Perfect. He said she was very happy. He was going to do the same for your Mamta . . .' the name makes Prem afraid for his elder sister. As promised he has said nothing to Lata Bai. *Oh, Mamta, be safe.* '. . . the one with the birthmark, but he died in a raid before he could find a man for her. He did the right thing. You must be proud of him.'

The woman is unimpressed. 'Mohit is gone. We need you at home.'

'Mohit Bhaia? Where?'

'I don't know.' The weight of defeat drives her into a squat. 'He left last night. I suppose he went to join Jivkant.'

This is his chance to say 'and Mamta'. The burden of the secret weighs heavily on him, but he keeps quiet. First Jivkant, then Mamta and now Mohit.

'There was nothing for him here. We are indebted to that castle over there,' she points at the Big House. 'Your bapu is finished. I can't

manage the tiny field we have. And Sneha, I don't know what's eating her. No one will marry her if you don't come home.'

'No one will marry her if I *do* come home,' says Prem. 'They hate everyone associated with Daku Manmohan. Here he is, trying to redeem himself, but do you think the villagers will give him a chance? No, they won't. How can anything change like this?'

'Prem, you always did have a heart as soft as cotton wool. What can I say to you? Nothing will change, my son. We are stuck in this quagmire that gets deeper and deeper the more we struggle in it.'

'Go, Prem, go with your mother.'

'No!' She is reluctant to ask her son to join her now that the bandit has given his resounding approval.

'My sister, please listen to me. Please . . .' the prisoner pleads for something more than her attention.

'Stay then! With this murderer!' Her fury is bottomless.

She turns without a second look, knowing that hurts more than words ever could.

'I want their loans forgiven. I cannot come to you and play this game any more if you won't cancel their loans. I have a link with this family. Prem's uncle worked for me. They have paid much in their lives.'

Singh Sahib isn't about to consider the bandit's request. He doesn't hold himself responsible for Daku Manmohan's moral health. He shakes his head from side to side. No.

'Then I leave you forever.' Daku Manmohan gets up to go. 'You are no different than your thieving son. Cut from the same stone. Why did I think you would change? It is because I have changed. How foolish of me. The world is never different.'

'My, my, look at you two, huddling together. How low the mighty have sunk. Bapu, how long will you hold out? Clinging to life through this murderer? Get out of here.'

Daku Manmohan doesn't move. He has learned to ignore Ram Singh's outbursts. Inspired, he says, 'Your father has forgiven Seeta Ram's loan. There will be no more collection of interest, grain and vegetables from that farm. You leave them alone.'

Cleverly done. How can I contradict him without taking my son's side? The thought of siding with Ram Singh is so nauseating that the zamindar nods once again, this time up and down. Yes.

'Throw everything away, why don't you? Cancel all the loans. Give the Big House away while you are it. Lokend is doing it, why not everyone else in this family? Squander my inheritance, my rights . . .'

'Nothing is your right till your father dies. Perhaps he *will* cancel all debts. Perhaps he *will* give the Big House away. What then?' It has become a game. The object of the game is long lost, the players tussle purely for the displeasure they can bring to the other.

11

Mamta knows to sit upstream from her defecating brethren so she has the least amount of waste running past her in the ditch water; she can sing nearly all the songs off Mrs D'Souza's radio; and she can pick out the thrashers by the Devi temple – small boys who will hold out a handful of peanuts to a monkey, only to thrash it with a big stick when it comes to eat from their palms. She is cautiously learning to stand up for her rights, but only in the company of her peers, and never, ever, in front of Mrs D'Souza.

Mrs D'Souza is a Goan who possesses the natural exuberance of her race, fuelled by the hottest curries and at the same time calmed by the most pious prayers. Steeped in Hail Marys, Mamta's memsahib is a great one to castigate herself for every moral slight, which keeps her mostly kind to Mamta.

Mamta has made friends with most things in Mrs D'Souza's house: Baby no longer menaces her, the flush no longer barks at her, the flowers no longer bedazzle her and the photographs no longer confound her. She doesn't spend hours, nose to floor, studying the broken marble embedded in the bluish terrazzo tiles smooth as cream with wear. Now she can recognise the shapes in them from a distance: gnarled and knobby faces, racing horses through mist . . . the tiles have the wonderful ability to fit her every mood, her every idea, providing an instant image of each one of her thoughts.

Mrs D'Souza is pleased with her. She thinks she has a bargain in her sweeper, who spends two hours cleaning her house unlike the others who spent a mere forty-five minutes. Plus Baby has taken to the girl in a big way. Her coat has never looked so good, and the last time she checked, Baby did not have a single tick on her.

And yes, Mamta does have a special relationship with the dog. At first she was afraid of Baby, but that all changed the day she took the dog in her arms to cross a wide ditch. It burrowed its face in her embrace and licked her cheek. Living without love for so long, Baby's affection released a torrent of feeling in her own heart. Every now and then she is tempted to explore further from Himalaya House, because she can always rely on her companion to bring her home safe. Plus she cannot forget that it's because of Baby's food that she doesn't have constant hunger pangs.

Mamta hasn't been able to find additional work in other houses; however, more and more, Mrs D'Souza gives her errands and odd jobs to do: wash the windows, post her letters, buy the kerosene for the stove, clean the stairwell once a week, and any other job that Mrs D'Souza thinks won't compromise the status of her household if performed by a Sudra. In truth, Mrs D'Souza, being a Goan and a Christian, isn't bound by the same strict caste rules as the Hindu families in her building. She even turns a blind eye when she sees Mamta wash her hands in the kitchen sink.

Her latest audacity includes putting Mamta in charge of her dhobi clothes.

Begumpet's dhobi-ghat – exposed stones by the big drain, sticking out like dark islands in a sea of drying white sheets – is possibly one of the dirtiest places in the city. Over the years Mrs D'Souza's sheets had maintained their stretched crisp cleanliness, washed daily in the city's ooze, fragrant more with frothy bubbles of fantasy than soap. But one week the sheets came back brown with the filth of reality. That's when Mamta made her case for doing Mrs D'Souza's heavy laundry, and her mistress quickly cut the usual cascade of clothes down to a drizzle and eventually phased out her old dhobi like a bad habit.

And so Mamta has become the first female dhobi in the area.

She is learning that there is a process to picking which clothes will be washed at home and which will be given to her, the new dhobi. The system of choice may seem arbitrary to the uninitiated, but it is anything but. Clothes too heavy to lift when wet are washed by the dhobi, as is all bed linen and clothes that need starching.

Apart from the dhobi clothes, there are the extras for Cynthia, Mrs D'Souza's daughter, the girl with the promising breasts and thickly painted lips, easily the most gorgeous girl Mamta's ever seen, even more gorgeous than any Hindi movie heroine painted on any poster. The well-rounded Cynthia has no need or respect for society's rules. She thinks nothing of kicking off her four-inch wedges and offering her feet to Mamta, the untouchable, to press. Pressing feet is something Mamta knows how to do; she did that job well for her husband.

Mother and daughter fight constantly. 'Mummy, Shalimar has a sale on. They're selling the latest jeans. I've got to get a pair. A hundred rupees, Mummy, that's all I want,' she says, sashaying into the room and ignoring her mother's open arms waiting to be filled with a hug.

Of course that's enough to get Mrs D'Souza going: 'All you come home for is money. Money, money, money. How about bringing home a good report card? How about not wearing so much lipstick? How about . . .'

The mother's litany always starts off as a record of her daughter's foibles, but it ends in the larger picture: the state of India's youth, the terrible education system, the lack of respect for the old ways, culminating with the corrupt government. In the end, she appeals to Jesus to save her daughter from certain ruin.

Mamta has heard Jesus' name for so long now that she's convinced of his power. Jesus the saviour, the loving, the forgiving, the charitable . . . The everything. Jesus seems a lot more holy than her Hindu gods, who enjoy their share of human weaknesses. She rationalises that it must be because he has a lot more to do than any of her gods, whose jobs are specific like those of humans. She includes a special section in her prayers devoted entirely to him. *Please, Devi, make Jesus strong enough to grant*

each one of Memsahib's wishes, make Sahibji a great politician, and oh . . . one more thing . . . keep Baby safe. She asks nothing for herself, because she believes she has already received more than she deserves.

With extra money from her monthly stairwell cleaning and her weekly dhobi clothes on top of her regular pay and tips from Cynthia, Mamta is dreaming of saving for a future and sending money home to her mother. But first she must pay for the privileges she has received.

'Honest Mamta! Word is out that you have started a dhobi business. Careful. Your village ways won't work here. Life in the city is not as free as it seems. They'll beat you to pulp if they catch you. Everyone's job is fixed in the city. We all have our boundaries. I wouldn't try cornering someone else's salt. Mind you don't take it too far,' warns Kalu. But she won't listen, her newfound status has made Mamta a free woman, she'll do as she pleases.

They drag her from under her stair and out of the building. Kalu doesn't help or say a word as they beat her holding a hand over her mouth.

This beating is very different from that of her husband's. It isn't without reason. To her there is some satisfaction in it. She is being beaten for something she has, something she owns, something she has created with her own industry. This marvellous idea gives her strength. Through the repeated pain, she knows she will survive to wash her memsahib's heavy clothes another day.

'Don't steal our salt. This will teach you not to steal our salt.' There are four of them, she is only one, and they stop only after she has parted with most of her husband's money. She survives because she has learned to twist her body in ways that shelter its delicate parts. She looks much worse than she feels.

'I told you what would happen. I can't help you if won't listen to me. You have to stop washing Mrs D'Souza's dhobi clothes. Come on, I'll take you to the dispensary.'

Her jaw is swollen, her forehead is gashed, and her eyelid has opened up along the old wound fault line again. Her words come

out as if she is speaking from under a blanket. 'I'm not going to pay for medicine,' she says, ignoring the dhobi issue altogether.

'No, no, you don't pay, it's free.'

'Huh.' Nothing is free.

He makes her stay hidden behind a red postbox till he manages to get them a motor rickshaw; the driver wouldn't have stopped for a bleeding woman. They jump in.

'No, no, out. I'm not taking her.'

Kalu hands him an extra five-rupee note. The motor rickshaw driver quickly grabs it. Committed, he says, 'Don't make a mess. Here, take this –' and he hands Kalu a piece of newspaper. Mamta's teeth chatter as she bounces on the newspaper, clutching the piping round the edge of the plastic seat cover, refusing to lean back for comfort. Her hands, supported by arms straight as poplars, tucked between her thighs, have wrung her pallav into so many creases that the cloth has left welts on her bleeding knuckles. This is her first time in a motor rickshaw.

The driver weaves through traffic guiding the contraption with the horn as much as with the steering wheel. She closes her eyes as her motor rickshaw takes a public bus head-on, unaware that it is a game, and that both vehicles know the rules. The lumbering mechanical behemoth has right of way, regardless of signalling policeman or colour of traffic light, but equally, the motor rickshaw has every right to flex its muscle, moving out of harm's way at the last possible second.

Kalu drops her at the dispensary, in a line of women, studded with a few screaming babies and fewer token men. The babies surprise her. In Gopalpur there was no time or medicine to get the babies well. She can see the neat rows of bandages and a cupboard full of awe-inspiring medicine bottles behind the far counter.

Kalu nods and backs out of the dispensary. He doesn't have the time to sit and wait with her. Her number will come up after three hours.

'Hello, Kumari, you're back again! So which piece of furniture did you walk into today?'

'Furniture no. I fell off the cycle.'

'Fell off the cycle today. Why, that's a new one. When did you get a cycle? We have to stop giving you medicines, that's when you will learn. What is it with you lot? You work. You give him your money. He drinks it away. He beats you. You turn up here with bruises. The day you don't show up, I'll know you are dead.' Kumari swallows the woman's words.

'Put your money in the Post Office Saving Plan while you still can. Take one of those forms.'

The forms hang, poked through by a thread, nailed to the wall. Mamta notices that the woman doesn't lean forward to pull one away.

'We should put a police case on the husbands of the lot of you. But what would that serve? Huh! Tell me, what end would that serve? You'd still go back to them and produce your babies.'

'What can we do? My husband is a Sudra, he exhumes cemeteries for a living. We make a living from the dead, and that too from corpses of Muslim people. He has to work at night. They beat him if they catch him. We are worse than scum.'

'So how many children has this scum given you?'

'Eight.'

'And another one in your belly. What will you have to feed them? They aren't goats or camels, able to suck nectar out of a dry stick, they will eventually need food and jobs.'

'They are God's gift. Who will burn our bodies when we die? Who will look after us in our old age? We Hindus have to have male children.'

Why male children? A distant memory of caring words lifts its comely head: *it may be a man's country, Lata Bai, but you will get joy only from the girls.* Should she tell them?

The tin bench is so comfortable that Mamta falls into a deep sleep.

'Next!'

Someone pokes her in an aching rib.

She knows to wake immediately. Stands right to attention, instantly alert, and runs to the counter.

'Name? Father's name? Date of Birth? Village? Don't know. That's okay. Half of you don't know where you've come from, let alone where you're going. And who hit you? Don't know. Where does it hurt? Don't know.' The woman answers her own rapid-fire questions with equally speedy answers learned over years of interviewing the battered. She adjusts the spectacles on her nose. Her eyebrows join together in the middle of her forehead in one straight line. Mamta has the urge to reach out and touch the stationary caterpillar.

'So did you also fall off a cycle?' asks Eyebrows.

'Huh?'

'Fall off a cycle. Did you also?'

'No.'

'No? What was it then?'

'No, I don't mean no, I mean yes. Yes.' Suddenly she doesn't have the will or energy to recount her story. She just wants her treatment and then to get out.

'Yes, you fell off a cycle. Very good.' She immediately adds, 'I'm telling you, leave him before it's too late. In the back. I will bandage you and give you something for the swelling.'

Mamta stays fixed to the counter, holding on with the tips of her swollen fingers.

'New, right? Don't worry, you don't have to pay. Here, we don't charge. Come to the back,' the woman repeats without a trace of softness or sentimentality. Her voice wraps round Mamta like a scratchy blanket of the worst kind of wool. Uncomfortable but welcome, it pushes her further into the dispensary. The woman's conversation pursues her like a snapping dog. 'They think I was born yesterday. "We can't do this. We can't do that. This is impossible. That is impossible." Anything is possible, I tell you, anything! I too came from the village, you hear? Anything is possible if you want to change,' says Eyebrows with the arrogance of someone who knows how the world works.

Her screed doesn't sound at all awful to Mamta. Wife beatings, who can escape them? At least in the city women work for money and they have the Post Office Saving Plan. In Gopalpur, they carry

water from four miles away and there is only the Big House that lends money for their dowries.

'She sounds bad, but she isn't. Come, let me bandage you,' says a woman in a silk sari with an oversized bindi on her forehead and a mangalsutra, the black beads of marriage, round her neck. 'Don't be afraid. I am a volunteer, I work Monday mornings.'

The volunteer, Mrs Seth, cleans her wound. The disinfectant is astringent and smarts like the bites of fire ants. The wound reveals itself, a straight clean slice that requires stitches. The volunteer runs to the front: only Eyebrows can stitch wounds. Mamta passes from Mrs Seth's hands into Eyebrows', who puts in three stitches on her forehead, then passes her back to Mrs Seth again. Mrs Seth bandages her forehead and finally places a single plaster across her eyelid.

Eyebrows confronts Mamta again. 'Take these. One every four hours. Don't miss a single dose. I give medicines here every day, that's only one half of the story, the other half is the taking part. Some of these women are so stupid, they feed their medicines to sick relatives or their babies. These pills are for you and you alone. They will make someone else sick. Every four hours, do you hear? Children?'

Mamta nods from side to side, the definite nod of the No.

'Good. Now don't become one of them. Producing child after child and old at thirty,' she says as Mamta turns to leave.

Minutes out of the dispensary, she takes off her bandage and rolls it carefully into a ball: she'll keep it for tying her bedroll. Pulling her hair over her stitches she then attacks the plaster, ripping it off, taking a few eyelashes with it and making her cut bleed again. The sticky bit isn't sticky enough to be useful any more. She throws it into the gutter, and looks at the bus number that the volunteer inked into her hand. She has learned to climb into any bus, fast or slow, crowded or overcrowded.

Her bus arrives carrying its own message: a family of four is painted on its side, an advertisement for family planning. Instead of stopping, it speeds up at the bus stop, taking its model-sized family with it. She leaps on to the next bus, desperately throwing herself towards the stairs as a champion swimmer might launch

himself off the starting block into water. This is the only way to get on a bus that would be overcrowded even if three-quarters of the people were taken off it. No one takes any notice of her, with her swollen eye and droplets of blood strung down her blouse. She wraps her sari round her tightly, even then, she can feel her neighbour's thighs seeking the sensual warmth of her hips. She looks up to see an oily face filled with acne, a stiff hairdo and loose limbs. He smiles showing her his broken teeth. She shows him her bloodstains in return. It is only then that he starts to avoid her rigorously, gyrating through the thick crowd friskily enough to make breathing diffi- cult, moving closer to the next woman, who shouts at him, 'Keep your distance!' and elbows him in the ribs.

She won't give up washing the sheets and towels. She will just find another place to do it. She's paid off those who beat her that morning. They won't return.

Mamta lets herself in with the house key. Slowly turning it in the lock till she hears the familiar and satisfying click. Mrs D'Souza had to give it to her months ago, when she was feeling so unwell that she couldn't get out of bed. She hadn't taken the key back when she got better, instead she'd kept an eye on Mamta for months, testing her, hiding behind the curtain watching every move she made after she entered the house. So months later, passing each and every one of Mrs D'Souza's tests, Mamta still has the key. Unknown to her, Mrs D'Souza still conducts surprise checks, hiding behind the curtain, sometimes tempted to shout boo at her servant, but instead she watches Mamta silently as she diligently cleans and cleans, only coming out of hiding when she hears the door click behind her sweeper.

Carefree laughter, light as a smell, propels giggle-driven air her way, loud enough to enter the neighbours' flats uninvited, unrequited. She advances with caution. Then she sees them, lounging in Cynthia's plastic-infested room. Entwined. Privy to something so illicit, her energies are immediately distracted by useless things. She sees the mesmerising rhinestone heart dangling on Cynthia's favourite stuffed dog, so realistic with hair falling into its eyes. She sees the crack clearly,

running up Cynthia's wall, and then down, down, down, diving behind a boy. A boy who has stayed too long. The teenagers cling to each other.

Mamta says nothing. Then the bell rings, the tweet of some untameable bird. Irony of ironies, the servant has the key, but the mistress doesn't. 'Cynthiaji,' she hisses.

Needing to rescue Love, Cynthia pushes him behind the curtain. The same one Mrs D'Souza has used as her hideaway innumerable times. The teenagers squeeze their entwined fingers once again tightly enough for residual pain, quickly securing their unfinished business for a generous serving in a safer setting, and then the boy disappears out of sight.

The bell rings again. This time Mamta answers the door.

'Hello, Ma.' Cynthia hugs her mother, whose eyebrows shoot up into her hairline with surprise.

'My, my, hello, my precious daughter,' says Mrs D'Souza, with grateful surprise. 'Here's a hundred rupees, go get your jeans.'

'That's okay, Ma.'

'Mrs Nath from downstairs wanted you to look in when you returned.' Cynthia looks at Mamta, impressed by how easily the lie slides off her untouchable tongue.

'Mrs Nath?' Mrs D'Souza is incredulous. Mrs Nath is the one who throws her garbage out on the street from her back window, and yet maintains the most airs and graces in the building: drinking tea with her little finger crowned with a bright pink nail extended to the sky, and pruning the solitary rose bush on her balcony from under the lacy shade of her embroidered parasol. Mamta has seen her little black servant boy tip a bucket of kitchen slime over the sill to tumble down in a nauseating cascade. No one mentions the muck, but people are fed up with having to skirt garbage all day and afraid that one day it will land on their heads. Mrs Nath got her comeuppance last week when her late husband's family came to visit from Haryana. They played cards all day and never flushed the toilet, and were probably the biggest contributors to the stair-well's filth. The stink that travelled right up the staircase into Mrs D'Souza's flat was unbearable.

'Oh, stop jabbering away to glory, Mrs Nath said it was urgent. Must be about the garbage,' says Cynthia eagerly.

'No time for a cup of tea before I go?'

'No, definitely not,' daughter and sweeper say together, leaving no room for argument.

'What happened to you? Did you get hurt?' Mrs D'Souza finally notices Mamta's swollen eye.

'She said it was urgent,' Cynthia reminds her mother, thankfully freeing Mamta from explaining her wounds.

Mrs D'Souza goes to the floor below to find Mrs Nath's door locked. The boy manages to escape upstairs and when he hears mother and daughter talking again, he leaps down the stairs three at a time, still savouring the taste of Cynthia.

'Promise you won't tell Mummy!' Having witnessed their intimacy, Mamta has an illusory upper-hand over her employer's daughter. 'Promise me!'

Had she been just any sweeper, Cynthia would have threatened her with dismissal, instead she cajoles her like a family member.

Mamta has become indispensable since Mrs D'Souza firmly relinquished certain aspects of the household to her. 'Promise me!' Cynthia is about to shake her into submission and physically extract the promise she wants. Mamta stands her ground. Somehow she knows this is the turning point in their relationship. 'Go on! Promise me!'

Mamta will never know why she said what she said next. 'Okay, but I want you to do something for me then. I want to send money to my mother, and a letter too. Every payday I will send a letter, but ever other payday I will send money. You must write this letter for me.' How else can she do it in this city where no one looks into your eyes?

'Is that all? And then you won't tell Ma about Vikram?'

'Yes, that's all and I won't tell Memsahib.' Mamta is well aware that her bargain would not receive her employer's approval. 'But, you two cannot do anything bad. Promise me you won't do anything bad.'

'We won't do anything bad, I promise, nothing bad.'

'Okay then, once a week.'

'No, twice a week. I'll die if I don't see him twice a week.'

'Once a week, and you'll sign your name on the letter.'

'You mean send the letter as if it's from me.'

'Yes, exactly.' It is a spontaneous act. She will have to pick her explanations carefully. He must not find her. The template of cruelty jumps into her vision again. This time she is not frightened, just determined. Yes, she will send money to her mother, she won't abandon them the way Jivkant did. She knows it will be dangerous, she will have to weave truth with lies, fantasy with reality to fabricate a life in which she is not a runaway, but one of those industrious village wives who has come to the city to fend for herself and her family with the consent of her husband. There are a few of those in every village, and they are both pitied and envied, pitied because everyone knows they are not 'true' wives, their husbands satisfying their carnal pleasures elsewhere, and envied because they are free.

'Don't worry, I'll make Amma understand it's from me.' Mamta isn't sure how much she can tell this soft city girl. She is afraid to shock Cynthia, to jar her warm innocence with the cruel reality of her disastrous marriage, her operation and running away. 'You must write it in Hindi. In Gopalpur people only understand Hindi.' Cynthia studies in a Catholic school where Hindi is the second language.

'Hindi? My Hindi is so bad.'

'Doesn't matter.'

'What about the money order?'

'That will be from you also.' It is time to tell the girl something about her past life. She knows her lie will meet with Cynthia's envy and approval. 'See, Cynthiaji, I came to the city to earn my own living against everyone's wishes. Actually, if you want to know the truth, I ran away . . .' Secure enough now in her job to let this secret go.

'You ran away?' She hears the predicted envy in Cynthia's gasp.

'Yes, I ran away. My amma had a hard time finding someone for me to marry because of my age,' says Mamta, mixing some truth in with the lies.

'Well, I won't be married till I am good and ready, and I will make sure he won't want me wearing saris all day. He's going to accept me as I am. I'll tell you this much, I am going to work in an advertising agency straight after school. Daddy's brother has an agency and he will give me a job.' The conversation moves to Cynthia, as it always does, but Mamta doesn't mind. The girl's life fascinates her. She is almost the same age as Mamta and still such a child in so many ways. Cynthia asks, 'So why are you sending money home?'

How can she explain the reason? Mamta's eyes shine with emotion, and it is Cynthia who looks away. 'I want my amma to know that I am happy and safe here in the city. I don't want her to worry about me any more.'

And thus Cynthia agrees to write Mamta's letters for her in return for the boy being allowed in once a week, but no clothes-off business. They both agree that the door to Cynthia's room will be left wide open. Still the lovers manage to get in enough grinding and feeling without detection.

All her letters will be about the city. But the first one, the hardest to write, will let her mother know that she is safe, living decently and earning, without telling her anything more about her life.

My Beloved Lata Bai, Namaste,
I am writing to you from Begumpet city. I have sent you one hundred and fifty rupees by money order. I will send you more whenever I can. I hope Shanti is well. I still have the lock of hair we cut from her head together. I hope Sneha is well and so are Prem and Mohit. What news of Ragini? I have a good job and a good memsahib . . .

By reading this much her mother will surely know that the letter is from her.

This place recognises no seasons and there is a lot of food to eat. It may be getting to summer, but you can still buy peas and

230

spinach, squash and cauliflower in the shops. I am still eating
apples and oranges in summer, can you imagine?

'You are writing this to your mother?' Cynthia chews the end of
her pen.

'Yes, she won't believe it!' Mamta giggles. 'The trees over there
are only producing mangoes. But here, your amma never changes
her menu. Rain, cold or heat, she eats what she wants. In Gopalpur,
it was spinach for months, wild mangoes for a whole season, or
cauliflower all three meals.'

This is what confuses Mamta the most. City time. Magnificently
elastic, making everything easy. How long did it take her to cook a
meal in the village? Sometimes as much as two hours. How long did
it take to eat the food in the village? Ten minutes. Here Mrs D'Souza
spends at least as much time eating her food as she does preparing it.

The mango must be in fruit in Gopalpur. Tell Prem and Mohit
to leave some on the trees for me for when I return.

 In this city everything is sold as powder: sugar, salt, spices,
everything. You can't imagine how quickly I can cook a meal.
And there are buckets too, light and airy, in any colour you
could want.

'Surely your mother won't be interested in *this* useless information?'

'This isn't useless information, Cynthiaji, my amma will be
stunned. Such things as powdered sugar or salt, or buckets made of
plastic would change her life. The clay pots we carry from the well
are so heavy. Imagine if we had two plastic buckets instead! Oh, and
I mustn't forget the ice. Tell her I've tasted ice. And tell her about
taps . . .' Cynthia moves her pen across the blue paper of the inland
letter form, writing about ice and taps.

I promise I'll send you a bucket with someone going to Gopalpur.
And I ride about on a bright blue bus all day. I am sure Jivkant
caught just such a bus to the city.

231

'Should I tell her about the movie? Or do you think she'll think me wasteful?'

'Wasteful?'

'We don't have a cinema in Gopalpur,' says Mamta, picturing the Rivoli cinema cum auditorium with its cake-decoration plaster, small balconies that stick out like bad teeth and red velvet chairs.

'No cinema? I couldn't do without the cinema.'

The movie at Rivoli had started with a drum roll. Then the elegant red curtain, moulded in beautiful loops, began its slow journey into the ceiling. Mamta had never sweated so much with anticipation, not even on her wedding night. 'Hai, what a movie!'

'Hindi movies are so unrealistic. What nonsense, showing all those flocks of birds flying into the skies or roses opening to dewdrops or lovely mountain scenery to mean that the hero is kissing the heroine. As if people really dance and sing when they are in love . . . and that too only in snowy hill stations! In English movies they show all that stuff . . .' Cynthia drops her voice. 'And in A movies they show even more . . .'

'Cynthiaji, it was *such* a great movie, I can't tell you.' Even now the memory is just too sweet, something akin to a first secret love. The hero's brooding eyes had caught her off-guard, she didn't know it was possible to become infatuated so thoroughly. She'd lined up to use the Rivoli WC during the interval, climbing up to squat on the Bakelite seat of a ceramic commode for the first time. The patriotic film had ended with the national anthem, and she'd stood still with the rest of the audience, sharing in the great sound, her heart bursting with pride for the flag fluttering on the big screen.

The folks from the delicate curved balconies of Rivoli got to leave first, their velvet chairs closing upon themselves with synchronised sounds like so many soft slaps on cheeks. Then it was the turn of the ones from the Lower Seating Middle Row, and finally her turn, seated in the Lower Seating Front Row. She was felt up by at least two men before she broke out into the starry night, but all in all it had been worth it.

'I could see a movie every day,' says Cynthia.

So could I. 'No, let's not write about the movie; Amma will think

only of the money I spent on the ticket. Let's tell her about the dispensary instead.'

And there is a free dispensary. Yes, here it is really free and they give out forms for storing your money in a post office. Don't worry, it's perfectly safe. I have started saving my money now, and who knows I may even have enough some day to buy my own piece of land. Intuitively, Mamta is a saver.

'Actually, don't write that. Cut it out,' she says, afraid of the words which go against every grain of Gopalpur society. But Cynthia is not about to be deterred in her task. Now at last this is a piece of information worthy of appearing in a letter. She pretends to cross out the words.

My mistress is very kind. I also have a good friend, her name is Baby. I'll write more next time when I am sure you are receiving my letters.
 Your loving Cynthia D'Souza

It was Nathu's daughter who first brought her the news at the well. 'Come quick, Lala is looking for you,' she said. Lata Bai didn't look up from her pitcher out of respect for Lala Ram's wife, taking no notice of the vulgar woman with the big dangly breasts who openly flaunted her status as Lala Ram's mistress.

'Lata Bai, don't act so coy, it's a money order. But of course if you don't want to pick it up, I can tell Lala to send it back to the city.'

Lata Bai hurried to Saraswati Stores in the rain to claim her good news, her empty pitcher banging against her legs without slowing her down. Lala Ram pulled out an official-looking piece of paper streaked with carbon marks from a purse dangling close to his heart like a necklace. 'From Begumpet,' he said, handing it to her.

In her confusion, she asked, 'Who?'

'From the city. Begumpet.' Then he peered at it to try to read the name: 'Chinta. D-Susa. Who's Chinta?'

'Give it here —' She plucked the money order from his hands before he could read another word.

'The post comes twice a week. Cash it with the postman on Monday, that's two days from now in the afternoon.' He enunciated his words very carefully and shouted them at Lata Bai, explaining to her as if she was a deaf mute who had to lip-read. 'Chinta D-Susa. I wish we all had a Chinta D-Susa in our lives.'

'I knew it. I knew he would send us money,' she said, crediting the money order automatically to Jivkant. 'I knew he wouldn't let us down.' She hurried away, clutching the money order inside her blouse. That was its destiny, to move from one heart-space to another.

For two days that piece of paper tucked between her breasts has heard her beating heart. Inside her there is the certainty that the money order is not from Jivkant. He would have put his own name down had he sent her anything. Who is this wonderful Chinta D-Susa, Lakshmi incarnate, someone who has showered her with good fortune? She rolls the name Chinta D-Susa around on her tongue, trying to get used to its awkward sound: Chinta D-Susa. *Thank you, Devi. Jai ho Devi, Devi jai ho.*

She almost can't stand the wait. How much money is in that paper? She looks at the money order, hoping to find something in the letters that might set her at rest, but she can't make anything of the symbols. From the numbers she can tell that there is a fifteen involved and a two joined together with a four. One of the numbers is the date, the other the amount Mamta sent to her mother. It is when she cashes the money order that she knows which one is which.

The postman pays her in dirty ten-rupee notes and one-rupee coins, the denominations he has the most use for in his job. He keeps five rupees for himself, both as a fee for his part in the deal and as a gift to himself in acknowledgement of Lata Bai's good fortune. Then he says, 'I have something else here,' holding out a letter. He reads it only when she parts with another two rupees.

My Beloved Lata Bai, Namaste,
I am writing to you from Begumpet city. I have sent you one
hundred and fifty rupees by money order. I will send you more

234

whenever I can. I hope Shanti is well. I still have the lock of
hair we cut from her head together . . .

She still remembers cutting her baby's hair. How could this Chinta
D-Susa person know about Shanti's hair? She'd cut off a lock and
pressed it into Mamta's hand before her wedding. So what has Chinta
D-Susa got to do with it?

The postman reads on: . . . *I hope Sneha is well and so are Prem*
and Mohit. What news of Ragini? I have a good job and a good
memsahib . . .

Sneha . . . Prem . . . Mohit . . . Ragini? This Chinta D-Susa seems
to know all about her family and her household. She misses the
rest of the words. Suddenly the puzzle is solved. She breathes in
sharply. Chinta D-Susa – Mamta? Mamta – Chinta D-Susa? Not
from Jivkant, or from some mysterious Lakshmi named Chinta
D-Susa, but her own Mamta? *Mamta in the city? Has the family*
moved to the city? Why is Mamta using another name now? She has
been without Mamta's voice for so long that she finds herself almost
answering her daughter's questions aloud in the postman's presence.
Oh, what shall I tell you about Sneha? Poor skinny Sneha, with no
offers of marriage. And Mohit? He's gone away too. 'Read on, Bhaia,
read on,' she says.

> . . . *there is a lot of food to eat. It may be getting to summer,*
> *but you can still buy peas and spinach, squash and cauli-*
> *flower in the shops. This place recognises no seasons. I am*
> *still eating apples and oranges in summer, can you*
> *imagine?*
>
> *The mango must be in fruit in Gopalpur. Tell Prem and*
> *Mohit to leave some on the trees for me for when I return.*
>
> *In this city everything is sold as powder: sugar, salt, spices*
> *. . . I have started saving my money now, and who knows I*
> *may even have enough some day to buy my own piece of land.*

'This is from a girl no? Look at what she says. Might even buy
some land. Buy some land, indeed! Where do you find these people,

Lata Bai, their ideas too big for their own good? If she was from around here, there would be no saving, the money would be going where it belonged, to her husband, so *he* could buy them a piece of land. I am a postman, and I've never heard of money being stored in a post office – and I would know.'

'Read on, Postmanji, let us see what other silliness she has to share with us.' Outwardly Lata Bai mocks the letter, but inwardly she shudders.

My mistress is very kind. I also have a good friend, her name is Baby. I'll write more next time when I am sure you are receiving my letters.
 Your loving, Cynthia D'Souza

The postman looks at Lata Bai, wringing his upper lip. 'You sure this letter is for you? Let me see –'

This time she plucks the letter right out of his hands, 'It's for me, all right,' she says.

The postman snatches the letter back. Clearly it is a valuable document, linked to the money orders, could be something more in it for him yet. 'Let me see the address. You're right, it is for you. But Chinta D-Susa, who is she? From Begumpet? Your daughter?'

'My friend's daughter.'

The up-down movement of his eyebrows tells her he doesn't believe her one bit. 'Tell her what I said about storing her money in a post office.'

Lata Bai's confusion has no answers, but it is quelled by the relief of the money. She doesn't dare ask her daughter what she is doing in the city. Too many questions can lead to far too painful a truth. Instead, she rationalises that at least Mamta's letters are cheerful. Some puzzles are just not meant to be solved.

Lata Bai has been very careful not to show any sign of Mamta's money to Seeta Ram. Outwardly her life goes on as before, but she is daring to dream some dreams. Already big plans are forming in her head, plans for Prem's education, for embroidery needles and

thread for Sneha, for Mohit's apprenticeship with the jaggery-maker when he returns home, and pickling jars for herself. In the meanwhile, the notes lie safe, stitched into her blanket.

She is looking forward to many long letters from her daughter, filled with stories of city life, stories such as she's never heard before, stories that some day she might repeat to Kamla and others, stories that will set her free. In the meantime, she waits for the anvil to drop because she knows that the money must be paid for. Nothing is free, this much Lata Bai can guarantee.

But must it be Shanti who pays for her good fortune?

What should she do with Shanti? *Oh, Mamta, what should I do about Shanti? Oh, Devi, what should I do about Shanti?*

Always able to stretch a meal, or a rupee into a concept, she knows with the calculated accuracy of one who has done the arithmetic over and over again that it may not be possible to save her baby daughter. What if she were to give her more food? Even then she wouldn't last. The free mobile government clinic that parks at the Big House to no fixed timetable isn't free like Mamta's city clinic. The clerk has to be bribed to dispense medicines. She's already been to Asmara Didi who'd thrown up her hands in defeat. 'I would help if I could, anything for Prem's sister, but she was born sickly. Her insides are rotting. Only Devi can save her.' But Lata Bai can't let it be entirely up to Devi.

Each time Shanti gasps, Lata Bai tries to console herself with thoughts of the next life, but this life keeps tugging for attention.

'Where have you come from? What is your name? Who are you?' She repeats the mantra in her daughter's ear. She'd forgotten to do that in her birth pain, and now Shanti is being dragged away from her bit by bit every day.

'Where have you come from? What is your name? Who are you? Don't go, don't leave.

'You are Veda Asi,' the mother whispers her daughter's eternal name into her ear. 'Veda Asi, immortal knowledge. Your earthly, passing name is Shanti, but you will be forever Veda Asi.

'Shanti, relinquish your past life, come into this one.' A dying

child is a sure sign that it remembers its past life and yearns to go back to it, passing through the twilight of death as it does. Did Shanti ever have any peace in this life? 'Forgive me, Shanti, forgive your mother.'

She discards all her plans for her healthy progeny and puts herself, heart and soul, into making Shanti better. Temples and extra food, Vedic verses and medicines, she does what is humanly possible and then has her endeavours underwritten by religious rites. But the child's heart isn't in it, and by the time the third money order arrives, Shanti is dead.

Lata Bai looks with disbelief at the body of her toddler slowly turning blue in her arms. A long low cat-moan comes out of her mouth and she can hardly breathe. She rocks to and fro like she did when Shanti suckled at her breast, smoothing her hair and singing to her softly. Kamla rushes over when Sneha brings her the news. But Lata Bai refuses to be consoled.

Grief in these parts is usually a private thing, especially for a baby girl. Her husband would never sanction the time for a fuss over the death of Shanti, a burden, someone else's garden. Lata Bai swallows her sorrow which swells in her belly like a growing embryo. She absents herself from life, and takes on the burden of guilt for the premature death of her daughter. How did she allow her fugitive emotion to take such a grip over her heart? How, when girls are supposed to be dispensable, did Devi dare to make her feel this much? For the first time she is realising that, indeed, the god-energy that governs her psyche is a female one. Devi isn't some distant goddess to be worshipped in an ancient derelict language, she is alive, and living in Lata Bai's breast; it is she who brings the tears to her eyes, and it is she who whispers 'I understand' in her ear.

She prays to Devi, propitiating each manifestation in turn. 'Hey! Kali Mata, black goddess, destroyer of all evil, maker of new cosmic energy, all fear and obey you, even Yamraj bows before you. Accept my daughter Shanti and teach her the lessons of Eternity. Hey! Varahi Mata, shining goddess, giver of life, governess of the Universal Flux, no one but you understands the perfect cycle of life. Accept my daughter Shanti and teach her the lessons of Time. Hey, Aindri Mata,

grace, wisdom and beauty are yours. Hold my daughter Shanti to your heart, take her one step closer to enlightenment, to live in that place that we call transitory heaven. Hey, Vaishnavi Mata, all sustenance, all perfection are mere reflections of your reflection. Accept my daughter in her manifestation as Shanti, promise her a better birth, bring her to the door of deliverance. Hey, Maheshvari Mata, cosmic order, infinity, you are the keeper of the cycle. Accept my daughter Shanti, let her realise her fate, free her from karma. Hey, Kumari Mata, mother of beauty and harmony. Accept my daughter Shanti, teach her to relinquish action. Hey, Lakshmi Mata, benevolent, giving mother. Accept my daughter Shanti, support her with your grace and strength as she searches for her true self inseparable from the Universal Soul. Hey, Ishvari Mata, mother of pure reflection. Accept my daughter Shanti, dispel every iota of ignorance that might hinder her journey to commune with Truth. Hey, Brahmi Mata, mother of divine speech. Accept my daughter Shanti and let her realise the immutable sound that knows no duality. Let her find you, One and All, and be joined with you, One and All, for all eternity. Ohm. Ohm. Ohm.'

The sages tell us that cosmic truths reveal themselves to us at certain times in our lives, the clearest revelation being at the time of death of a beloved. For a brief moment, holding her dead child in her arms, Lata Bai feels one with the universe.

Now more than ever she wants to tell Mamta, but she won't say a word about Shanti. Mamta is so far away, working so hard, what's the use of breaking her heart too?

My beloved Chinta D-Susa,
Thank you for the money you are sending, I can't tell you
how much you have helped us. Mamta's father is sick and it
helps to pay for his medicines. Thank you. I hope you are
looking after yourself. I want you to have a good life. Prem has
a permanent job at the Big House now, and Lokend Bhai, our
great zamindar's son, is very kind to him. It is his responsibility
to guard Daku Manmohan. Singh Sahib has moved him to a
jail on his own property. At last Gopalpur is satisfied. At least

239

*that's what the villagers say, but I think not. That man should
see the inside of a real prison, but Prem says he is a good man.
I suppose, with this wonderful luck that you have bestowed on
me I should start looking for the good in every man. Thank you.*

*The summer here is fine, and the mango is in fruit. I must
start pickling soon, but there is no one to collect the mangoes or
the tamarinds for me. We are hoping that the wind will be kind
this time, I don't know if Sneha and I can replace the roof by
ourselves. That is if Sneha is still unmarried by the time the big
wind comes.*

*Now my final duty is to find a husband for her. Should you
see someone suitable in the city, be sure to send him to us! I pray
daily to Devi for a good husband for her.*

*But tell me about yourself and your husband. Have you any
children? I long to hear about a little one. We still haven't heard
from Jivkant since he left. Perhaps he is in your city. If you meet
him tell him Mamta's father thinks of him all the time. I am
deeply worried about Mohit. He too left for the city just like
Jivkant. You must look out for those boys.*

May God keep you happy, your loving Lata Bai

Mamta makes Cynthia reread Lata Bai's letter out loud four times,
each time asking the girl to skip the husband and children part. The
mention of Lokend's name has her all aflutter. As long as she has
him . . . albeit unilaterally, she is safe, she needs no acknowledge-
ment of her devotion, and expects none from someone so above
her in every way. As such, he is her precious amulet, put away in a
safe place closest to her being.

Immediately she dictates a reply. She must squelch the need for
information swiftly and conclusively. There must be no more talk
of her husband or her unborn.

My dear Lata Bai,
*Please send me more news of Prem and his important job in the
Big House. Is Daku Manmohan as brave and handsome as
ever? All the village girls were mad for him, even more so than*

Guru Dutt, if you can imagine that. I might as well tell you that I have seen the inside of a cinema hall and it is wonderful. But you need not worry; I won't be doing that again, as I am saving every rupee I earn.

Also don't worry about Sneha, I am sure there is someone waiting to marry her, and will come to get her soon.

Her optimism is for her mother's benefit, she knows first-hand how hard it is to find a husband.

Lokend Bhai is a big hero here in Begumpet. [She cannot resist saying his name out loud.] *His posters are plastered all over the city. It is quite a good likeness. They say he is going to become a Netaji and do wonders for our city. You tell Prem to tell Lokend Bhai that we are waiting for him here in Begumpet. Tell him we need him here, and that we pray for him every day. And what about you? You never send me any news of you and Shanti.*

'I have a baby sister, she must be walking by now,' she says to Cynthia D'Souza.

Tell me about the well. Is there still water in it? Do you still meet Kamla Masi?

Her letter is filled with questions.

'Do you miss your mother?' asks Cynthia, unexpectedly reading her thoughts.

'Yes, I do, but my life is here, with you all, Cynthiaji. Please write on:

What about the bandit raids? Have they stopped now that Daku Manmohan is in prison?'

'Bandits?' the city girl can't believe real bandits exist, she's never heard of such a thing.

'Yes, Cynthiaji, they were terrible in my amma's time. Now they have surrendered and the chief is in jail in Gopalpur. All the girls were in love him.'

'Yes . . .' the city girl licks her lips.

'And what's to tell? My brother guards the chief bandit Daku Manmohan, handsome as a film hero, in his cell at the Big House.'

'Gosh, your life sounds so exciting.'

'It's just life when you are living it. It's yours that sounds exciting to me.'

I will go and see my lady doctor, the one I met at the dispensary, next week to start putting away money in the post office. Men and women are allowed to do that. It's so different here in the city, you can do what you like. Everyone is so rich, they don't care for rules like they do in the village. That's why Jivkant and Mohit left for the city. Don't worry, I will look for them.

With deep respect, Cynthia D'Souza

May is ripped from every calendar. The season has started to change. The heat is suffocating. In the village she would be picking wild mangoes off trees. She was such a good climber that she always managed to get the most. There is nothing in the city like those round mangoes, sour enough to put one's teeth on edge.

She has begun dreaming dreams of going back home. The two things she'll take home are plastic buckets – two of them – and powdered salt. Plastic! Already Mamta has collected bits and pieces of all kinds. Thick plastic, thin plastic, leathery plastic, rubbery plastic, scaly plastic, smooth plastic . . . on her side of the staircase. She hides it from thieves under a rotting piece of cardboard when she goes to work. Besides her monthly wage, which she puts in the Post Office Saving Plan, that plastic is the only thing of value that she owns.

Mamta has come a long way from sharing the space under the stairs with Kalu. Now she sleeps just outside Mrs D'Souza's flat, and it is habit that brings her down from time to time to chat with Kalu, add to her hoard of plastic bits, and pass on a bit of betel-leaf to

him. 'See that one, she's as spicy as a hot Kerala curry; and that Maharashtran one is saucy, like thickened coconut milk; and Shobha the Punjabin, Lord, she's sweet like a jalebi; now don't ask me to tell you about one who cleans the first-floor pots and pans, she's succulent like a fresh gulab jamun . . .' Kalu has an imaginary affair going on with every woman in the building. He's never had a woman, just like he's never tasted the food he compares them to. Kalu will have to settle for someone like herself from the ditch-side latrine.

'Arey, Kalu, shut up. Why do you compare the women with food? They're the ones who get the least of it,' says Mamta playfully. 'I'm going back upstairs, I have work to do.'

'I know about your plastic, Mamta,' he shouts at her, lifting the corner of the cardboard.

'Leave that! It's mine! It's for my mother. I will take it home when I leave.'

'What will your mother do with a broken mug or a piece of string?'

'Huh, you city types! Amma can find use in anything.'

'Arey, don't be angry, don't start fighting, come here. Come on, come back here, I have a story to tell you.' Kalu can see the change in Mamta, there is an eagerness to her gait. Mamta returns and squats beside him, staring at the floor. 'Mrs D'Souza's old sweeper also used to collect useless things when he came to the city, in his case it was fused lightbulbs. He was so excited by them that he used to pick the fused ones out of everyone's garbage and save them. He even used to wear one round his neck. He worshipped those things. Then one day he had the bright idea of planting money plants in them and he hung one up in Mrs D'Souza's bathroom window.

'You must have seen it, so tiny, full of hairy roots. He might have started a fashion, that's why every flat in Himalaya House has a money plant growing out of a hanging lightbulb in each bathroom window. Poor fellow, I wonder where he is now. I bet you he's running with the kabari-man, shouting for people's bottles and old news-papers . . .'

'. . . and fused lightbulbs,' Mamta says, giggling.

'Yes, yes, and fused lightbulbs. What's a living to some is clutter to others.'

'Well, money plants or no money plants, lightbulbs or no light-bulbs, I'm taking this plastic home.' She clutches her mother's letter in her hand. Why does she miss her life in the village so much? It brought her only pain. Is it for the familiarity of it or the chance to go back and show everyone how well she's done for herself? That's human nature. No one wants to make a good life unseen and unheard. A life unshared is a life wasted.

'See what I have written to my mother today . . .' She speaks from memory, but runs her eyes over the letter as if she is reading it. Kalu is impressed.

'*My beloved Lata Bai. Namaste. The city is a big place, but if I meet Jivkant, I will tell him to come home soon. And, if not, to write to you.* My brother Jivkant left home before the planting season years ago. That was before my wedding. He said he was going to become an engine driver. But we never heard from him again, and he didn't send Amma even one rupee. Bapu thinks he's dead, but Amma thinks he's lost in the city. Now my other brother Mohit has left to join him too. In her last letter Amma asked me to look for them.' She giggles, 'Amma has no idea of the city. She thinks you can just bump into people here like you do at the well in the village. How long have I been here, Kalu, and still I only know you and Mrs D'Souza and Cynthiaji. Find Jivkant, find Mohit – as if. They're lost, but Amma won't give up hope.

'Tomorrow is my day off, I am going to get a form for the Post Office Saving Plan from the dispensary. Shall I get you one? Then you too can start saving and change your life.'

'A form? Savings? I don't have anything to save. I don't have a fancy job like you,' he says, half joking.

Mamta jumps on the number 210 bus which takes her to the dispensary.

Eyebrows is there, shouting orders. 'Everyone who bumped into furniture today stand in this line. Those with cuts in this line . . .' The scene hasn't changed much, except for two new posters up on the wall. The smaller one is of a baby studded with dots: smallpox. In her village the afflicted were looked after by their mothers, because

244

everyone knew that mothers were the only ones immune to the disease. Mamta regards the pus-filled spots with deep concentration, committing their exact shape, size and scabbiness to memory. Every bit of city knowledge is knowledge that might save her in the village one day. Nothing is wasted. The larger poster has two pictures on it, one of a back with patches of faintly noticeable discoloration poked at with the tip of a ballpoint pen, and the other of a face with a collapsed nose. Mamta looks at the nose and touches her own beautiful bridge. Yes, her nose is lovely, but perhaps she should poke a ballpoint pen into her birthmark. She'll ask Eyebrows.

'Didi . . .' elder sister, it holds the right degree of respect.

'Your number hasn't been called, to the back.'

'But I only want a form . . .'

'To the back, wait for your number. Can't you see I'm busy? I am just one person here. Today the volunteer hasn't shown up either. So where are all these unemployed? We are supposed to have millions of them, but do you think you can get even one person to do a job when you need them to?' No answers are given. None are expected.

Feeling like an impostor amongst the wounded and dying, Mamta takes her number to wait in line.

'Side, side.' The women look up, jerked out of their reverie by the commotion. A body shows up on a stretcher covered in a sheet. It is moaning and stinking. The waiting women put their pallavs to their noses.

Eyebrows knows exactly what to make of it. She tries to throw back the sheet, but it sticks in places to the moaner. She tugs harder then gives up. The waiting women have seen enough of the burned flesh to conclude that the woman is wounded all over. 'So what was it, a cooking accident? Is she your daughter?' she asks the dazed man and woman who brought the body in.

'Yes,' they cry, 'yes, she's our unfortunate daughter.'

'Why don't you put a police case on her husband and her mother-in-law?'

'She wants to go back when she's well.'

Eyebrows laughs a disgusted laugh. 'And you don't mind that? You'd send your daughter back to the monsters who did this to her?'

'Didi, what can we do? We paid him the dowry. We have nothing left now. What should we do with her? You are educated so you can talk like this, but for us there is no choice. We are grateful that she wants to go back.'

'You see this? You all are to blame. You, you, you. I am to blame. The world is to blame. I have no pity left in me for you lot.'

'We had to bring her here. We tried to cure her, but her moans are making us mad. This happened ten days ago. Some of her burns healed, but these others, they are just too deep. We can't care for her any more. I am a shoemaker, people from our slum have stopped coming to me for shoes because of her smell. We can't survive like this. Take care of her. Please, Didi, take care of her.'

'Yes, make her well so they can take her back and finish the job,' says Eyebrows, grabbing the victim's hand, still finely decorated with fading henna pattern, the one part of her body that's escaped burning.

The parents shuffle out of the clinic, they are too tired to tangle tongues with Eyebrows any more. They leave their burned daughter, a hopeless case, in the hands of a total stranger. Their daughter will never see them again.

'I will send you to the hospital, don't worry.'

'No . . . no . . . no,' the woman can barely speak. 'No . . . hospital.' The waiting women shake their heads. They understand completely. A hospital means shame, might even mean a cure. Yes, the woman wants to go back *if* she is cured, but she doesn't want to be cured.

'You can't stay here. I can't take care of you properly,' says Eyebrows.

'No . . . please . . . plea . . .' The victim's words, released with such great effort, have no effect on Eyebrows.

'See this woman?' She shows off the patient, opening her arms wide to include her whole body. 'You can stop it. Fight it, I tell you. Why is it that such a thing can happen in our country? In a land of saints, where so many great beings have lived? Is this not the land of Gandhi, of Mahavir, of Gautam Buddha, of Kalidas, of Sudama, of Guru Nanak, of Nizammudin Chisti? Where are these saints now? Are you listening? Do you hear me?' Eyebrows is the rare type of woman who will not be numbed into silence by repeated scenes

of pain and suffering. Her mind will stay alert and she will rant to anyone who cares to listen. Some call people like her Fools, others call them Warriors. 'The sages may tell us that enlightenment is where solace lies, but in the meantime what does she do? Die slowly? Scripture cannot provide a cure; it is only a grindstone that pulverises pain, making it easier to swallow,' says Eyebrows loudly. Every woman there is compromised enough to happily settle for an easier pain to swallow. Eyebrows' face is red; in that moment she is one with the dying woman.

Then after a long time, someone says, 'The saints tell us that there is a reason for everything.' The woman is diffident with her explanation. Each one present is a speck of dust stirred up in the swirling eddy of Eyebrows' rhetoric, they are all looking for an answer, and if not an answer, then at least stillness so they may settle again. 'All this is happening to take us to the next spiritual level. It is only when things get unbearable that God comes to us. It is no coincidence that Buddha or Mahatma Gandhi or Kalidas or a million saints were born in *this* country.'

'So you think those that burn their wives are doing us a spiritual favour?'

'No . . . no,' the woman has lost her footing, she's never disagreed with anyone before, not even another woman. 'No, it isn't like that. We all have to act in the plays of our making, according to our karma. With great injustice comes great compassion, great understanding, great enlightenment.'

'Whoever told you that sold you worm-eaten wheat.'

'Then how can you explain saints like, like Buddha, like Mahavir?'

Mamta knows the answer already, otherwise how could she have come this far?

'Okay, where is the patient?' The ambulance driver and his assistant have arrived to take the moaning woman away. Eyebrows is busy bandaging someone else's arm, and doesn't look up to say goodbye.

'Next!' she shouts.

'I just wanted the forms for the Post Office Saving Plan, and oh yes, one other thing. I think I have that disease in the poster.'

247

'Leprosy?'

'Yes, on my forehead, see this red patch? You have something for it?'

This time Eyebrows laughs. A genuine laugh. 'No, you don't have leprosy. You wouldn't be able to feel your birthmark otherwise, and I can see that you feel it quite a bit. Go home, you are a lucky one. Hey! I've seen you before. You came here with a cut eyelid, right? What did you do with the stitches? Took them out yourself, did you? No bruises today, I see. Good girl,' she says as if Mamta got high marks in a very difficult exam. 'Good girl. Here, fill these out and bring them back. I'll take them to the post office for you. Can you do fifty a month?'

'Fifty?'

'Fifty rupees? Every month can you put fifty rupees in the rolling scheme?'

'Yes. I think so.'

More than a year into her service, and Mamta knows she is happier than she's ever been. She is definitely more than a sweeper now, she is a servant, the highest position she can hope to reach in this life-time. She sleeps on the landing and has stopped eating the dog's food because she gets so many leftovers from the table.

Mamta may miss the familiarity of her old life. She may even resent making her life here in Begumpet unseen and unheard, but sleeping on the floor outside the kitchen door, inhaling the smell of Baby's food with each breath and feeling Mrs D'Souza's latch-key dig into her hipbone, Mamta knows she is finally secure. If she is to look at things objectively, she'll know that her new better life has begun to heal the old bitter one.

And then there is the dispensary. She goes to the dispensary once a month to give Eyebrows her savings to place in the Post Office Saving Plan. While she's there, she cleans the dispensary's bathroom for an extra ten rupees.

Each month she tots up her mental list of all she sees: two beatings, seventeen bad beatings (hard enough to cause broken bones), innumerable venereal diseases, the odd case of leprosy, some other

confounding ailments which result in sores of all sizes, eight minor burns and four major burns. Major burns are inconvenient. The girls have. to be taken to the hospital and Eyebrows is required to go to the patient's house with a token policeman in tow.

Each time Mamta returns home, she says her prayer to Devi mentioning the sick and diseased by number. Then for good measure she bows before Mrs D'Souza's statues, repeating her prayer for the patients, this time to the Madonna.

During her third summer in the city, her husband manages to suppress his shame and borrow enough money to come looking for her in Gopalpur. 'If I catch her, she's a dead woman. Six sacks of wheat are what I want from your family. And mind that it's good wheat, not some worm-eaten grain full of chaff.'

'We will give you news if she turns up,' says Prem.

'Let her just set foot in this region, I will break her neck. I don't want her back, I just want the wheat.'

'Where are we to get wheat for you? Look at the fields, fallow. The Big House takes all our produce,' he lies. 'Can't give you wheat, can't even give you chaff.'

'Then you better start giving me some information. Tell me where she is.'

'I don't know where she is, but I will try my best to find out.' The conversation reaches an impasse, the man has to accept crumbs. 'But only if you promise to keep it quiet.'

'Keep it quiet! As if! She has disgraced Gopalpur. I will tell that fellow from Saraswati Stores what your sister has done and then the whole world will come to know. She is a runaway, no one can save her now. Not your bapu, not your amma.'

'So what did you do to her?' Prem has assessed the situation shrewdly. His time protecting Daku Manmohan has been well spent.

'You pet dog! You dare to question me? Your sister is a bitch, a worse she-dog I never saw in my life. I clothed her, fed her, and what did she do to me? How did she repay me?' For all his blustering, Mamta's husband has to leave unsatisfied. He came to find her and his money, failing which he would have settled for some wheat, but

things went worse than he expected. He is leaving empty-handed. He dare not talk about the stolen money, or about what he did to Mamta. Cut out her flesh and sold it, and she had the audacity to steal *his* money and run. Bitch!

All of Gopalpur eventually hears the news. Seeta Ram is told under the banyan tree. 'That she-devil, born to disgrace us, born to strip us naked. Your bloody daughter, a runaway. She left her husband. If I catch her, I will kill her. For me she is already dead. Dead. Dead. He should find her and slice the nose off her face. A runaway!' He assaults Lata Bai with his words.

Lata Bai has no defence. Her words are dry and dusty, a hindrance like the Gopalpur wind. She is furious, but for a different reason. Seeta Ram's anger is guided by under-the-banyan-tree rules, but Lata Bai's stems from the disappointment of disgrace. By running away Mamta has made her own rules. She has betrayed not just herself and her mother, but all womankind. Lata Bai has no option but to be equally murderously indignant with her daughter.

'All this time I thought your sister was in the city with her husband's consent. She won't last, with her husband and her bapu out to kill her, she won't last, and it will be her own fault,' she tells her remaining children.

'Amma, have you ever thought that she might have had a good reason to run away?' Prem can still hear the desperation in his sister's voice. *You must tell no one. No one.*

'A good reason to run away! Do you think I never had a good reason to run away? To leave all this –' she sweeps her arms across the horizon, encompassing and rejecting her home at the same time. 'Don't you think other women have a *good reason* to run away?' She is condescending, speaking to him from her position of the stronger sex. What does he know of endurance, or reasons to run away? He is a man, a weak man. 'But that doesn't mean we do it. Duty, Prem. Duty!' Duty is the one thing that's been dinned into their heads generation upon generation. Earthly duty, karmic duty, divine duty. It is the one (and possibly the only explanation) that justifies many things in their lives, including their place in the divine order – the

caste system. People are picked for a duty and their skills are honed over generations for that duty alone; that's why there are whole communities of mathematicians who can multiply six-digit numbers together in their heads from a very early age; and weavers whose early warp and weft acrobatics led to the unknown invention of the computer in far-off lands across the seas; and sea-children born with permanently bowed legs for their forefathers seldom having walked on land.

'Duty, she should have done her duty. We are born to perform a duty, no matter how disagreeable. To run away from your duty is to spit on our divine teachings. I deserved more for all I taught her.' Mamta's running away is a personal insult to her mother. 'Your bapu was right, I spoilt her. She should have stayed. She was married before Devi, and now to disgrace us like this . . . you with Daku Manmohan, Mohit . . . and now Mamta deserting her family. What did I do in my past lives to deserve this? You children won't be satisfied till we are drummed out of this village with shame biting our backs!' She is surprised at herself, at how much she disapproves. She is in the unfortunate position of being the one who understands but cannot accept.

Prem holds his tongue, not because he agrees with his mother, but because there is no use in prolonging the disgrace through discussion. His mother presses Mamta's letters into his hands. 'I foolishly saved these. There won't be any more coming. Go, burn these letters, I have no use for them.'

The next time Lata Bai goes to Saraswati Stores Lala Ram asks after Mamta. 'Any news of your girl? How come her husband came here looking for her?' The only reason Lala Ram doesn't know the whole story is because he was too busy to attend the under-the-banyan-tree meeting. But he will come to know, if not today, then tomorrow. But not from her.

It is all becoming clear to her, the reason Mamta hid her own name, because she was a fugitive, a runaway, just like Sharma's wife, raped and shit-smeared. Worse even than Sharma's wife, because she got away without any retribution.

251

The mother has no choice but to cash the money order to pay the postman to write a final letter to Chinta D-Susa, parting with five rupees.

> *Chinta D-Susa,*
> *Namaste!*
> *I know everything. Your people told Prem everything. Go back where you belong. Nothing can come of living in a big city like Begumpet. Why did you leave? Your mother is so ashamed of you, shirking your duty and deserting your family.*

The words are uncharacteristic of Lata Bai. Never before has she openly blamed one of her children for her own discomfort.

> *Go back, the money we can do without.*

'Lata Bai, are you sure you want to write this? If your cow is giving milk, why not drink it, Lata Bai?' She wants to kick the postman in the shins, and tell him it is none of his business, it is a matter between mother and daughter. Instead she demurely says, 'You won't understand, Postmanji.'
Everything has changed here. As you know, Mohit has gone to join Jivkant, and we haven't heard from the two of them. Shanti is dead. She wants to twist the knife. Why should she spare Mamta the sorrow when Mamta didn't spare her the disgrace? *We are still looking for someone for Sneha. Every day it gets harder to marry off my daughter. There are no offers for her, and now things are worse than ever.* Lata Bai knows no one will marry into the family of a runaway wife.

> *And Prem, he is still the important man working at the Big House, looking after a murdering bandit. Mamta's bapu is sick and I am also sick, not in my body, but in my spirit. You must go back now. It is your duty. Remember the gods, remember Devi. This is my last letter to you. Go home.*
> *Never write to me again. Never send us money again. We will not be cashing any more money orders.*

For the sake of your mother, for the sake of Devi. Go Home.
Lata Bai

This time it isn't for lack of courage that she doesn't sign Amma, but for the shame it'll bring her family.

The letter leaves the postman more disappointed than confused. He can see his own milking cow dry up before his eyes.

'Why is your mother saying all this?'

She can't bring herself to tell Cynthia the whole truth, the beatings, the kidney. She deserves it for deserting her stepdaughter, no? She left her behind, so her own mother is abandoning her now. Love for love.

'It's all right, Cynthiaji, don't worry about it, it's all right.' *Another debt repaid,* her mother's very words. Words of consolation when anything bad happened to her. *Oh, Mamta, consider it another debt repaid.*

But it is the *deserting your family* part that hurts her most, even more than her mother's diatribe. Yes, she is a deserter. In the two years she's been in Begumpet, she has managed to bury her guilt and pain under hard work and the frantic pace of the city, but she has been waiting, listening behind the door all this time for blame to show its face. And here it is, from her own mother. From that one corner from which it was least expected. It had to happen. Life was becoming too good. It was time to learn a lesson. She blames her complacency. How did she ever think herself lucky, or privileged? Maker of her own destiny?

'Read it to me again,' she says, 'one last time, please, Cynthiaji.' She never wants to forget the words. She wants to hurt as much as Lata Bai, to pay off her debt well.

It is only in the second reading that she understands the words *Shanti is dead,* and realises that she has no grief left in her for her baby sister's passing.

12

Asmara Didi discovered his body on the floor. He had slipped as he had tried to reach for the chess set. She sent a telegram to Lokend:

Bapu expired. Come home.

Ram Singh stands in the doorway greeting all the mourners with a pretence of humility, completely in command. Even Asmara Didi must take her cues from him. She has taken all morning to prepare the body.

Lokend is unchanged, calm, in white as usual. Raja runs back and forth across his shoulders eliciting suppressed laughter from the crowd. Singh Sahib's body lies on the raised divan bed in the public downstairs, his face whitened with flour. Asmara Didi put the final touches to his lips with a borrowed lipstick, the colour of ripe tomatoes, with not a very steady hand. His head is ringed with rose petals, enough to ensure that she will not make her delicious rose jam this year.

Asmara Didi wants Singh Sahib's funeral to be filled with music because he considered music to be the greatest of all arts. She has hired a rudali to coax the tears from watching eyes. An accomplished singer, she is a professional mourner who will leave nothing to chance. She starts slow and easy, swaying to her lament. Her tears

for sale, she may never cry for herself, and if she does, she will be considered tainted and no one will hire her again.

She is a good rudali, but she cannot bring Ram Singh and Lokend to tears. They both feel no grief for their dead father; one's estrangement shields him, while the other's spirituality protects him.

The whole village is here to pay its last respects, even though they held him responsible for their debts. They join in the prayers the minute they arrive, dovetailing into exactly the correct place in the Gayatri Mantra.

Asmara Didi is the only one thoroughly altered by the death. On this one occasion, the words of the *Bhagvat Gita* that held her like a life raft through her husband's untimely death – *this dweller in the body is invulnerable; therefore you should not grieve for any creature* – have let her down. Singh Sahib was more than an employer to her.

The tears glisten on her cheeks like jewels reflecting the sunlight. Her pallav blows off her head, and for some time she is lost, unconcerned with the fact that people might openly stare at her face. Then she turns her back on the mourners to fuss over Singh Sahib's body. Her hands float softly over the corpse's face as she adjusts a wisp of hair, then to the shoulders to straighten the sheet and all the way down to the toes. Her hands linger on the toes a long while, then she pulls herself together, rises, and goes into the kitchen to supervise the tea for the mourners.

The mourners coagulate into groups defined precisely by caste and sex. The upper castes stay in the house closest to the body, while the lower castes spill out over the veranda on to the steps and into the dust of Gopalpur to share the shade of the mango tree with the jeep. Many are already asleep in spite of the hymns and the rudali's chest-beating, because it isn't often that they get a break from the fields this early in the day.

Asmara Didi brings the upper-caste visitors endless cups of tea in Bibiji's good china cups, the ones with the shiny gold rim and flowers on the outside and inside. For the others, tea is served in earthenware cups which are destroyed straight after use. Some have never tasted such tea, thick with sugar, and flavoured with cardamom

and clove. They hang about all day, sipping from the earthenware till the cups all but dissolve in their hands.

Wisps of grass seed are floating in the wind. The men know the signs well, their superstitions are based on long years of observation. Come the wisps of grass seed, they start lashing down their roofs. They believe the roofs will float away to follow the seeds on their adventures, but really it is because the seeds herald a change in temperature, forcing a change in air pressure and therefore the winds.

Ram Singh stands to one side hardly participating in his father's last rites. His shaven head hasn't dulled his good looks.

He idly rotates his feet to ease the tension in his ankles – left, right, left, right – and fixes his younger brother with a stare, but looks through him to a life beyond his father. Of course Lokend will leave Gopalpur. What is there for him here? He'd left the Big House in spirit years ago. The whole estate is now conclusively in his hands. The elder brother sighs, deeply satisfied. Stilled in his impartial haste, for the first time he can ignore the world that has so plagued him; it is as if someone has switched off the tinning sound in his head after years of cacophony. There is no one to shout 'Honour before Life' at him any more.

Lokend seeks out Prem over the head of the priest and beckons to him. The boy understands and wades through the crowd, treading on fingers and toes, his ears burning with anxiety. He plucks Raja off Lokend's shoulder and stuffs him into his own kurta and runs off. The silent tableau bears testimony to their friendship.

In the group of farmers one voice whispers, 'My boy, that's my son,' with great pride. This is the first time Seeta Ram has seen exactly how close Prem really is to the members of the Big House.

Suddenly there is silence so strong that Asmara Didi urges the rudali to cry some more. The rudali smiles inwardly, extra tears mean an additional fifty rupees for her. The tabla player taps his fingers faster and harder against the twin drums at his feet, until the sound of the clay gourd resonates with his breath, and the sharper sound of the wooden gourd flutters with his pulse. The rudali sings on.

At last Lata Bai feels the tears on her cheeks. First for Shanti, the

baby who gave her so much pain at birth and then left her holding nothing. Then for Mamta, the runaway daughter who gave her so much pleasure as a young girl, but has now destabilised her so thoroughly that she honestly doesn't understand what she is feeling.

She is glad she stands apart from her husband. Tears in front of her husband for something as frivolous as sorrow? He would think them a resource wasted. Sneha sneaks a sideways glance at her mother. Her daughter's instinct has forewarned her to be discreet. Her mother's tears make her afraid for herself. Is there something there that might make her cry too?

Prem returns holding Daku Manmohan's hand, but he dare not show affection in his grip. Daku Manmohan is unrecognisably changed since the day he surrendered in front of Saraswati Stores. Luckily, few make the connection. The boy drags the bandit behind him like a man chained. The bandit understands the boundaries of their relationship. He follows. There is no strain on either's arm. Once again Seeta Ram says, 'That's my son.'

The bandit and boy join the outer circle of retainers, family and friends. Lokend beckons them closer, Daku Manmohan advances and stands by the corpse of the zamindar. The boy is no longer in the picture, not even standing on the border, he is outside the frame.

The farmers may not have reacted to the bandit in their midst, but Ram Singh will not tolerate him. 'Get rid of this man, he has no right to be here,' he whispers viciously. The boy runs back to grab Daku Manmohan's hand, and tries to escape with his ward to the outer edges of the circle. But he is cornered by Ram Singh.

'Out, out. Get out, you murderer!' As the words leave Ram Singh's lips, the crowd recognises Daku Manmohan.

The tittering starts on the women's side, chased by gruff disbelief on the men's. 'That's my boy. Fearless chap. My boy Prem,' a father's voice once again praises his son.

'Your son with that bandit? If that motherfucker was my son I would have beaten the skin off him.' Now the father is unsure of what to say. Seeta Ram is in a precarious position. In the weight of the crowd pressing round him he once again recognises the under-the-banyan-tree rules.

'Get back in your cell.'

'Ram Bhaia, he will, he will . . .' Lokend is firm as he smoothes the ruffled tone of the proceedings. 'Let him conduct the last rites. Bapu wanted him to do it. Please, respect my father,' he says loudly to those gathered. 'You have come here to bury Zamindar Singh, this man was his friend. This is a sacred time for us all.'

Coincidentally, the rudali is in her most dramatic trance, swaying and singing, her long hair thrashing to the floor with each salutation. The tabla plays faster. Her drama might save them all, the farmers are mesmerised by the creature, at once repulsive and eerie. Lokend decides to cut short the formalities and light the pyre straightaway, even though most people have not had time to pay their respects.

The Big House's servants move their employer's body from the divan and lay it over the bier, sticking out of the flat packed earth like some giant bird's nest. The rudali shrieks, 'Hai, hai,' letting loose a thick stream of ersatz tears. 'Hai, hai,' cry the mourners, whipped by the fake sadness into a more real frenzy. Every pore of Gopalpur opens to accept the sound of sorrow. 'Hai, hai,' say the people. 'Hai, hai,' the land replies.

Most fathers place their small sons on their shoulders for a better look. All of a sudden the rudali goes quiet, the tabla goes silent, the women's cue to leave. Now mothers start herding their daughters back to their farms. This is no place for women. Lata Bai pulls Sneha behind her. 'He never did anything for us, why should we shed one tear for him?' she says bitterly.

'But Prem is there . . . and, what's more, he's holding his hand,' Sneha says with envy. She still nurses her infatuation for Daku Manmohan, a man with a beautiful wife and a tragic life. There is no figure more romantic than an honourable man forced to live in a dishonourable world.

Lata Bai says nothing. She walks back to her field. Sneha follows her mother, but turns around for one last look at the body. 'We must tell Mamta,' she says. Mamta's name emerging from Sneha's mouth at exactly this time is just more proof that everything in the universe is connected.

'Mamta!' says Lata Bai. 'None of this concerns her. She has aban-
doned her family for a big-city job. She has run away. She is dead
for us. You must never speak of her again.' *One son with a bandit
and one daughter run away from her husband.*

'A big-city job. Oh, how lucky, how lucky, lucky, lucky. Oh, Amma!
The city. Can I go too?'

'Stop it! Stop it!' She shakes Sneha by the forearms. 'Don't you
start getting ideas beyond yourself. It's because of her that there are
no offers for you. As if someone would marry the sister of a runaway
wife.'

'Amma!' says Sneha. 'Don't worry, I'll stay married. Don't worry.'

'That is, if any man will have you. Mamta has strangled your
future by leaving her husband,' says Lata Bai.

'Amma?' she looks at her mother, eyes wide with betrayal. Her
mother always stood up for them.

Mothers have to be soft and hard, bitter and sweet. Lata Bai
gathers Sneha in her arms, and presses her face gently to her chest.
'Now you be a good girl,' she tells her roughly. It isn't often that
Sneha gets to feel this close to her mother. The funeral doesn't seem
that impersonal any more. She wants to cry. 'For your amma's sake,
you be a good girl. Forget about the city, it isn't for you. We will
look harder for a husband, that's all. You just get married and be a
good wife,' says Lata Bai.

The rudali stops her musical antics so the prayers can start. The
retinue of Singh Sahib's retainers shoo the little children away as
Lokend approaches the bier with a burning branch. Burning the
father's body is the eldest son's prerogative, if not duty, but Ram
Singh has made up his mind: no union, not in life, not in death.

The fire is born mature, like a god. The body catches fast and is
a surprisingly noisy thing. It's as if it sings with its last voice, the
final thread that connects it with this life.

Very quickly, the mourners cannot see the body for the flames.
The heat from the fire forces the farmers to take a step back, but
the bandit and his little companion stay standing where they are.
Prem shields his eyes and then hides his face in his folded hands.
The orange flames reflect off Daku Manmohan, turning his whole

being luminous. Singh Sahib's body sighs and clicks almost to the very end. It seems that coded messages pass between the dead man and his friend.

The bandit stands planted in the soil as firmly as the mango trees. He knows what this funeral means. It is the end of him too. He thinks of their long chess games. Neither had wanted to be alone, separated from the other in the thickening of his life. What was he to Singh Sahib? What was their connection? How can he explain the circumstances that brought him to this particular place on this exact day? Even destiny seems like a feeble excuse, there has to be more of a reason.

What if the future asks nothing more from him than just having been?

It is a time of death, he rationalises, such thoughts are bound to burble to the surface like a new brook finding a crack in turned earth. *You changed my life. If you must measure your life by some standard, know this, you changed my life.*

Lokend urges a stick into Daku Manmohan's hands and steers him towards the bier. 'Go do it,' he whispers. 'Go on,' he says.

'But . . .'

'He would have wanted you to.' Asmara Didi does not challenge Lokend.

The bandit advances with the stout stick. 'Accept his soul, oh Devi. Release us all from the bondage of rebirth.'

Asmara Didi clutches her prayer beads even tighter as Daku Manmohan tries to crack open his friend's skull with the stick. The ritual gets to her every time. The burned body starts to fracture and crumble. The head, black as a burned coconut, lolls drunkenly to one side.

Thwack! goes Daku Manmohan's stick again, but this blow is weaker than the last. The audience will stay till the end, when the skull is finally split open to set free the soul. They've seen this done many, many times before. Thwack, thwack, thwack. There is a loud crack.

The priest drops his hand like a referee giving his approval. Daku Manmohan has released his friend's soul to commune with the

Eternal. The rudali resumes her dirge. This time she sings alone; the farmers are walking back to their fields and the servants back to the Big House. Ram Singh had walked away as soon as the pyre was lit.

Then the rudali falters, she can't sustain the holy music much longer.

In that collapsed moment, the bandit starts singing. His music fulfilled the zamindar almost as much as it irked Asmara Didi. But today, they are all grateful for his song. His voice is a rivulet, racing out to meet others like itself in the voices of Asmara Didi, Lokend, the rudali and the remaining gathering of farmers, becoming first a brook, then a stream and finally a grand shining river.

> 'Oh innocent heart, oh innocent heart,
> What is your desire, what is your destiny?
> In this material world,
> You are a lost soul,
> Oh ignorant heart, oh ignorant heart,
> What is your desire, what is your destiny?'

Still singing, the bandit walks closer to the smouldering heap. His voice falls low, becoming a whisper. He sings exclusively to his friend. As the song finishes, he tosses Singh Sahib's chess set into the fiercest part of the fire. His duty complete, Daku Manmohan turns with the smooth grace of a dancer and walks back to his cell with Prem holding on even tighter to his hand.

Used to hearing her children's slightest sounds, Lata Bai senses the weeping in the hut that night. She knows that Prem is crying silently, secretly in his corner. She reaches out to touch her son's shuddering shoulder, then draws her hand back mid-mission.

Prem's shoulders shiver with each jagged breath, long and tortured, matching his thoughts, and his mother's feelings. He cries for Daku Manmohan, for his scarred back and his tiny cell; he cries for Lokend Bhai, achieving so little with such great sacrifice; he cries for Asmara Didi, coping in a mansion full of loss; he cries for Singh Sahib, for

his restless and broken spirit; he cries for Mamta, alone in the city; he cries for Lata Bai, grieving her children, both dead and alive; he cries for Sneha, without offers of marriage; he cries for Jivkant, and the disappointment he caused them; he cries for his lost brother Mohit; he cries for Gope, destroyed by the bandits; for Kanno, struck dumb by fright; for his dead baby sister Shanti, for his father, for the rudali, for the mourners, for himself.

Lata Bai wills him to stop. She doesn't want her son's sorrow to wake her husband. She feels safe only when Seeta Ram is sleeping, as she can no longer predict his actions. Seeta Ram had taken a stick to her when Lala Ram told him about the money orders. The beating was severe, the words too terrible to remember, but it was expected. What wasn't expected was that his anger would spill over to Sneha. 'Let that daughter of yours pay my share. I'll send her to the Red Bazaar. She has no offers of marriage anyway.'

Lata Bai leans towards Prem, absorbing his shudders like a buffer. By clasping the boy in her arms, she doesn't feel so alone any more, her son's tears somehow wash her own pain away. She lies immobile, considering the night, both softened and hardened by defeat. 'Go to the city,' she whispers her consent. 'Go and find your life. Take Sneha with you. There is nothing for her here.' She will no longer interfere in her children's lives, better for Sneha to go to the city than to become a prostitute.

When Prem finally stops crying, his mother gets up and goes outside to cough in peace.

The day the zamindar died, Ram Singh took over the Big House and vowed things would be different in Gopalpur from then on. Lokend granted Daku Manmohan his official freedom as he knew it to be his father's unspoken dying wish. However, once again the bandit chose to stay in his cell.

A week later his body was found on the garbage heap close to the Red Ruins. Prem went to see the corpse just to make sure it was Daku Manmohan and not someone else. His right hand was holding the black queen so tightly that the boy couldn't free it for himself. That night all across Gopalpur the village girls broke their bangles

for their saviour. Many had seen him at the funeral, and had bitten their knuckles that night for the curls in his ash-coloured hair, the light in his eyes and the straightness of his back. The finality of his murder left the village girls with an unfinished story which they concluded in their secret language of romance. Each woman had her own version: hoping to become his redeemer in the telling of his story. In time, his legend will be borne by the few who will carry the news of his chivalry to the well-side, and sustained by the many who will give him a great reputation as a man of honour.

'Now that Daku Manmohan is dead, what will I do? The village is lost to me. They see me as a traitor, where will I go? Take me to the city with you.' Prem's plea isn't just about self-preservation, it is also about forgetting the past.

'Don't worry now. Go back home to your mother,' Lokend re-assures the boy whose life has been so intrinsically scarred by association.

'Take me with you to Begumpet. My mother has agreed to let me go. The word is that you are going to become a big politician. Become a big politician for our sakes, Lokend Bhai. For me and my sister's sakes. Sneha will have to go to the Red Bazaar if I don't take her to the city. My eldest sister is already in Begumpet. You remember her, don't you? Mamta. You helped her that night.'

He can recall the scar along her side, and suddenly, the smell of buttered chapattis. It seems like yesterday. 'Yes, I remember her well.'

'Her husband came looking for her, but I said we didn't know where she was. Take me, take Sneha.'

Lokend looks into Prem's ardent eyes and pats his head. 'You are getting tall. Becoming a man. All right then, little man, we will go to the city. Get Sneha packed.' There is just one thing left for Lokend to do before he can leave for Begumpet.

'When?' Daku Manmohan's wife asks even before Lokend enters her hut. She has been so tuned in to the circumstances that would bring about his death that she knew precisely when it would happen.

'They found him this morning.' Lokend offers no solace. She must

263

stand alone. 'I see you have done more.' The steam rising off boiling pots of thickening cane juice sweetens the air. The smell of festivity doesn't fit the news.

'Yes, we sell our jaggery at Saraswati Stores now. Can't make enough of it.'

'And the embroidery?'

'Still sells in Begumpet. We have three new girls.' She is a natural-born leader, just like her husband was. She has turned the opportunity offered her into a thriving business, employing not just the wives and daughters of other bandits, but girls from the village as well. Still, she does not see the miracle in her achievement. 'Lokend Bhai, I envy you your peaceful place where no one can reach you. If you ever fall in love, you will understand. I knew I would never see him again, and yet . . .'

'There is no end in Death,' he says.

'It isn't end enough, that's the problem,' she replies. A boy comes running towards her, he is a little smaller than Prem. 'Say namaste to Lokend Bhai, your father's friend.'

'Namaste,' says the boy.

'Abhay?' The boy nods. Abhay, the fearless. His father was proud of his choice of name.

'He's gone,' she tells her son without ceremony.

'Who?'

'Your father.'

The boy doesn't know where to look, and less how to act. He should cry, he should feel something, he should . . . Lokend takes his shoulder. 'I am going to Begumpet. Would you like to come with me? You will have a friend, another boy, Prem, almost the same age as you.'

The woman says nothing. The boy steals a look at his mother for some sign of approval or otherwise. Their relationship has been distant. She did not replace the man in her life with another.

'No, I'll stay with Amma.' Again he seeks something from her, a sign that he's made the right decision. She does nothing.

Lokend pats his back. 'Abhay, remember your name,' he says, 'there is power in names. Abhay the Fearless One. Your father was

a fearless man, perhaps that's the legacy you have inherited from him.' The boy scrapes the floor with his toe, making half-moon lines, back and forth.

'Abhay, Abhay,' a voice calls out to him. Lokend and the boy look towards the voice. They both know it well.

'I'm glad you are here with them,' says Lokend.

'Taste this,' says Asmara Didi, putting a small piece of jaggery in each of the three open mouths like a mother bird feeding her fledglings, 'the next thing she's going to start is pickling.'

Dear Mamta,

There is big news in Gopalpur. Singh Sahib is dead, and Ram Singh is Gopalpur's new zamindar. Amma says things are not good. Daku Manmohan is also dead. They found his body thrown in the rubbish tip by the Red Ruins. They murdered him just one week after Singh Sahib's death. Can you imagine? The Red Ruins are now redder with the blood of grieving girls for all the bangles that were broken. I think Sneha secretly broke her bangles there also.

I don't know if Amma told you that Mohit Bhaia is in the city too. He ran away to join Jivkant Bhai. Everyone in the village knows. We haven't heard from him. Asmara Didi has moved out to live with the bandit wives. She didn't stay with Ram Singh. I too will be leaving soon. Thank God, Amma has given her blessing. I cannot stay in this place a minute longer. Everywhere I look I am reminded of that great man. He may have murdered and killed and maimed . . . he may have done many bad things, but in the end he was a good man. You have to believe that.

I will come with Lokend Bhai to the city. He is a saint. He looks after me better than Bapu ever did. Lokend Bhai is to become a big politician. Who knows, I might get a position in his office one day. I have learned to read and write thanks to Daku Manmohan, that's why I am writing this letter.

You must never give up your good job in the city. Never come back here, especially now that Bapu knows about the money orders. Bapu went quite mad when he found out that Amma

had taken all the money you sent. He beat Amma, and then started on Sneha. It is the worst for Sneha, we have no offers for her. You should see her condition, she begs at Lala Ram's for food. Though our loans are forgiven, the rains failed again, and we have no money. The thatch is gone from the roof and the floor is always wet. I know Bapu's planning to sell Sneha in the Red Bazaar soon. But I think I can save her by bringing her to the city. Amma says I am her only hope now. Sometimes I don't know what I am supposed to do. Thank God we will be coming to the city soon.

You must look out for those brothers of ours. If you see them, send them back to Amma. Please come and see our new Netaji Lokend Bhai when he comes to Begumpet,

Your loving brother,

Prem

Netaji Lokend Bhai. She can recite an opera to happiness and apprehension. The slippers, the look, the hands on her shoulders. She thought they were to remain a distant sweet memory, but the mention of his name has caused the best part of her past to spring to life. Mamta stays holding the letter. She feels a moment of pride. 'My brother wrote this letter. Can you believe that?'

'The Red Bazaar?' Cynthia D'Souza has her own questions.

'It's near the old quarter where all the tanneries are.'

'Is it bad?'

'You ask your amma about it.' Mamta doesn't elaborate.

'Oh, it's one of *those* places, is it?' She is just worldly enough to hint at the reality of prostitution. 'So what will you do about your sister?'

'Nothing. What can I do about Sneha? How can I look after her here? Where will I put her? Under the stairs?'

'Ask Mummy to help you find her a job.'

'Do you really think I should?'

'You can't let her stay in that place. Shall I write the letter?' The girl with large breasts and finely painted lips, who only eats with a spoon and fork and never anything she doesn't like, pleads on behalf of hair-slowly-turning-orange-soon-to-be-sent-to-the-Red-Bazaar Sneha.

'Yes, please write the letter. How will I send it to my brother?'

'Oh, that's easy, we'll send it care of this Lokend.'

'But he's such a big man. Why would he give Prem the letter?'

'Well, is he or isn't he a saint?'

Mamta giggles. 'All right, we'll send it to Lokend Bhai.'

Cynthia jumps straight into a cross-legged position on her bed. She writes quickly. Mamta stares up at her from her squat. She pulls Mrs D'Souza's donated sweater closer round her. The thought of becoming her sister's saviour makes her cringe.

'You'll get sick, wrapped up like that in this heat. Get sick and die before you can see your brother or your sister at the rally.' Cynthia has never understood her sweeper's aversion to wind. 'God, I hate the heat. I don't remember another year when it was this bad.' For a brief moment the girls hold the letter together at either end and peer into its heart. One smells of rose soap, the other of phenol.

The letter will arrive days after Lokend, Prem and Sneha have left for the city.

No one else in the building seems as stirred up as Mamta with the prospect of a political rally right in the heart of Begumpet, so she has made it her personal mission to round up as many people as possible to go with her. She must pick amongst her own. The rich will watch it on television.

She starts with Kalu. 'You must come and hear him speak. You will be a changed man by his words. He's from my village. I know him.'

'You mean the man who is standing against a hijra. Now that's not what I call fair play. Someone with balls standing against someone with none! The people say they will vote for the hijra because all those they've voted into power before didn't use their balls.' Kalu holds himself between his legs with two fingers to make his point; he gave up coddling Mamta's coyness ages ago. 'Maybe this time someone without balls will surprise us. Hijras are rejects of society, they have no families, with fewer mouths to feed, they won't need as much in bribes. Now that's logic even I can understand,' he says.

'Logic, phah! It's an insult to someone like Lokend Bhai. No

matter, no one will make a better politician than my Sahibji. He is a saint. He came to my wedding.' It was six months after she met Kalu that she told him she was married and a runaway. He didn't show much interest in her story then and hasn't up to now.

'Go on, making up your grand stories. Why would he come to your wedding?'

'Kalu, I'm telling the truth. He gave me a box of sweets . . . cashew barfi, the most expensive kind.' She stops. The box with the face of the goddess. *Jai ho Devi, Devi jai ho. The box I left behind with her.* The suppressed memory of a child abandoned becomes vivid again. An involuntary bleat slips from her lips.

'Not crying for our Netaji, are you?'

'Of course not!'

'Once he is elected, the bribing and corruption will start. You just watch. They all change, even the best of them.'

'No! Not him. He's a saint. He'll never change. He's helped so many people. He's dead against the dowry system. He cares for us. My brother works for him now. He made Gopalpur safe. He did so much for the victims of the bandits. He gave his lands away. Now tell me how many zamindars would do that?'

'He has given away his lands to fool people like you. Come to the city, but you still remain gullible.' He doesn't bother hiding his disappointment in Mamta. 'He's given away his lands in the hopes of earning something better. Power.'

'I don't care what you say. I'm going to tell my amma . . .' *Tell my amma,* the comforting phrase jumps to her lips before she realises that option is no longer available to her, 'about the posters that hang above the number six bus stop.' More posters have been painted by the star makers, their colours heightened to add allure to the man. Lokend Bhai's eyes hold Mamta in their gaze each time she walks past, and she hugs those eyes close like a lovesick fan.

'He has a pet mongoose that lives inside his kurta. Imagine that. Only someone saintly like him could tame a wild animal like that. I tell you, Kalu, if you tried putting a mongoose inside your kurta, it would tear your heart out.'

'Really? A mongoose?'

'Yes, and those animals are dangerous. After all, they do bite the heads off cobras.' This is how legends are created, in innocent conversation.

'A mongoose,' he says, filled with awe. The legend takes root.

'And mind you, it's a big black one, not one of those skinny ones that the snake men drag behind them like cats on a rope.' The legend becomes a myth. 'He's bringing my brother to the city with him and my sister too. Come with me to listen to his speech. Then you'll change your mind.'

At first Lokend used to return to the Big House only because his father wanted him to, then it was because Asmara Didi needed to see him, and finally it was for Daku Manmohan's sake. Now, with his father gone, Asmara Didi living with the bandits' wives, and Daku Manmohan murdered, he has no reason to return.

'Ram Bhaia, I'm going.'

'I know you think I ordered his death,' says the elder brother.

'Ram Bhaia, it is not for me to say anything. What's done is done. Forgive yourself if you feel the need.'

'It's easy for you to say that. You were his favourite. How dare you stand there and accuse me of Daku Manmohan's murder.'

Words are useless, Lokend knows. Anger swallows a man's judgement. He hugs his elder brother. 'You know I've found love to be the best protection? Well, maybe love is too strong, try liking first. Like the person you would otherwise despise, like the person you would otherwise shun, like the person you would otherwise resent. Like them, and suddenly their deeds lose their malice, their actions become full of enjoyment, full of fun, full of laughter. Do this and you know you have the Power. Do this for long enough, and you know you *are* the Power.'

'You and your lecturing, you think you have an answer for everything and everyone. Well, I'm not looking for answers, I'm not looking for sympathy . . . I just want to be heard.'

Lokend squeezes his brother close one last time. A time will come, he knows, when information will turn into knowledge with

experience, and finally into wisdom with understanding. That is the path of all evolution.

'Here is the great Lokend Bhai himself, the son of a zamindar, from a long line of illustrious nobility, but he chooses to live like a common man. Now who wouldn't trust such a face?' Mrs Sahai is an avid campaigner for the Party. Hers is a tidy story, the daughter of a national hero without enough charisma to make it to the top, she has developed a knack for spotting new candidates. Not one of her 'finds' has ever lost an election. 'Lokend Bhai –' she stresses the Bhai '– I thoroughly approve of Bhai. It has just the right ring to it. It is better than Sahib, better than Abba, better than Bapu. Bhai. Brother. Too long have politicians distanced themselves from the voter, but Bhai makes you one of them . . . brother to all people.'

All this time, people round him assumed Lokend would never enter politics, but they had their hopes, and they thought their hopes enough to fashion his destiny. Without his consent, Mrs Sahai put his name up as her party's candidate. Without his knowledge, Ram Singh announced that his younger brother was leaving Gopalpur for the city to become a big politician.

Mrs Sahai is responsible for the larger-than-life posters of Lokend in pinkish hues all over Begumpet. The very ones that have Mamta all stirred up. So how did she swing this one? The story goes that one of Lokend's grand aunts hailed from the outskirts of Begumpet. It was an important connection. The opposition tried to knock it down, but she had the papers prepared to prove that he had Begumpet blood, albeit two drops of it, flowing through his veins.

From all the candidates Mrs Sahai has found in the past, she knows this one is the most promising. His history is so compelling. Freeing the bandits first catapulted him to fame, then what he did for the bandits' families propelled him higher, but what he did for the victims of the bandits was unquestionably his crowning glory.

But what of Lokend? What has prompted him to join the Congress Party? What has brought him to this decision which forces him to mire himself in the most corrupted temporal situation imaginable? Why now, when at last he is free of the Big House, free to work

unfettered, binding himself to no one, giving help where it is needed, is he consenting to live by other's rules?

Could it be that he wants to put himself to a test? Or is it guilt? Guilt for the pain he caused, guilt for the pain he could not erase, guilt for the pain he ignored? No, it isn't a test or guilt that charges his actions, but a seeking mood that has fallen upon him like night, taking him deeper into the depths of self-exploration. He needs to know if he is a true yogi, someone who can perform action, live in the temporal, and still attain bliss.

Mrs Sahai finds him most perplexing. Sometimes he seems lost and she feels the need to wave a hand in front of his eyes. He asks the most peculiar questions and never accepts the answers for what they are. His is a strange mind that works in a mysterious way. He was very keen to meet his rival, face to face, over a cup of tea.

All of Mrs Sahai's dilly-dallying has got her nowhere. Lokend won't be deterred, he will meet his rival, the hijra Nirmala Devi, even if he has to go and find her himself. 'Now, Lokend Bhai, don't be put off by what you see. Your opponent is a hijra. What can I tell you? They make such a mockery of the election, pitting a hijra against you. I know it isn't worthy of you, but a landslide victory will convince them. You just wait and see,' she speaks to the whole city, 'make a mockery of what we stand for, will you? Make a mockery of me?'

'Oho, Mrs Sahai, leave it. Hijras are very strong people. They belong nowhere. Adversity is their lot right from birth. I bet you she is fighting fit. No matter, let's see what she has to say.'

The meeting is on neutral ground, at a teashop, and not at the Congress Party office, which Nirmala Devi's assistant refers to as that pit of snakes.

The tea arrives simultaneously with Nirmala Devi. She has on the most boisterous pink in an effort to look more womanly than the most bona fide female. Mrs Sahai wrinkles her nose. She hopes there won't be any embarrassing clapping. 'Let's keep this short,' says Mrs Sahai, poking another pin into her bun.

The two women regard each other. One thoroughly adorned, the other fastidious, almost mousy.

'Of course we will keep it short, madam. After all, my time is most valuable.' Nirmala Devi has the affectations of a silent movie actress. Mrs Sahai breathes deep, stifling her words. She is pleased that she managed to convince Lokend to leave his mongoose behind with his servant, Prem. What a combination that would have made, a richly painted hijra and a man with a mongoose up his kurta. She almost chokes on the picture.

'Lokend.' He folds his hands exactly before his heart. 'Namaste', he says.

'Namaste,' she replies without folding her hands. 'I have heard of you. You got the bandits to surrender, didn't you?'

'Yes, you could say that.'

'So where are these bandits now?'

'Daku Manmohan was murdered, his two chiefs are in jail in New Delhi, and the rest of the gang is in various jails in these parts. Except for the two chiefs, they should be out in three years. But surrendering is not what it was about. It is about making sure we don't create any more bandits.'

Nirmala Devi crosses and uncrosses her legs. Her chiffon sari, as soft as dew, climbs like a creeper over her stuffed bra. She wants to dislike her rival.

'So that's your platform, is it? No more bandits?' She sniggers broadly on the inside, her assistant sniggers visibly on the outside.

'Yes, that is my platform. No more bandits. No more thieving in any form, not by the weather, not by acts of God, not by politics or politicians, not by bureaucracy, not by society, not by custom, not by religion, not by any other man, not by industry – nor the lack of it – not by husband, not by in-law. That is my platform. No more thieving.'

'Look, don't try and deceive us with your oily tongue,' says the assistant, lashing him with her looks.

'Champa!' Nirmala Devi is appalled at her assistant's rudeness. She releases a long sigh, searching for something that will establish Lokend as a phony in her eyes.

'You know how I came to be here?' She feels the need to explain: 'I used to roam from house to house dancing for food, just like any

other hijra, threatening to show my privates at marriages and births if they didn't pay me enough to leave, and I would have gone on like that forever, if it hadn't been for one irate father of the bride who beat me hard with a stick and shoved me off his property saying, "Find a suitable job instead of peddling your filth in front of decent folk." A suitable job for a hijra? What's a suitable job for me then? I'll tell you what it is. A politician's job. The whole political system is emasculated anyway, so I don't need balls to fit in. No matter how much money I make, it cannot change what I am. I will forever be a hijra, an outcaste, and therefore, best suited to be a politician.'

She has him now. She can establish her legitimacy. 'You don't understand, do you? You family folk never do. As an outcaste I have no reason to take bribes. Who would I take the bribes for? For myself? Money won't buy me one true friend, money won't make me belong. I will have to earn people's respect, because I can never earn their love. People are afraid of hijras. They can't understand someone who willingly gives up his balls to become a she. I could have died during that operation, you know. We perform it amongst ourselves, in secret, with a razor blade and a prayer.'

Mrs Sahai is appalled at the depth and nature of the private information being shared over what should have been a formal, quick cup of tea, but she won't let on. 'Do we have to listen to your life history? Lokend Bhai doesn't have all the time in the world, you know.' She downs her tea in a single gulp, leaving no reason to stay.

'What do you think you people are?' The choice of *what* instead of *who* isn't lost on Mrs Sahai. 'At least our life history has been created by ourselves. Look, madam, every day we have to fight women like you and men like him to stay alive, so don't try and shake us with your words,' says the assistant.

'Oho, Champa, you take everything to heart. It's just a job,' says Nirmala Devi, but she too has taken things to heart, and the prospect of a win grasps her ever tighter.

'Look, your time may not be precious, but . . .'

Lokend stays Mrs Sahai with a slight movement of his hand. 'People must have room to speak.'

'Oh, I *will* change this city with my work. I will work for these people, so that in time I might affect a miracle and earn their love. I have never felt love in this life and you don't know how far I'd go for it. Not like you, who have been surrounded by love all your life.'

This time Mrs Sahai points to her watch with a swing of her eyes, like a long-term spouse signalling to her overstaying husband at a Delhi dinner party.

It is a different conversation that leaves the table. 'I came here prepared to fight him. But I find myself on his side.' Nirmala Devi turns to her assistant and applies a fresh coat of lipstick. 'Did you see that something in him? I almost wish I could join him.'

'Oh, Didi, you can beat any man.' The assistant lets her voice go, it falls to its natural masculine pitch like a weight on a rope. 'He is only a man with limited experience. You have created your-self, changed your life in an unimaginable way. Don't be beguiled now, you have come too far.' She knows Nirmala Devi isn't one who shares her words lightly. That Lokend has really got under her skin. The assistant feels molten hatred coursing through her veins; for whom . . . Lokend or Nirmala Devi? The force of her feeling unsettles her, she needs some urgent words. 'What will we do if you change your mind now? What will *I* do if you change your mind now?' She is thoroughly invested in Nirmala Devi's campaign. The prospect of one of her kind ever making it in a defined-sexes world is a dream she will never relinquish. She has known Nirmala Devi since she became a hijra. It was Nirmala Devi herself who performed the illegal operation on her, and it was her face she had awoken to.

After becoming a hijra, her return to the world she'd left as a man had been tragic. Her mother had killed herself and her brother had tried to kill her. If that wasn't enough, both her sisters were soundly rejected by their husbands. That had been the hardest for her, because she'd had that special connection with her sisters that many men who completely understand the inner workings of a woman's psyche develop. Eventually, her father had conducted a funeral for her, letting his village know that his son was dead. And now, with victory, respect, and possibly acceptance within her grasp,

for the first time in her life she feels like a whole person. And she can't, she won't, let that go.

Both eunuchs slide into the waiting ambassador car.

In another ambassador car, Mrs Sahai chivvies Lokend towards a win. 'You're not thinking of softening up, are you?'

'So you thought she was wonderful too?'

Mrs Sahai wrinkles her nose. She is not going to dignify his question with a response. *Thought that hijra was wonderful, my foot.*

'Let me tell you a story, Mrs Sahai. There was an orange seller who used to roam the streets from morning to night in the season selling his oranges. Already an old man, he would complain about pain in his back from carrying the basket on his head and corns on his feet which bled from walking too long. Early one morning the orange seller had the good fortune to meet a gentleman who wanted to buy his entire basket of oranges. The seller was flabbergasted, he'd never been asked to sell his whole basket of oranges before. The gentleman explained that he was late for a wedding and didn't want to arrive empty-handed, and a big basket of fresh oranges would make the perfect gift. The old orange seller thought hard while the gentleman impatiently waited for an answer. After a few minutes he said, "*All* my oranges, why not just take a few?" "I don't want a few, I want them all, any less than the whole basket wouldn't be enough," replied the buyer, thoroughly irritated. "So make up your mind: how much?" Once again the orange seller thought about what to charge the buyer, and finally, his mind made up, he said, "No, sorry, I can't sell you all my oranges, take a few kilos." The buyer became very angry and started shouting at the seller, "I don't want a few kilos, I will have all your oranges or nothing." Then the seller said something very surprising, he said, "It has to be nothing then. If I sell my entire basket of oranges this early in the morning, what will I do for the rest of the day?"' Mrs Sahai looks at Lokend. 'A true story.'

'Hmm,' she says.

'We are like that sometimes, unwilling to relinquish our burdens. We just drag our thoughts – oranges – around with us on our bent backs and bleeding feet day after day.'

Such a perplexing creature and a most odd human being, naïve too, she thinks.

The Congress Party's office in Begumpet is an untidy nest of papers. It is just weeks to the elections. Campaigning must go on day or night. Jeeps in camouflage green have been commandeered for the job. The Youth Congress volunteers are busy attaching loudspeakers and searchlights on the tops of their hoods for maximum impact.

Prem and Sneha are waiting at the office.

The boy is wearing pitiful socks that roll wilfully below his ankles, the elastic no longer strong enough to grip his flesh, with a pair of sandals. His hip bones boldly declare themselves through his trousers, which sit uncomfortably on his waist held up by a large safety pin. For the first time, his four-metre dhoti put away, it is easy to see how bony he really is. These accoutrements of city life, given to him by Mrs Sahai, define his standing. His sister has received no new-old clothes.

'How was it? What was the hijra like? Was she strange? How will she give a speech in public? In Gopalpur we would have beaten her off the platform with a stick. I can gather stones, if you like. One stone from me will be enough of a lead,' Prem says in a rush before dribbling into silence in the assertive presence of Mrs Sahai.

'No. She is a good person. I wish she was on our side. Forget about the election, the speech. Let us do something constructive. How will we contact your elder sister?' asks Lokend.

Sneha releases her head from under her pallav. She has been hiding since she came to Begumpet. Mrs Sahai squeezes past her. The village girl breathes in to make way for Importance.

'I hope Mamta Didi comes to the rally,' Prem answers.

'And Sneha? What about Sneha, if she doesn't come?' Mrs Sahai points out the foolishness of their hasty pilgrimage.

The boy shrugs. The future has no meaning for him. Sneha's eyes are dry, she looks from man to boy, searching for some sign of certainty. She finds none. Her mother cried to see her go. Why did she come here? How could her mother think her life would be better here in Begumpet? Life here is a flurry, like the leaves tousled by the

276

Gopalpur wind. Where on earth in this crazy place of people would she find her sister? The Red Bazaar would have been better. Her father will surely kill her if she goes back home.

'Don't worry, we'll find her. We'll think of something.' She reminds him of another girl, shivering and vulnerable. Lokend speaks Sneha in her own dialect. Even her brother has abandoned this mode of communication in favour of sophisticated city Hindi. Her insides are knotted so tightly that she hasn't passed a motion in two days. The bathroom frightens her. What should she do with the commode, and the chain, and the mug, and the tap? Slogans that she cannot read rant at her from the walls. She is sure they are instructions for other novices, but not for her, they belong only to those who can decipher them. She is tempted to ask Prem what they mean, but she does not see him as her brother any more. He has left her behind. She must seem very small to him, trouser-wearing, I-can-read-and-write Prem.

Prem is thinking his own thoughts. He cannot waste time on Sneha. It is better that she comes to grips with the city sooner rather than later. His worth is still a tenuous commodity, he has to prove it every day to the Party cronies. No one cares that he risked his life to carry messages between the bandits and Lokend Bhai, no one cares that Daku Manmohan treated him like a son. Here he is a guileless villager filled with an eagerness to please. He hasn't time to think of Mamta or Sneha.

'Oho, stop wasting time,' says Mrs Sahai. 'We need to go over the speeches once again.' She pulls Lokend into a huddle with twenty of her cronies. Some have eyed Sneha and found her wanting. They won't look at her again, and if they do, they won't see her for all the looking they've done. Prem brings the men tea. They haven't that sense of formality that one reserves just for equals with him. He may not be one of them, but it is clear to the group that their leader depends on this village boy, so they tolerate him, exaggerating their compliments. Some try to sound sincere, and others, just the opposite.

That night, lying down on the floor between the olive-green steel tables, Sneha can hardly remember her elder sister Mamta.

* * *

'Didi, you will come tomorrow, won't you?' Mamta has rushed all the way to the dispensary to remind her friend of the rally. Eyebrows shrugs, her standard response to most things.

'Which party are you supporting?'

'I am with Lokend Bhai.'

'Yes, but which Party?'

'Party?'

'Look at you, so eager to go to a rally, but you don't even know what your precious Lokend Bhai stands for. Oh, to have such faith in a person must be a wonderful thing.'

You have been helping people for so long that you have lost your humanity. 'You have been helping people too long . . .' Mamta says out loud. Her judgement cannot be underestimated, it is not a simple thing that just jumped into her mind. It is a culmination of her newfound self.

'Yes, you could say that.'

'Your charity has made you . . .'

Eyebrows doesn't let Mamta finish, she pounces on her words as quickly as a cat on its prey. 'You must understand, Mamta, I don't believe in charity. Yes, it may come as a surprise to you, but really I don't believe in charity at all. Too many people don't, won't or can't distinguish between charity and giving people an opportunity. I simply create opportunities for people so they can help themselves. Giving charity is cutting their feet from under them.'

Mamta has come to this dispensary precisely twenty-four times to give Eyebrows her fifty for the Post Office Saving Deposit Plan. She has shared countless cups of tea, pouring half of it into a saucer for Eyebrows, retaining the cup for herself. No one else would have simply accepted a saucer of tea from Mamta (let alone insisted on it), this thought used to make her hand tremble as she poured, at first spilling more on to the floor than into the saucer. The saucer was always Eyebrows', its wide surface offering up the tea for hasty cooling gave her a sense of security, she knew if need be she could get back to work, swallowing the dregs at a moment's notice. *So many shared cups of tea and yet I know nothing of you.*

'So why do you do this work? I mean . . . I mean is it the money?

Can't be for the money, Didi. Kalu says that if you become a private doctor there is a lot of money in it, but working in a free dispensary . . . Why?' Suddenly Mamta needs to know.

'My destiny maybe. Maybe because it was in the stars.' Eyebrows shakes her head. 'Look at me, talking about stars. I don't believe in that bunkum.'

'It's not bunkum. The heavenly bodies do govern our lives. What else is there? Our female cycles are synchronised with the phases of the moon. Do you think that is a coincidence? Or that we stay pregnant for exactly nine moons, what do you say to that? The whole world is guided by some star, some planet, some sun. You know there are these people called the Nadiwallas, who can tell your past and future just by looking at your left thumbprint. They came once to Gopalpur, so Bapu brought them home. He showed them his own thumbprint, but not ours. He didn't think we'd amount to anything. They foretold his future and saw his past, I tell you, absolutely everything. His mother's name, his father's names, everything. They said something bad about Bapu's father and said that Bapu would have to atone for his sins. They said Bapu had married a woman with two names, one starting with La and the other with Ba. My mother's name is Lata Bai. They said Bapu would be blessed with seven children. Now tell me, how could they have known that? Only I was born at that time. They said he had a daughter with a mark, that's me, but that her mark would disappear when she became older. I hope so, Didi, I hope so.'

'Oh, for every one of your stories I could tell you a hundred. But does that make them true? I came here because my father survived lightning. Yes, don't look at me like that, it's true. My bapu got stuck to an electric pole in the monsoon time, you know when the streets get so flooded and you can't see the open manholes. Every monsoon one or two people disappear down those same manholes, probably swept into the blessed Ganga washing their sins in the river with their dying breaths and achieving nirvana if nothing else.' Mamta reaches a horrified hand almost to Eyebrows' mouth to stop her blaspheming, but stops short, suddenly remembering the difference in their status.

'Anyway, no one dared to free Bapu because they knew the minute they stepped in the water the electricity would grab them too. Right then, as he was shaking on the pole, eyes bulging and arching into backbend, lightning struck. Instead of finishing off poor bapu, the lightning knocked down a workman's ladder from on top of the electric pole which fell so hard on his arms that it broke his grip on the cable. My bapu was thrown free of the pole and the water.' There is mirth in her eyes. 'I'm told the people in my village now routinely leave ladders on top of electric poles. After all, who is to say which one of them will need saving next!

'I was a very small girl then, but I can clearly remember how he looked when he got home. His hair was spiky like an angry cat's tail, he was shaky, and had two black patches on his palms.

'When he touched my amma, she jumped away from him, screaming, The current has caught me, the current has caught me. After that, she wouldn't let him come near her. But four days later she realised that her backache had disappeared, and she said it was because of bapu's shock treatment. So he started giving shock treatments to people to cure them of all kinds of aches and pains. He received such joy from helping people that he wanted me to do the same. My mother would have been happy to keep me ignorant on the farm, but not my father. I am what I am because of him.'

Mamta's eyes glisten and blink, she looks to her clasped hands and then around her. The dispensary is empty. Eyebrows has put up the Closed sign on the door, not that it stops the worst cases. The smell of disinfectant is fresh and clean. It is the first time that Mamta has seen the countertop folded upon itself, simultaneously sandwiching a roll of cotton wool and creating a strait between the erstwhile separate spaces of pharmacy and waiting room.

'And that's that. It was a miracle, all right, that brought me here, but now I have an ordinary life.' She holds out her hands. 'Oh, you are disappointed. Disappointed because I say I have an ordinary life. What is an ordinary life worth, you ask? In our own ways, we all have ordinary lives.'

'Not me, Didi. I don't have an ordinary life. It is because of someone . . . someone very special that I have this life. Come with

me, just this once, come with me. You'll see for yourself.' Her pleading costs her. She cannot plead as an equal, it sounds like begging.

'If you didn't so hate the male race, I would say you were in love with this Lokend Bhai of yours.'

Now Mamta laughs loudly; her mirth, released from bondage, is a blithe young thing. 'Love that saint?' She shakes her head from side to side. It is not a no, but an acknowledgement of absurdity.

'Well, think of it. It's always Lokend Bhai this and Lokend Bhai that. Lokend Bhai gave me sweets on my wedding . . .'

She says the word *wedding* as if sharing a secret bordering on a lie. That much Mamta has told her, but nothing of the scar, nothing of her stepdaughter, nothing of her husband – who Eyebrows thinks is a fabricated character, an invention that brought her friend from the village to the city.

'I don't think I can ever love anyone. I don't think it is in me,' Mamta half-lies to protect herself from her own emotion. If you don't climb high, you never have to fall; if you don't have anything, you never have to lose.

'Everyone can love if they put their mind to it. It is a skill,' says Eyebrows, secure in the knowledge that she has no intention of putting her words to the test.

Mamta is so tempted to let this woman, who, over the past two years has become closer than family, see her scar and tell her of that precious night when Lokend protected her. Instead she presses her lips tightly together, unable to pass her tongue between them, afraid to let runaway words tumble from her mouth.

'All right, I'll come. By the way, it's the Congress Party, of the flag and palm symbol. Your man Lokend Bhai is standing for the Congress Party, though you are right to ignore the Party. In this case it might be better to put your trust in a man rather than an organisation.'

'Your man Lokend Bhai' – she likes the strength of those words, or is it the weakness? 'He is bringing my sister Sneha,' she says, changing the subject. 'I didn't tell you because I didn't want to jinx her coming by talking about it.'

'What superstition. You people only ever say something unflattering by way of a compliment.'

'Remember when Sadhana said how nice your sari was, and you spilt daal on it straightaway. Remember? Remember?' She is bullying, she wants to win a fight on some level. Any level.

'Come, come now,' Eyebrows says, cajoling. She is very fond of Mamta, but it will never be in her nature to show it. 'Come on, let's go or we will be late.'

Lata Bai's hut is empty of purpose, of industry. She coughs into her pallav. Her husband lies on the straw mattress, occupying it all. She has taken to the floor. She hardly goes to the well to draw water. With just the two of them, once in four days is enough. That's enough cooking too, especially with Mamta's money orders halted. She turns her thoughts away from her runaway daughter.

She can hear him shift and moan, trying to get comfortable in a body that's badly let him down. Who is this man? A collection of aspirations, dreams, emotions; a representation of something so familiar that all meaning's lost in the comprehension. He must have felt the same breath of winter wind, slowly turning summer away in gentle parts of nights. He must have rejoiced in someone's touch, felt a rush through his frame sometime in their youth. He must have cried for at least one other person, perhaps in secret. But what did he stand for?

She is glad he is dying. This is her retribution for what he did. She has waited for this day from the time he beat her into a huddle on the floor.

With his body, his beliefs are also dying. His corn-husk skin covers bent bones that connect awkwardly, he stands half-erect like a praying mantis on its hind legs. Now each time she coughs, he winces, hoping she won't die and leave him to his dusty, brittle body. She has that over him. Her coughs make him shudder. At last her actions evoke responses from him. But so what?

No one comes to their hut. They are not shunned, simply forgotten. His will be a flaccid death, a slow release of energy, like the dying sigh of a doused fire left to smoke, collapsing into itself without control.

Except for her cough, she too is softly silent. In this place, she

mistakes the wind as weeping for her lost past when in fact all it seeks is a new pitch. Nevertheless, there are times when she doesn't truly believe she has been wronged. Whenever she met her life, it showed her a different face: a daughter, a sister, a bride, a wife, a mother, a friend. Life tolerates no excuses, it only recognises finality, an exact computation. And in her life of fixed paths she has dreamed up many final reckonings. But reality is not an intuition, it isn't a thought or even a fruition of the past, it is a wilful creature aimless in its wandering. Acceptance is the only defence, the only sanctuary left to her.

'Lata, Lata.' His voice still has a modicum of bullying force. He will be heard, it is his birthright. 'Lata, Lata.' Bloody woman.

She looks at the body, calling to her, head thrown back, lips open, producing a sound she carries in her pores. How many times ... and yet today she sees it as something new. She almost wishes she hadn't given her best green sari to Sneha to take to the city, she thinks she would have liked to have worn it. She stays staring from outside the hut, head held up like a burden, her gaze loose but not locked.

'Lata, Lata,' he calls again. 'Lata ...' he is about to start with the words, but she doesn't let him. She walks away, taking her cough with her. Later, when he is asleep, she will leave food for him within reach. She will not allow a shadow of discomfort to befall him, except the withdrawal of herself, her spirit, her presence.

Each time he wakes, he recognises the bitterness that has seized his heart. At first it was for her, but with her gone, his bitterness has turned on himself. Not as an apology for his actions, nor regret or disappointment, but more because he doesn't understand why she has stopped talking; and why, when he needs her most does she choose to find a lone place somewhere where she can hear his voice but not listen.

The breath slips out of him, each time with a softer 'Lata'.

She has an illicit urge to look in the cracked mirror. Will she even recognise herself? All this time she has lived for others. Suddenly she wants to be something, someone. Someone not so much wife

and mother. A daughter, a sister, a bride, a wife, a mother, a friend and now a widow.

She carefully wipes the sindhoor out of her middle parting, wetting the pointed end of her pallav in spit for the final erasure. She meticulously takes off her lone bangle, and slides off her toe ring. She will never have use for the trappings of marriage again. Not in this lifetime. Lata Bai believes in the next life as firmly as she does in this one. That's why she is not surprised by the gentleness of her husband's death. Of course he'd deserved worse, but who is to say what lies ahead. 'Jai ho Devi, Devi jai ho.'

She should be singing a prayer for her husband's soul to ride on. But she cannot. She looks at the twigs in her earlobes. The left was pierced crooked. That is how it always is, one ear is pierced perfectly, and then, for the other, the head anticipating pain, moves. A crooked, jagged hole. It will bleed if she wrenches the twig from it. Her gaze slips to the reflection of her eyes. Still clear. Still alert.

Very little of her face is familiar. Before Mamta was married she would look at the photo to remember what she used to look like, but with the photo gone, she has nothing but the mirror to tell her things.

'Lata Bai, Lata Bai. Are you there? Arey-oh, Lata Bai.' The widow Kamla arrives, bringing sound and life with her. Should she reply? Should she dive under the blanket with her husband and pretend that she's dead too? Should she cover the corpse with a reed mat and pretend it is grain?

'Now what are you shouting at the top of your voice for, loud enough to wake the dead?' A sudden giggle escapes her lips, unintentional as a stubbed toe, irreverent as an uncovered head, festive as a noisy wristful of bangles, and loud, loud as freedom itself.

Kamla has news. 'Arey-oh, Lata Bai, that Lala Ram has finally done it. The bank's open. Right here, right now, you can go and get a loan from the Bank of India. Even I can. Can you imagine? Me – a widow. And the best thing of all, the manager is a manager-didi, a woman. A woman running a bank in Gopalpur. Now we'll see where it gets that dog Ram Singh.'

'Seeta Ram is dead.' She says her husband's name for the first

time. Still mired in reverence, she points to her hut and the body it contains respectfully with her thumb instead of her forefinger. Even from the dead her husband commands her actions.

'Bastard, he's sucked us dry for the last time. What!'

'Yes, I am a widow too.' She shows her scalp to Kamla, standing perfectly still, pulling her hair apart, waiting for a critique from someone with experience.

'The funeral?' Kamla ignores the scalp, pink as the underbelly of a newborn rat.

'I'll not take a loan for it.'

'So then?'

'I'll think of something.'

'What about Mamta's money?'

'Don't mention her name.' Now it's a habit, this rejection of her runaway daughter. 'There is no more money.'

'What will you do with your life?'

Lata Bai looks away. 'My life . . .' She pauses a long while and then says, 'Live it, I suppose.'

The lightning is shrieking around them. No one will be out on such a night. Two figures balance a corpse unsteadily between them. Not because the body is heavy, but rather because the deed is.

'Come on!' Kamla is in command, even though it isn't her husband's body they are disposing of. As the person in charge, she has the legs, the lighter side.

Lata Bai hoists the head further up her arm. Its weight bears down on her. For a brief second she's afraid her husband is alive, pressing down on her. He slips from her grasp, she catches him mid-fall by the upper arm.

'Uffo, come on. Do you want to spend all night dragging this' – Kamla doesn't know what to call it: thing, body, corpse, husband, Seeta Ram – 'this . . .'

'It isn't so easy, I have the heavier side,' the wife complains. 'He's stiff.'

'He would be stiff, no. Never did do what you asked of him in life, why should he start now?' Kamla laughs.

Suddenly the thorough absurdity that usually lies concealed in truly dangerous situations is revealed to them. They both laugh so hard they drop the body on the ground. The lightning illuminates their burden. They are convulsing now, doubled up, genuflecting with mirth, paying obeisance to the Goddess of Glee.

'Jai ho Devi.'

'Jai ho Devi.'

'Devi jai ho.'

'Devi jai ho.'

The river is low and Lata Bai has to wade deep into its centre to let Seeta Ram go. She has earned herself a heap of sins in this lifetime for not giving her husband a decent funeral. But it has been well worth it.

Kamla pulls her up the bank. She slaps her wet hands together, as if dusting them of flour. 'That's done.'

They will tell no one about her husband's death. Lata Bai will be able to continue to wear her coloured sari till someone notices the absence of sindhoor in her hair, the bangle on her wrist or her missing toe ring. Most will believe that Seeta Ram walked out on her, just like her two sons did.

What would women do without other women?

Jai ho Devi, Devi jai ho.

13

THE CROWD, CULLED FROM THE LOWER middle class and below, is the backbone of the electoral process. These are the people who believe a leader chosen by them will truly change their lives. They haven't yet acquired the paralysing, protective cynicism of the upper classes, who will never deign nor dare to go to a rally, but take up the political baton at a dinner party or club somewhere, pontificating seated in overstuffed armchairs, over a whiskey soda and pipe, lamenting that it makes no difference who wins in the end.

They have come dressed in their dignified city best, shirts and pants for the men, and Punjabi suits and saris for the women. There is not one ghaghra choli to be seen, no swish of a skirt made with nine metres of fabric, no scarf making its way from the waist to head and back to waist again, no bare bellies folded sensually over mirrorwork belts. It is a crowd made up of office boys, shopkeepers, servants, rickshaw drivers, ayahs, sweepers: all working class.

The ones who won't be here are Cynthia and Mrs D'Souza. Cynthia is with Vikram, though she has tired of him somewhat. She made her story convincing enough for her mother to let her go, but she felt no victory in it. She has on her midi. It swishes past her knees. Her skin feels like silk, she waxed herself and has vowed she will never take up a masculine razor again like other girls. Her mother will be at home, watching *Chitrahaar* on TV. The continuous string

of popular Hindi movie songs will have her poised for dance herself. She won't even bother tuning into the rally. What have politicians and parties got to do with people like her? She lives off her husband's army pension and owns her flat.

Prem and Sneha have been left behind at the office. 'Come in the next car,' they were told. He tried so hard to fit in. Joked and back-slapped with the rest of them. So why has he been left behind?

The large gathering of potential consumers has attracted all sorts of entrepreneurs: entertainers, letter-writers, fruit sellers, inde-pendent portable restaurateurs, miracle workers, fortune tellers, ear cleaners, sadhus . . . selling anything and everything: sweet paans wrapped in silver leaf, camel rides or head massage. The trees to one edge of the field have become male-only urinals. It doesn't matter who sees them pissing against the trees.

Mamta squeezes herself closer to the snake charmers. On any other day she might have lingered, but today nothing seems to hold her attention. She moves through the crowd, her arms wrapped tightly round her chest. Eve-teasing is not discriminating. Pretty, ugly or plain, men and boys alike will seek out their targets efficiently and ruthlessly, taking a squeeze of a breast here, a pinch of a bottom there, and if they are really lucky, two fingers squeezed through tightly pressed legs.

While Mamta would never aggressively defend herself against the predators, her companion will lash out at anyone who even thinks of touching her. Eyebrows is not intimidated.

Kalu stands two paces behind Mamta and Eyebrows, close enough for them to know he is there, but far enough to escape association. He has come here hoping to sample one of those tasty servant girls he's had an eye on for so long.

Mamta searches the crowd with flitting looks, afraid to miss a familiar face. 'What if they don't come?'

'They'll be here,' says Eyebrows.

They'll be here. Mamta is charged. Memories of Gopalpur pull at her as she searches for her brother and sister. She won't let this girl

down like she did her stepdaughter, but what can she offer the sickly wretched unmarried Sneha? The yeast of anxiety is fermenting her being. *Please come, my sister.* Eyebrows grasps her upper arm.

'Stop behaving like a lovesick girl. Don't worry, you will see him soon enough.'

'It's not for him. My brother . . . my sister. Oh, Didi, Prem helped me when I ran away, he is working for the Big House, I haven't got a job for Sneha yet. I thought I'd wait to ask Mrs D'Souza. What if they don't show up? What will I say when I see him?' All her concerns tumble out of her mouth like water from a gushing tap.

'No one has this many shivers for their sister or brother. It's for him. Once you see him, you will know. Lovesick idol-worshipper,' says Eyebrows, grinding her knuckles into her friend's head.

'Let's go.' It is Mrs Sahai. 'He sent me here personally to get you two. Tch. Tch. Why that man has to take the burdens of the entire world on his shoulders is something I'll never know.'

Mrs Sahai rolls down her window halfway, fastidiously arranging her sari. She has chosen a beige one with a rich border. The beige is neutral, it won't set her apart, and it is ethnic enough to be considered in good taste in the city. Yes, she did well with it. She bought Lokend a new, startling white handspun khadi kurta pyjama.

Raja is rattling around on the backseat between the boy and his sister. He has become almost as comfortable with Prem as he is with Lokend, and now happily hides in the boy's shirt. But today, Mrs Sahai said definitely not. The mongoose had to be caged. This rally is much too important to have a wild animal running around all over the place. She brought the wire box to the office herself this morning. Prem pokes his finger into the cage and pets the ridge of the animal's nose. Raja is stilled, but not calmed. The cage is too small for him. In the few hours he's been in it, he's managed to rub the fur and some skin off his side.

'Out of sight, remember. Stay out of sight, you two. I don't want anything distracting him today. It's an important speech for him.'

Prem looks at Mrs Sahai with his big eyes and nods. Sneha says, 'Yes, memsahib.' She can't understand why Mrs Sahai hasn't offered

her a job. She has made it clear she'll accept anything, sweeping the Party office, anything. She wants to be like Mamta. She knows word for word what Mamta had written to her mother in her letters. Prem didn't burn them, instead he saved them to read to Sneha. How had her sister become so lucky, to be living in a house full of fake flowers, with powdered salt and plastic buckets? *Please, Devi, please. Jai ho Devi.*

The crowd is slowly congealing around them like boiled rice pudding. Eyebrows and Mamta have reached the podium with Kalu making room for them with his elbows. Kalu will leave them soon, he's spied his saucy Maharashtran at the edge of the crowd.

Mamta bites her knuckles. Eyebrows thinks of taking her hand, but changes her mind. She can't risk that much intimacy with anyone, not even one as dependable as Mamta. 'They'll be here, they'll all be here,' she reassures her nervous companion.

Mrs Sahai gets out of the car. 'Remember, out of sight, I don't want any distractions today.' She knows these village types need to be reminded a hundred times at least, if not more.

Prem drags the cage with him, it gets stuck in the car door. The boy is gentle with the cage and the car. He manipulates the wire contraption, sliding it up and back, sideways and down. Raja tumbles inside, his world more topsy-turvy than ever before. The boy tugs a tiny bit harder, his world as topsy-turvy as the animal's. Eventually, Mrs Sahai says, 'Leave it and get out.' Prem is distraught, he is a failure, the cage is left stuck in the car. Mrs Sahai walks to the back door, deftly opens it a little wider and easily slides the cage out on to the pavement. Raja falls to the floor inside the cage with a thud. She points to the mongoose. Prem awkwardly picks up the cage, confirming he is still a bumbling village boy.

Lokend is inside one of the Party's vans. The Youth Congress members are leaning against the vehicle, nonchalantly smoking. Inside, a senior member is waiting for Mrs Sahai to show up so she can rehearse Lokend's lines with him. He hasn't the courage to tackle Lokend's charisma head-on.

Prem and Sneha are separated from Mamta by layers of humanity.

Prem looks at Sneha, Raja is rattling his cage, jumping up, down, up, down. It is becoming hard for her brother to hold it. Sneha helps, grasping it from below. Raja lets loose a nervous stream of pellets, they drop into Sneha's hand. Dirty, filthy, smelling to high heavens, and now this, a handful of mongoose pellets. *Please help me, Devi. Please help me, Mamta Didi. Come and get me.*

Lokend emerges from the Party van to take his position behind the mic. 'Brothers and sisters . . .'

'See, that's him,' she whispers. His hair is thick and bristly. It is almost fully grey. 'Brothers and sisters,' Lokend says again, folding his hands before his heart.

'That is Mamta's saint. Mamta, my sister,' says Kalu, making an impression on the saucy Maharashtran.

'Lokend Bhai zindabad, Lokend Bhai zindabad, Lokend Bhai zindabad . . .' The Party boys will continue to repeat the slogan, Long live Lokend Bhai, till the crowd takes up the chant, then and only then will Mrs Sahai give the signal for the speech to begin. She doesn't think the crowd charged enough yet.

It is that instant of time when everything is stretched taut, silent and slow. That piece of time that people will invariably recall in different ways.

It all happens so quickly.

An apparition of a strong, wiry woman makes its way quickly through the crowd, along the outskirts of the throng, up the podium. Suddenly Lokend is left clutching his side.

'It's the assistant!' Mrs Sahai screams. 'The hijra assistant. Get her. Grab her. She's stabbed him! Stabbed Lokend Bhai! He's bleeding!'

The crowd grabs at the hijra, but she is able to break every grip, strengthened by righteousness and hatred.

'Get these people out of here. Where is the security? I said we needed more security!' Mrs Sahai will not be distracted from the practical details, these are lessons she must commit to memory for the next time.

Lokend collapses into waiting arms. Stabbed, wounded, dying. No, no, no . . . Mamta is gasping harder and faster than him.

291

'Air, give him air,' shouts Mrs Sahai, before going to the van to radio for an ambulance. Not more than one minute has passed.

Mamta has willed herself standing, though in fact she is close to collapse, and not because she's unused to blood. There was the time that Mohit had cut his shin so badly from falling into the gutter. For days they didn't know whether he would lose his leg. She'd changed the dressings, she'd washed the blood and taken her brother on her back to the mobile government dispensary parked at the Big House for his injections. She'd stitched God knows how many cuts on her sisters' and brothers' arms and legs. And then there was the night her grandmother's cow needed help delivering its calf. She'd put her hand inside it right up to her shoulder and yanked the calf out dripping with mucus and blood into the lamplight.

Her mind has shut down. She can't bear to see him bleed. She looks at his feet, his toes, encased in familiar slippers. His almost white hair. The lines in his face. If she didn't know it was Lokend Bhai, she would think him an old man.

'Yes, get her here. Here up on this podium. Grab her tight.' Mrs Sahai holds her sari pleats close to her shins to avoid soiling them with blood. 'We will get you the death penalty for doing this. Hijra! Hijra! Outcaste. Filthy bitch!' Mrs Sahai is a changed woman. The words coming out of her mouth should never taint the lips of someone dressed fastidiously in a neutral beige sari with a rich border.

'Sssss . . .' The hijra hisses at her, sending Mrs Sahai shrivelling into herself and flying to the back of podium.

'L . . . et her . . . go.' Lokend has found his strength. He speaks from his supine position on the floor, through his wound, from deep inside his pain. 'L . . . et her go . . .' The words are almost inaudible. He is losing his strength.

'No!' The hijra is petulant, she will not be beholden to this man, her nemesis. Of course she had no choice, she could see him ruining everything for her. All the things she had worked for. The prospect of respectability at last in her grasp, but waiting to be squandered by Nirmala Devi who was seriously considering letting Lokend Bhai stand unopposed. She wasn't about to let anyone tamper with her dream. She planned to kill Lokend Bhai for all the hijras, to show

the world that they were more than just open-fingered-clapping performing monkeys. And she is willing to die for it. Just as she was the night she'd handed the razor over to Nirmala Devi to castrate her in the light of a petromax under a giant spreading banyan tree.

'Take me to jail! Get me the death penalty! I am not afraid of death! You think you can stop us? You think you can treat us like scum because we are different than you?'

'Let her . . . go . . . go . . . go.' The party workers lead their prisoner away so Lokend doesn't have to struggle to plead with them any more.

Two men bearing a stretcher rush on to the podium. The crowd immediately starts to thin. The spectacle is over. There will be no speech today. Kalu elbows his way out just as he had in. He leads his ayah away, they weave like two dancers through the swirling people. He has been lucky today. The sight of the blood sent her trembling, which he was able to quell not just with words, but with his hands. In her caste, once a man's hands were on her they were practically married. Tonight, tonight would be the night. She won't make such a bad wife. A gorgeous body with ample child-bearing hips, an endless length of hair and a good job in the next building on the second floor as an ayah to two young children. *Oh, Kalu, you lucky devil, what have you done to deserve this, you motherfucker?*

There is a special way to load a stabbed man into a stretcher. Mamta watches, not breathing, teeth chattering. They place a mask on Lokend's nose and mouth. It frightens her, it means he is for sure going to die. Without thinking she places her chin on Eyebrows' shoulder and shuts her eyes.

'It's for air. He's not going to die. He has a strong pulse.'

Her chattering stilled, she thinks she reaches out to the wounded man, and manages to brush the edge of his kurta that's dangling off the stretcher before she sees his body disappear into the ambulance. In fact, her hand hasn't moved from her side the whole time.

14

EYEBROWS HAS ALREADY TAKEN NOTE OF the name on the van:
Sai Sidhi Hospital. It would have to be that one, it's the only decent
one in Begumpet, the one she takes her badly burned victims to.

Prem and Sneha have gravitated little by little closer to the stage.
They spot Mamta. 'Mamta Didi!' The crowd is too thick to pene-
trate with their combined voices. Even from that distance, they sense
their sister's desperation, bordering on madness.

'Didi!'

'Didi!'

Mamta has awakened in a dream, *Who are these people and why
are they here?* 'Didi,' there are tears in the voice. A small, pretty,
feminine voice attached to a plain, intensely familiar face. 'Thank God
we've found you.' And then it's over. The bubble-skin of unknow-
ingness is broken. She hugs her siblings close, one arm around each.
Her sister nestles into her shoulder, releasing tears of relief. Now
everything is all right.

'Lokend Bhai . . .?' Eyebrows' question brings both of them back
to their senses. Everything is not all right.

'What will we do?'

Mamta grasps her left hand with her right and squeezes.
Unexpected waves of softness break under her skin. 'We must go to
him,' she says. *What will I do if he dies?*

'Sai Sidhi Hospital, that's where they've taken him. I know it.'

Eyebrows wastes no time, she grabs Mamta's arm, she will pull her the whole way there if she has to. She sees herself as the maker of Mamta's destiny. All this happened so she could help. At last Devi has set her a worthy challenge. God, if she'd thought up such a scenario in her dreams it would have been illicit enough to make her hide her conniving head under her pillow, but Devi has handed it to her on a silver tray: a dying man, bleeding to death, with only her as his saviour; a broken woman, desperate to save her beloved, with only her as a guide. The glory of service, the marvel of self-sacrifice is irresistible to her. She will save Mamta. She will save Lokend Bhai. She will save them both, help them find their way in this world, keep them whole, force them to survive. She will give life.

Prem grabs Mamta's other arm, and Sneha his. The whole chain waggles forward.

'The number 35 bus will get us there. We'll get off at the water tank and walk from there. It'll be faster.' Eyebrows is familiar with all the bits and pieces of the city.

For the first time in months, Mamta furtively runs her fingers over her kidney scar. *How is his pain? What is he feeling?* His wound is an almost exact mirror image of hers. *Now our scars will bind us.* She looks around, afraid someone will discover her thoughts. *Save him, Devi. Jai ho Devi, Devi jai ho.*

Lokend would have thoroughly disapproved of his private room, had he the strength.

Mrs Sahai, positioned like a watchdog in the doorway of ICU-1J, plans to control what happens in the Party. She casts her eyes down the corridor, filled with Party people. She shrugs. Two or three more won't make a difference. They'll get chased out by the staff one by one anyway. In the meantime, she has the best seat in the house, close to Lokend Bhai. Anyone wishing to see him must check with her first.

Lokend Bhai . . . Minister Lokend Bhai. The hijra might have done her a service. He will definitely become a martyr if he dies, and if he survives, why then the elections are won for them with an over-whelming landslide victory. What a wonderful situation. She picks

at a piece of food stuck between her teeth. Now who can she ask to get her some magazines? Some tea? The newspaper?

'No visitors, not allowed. Come back tomorrow between nine and eleven,' the nurse on duty barks at Mamta.

Come back tomorrow? What if tomorrow doesn't come? She cannot move.

'Didn't you hear me?' the watchdog asks with unassailable authority.

'Didi . . .'

'Tomorrow.' The watchdog moves purposefully towards the room, chart in hand. 'Rules are rules.'

'We can't stay here all night, Didi,' Prem whispers roughly. 'Find a place for us,' he says without saying.

Where can she put them? All she knows is that her Sahibji is in hospital. *Where can I send you? My only place is Mrs D'Souza's home.*

Mrs D'Souza's home! It's almost three o'clock. She must not be late for work. She cannot afford to lose her job. 'Didi, I have to go to work. What bus? What number?'

She leaves the hospital. Once again the chain, Mamta, Sneha, Eyebrows, Prem, and the mongoose cage, shuffles forward.

It is the one day that Mrs D'Souza won't care if her servant is late. It is the day that her daughter has come racing home, straight into her mother's arms, adrenalin-shaken and fragile from her meeting with Vikram. Cynthia D'Souza wanted to tell him of her intention to break up. She'd tried to be gentle. She told him they were young, that they should live a little, that she wanted to be free for the sake of freedom, but Vikram refused to understand. He'd grabbed at her arms, her hair and her clothes, and she'd managed to escape with her dignity intact only because his mother returned early from her boring card party.

Cynthia D'Souza put her head in her mother's lap and cried. She vowed to herself that she would never leave the family fold again and argue with her mother over boys. Thankfully the blue marks, dead giveaways, were well hidden under her skirt. Her mother put a quiet hand on her head and soothed her hair. It had to be one of

those explicable female moments. Mrs D'Souza can remember them from her own youth, the tears suddenly appearing in her eyes, her heart pain growing strong enough to split her chest and her need to cleave to her own mother, a creature so distant and antiseptic it was a wonder she'd had a child at all. Yes, Mrs D'Souza, running her fingers through Cynthia D'Souza's thick hair, realises her daughter is growing up.

Mamta knows what she must do as she climbs up the stairs with her sister in tow. Surrounded by vulgar anatomical graffiti that neither fully understand, Mamta helps Sneha awkwardly change into her only spare sari. She remembers this same sari resting on her mother's shoulder on the day of her wedding.

Her sister carefully groomed, they run up the stairs. 'Memsahib,' there is a gasp in her voice.

'What is it?'

What can she tell her? What can she say? Her life is filled with the sound of one word: Lokend Bhai. Her world is just that. Lokend Bhai. She needs to be there for him just as he was for her. 'I have to go . . . go somewhere, could be for one month . . . or six, I don't know . . .' She is shocked by her own words. 'My sister,' she steps aside, revealing Sneha standing behind her, like a magician's assistant. 'Can she . . .? Will you . . .? I wanted to know if she could . . .?' Mrs D'Souza is in a remarkably listening mood, it has been a good day. She will make tea for her daughter soon. She waves a magnanimous hand at Mamta.

'Of course she can take your place. But come back to me, Mamta. You are like family here. Cynthia adores you. Does your sister know the job? I won't pay her what I pay you. After all, she has no experience.'

'Yes, memsahib. Of course, memsahib.' Facing her mistress, she quickly retreats to the door, while Sneha is ready to dive down and grasp Mrs D'Souza's feet. The sisters run down the stairs to where Prem is waiting for them holding an empty cage. His city shirt doesn't provide good shelter for the mongoose. Raja is clinging to his back, digging his claws in, making the boy wince with each move. 'Come, let me show you where you will sleep. Be on time! And no

297

stealing at all. Please don't disgrace me.' Mamta needs to spell out the rules for Sneha. 'Oh yes and one more thing, be nice to Baby.'

'Baby?'

'Mrs D'Souza's dog,' she replies, giving Sneha a quick squeeze with her arms. 'Say my hello to Kalu.' Now it's Sneha's turn to sleep under the stairs.

'Kalu?'

'He's nice. You see that bedroll, it's his. That's his space over there, you sleep on the other side.' Sneha nods. Her anxious hands clutch her things tied in a bundle with a piece of brown cloth. 'Chacha, my sister,' Mamta calls to the man in khaki. Chacha looks at her, he has been in close conversation with Eyebrows. 'She is with Mrs D'Souza now.' Mamta offers no other explanation and Chacha doesn't demand one. From the day she arrived he's been consistently taciturn, dependable.

Sneha clings to Mamta. More than anything she wants to stay close to her sister, to all that's familiar. Mamta had nowhere to go when she first came to sleep under that stair, and she was grateful for its shelter. The same shelter terrifies Sneha who has had much too much time for plans.

Mamta walks out of the gate and melts into the night, just as Kalu did a long time ago. She had promised herself she would mark the day that happened, but she couldn't tell you when she'd simply begun walking out of the gate with the same artless confidence of her under-stair companion. It is dark, the neon is blinking on the far side of the street.

Sneha runs after her into the rain. What does she care about staying dry? The rain camouflages her tears, now streaming down her cheeks, cleaning them of village dirt.

If you look into rain at night, you can see the individual drops come toward you before they disappear as water in your eyes. Mamta watches the rain for minutes. Should she go back to Himalaya House, under the stairs with her sister? Go back to the dispensary? She would be accepted, even welcomed, in both these places, but her life is here, at the Sai Sidhi Hospital. Forever. Her life is here.

She feels outside of herself, she must. She sees a story in her life, she must; otherwise the prospect of sitting in the rain, uncovered, would seem ridiculous enough to her to want to change it.

The only living things undeterred by the rain are the tenacious ants. Just like the ants, they won't be able to stop her. She sees the ants, fleeing from forming puddles, but always surviving, rising to the surface on their last dying breaths, the bubbles clinging to their bodies like jewels. Hundreds of ants survive the night in her puddle alone. As they rise to the surface on their private air bells, she rejoices for them.

The morning is fresh, clear and innocent, like a washed and combed child. She realises that, though her life is unchanged – she will continue to eat, sleep, and come awake as before – nothing will ever be the same.

The hospital is still dark, but she is able to look in through the glass criss-crossed with reinforcing steel on the upper half of the front door. There is no one at the desk. Mamta stays looking, nose flattened against the transparent surface. She pushes the door open and walks in. Her throat is dry, but she remembers the pattern of the English letters burned into her mind: ICU-1J, ICU-1J, ICU . . .

Everything that looked familiar yesterday suddenly seems treacherous. She is lost. She gasps. *What if he dies? What if he is dead? Don't think about that.*

She sees a man talking on the hospital phone and waits for him to finish. 'Tomorrow . . . sweets . . . don't forget.' He is excited, cradling the phone, shaking his head with disbelief.

'Babuji, I, Shi, U?' The new, proud father of a baby boy looks up, his eyes still wet with happiness and points to the end of the corridor, where it divides into a T.

There may have been no guard at the door to the hospital, but there is an orderly at the head of the T. Behind the orderly she can see two families, children in arms, all waiting, sipping tea from thermoses brought from home.

'Not here,' the orderly shouts at a couple of stretcher-bearers behind her. She presses face-up against the wall, trying to hide. 'Can't you see the signs? ICU –' he points with an insolent forefinger '– is

over there. Get out, come round the other side. No one can go through here.' She leaves the screaming and follows the stretcher-bearers dressed in white Nehru caps and striped green uniforms, like lifers wear in prison. The body of the patient is almost covered up to the forehead in a green sheet. She has the urge to pull the sheet away from his face. It isn't a good sign, to cover a living person's face. *What if he dies? What if he is dead? Don't think about that.*

She follows the dying man.

Suddenly the stretcher-bearers notice her walking close behind. They are out of the building now, back down the steps, going round the other side as they have been told to. 'Family?' the orderly in front asks without turning round to look at her.

She lies with a nod, then says, 'Yes.'

'Who?'

'My . . . uh . . . my man.' The words manifest her dream. *What if he is dead? Don't think about that now.* She walks quickly past the stretcher and yesterday's litter, suppressing an urge to sweep away the plastic bags, sweet wrappers and bits of rotting food along their path.

Then she sees the letters I – C – U carved solidly into wood. It is dead quiet. The nurse is on her rounds, or in the bathroom, or nodding sleepily, but she isn't here to stop Mamta entering. She walks into the ICU, a corridor with doors on one side. She looks up at each door, 1E . . . 1F . . . 1J. She knows the curve of the number-letter combination as intimately as her own birthmark.

She pushes door 1J open a sliver. The sliver becomes a crack. The crack becomes an opening. The corridor light leaks into the room. She can see the sheet stretched even across the bed. A green bed. A sheet stretched even.

The bed is empty.

Her hand stays on the door handle. He's gone. *Gone . . . gone . . . gone. Dead. Gone. Dead . . . dead . . . dead.*

She has pictured this scenario so many times in the last few hours that her reaction, or lack of it, surprises her. She will never have reason to be happy again. It is a deep bitterness she encounters. What on earth made her mad enough to think herself so lucky?

Those hands that led her back up to standing and fed her buttered

chapattis were her thatched shelter from the rain, fine sand at the bottom of a tamarind tree waiting to break her fall, a memory of quiet, even joyous, retreat. All this time, it was the feel of those hands that reminded her she was a person.

And now . . . gone . . . dead. At least now she doesn't have the added agony of loving him in person. At least now she can hoard her fantasies, and in her fantasies she has held him in her arms, melting into him like warm rain in parched earth.

'Don't forget under the bed. Strange man, didn't want a private room. But it'll fill up soon enough, they don't lie empty for long. Here, take this.' The nurse stands out as clearly as one of Mrs D'Souza's Christian calendar angels in her crisp white uniform and funny crown cap, her hair pulled back into a severe bun beneath it. She tosses her a green sheet and bobs her capped head at her. 'You're new?'

Of course. She's been mistaken for an employee, she has that air of service. Mamta nods, noticing the nurse's skin, glowing black in contrast to her uniform.

The nurse can tell the cleaning woman is tired, but her day must go on. She has three more hours to her shift, might as well talk to keep her awake. 'He came in with a stab wound this morning. Some kind of politician. I had to chase his watchdogs out of here. That woman just refused to leave. Said she'd alert her father – someone high up, said she'd call the police . . . sat right in the doorway . . .' The nurse struggles with the language. She'd railed against being posted up north, the place of spoken Hindi and chapattis. ''Till I told her. I told her, "Madam, if he dies it will be your fault for obstructing the door to his bed."' She wrinkles her nose slightly.

Mamta nods, she isn't sure she's heard right . . . *if he dies, if . . . if . . . IF!* 'So where is . . .'

'In the next ward, Ward A. Lucky for him, Dr Pande did the operation. He's the best.'

Mamta holds her muscles in place until the nurse leaves, then squats beside the tin chair, the one that was used by Mrs Sahai, arms held straight-elbowed in front of her for balance.

She quickly walks to Ward A. This time no one tells her to stop. There are so many others like her in the hospital, also stinking,

having spent the night somewhere without shelter. She flattens her hair and walks on.

Mrs Sahai is standing right up close to his metal bed, giving him the election news. Lokend's eyes are closed, he looks wan, it is the first time one can see something of his father in him. Mamta watches from the door, shaking from her own trembling and the shoves of passing shoulders.

She can see the curve of his forehead, almost count every laughter line, follow his profile up to his neck, and after that the hospital green sheet all the way to his toes, the same toes, once encased in leather slippers. *Help me, Devi.*

Mrs Sahai looks up. 'Let him rest,' she whispers, gathering command. 'Don't disturb him. If he could, he would make it his business to take on the ills of the whole world,' she says, trivialising their meeting. 'You'd better go back.'

Go back to where? Where she came from? Mrs D'Souza's? Gopalpur? To her former life? She daren't ask. She daren't think. The hospital is the only place for her now. *What if Lokend Bhai dies?*

Lokend opens his eyes. 'I . . . know you.'

Somehow she finds herself close to the green sheet. She touches the sheet, feeling the toes through the cloth. A deep sense of being alive pours through her fingers. *Yes.* She is by his side.

'I . . . know you.' He only wants her. They are in their own circle of light, all the others are forced to step back. They are the only two people in the room, Mamta and Lokend. The rest have swirled off into nowhere, water down a drain, leaves in a hurricane, sparks in smoke.

'Yes, I am from Gopalpur. Prem, my brother, Sneha, my sister, you brought them here.' She holds her hands out to him, soiled from her night under the stars, palms folded in prayer, Namaste, what a wonderful greeting, acknowledging the divinity in the other's soul. 'The box of sweets,' she tries to explain again, 'at my wedding. You came. You gave me a box of sweets with a picture of Devi on it. I remember it was cashew barfi' – she can recall everything in fine detail – 'and buttered chapattis.'

'No . . .' he grasps her hands tightly. Mrs Sahai visibly twitches

with revulsion at the filthiness of Mamta and the stale odour of her skin. The painkillers have made him groggy. 'Not Gopalpur.' And that is all his body can manage for the day. He has lost much blood, and though stable for the time being, the situation could turn in an instant.

Their fingers entwine. She closes her eyes, out of his line of sight. *Oh, Devi, let me rest in this moment.*

Mamta has been taken, used, reused, discarded and defiled, in so many ways, that this sensation of holding a man's hand, purely and simply, without thought or panic is utterly new to her. It is the one action capable of erasing her husband's face, the template of cruelty, from her mind.

15

MRS SAHAI CONCLUDED THAT HE WAS a hopeless case. All month long she tried to convince him to take up the political baton again. That damn village girl showed up to kill her plans. She saw the election zeal, if she could call it that, seep out of Lokend's pores. He would never become a politician. There was no reason for her to waste her time on him.

Once Mrs Sahai left, the others deserted him too, starting with the Party members, then those who had to return to Gopalpur, and finally the stragglers who had once been mesmerised by his charisma. At Eyebrows' urging, even Prem deferred his hospital visits, bequeathing a long tender healing time to Mamta.

At first she was just content to stand in the doorway and look at him. Then, when Mrs Sahai left, she moved to his bedside, arriving before every other visitor and staying till the close of visiting hours. Each time he woke, she was to there to meet his needs: rearrange his pillow, feed him, wash the night clean off his face. The nurses rewarded her diligence and consistency with their trust, and every now and then they let her bathe him, change his bedpan, help dress his wound. They didn't know what to make of the village woman, obviously decades younger than the patient. First they conjectured that she was a Party supporter; then that she was family; and now

they are confused, because her attention is so close to that special kind of service – both greatly loving and impersonal.

There were nights of terrible pain for Lokend, who struggled for a long time with death. His dreams suddenly turned into nightmares of deep, drowning red. At such times his arms would rise involuntarily out of the sheets aching to hold on to something real. And Mamta was that reality, standing steadfast as a lighthouse, her shoulders an impersonal crutch for his flailing arms. Night after night.

One night on its way back down to his side, his left hand had brushed her skin at the dip in her neck, and continued its intimate journey down her breast. That touch, unknowing in Lokend, had left her in a heady panic from something akin to ecstasy, and she was only able to set her world right side up again by taking his limp hand in her own.

Only a life-threatening trauma could have pushed those two from their separate and unfelt lonely spaces into each other's lives. Was it he who took her hand, or was it she who offered it? It couldn't really have been that she made the first move. The times wouldn't have allowed it, such public intimacy with a man; her caste wouldn't have allowed it, touching someone so far above her; her being wouldn't have allowed it, this much pain for someone she hardly knew. But the times did allow it, her caste did allow it, her being did allow it. All that stolen, perhaps wrested, possibly sanctioned, and now here she is, grasping his hand.

She realises she is ready to accept the companionship of another man. In fact she is ready for more than just companionship; she is prepared to love him, having already loved him for so long. But the thought of a relationship with even one such as Lokend who she *knows* will never betray her, remains a looming abyss. She has no idea how deep the darkness is or might become.

But the long and lonely hospital visits and Lokend's endless pain have made a friend of that abyss, and she finds herself whispering stories into his unconscious ear, purging herself of the poison of history. She shares her most intimate thoughts with him, tells him of her loveless marriage, of her stepdaughter, of her father, of her

benign dreams in a world of dread. She believes he hears her, perhaps not with his ears, but with something deeper. And as she speaks, her fear evaporates.

How does one go from loving to declaring; from declaring to hoping for love in return?

She is happy just to love. It is an intensely familiar emotion. It has been her enemy and her most faithful friend. *Oh, Devi, let me love him. Just love him.* He has been with her through her life, she let her thoughts stray back to that quiet look each time destiny knocked her in the dust and it was to him that she returned with every piece of good news.

And what of Lokend? Why does he love her? Perhaps because the moment they touched, he felt that Mamta needed him far more than any creature ever had before. For Lokend, all female kind, indeed the world, had coalesced into her being. In that instant, she became Devi, universal female energy, absolute divinity. That could be one explanation. Perhaps there are other, more mundane ones. Perhaps he is committed for planting those sweets in her trembling hands at her wedding, or for seeing her at her most vulnerable – beaten by her husband, the under-the-banyan-tree rules, and by social mores. It could be for anything. Who is to know why two souls come together?

Still holding her hands in his and tracing ever so softly, he asks, 'Why do you come every day?'

'People would die for you, Sahibji. You know that.' *Don't tease me.* Her throat can hardly move, the words sound as if they are coming from far away. 'I . . . I, I am just a small person, nothing . . .'

'Let no one tell you who you are or must be.' He offers these words to her with gratitude. For the first time in his life, he feels that he might be of this world. If she lets go, she will be able to fill the room with her tears.

'Lokend Bhai, Lokend Bhai.' Prem dashes into the ward. He whips the sheet off Raja's cage as he approaches. 'Raja missed you more than all of us put together, I think,' says Prem, assured, mature and comfortable in Lokend's presence.

Raja pokes his nose out of the cage; the bars allow him to get as

far as his whiskers. He leans forward, bringing all his weight to push him through, till his flesh is doubled back on itself. Lokend puts two fingers into the cage, giving the struggling animal some respite. Mamta looks on, she looks at the fingers, Raja's cheek against them, and she is happy for them both. She herself has been found. She too has stopped straining against her bars.

16

ON THE DAY HE WAS DISCHARGED, she packed his things in a small cloth bag and they left just like any other couple. Without hesitation, she took him to Eyebrows' dispensary. There Prem had knotted a sheet between two nails on opposite walls to give Lokend his own room. The brother said nothing when he saw his elder sister help Lokend on to the cot and place his clothes and her own, some side by side, and some – one on top of the other – in the cardboard box he'd set aside for Lokend's cupboard.

But companionship is easier to share than intimacy.

Mamta made sure she was never exclusively alone with Lokend, she would pull back the sheet and tie it to one side during the day, and would find some reason to ask Prem to share their evenings. It cost her to set up her life so precisely, she was constantly in turmoil, much as she had been in her husband's hut, this time for not wanting to accept love too eagerly, wanting to delay its guaranteed caprice a little longer.

And so the weeks passed, with Mamta and Lokend living side by side, but not together, and helping Eyebrows in the dispensary. While bandaging arms and legs and cleaning wounds, Mamta often allowed Lokend to look into her eyes and smile with the knowingness of lifetimes. It pleased her when his arm accidentally touched her own, without eliciting a hint of acknowledgement or a tremor

of a response. He simply asked nothing of her, bringing a normality to her life that was extraordinary.

Their roles are precisely defined. Mamta does the cooking, cleaning, sewing, mending: all those things she learned in the village, leaving the purchase of medicines to Eyebrows and Lokend. The regulars remark at how the dispensary smells more of impatient spices than disinfectant, most definitely a change for the better. And so, Mamta starts preparing two sets of meals, one bland for Lokend and the other, village-style, for herself and Eyebrows and all the other hungry patients who come to their door at two in the afternoon hoping to share a bit of the trio's lunch. Once again she is excellent with clothes just as she was as Mrs D'Souza's unofficial dhobi.

She works every waking moment, even harder, if that is possible, than she did in Mrs D'Souza's house, because she tells herself that the dispensary is her own place. But really it is because she wishes to stay busy, distracted, much too busy to think about him and her, the one thing that occupies her every waking moment.

But life wins in the end, as it always does: wins over death, over hurt, over anguish and, most importantly, over fear.

It happened the night a baby was born at the dispensary. A pregnant girl, still in her teens, had knocked on the door hours past closing. She was gasping, as if she had run a long distance. Sickly thin, she looked hardly five months pregnant, though she was close to delivering. She must have known she would die without help, so she'd rushed to Eyebrows' door, the place she'd heard about from her battered sister.

The banging had woken Mamta first. She always slept the sleep of a new mother, able to rise at a moment's notice and able to fall asleep equally quickly. Mamta reacted instantly; she'd seen many babies born casually in her village.

She let Lokend sleep, she knew night time was his only relief from constant pain. Instead she woke up Eyebrows and together they prepared the girl for her difficult birth. The birth canal was too small, the girl too weak, her will too vitiated. Whatever the reason, the baby was stillborn. By then it was morning and Eyebrows

had to attend to other patients, so Mamta was the one responsible for sending the girl home.

The girl hadn't cried, and Mamta had held her hand, looked into her face and said firmly, 'It's better to cry,' sanctioning her grief.

'I know,' the girl had replied with a wilted smile, 'I know, but I don't feel anything. Is that bad?' Then the girl said something that changed Mamta's life. She said: 'What would I have done with this baby? In a way I am saved. I can go back to my old life now.'

Mamta felt a sensation of enormous loss on the girl's behalf. She realised that she mourned not so much the death of the baby, but the death of the girl's future. The instant she delivered that dead baby, the girl knew that she would go back to her old life, her future unchanged. She gave up the one moment capable of shifting her life-scenario from one in which she was a helpless child-mother to one in which she was a strong woman, in charge of her own destiny.

The loss of belief in the girl's future had brought her own future into focus. Unlike the teenage girl, Mamta realised that her old life did not have a hold on her any more. She had to go forward, so she decided she would go forward with him, her heart-keeper, Lokend.

Go forward.

They were meant to be lovers.

He'd clasped her hand and pulled her close to him. She'd slid beside him, carefully avoiding his wound. He'd folded her in his arms without speaking and kissed her birthmark. His caresses were tender and immature, unpractised and gentle. She tried to stop the comparisons, the flashbacks, the coupling without preamble, but her body finally tuned out the pictures of her previous sexual experiences. Trembling, she'd given in to him, flowing with him, dancing with him to the fugue of small, silent, discreet laughter; laughing that little laugh that occurs in physically intimate situations only in the context of complete trust. There are lovers who go through lifetimes without the company of such healing, shared joy.

She'd fallen asleep cradled in the crook of his arm, into such an unusual and deep sleep that left her satisfied, swollen and rumpled when she awoke. That day she knew she had slept in a place of absolute safety for the first time in her life.

17

Every morning, her love slides across the table, warms the tea and butters the chapatti. She does the same things her mother did for her father, but with a difference. Her actions aren't automated by habit or dictated by duty, but burble from her laughing heart that dances with the passion of a rose in a monsoon wind. At last she is able to give in to her great lilting love that has shattered her peace only to put it higgledy-piggledy back together till she has to stop herself from giggling at the thought of them together.

But she cautions herself that this much happiness isn't a good thing. What has she been taught? Never laugh too much, never expect too much, never ask for too much, never, never, never. Laughter and tears will be hers in equal part. Cause and effect. But she can't muzzle her delight. No place can contain her big love, so close to worship, that the gods might surely be offended if she didn't placate them with prayers three times a day.

Now that she has been with him for almost a year, she can hardly remember a time when they were apart. She has been his companion longer than he has been hers, but now, it seems they are one. For her part, she's learned his lessons well, that is the gift she promised him, silently inside her heart: to live a better life, not for him, but for herself.

She feels so much a part of him that she has never fully realised

the truth of their commitment. She is devoted, that's all she knows. She is grateful, that's all she knows. If he were to leave her without a word, she wouldn't be devastated or hurt, she wouldn't question, she'd accept.

But he does love her.

She senses something tragically magical in his feelings for her and she shudders with guilt each time she sees the crinkled corners of his eyes and his big white teeth shining through his smile, thinking how hard it must have been for him to give up his world of lofty, unseen bliss for *this*, her fickle world of Maya, illusion, the dream of duality in the empirical universe. She thinks he is able to visit her world, the place of pleasure and pain, only because he can very clearly see a finite end to his life. She imagines his spirit struggling with his feelings by day, and each night, triumphing over her world of duality, returning to the heavenly heights of those ascetic places which she still imagines as lonely and cold.

He smiles more on the outside now. For that he is grateful to her, and in turn, she is indebted to him for allowing her to think herself deserving of a pout on her lips and an angry tear in her eye because of some imagined slight, just like any other woman.

When they lie entwined on their mattress, Lokend talks about his day. They dissolve into each other like honey and warm water. She feels a solid sense of companionship, so different from her mother's warnings about love, pregnancy and childbirth. Her mother was right on every account, but for the fact of the incredible love that overwhelms her. At those times she wishes to climb under his skin, till there is no one who can say which body is which.

And yet, outwardly, theirs is an ordinary union. Mamta has that untidiness of appearance that goes with so many women who have never felt attractive in their lives. She spends no time in front of the mirror and even less pulling her hair into a knot at the nape of her neck. She knows it isn't for her looks that he is with her.

For a year now they have lived out of the back of Eyebrows' dispensary.

For a year she has tried to contact her mother, first through

Cynthia D'Souza, and then Prem. She has described her miracle-life in florid detail without mentioning Lokend in her letters home. But there has been no reply from Gopalpur.

Mamta has sent a box of sweets to her mother, a box with the picture of Devi on it, the same kind that Lokend gave her on the first day they met. Mamta thinks that sweets on Diwali – their favourite festival of lights, firecrackers, fancy food and prayers – will turn her mother towards her. But she is wrong.

Lata Bai has made a hard-headed pact with herself not to forgive – and that is the word she uses each time her thoughts stray to Mamta – her runaway daughter. For Lata Bai, Mamta *is* Sharma's wife, shit-smeared and raped, a disgrace. She has kept the news of Mamta's newfound freedom to herself just as she has news of Seeta Ram's death.

'This is the first time I am celebrating Diwali on the correct day. For our kind, Diwali always came one day later than for the rest of Gopalpur. The morning after, we bigger ones would head out into the forest and fields looking for unspent firecrackers, while the little ones waited in line at the back door to the Big House's kitchen for leftovers,' Mamta says.

'Yes, I remember that, the queue outside our kitchen. Asmara Didi was always so kind.'

'Yes, it's easy to be kind when you have everything,' she says, bitterness tainting her words. She bangs the side of her hand into the floor, furiously beating out a pattern. Then she quickly checks herself. 'We knew you were home if the sheets were dragged into the courtyard laden with sweets! Oh, how we wished to see you.' Thump, thump thump, go the prints, just like someone walking, emerging first as toeless soles. She paints the toes with the tips of her fingers, first the thumb, then the pointing, middle, ring and finally the little finger. 'Amma used to do this every year. Each year she would invite Lakshmi into our house.' The baby footprints of Lakshmi, the goddess of wealth, have started their journey at the front door, snaking deep into the dispensary. Thump, thump thump, fine red dust escapes from under her hand like warm breath to

313

shower her blouse, 'but the goddess never came, instead we listened to the sound of other people's firecrackers and dreamed of leftovers from your kitchen. The night after Diwali, Amma would light a single oil lamp once again, and take down your sweets from the rafters. We would eat your sweets and pray all over again, begging Lakshmi to come to our house . . .' She starts on the rangoli, a special painted square filled with secret meaning, its esoteric pattern rendered in edible powders: turmeric, rice flour and crushed rose petals. She clamps her tongue between her lips, the lines must be unbroken, drawn accurately by a steady hand, without any mistakes. She carefully releases a stream of coloured powder from between her thumb and ring finger to form a pencil-thin line. '. . . But she never did.'

Her words are tinged with sadness. He knows it pains her that her mother doesn't approve, doesn't write. 'Mamta, Lakshmi is here today,' he whispers, just loudly enough to calm her soul.

'She knows nothing about us, you know. I can't write to her about you . . . I . . . I . . . won't allow them to . . . to . . . I won't allow her to . . .'

'Mamta, it is beautiful,' says Eyebrows, bounding in with an armload of oil lamps. 'Prem is coming over to light these this evening, then we will burst crackers and feast.'

The dispensary is filled, floor to ceiling, with presents from grateful patients, new mothers, old wives, grandparents: clothes, sweets, crackers, pots and pans, even a milking goat tied outside. Eyebrows will start giving away everything tomorrow, barring what they use. It is the same every Diwali. The givers come back the next day as receivers. It has become a game. 'And tomorrow we will have to clean up this mess,' says Eyebrows, always practical, 'and treat the burns and the chest infections from poisonous smoke.'

'Poisonous smoke?'

'Of course. You just see the drains tomorrow, filled with bodies of chickens, dogs and cats all dead from cracker-smoke asphyxiation. Wait and see, Mamta: Begumpet will go mad tonight. There will be so much smoke from the firecrackers that you won't be able to see your hand in front of your face.'

'Can we go watch?'

'Yes, of course we can, and let's ask Prem to join us too.'

'I wish Amma was here.'

'Amma, Amma, Amma, is that all you can think of? So why does she shun you? Because you have rejected the mores of society, poked a finger in the eye of her tradition. For that alone you should be lauded,' says Eyebrows, a consummate anarchist at heart.

Mamta's eyes fill with tears. 'You have no idea what she did for me, Didi. She may not accept me now, but it was different . . . we were different when I was small.'

'Mamta, there will be a time for reconciliation. Don't beat against the tide. Your love is a flowing river and, just as determined, it will reach its ocean,' Lokend says and puts an arm around her shoulders. More than anything, his affection confounds her; she has never been at the receiving end of unnecessary human contact. Mamta squirms, physical displays of affection in someone else's presence always leave her feeling giddy-headed, and very, very embarrassed.

'I am going to write to her anyway,' she says, her face beetroot red.

Lata Bai has received the sweets, and resolved not to eat even one. But she has. She has tasted a tiny corner of milkcake and found it excruciatingly delicious. It is the same dilemma with her daughter. How she wishes to enfold Mamta in her arms, but she knows she must stay true to her word with an equal strength.

Tonight she will hear the revelry, but she will do nothing. She will sit and contemplate the night in internal silence while the whole world celebrates round her with prayers and crackers in noisy delight.

'We'll be back by eight for the pooja,' shouts Mamta over her shoulder as she navigates through the gift boxes. 'You sure you don't want to come with us?'

'Yes, I'm sure. Someone has to stay to tend the stupidly wounded,' Eyebrows laughs. 'And there will be lots of those tonight.'

Mamta and Lokend are off to the bazaar. For the first time in his life, Lokend has use for the small amount of money he kept from

his inheritance. 'It's going to be so exciting,' she says, clinging to his arm through the gathering throngs. The city is already shuddering with the sounds of exploding crackers even though it is still light. 'In Gopalpur we never lit anything till after sunset.' She has got used to the crowds and doesn't comment on them any longer, but Lokend tightens his grip on her hand. He too is from the village, the place of open spaces, long bicycle rides and plodding bullock carts.

They sidestep on to the curb to escape the sweeping current of the crowd. There in the nook of a tree is a vendor selling bathashas and kheel, treats only available during Diwali. Lokend purchases some for her. The bathashas, fragile white discs of pure sugar, melt on her tongue, she quickly follows with a chaser of kheel, crisp puffed rice. 'It's all for you,' he says, delighted by her attempts to speak through mouthfuls of food.

'It's so good. Kamla Masi used to make this for us, but I never had nearly so much before. Let's take some back for Didi and Prem.'

'Don't forget Sneha.'

'Yes, and Sneha, poor thing, she won't even get the day off from Mrs D'Souza's.'

The crowd thins, moving towards the city square. Each street is lined with little stalls. The buying is furious. This is the last night of the Diwali mela, the shops will be gone tomorrow, whisked away as conclusively as a clean-up by a jinn.

The bhajans play on, the whole street bows to the devotional music, designed specifically to stir the conscience and alternatively settle and unsettle the soul. It is a night of ritual. The prayers are eternal, tributes to various gods and goddesses. Mamta and Lokend recognise many of the singers – beggars on other days and regulars at the dispensary.

They walk through the north street, dedicated to feminine adornment: bindis, bangles, parandis, henna patterns, saris, kohl sticks, incense, pooja paraphernalia. She buys a turquoise blue parandi. She will thread it into her plait tomorrow, so that it comes right down to her hips, and when she sits it will be as if she is sitting on her own hair.

'Let's go,' she says, leading him by the arm to the outskirts, 'let's enjoy the crackers from here.' And so the evening offers itself for exploration. Mamta's little-girl energies are rekindled with the gusto that only familiar scenes from the past can achieve. Without her knowing it, her frame of reference has shifted, gone back in time. And in this incarnation, her past is a happy one.

What is life if not a series of experiences? Lokend has given Mamta a second life, because he has made it possible for her to experience her life and understand her past in a new way. It is all a matter of perspective, even something as paradigmatic as the earth looks like something else seen from a long distance away.

The singers have dived deeper into the mêlée. There will be much pick-pocketing tonight.

> *Oh innocent heart, oh innocent heart,*
> *What is your desire, What is your destiny?*
> *In this material world,*
> *You are a lost soul,*
> *Oh ignorant heart, oh ignorant heart,*
> *What is your desire, what is your destiny?*

'He loved that song. Manmohan loved that song.' For the first time since he left Gopalpur he thinks of the bandit. 'He was a man caught in the caprice of destiny, and he made the mistake of thinking he couldn't do anything about it . . . He was a good friend to my father.'

'The Big House. I never dreamed . . .' This is the first time since their union that Mamta realises just how close she is to the Big House. Suddenly she thinks she needs to be formal with him. She takes a step back into his shadow, the exploding crackers continue their cacophony.

'No, no –' he takes her hand and smiles '– the Big House is all but gone. Are you still scared of it? We aren't in Gopalpur, you know. You are with me. What can't you do, there are no limits . . .'

'. . . except the ones I impose on myself,' she completes his sentence.

317

'Yes.' He laughs out loud, enfolding her in his arms, digging his chin into her back to make her giggle.

'So tell me about your Daku,' she says, playful again.

'Yes, I must. I will tell you everything.'

She rests her head on his shoulder for a brief second, looking up into the sky, spark-spangled from exploding rockets and lanterns. The sparkle is reflected in her eyes. Lokend breathes in, he knows he doesn't have many Diwali celebrations ahead of him. He wants the woman beside him to stand on her own, to find her own life. He takes a sideways step, placing an arm's length of distance between them. The sparkle remains in her eyes, her head stays tilted to the sky, her face catches the light, turning pink. She is supremely alive and strong.

Mamta can feel the start of a dream deep inside her – a dream of being a mother soon. Her body is bursting with fertility. But she hasn't dared to share her news. Eyebrows abhors talk of children. She doesn't approve of new souls being added to the burgeoning population by people who have much too little to live on themselves. But now, Mamta has run out of time, after all, how long can she conceal the pregnancy?

'Why? Why would you want to bring a child into this world?' Eyebrows has seen too much, her cautioning isn't merely cynicism, but genuine concern.

'Oh, Didi, I want it. With this man, I want it. I want to see something of him spring out of my body. When I was married, I never thought about children, perhaps because I was a child myself, but now, oh now . . .' Eyebrows looks at Mamta, intimacy overpowering the smell of disinfectant. She looks away.

'Think carefully, what can you give a child? Look at the times we live in.' The women don't have to look far. It is after hours, but there is woman knocking on the glass door with her elbow, a leper, whose bandages need retying. Uncharacteristically, Eyebrows shoos her away.

'Look at that. Needs her bandages tied neatly so she can beg tomorrow. She says the do-gooders turn away from open wounds,

but give generously to bandaged hands. What is the meaning in that?'

'Didi, you ask too many questions. Just learn to leave things alone.'

'If we all left things alone, then what . . .?' The knocking won't stop, the leper has started banging a stone against the pane.

'For God's sake,' says Eyebrows loudly into the room, half rising from her stool, throwing her body behind her words in a single action that says: Go Away. 'Shoo. Off with you. Tomorrow, come back tomorrow!'

'Look at that woman, no hands, no hope, and look at me . . . filled with . . . with what? I don't know how to describe it. It is what I used to feel when I prayed with Amma at the ruins. Oh, how I wish Amma could see me now. She would be so happy for me. So proud. I love him so much.' Mamta's eyes fill with tears.

'That's a sentimental heart if ever I saw one. Lovesick silly girl. Oh, go on, have your baby then, who am I to stop you? But don't bring your amma into it. The way your own mother has shunned you, why, I wouldn't treat a dog like that,' says Eyebrows, realising too late that she should have bitten her tongue.

Mamta physically shakes the hurt off her face. 'What shall I tell him? I hope he will be happy. *I* am going to have a child. I can't believe it Didi, *I* am going to be a mother soon.' In spite of all her cautioning, Eyebrows feels the beat of her own heart in sympathy with her friend's. She hugs Mamta, who says, 'I'm months along. I didn't tell you, but the smell of that red medicine makes me want to throw up. Did you notice? I used to leave all the bandaging to him.'

'What am I going to do without you two?'

'Nothing, you won't have to do without us. We're not going anywhere.' Just then, they hear the key turn in the lock and Lokend walks in holding soiled bandages. He puts them in the to-be-burned garbage pile.

'So she managed to convince you to change her bandages?'

'Yes, luckily I'd bought these for the dispensary –' He holds up a bag. 'She said she had no way . . .'

'. . . to earn a living without clean bandages. Yes, I've heard it all before. She is going out begging tomorrow.'

'We all have to find our own ways to live, right, Mamta?' News of Lokend's healing touch has spread throughout Begumpet. More and more come to the dispensary, not for bottled medicines, but for Lokend, the prince who gave up his kingdom to come here to help the destitute, sick and dying. Even so, Eyebrows now has a second line of defence – boiled water and vaccinations.

'Mamta has news, has she told you?'

Without warning, Mamta becomes infinitely shy. A trickle of sweat starts to wind its way down the nape of her neck.

'Go on, tell him.' Eyebrows walks to the front to put away the medicines and bandages and give them privacy.

'How are you?' Useless talk. Wonderful useless everyday talk between husbands and wives.

'I am well today. But tell me your news.' He pats a space beside him. She sits. Gingerly. He pulls her close, her head rests on his chest. Her hair tickles his nose.

'I'm going to have a baby,' she says at last, lifting her head to look in his eyes. 'I am going to be a mother.' He drags her to him, holding her tight, allowing time for many thoughts to pass. She is forced to shift in his arms just to breathe. 'You are happy, no?'

He is of this world! Oh, how he *is* of this world. She is glad for the ripples she has caused in him, this still pool of a man from which people have got used to slaking their thirst. 'Tell me you are happy,' she says urgently.

'Yes, yes, yes! Enormously happy,' he says, tangled in the shadows of her hair.

'I want to go home after the birth,' she says spontaneously.

'To Gopalpur?'

'Yes, to Gopalpur. I want to tell Amma everything. I want my child to have a grandmother. I want Amma to know you . . . To meet you.'

'Where should we stay?' She doesn't dare say the Big House. She'd just assumed that's where they would go. 'Not the Big House. It's my brother's, we can't go there. We must make a life of our own,' he explains, as if reading her mind.

'Like the woman with the bandages.'

'Yes, just like that woman with no hands. Look at us – between us we have four, we will be all right.'

Her face has relaxed into gentle plumpness with the new weight of pregnancy, pushing her birthmark into her hairline.

As Mamta's belly grows, so do the hopes and well-being of the patients at the clinic. The entire community of raggle-taggle sick women and children, who come to the dispensary more for solace than a cure, is bearing this child with her. The women find her bump irresistible, and they refuse to leave her alone, filling her ears with advice that her mother might have given her in other circumstances. 'Wash your hair under the tap with cold water when you feel the pains. Your baby will pop right out like a mango pit,' says a mother of twelve. 'Drink a tender coconut every day, your baby will be white as the full moon,' says the South Indian with bruised midnight skin. 'Sleep on your right side, it will be a boy.' 'Be consistent with its inoculations. Starting within the first three days of its birth,' says Eyebrows. After the burn victims, the battered women are the ones most delighted with her pregnancy.

Sometimes she is peeved by their consistency and their dogged faithfulness, but for the most part she is grateful for her extended family, women who come to the dispensary for medicines and bandages, but instead give generously of themselves.

Weeks before her time, Eyebrows insists she stop caring for the sick. Instead, Lokend cares for her, pressing her dimpled heavy feet and rubbing the small of her back with hot oil. She never remembered her mother being off her feet for one second before the births of any of her brothers and sisters.

Why wasn't her mother allowed any rest? The guilt makes her grab Lokend's hand. 'Just relax. This is your time. Enjoy it. When the baby comes, you can get busy again,' he says.

She cries so easily now, her tears just gush for want of reason. Pregnancy makes you soft, says Eyebrows, changes your body from sinew to weak quivering flesh, and turns all your bodily fluids into

tears. That may be so in the city; in the village when did a mother have time to hope for her unborn child, let alone cry for it?

She is not afraid of the birth. There is no forewarning, no talk about this being the night, no distress or anxiety. She is in safe hands. Once her waters break she knows it'll be soon, not because of what she's been told, but because of what she has experienced with other births, both animal and human. Her confidence is born of participation, not learning.

The baby is born at night. A boy. Eyebrows cuts the cord, cleans the baby and wraps him in a bundle, handing him to his father. Lokend cries seeing the baby, who is no more than the size of a packet of Brooke Bond tea. Eyebrows also cries, but because she knows Mamta and her family will leave soon.

'Manmohan, Manmohan,' Lokend whispers, naming their son in memory of his friend. At that moment, Mamta acknowledges to herself that, ceremony aside, she is truly Lokend's wife, and he, simply Manmohan's father.

'Yes, it's a good name,' she says. 'Manmohan.' Manmohan, beloved of the heart, another love word.

He pulls her up the step, his hand in hers. Manmohan sleeps happily in the crook of her arm. They settle into the back seat of the bus. She wants to see her sister and brother before she leaves Begumpet. She gets off at the stop she knows well, Lokend is accompanying her only because this is the first time she is travelling as a mother. She runs to the building, pulling her pallav over her eyes.

'Chacha!'

The man turns, his hair considerably more grey. With great reason the corners of his mouth turn up. 'Mamta!' He is pleased to see her. 'That yours?'

She nods. 'Where is Memsahib?'

'It's early yet, she must still be upstairs.'

She knows not to talk much. 'May I?' She points towards the building with her thumb.

'Of course, go on. It's practically your house. That sister of yours

322

is doing a good job,' says Chacha the Taciturn, foisting more words on her than he ever has before.

She skips up the steps, a lot less agile than a year ago; the new weight has made her clumsy, she holds on to the wall, realising it is clean, and free of graffiti.

The door to the kitchen is open. Mrs D'Souza's hand is doing the familiar twist motion alongside her right ear as she makes tea on the stove. Hindi music is filling the corridor. Mrs D'Souza is mouthing the words along with the radio's song.

'Memsahib.' The music is too loud. 'Memsahib!'

Mrs D'Souza turns her bulky frame, her buttocks moving independently of one another. The glassy film visibly vanishes from across her eyes. 'Mamta?' She closes the gap between her and her former servant, but stops short of taking her in her arms.

'Didi?' Her sister's voice greets her from inside the house. Sneha squats on the floor, mop in hand. Her hands are too dirty to give her sister a hug. It's Baby who makes things comfortable. Older and slower, she comes out from beneath the table, jostling a spray of blue flowers, shuffles up to Mamta and starts licking her, proceeding to Manmohan's face.

'See, she hasn't forgotten you.' The women laugh. Mamta shows off Manmohan like a prize, holding him under the arms. Baby quickly grabs Mamta's empty lap.

'Lovely child. Oh, Mamta, I finally had to get a new dhobi.' The subversive complaint about Sneha's work isn't lost on Mamta. 'I suppose now I must give up my dreams of having you come back to work.'

'Where is Cynthiaji?'

'At work. Would you believe it? She's taken a job in an advertising agency. She's a changed girl. You remember how she used to talk back all the time? None of that now. No skivvies, hardly any lipstick, and she even cooks now and then.'

'Can Sneha come downstairs with me? Not long, memsahib, I'll send her back up in fifteen minutes.'

'Take your time, take your time. I'm sure you sisters have a lot to catch up on. She's not the cleaner you were,' says Mrs D'Souza, ignoring her sweeper's presence. Sneha looks to her feet.

On the stairwell she says, 'I work hard, I tell you, Didi, I work hard. I've done nothing to disgrace you, and still she says those things.'

'I know, I know, don't worry, Memsahib has to have something to complain about. Keeps her young. When I was here she had her fights with her daughter. Now, with Cynthiaji reconciled, I suppose it has to be you.'

'You must be right. A baby boy, Didi, you are so lucky.' Sneha holds Manmohan with straight arms at a distance and looks at him.

'We are planning to go back.'

'Go back! Don't be crazy, Didi. Why are you going back? You aren't married to him.' Gopalpur is too fresh in her younger sister's mind to warrant romanticism. 'You have such a nice life here. You have the best husband, I mean man, and Prem and I are here. Granted, we don't meet much, but still.'

'Oh, Sneha, I can't tell you what it means to be a mother. I am longing to go back. Gopalpur is calling for me. I want to show Manno to his grandmother. I want Amma to meet Manno's father. I want her to accept our family. Amma knows nothing about us. She doesn't even know I have a son. I want Amma to hold my son.'

'Don't be silly!' Sneha says with the authority of an older rather than younger sister. 'You are married to another man. They will never let you stay. They will beat you out of Gopalpur. Even Amma won't accept you. She will disgrace you. Disgrace that saintly Lokend Bhai of yours. If I were you, I couldn't bear it. He has given you everything. What's in Gopalpur?'

'I can't explain it, Sneha. Even if I have to fight every person in Gopalpur for my acceptance, I will. I just need to do it.'

Sneha has never seen such confident zeal in her sister's eyes before. She feels a pinch of envy. It is now that she realises just how much Lokend Bhai has actually given her elder sister.

'You know Amma told me to go back to my husband in her last letter. But that was then, I didn't have him then' – the girls look at Lokend from under the stairs – 'but when she sees him, all her reasons will leave her, the village will mean nothing. He is something . . . someone . . . he is . . .' Mamta has no words for her love.

'I will make her accept me. I will make them all accept me. For him. For us,' she says, taking Manno out of her sister's arms. 'She won't be able to resist. Have you ever seen a grandmother able to resist her grandchild?'

Sneha has to stop fighting against her sister's gathering strength. 'For me, Lokend Bhai has always been a saint,' she says, nodding towards him. 'Without him I would be dead.'

'Yes, yes, I know,' says Mamta, hugging her close. 'Forget those days. Here, none of that matters. And what about you? Do you have someone?'

'Hmm. Uhuh.'

'Who? Come on, who is he?'

'Kalu.'

'Kalu? My Kalu? Kalu from under the stairs?'

'He's lovely, he takes care of me.'

'What happened to his Maharashtran then?'

'Oh, her? She was too high class for him. Thankfully, she broke his heart, that's why I have him now.'

'Tell Prem to come and see us,' says Mamta as she leaves.

'You know he won't come. But I'll tell him anyway.' Prem is holding down two jobs and apprenticing to be a machinist. With every cell in his body he has become a city boy, lapping at every opportunity that comes his way. He shares a room with another village boy three miles out of town and rides into Begumpet every day on the second-hand bicycle that Lokend managed to arrange for him. His time, each second of it, is accounted for, and he has none to spare for social calls.

In the end, Eyebrows convinces them not to leave for Gopalpur before Manmohan is a year old. She says the city is a better place to be to make sure Manmohan is inoculated right. But each day that Mamta spends in Begumpet her dream to return to Gopalpur becomes stronger. Her heart has already fled Begumpet, and one year later, almost to the day, she packs their bags ready to leave.

The bus to Gopalpur is full and people are dragging their luggage to the roof. They put the soft bedrolls on top of tin trunks like raisins on rice pudding, making a soft seat for themselves.

'Shouldn't we go see what they are doing? I mean, is our luggage safe?' Mamta has never had something of monetary value to protect before.

He waves a hand, what will be will be, he has never been attached to things, and what's in their luggage anyway? A few clothes, and some gifts for her mother.

She pulls her pallav low over her eyes, opens her blouse and lets Manno suckle all the way out of Begumpet. The city is almost unrecognisable. In the five years she's been in Begumpet, the slums have spread way beyond the outskirts, past the railway station.

The scenery streaming past, the wind on her face, and the disquiet in her heart opens it up to lost thoughts. Outwardly she is just another nursing mother, but her being is molten with trepidation. It was her decision alone to return, she is making this journey against everyone's advice. 'I wish the buckets hadn't been so expensive. Anyway, I managed to buy Amma some salt and sugar. I wonder if she will know what to do with it,' she says.

He laughs, delighted by her naïveté. It never occurred to him that powdered salt and sugar could be so precious. In the Big House, they always had sugar cubes, nice neat white ones, for their tea. He looks at her, fully covered from head to toe like a fresh bride, suckling their baby. He leans over to take a look at his son's face and is overwhelmed with love for his family. 'I'm glad we're going back,' he says.

It is impossible for her to enjoy the journey. Whenever her heart steps out of her chest to dance with the clouds, her mind quickly pulls it back to the real possibilities of village-style reprisals. As a married woman, living with another man is unforgivable. It goes against every rule, every system. She is still her husband's possession. In Gopalpur she will need Lokend's protection more than ever. 'What about my mother, what do you think she will say about us?' she can't hold the question any longer.

'You will be safe with me,' he replies. That's all he can offer, guarantee for her safety, but he cannot change anyone's opinion.

It isn't enough. She wants approval. Immediately Mamta rationalises, 'I know Amma. She will not say one word against me.' Her words are filled with hope, but she knows hope can be a false friend.

'We will live with Manmohan's widow, with Asmara Didi.'

Now she has reason to fret about something else. 'Asmara Didi? Do you think she'll accept me? She is like a mother to you. We aren't married. So many mothers-in-law hate their legitimate daughters-in-law, so what chance do I have?'

He laughs. 'Asmara Didi has been after me my whole life to get a wife, she always said she wanted a grandson. Well, now she has her wish. Do you think she will reject it?' *A wife, wife . . .* that word appeases her. 'Look, I kept this,' he says, taking out a piece of news-paper from his pocket.

At first she doesn't know what to make of the shrivelled-up dirty string it protects.

'It's Manno's.'

Of course, her son's umbilical cord. She is flooded with gratitude. Lokend is not a superstitious man, but he remembered her needs and saved the cord for her, knowing she would want to plant it in the courtyard of the home she chose for her children.

'Now Gopalpur can truly become our home,' she says, clutching the cord tightly in her hand.

18

LATA BAI HAS BECOME ONE OF those who gamble with destiny to pass the time. If today the wind takes my roof, Jivkant will come home to find my dead body. If a bee enters the house before the dog barks, then there will be a letter at last from Sneha. If there is rain, Ragini will send for me. If I hear the wolves tonight, Mamta will come to her senses and return to her husband. If there is an electric light at my door, Mohit will come home. She plays the wind game in the stillest season, the bee game when there is not a flower blooming for miles, the rain game during the drought and the wolf game because she knows the wolves left with the bandits, and as for the electric light, well there will never be one outside her door. And so, Jivkant doesn't come home to her dead body, there is never a letter from Sneha, or a summons from Ragini and no word of Mamta or Mohit.

Mamta finds her mother dressed in widow-white, her sari old, soiled and rumpled as if she put it on years ago.

She has come to her old hut alone, separated from Manno for the first time. 'Amma,' she says with overwhelming normality in her voice.

'Mamta . . . my daughter . . . Mamta! How did you come back? When did you come back? Your sister, your brother?'

Is her mother angry, disappointed, approving, betrayed? She can't

328

tell from the tone of her voice. Mamta crushes her mother against her chest without looking into her eyes. It has always been the other way round, with her waiting for Lata Bai to invite her into her arms. But no more. She feels a spike of defiance; she is done with waiting for the world to offer her things. She will create her own destiny. She can feel her mother's bones through the sari. Her mother's back is slightly bent, and she has faint lines around her mouth where her gums have started to recede. It is a deeply satisfying embrace, and she relaxes into it with cautious contentment.

'Amma, we are all all right.' The smell of her mother is unchanged. The smell makes her a little girl again. This parting has been too long.

'Shall I bring the water today?' It is that evening time. The women would be going to the well to fill their pitchers, a stream of psyche-delic shapes.

Lata Bai shakes her head. 'It's only me, I go once a week.' She chews on the end of her pallav; she is tempted to lie, but so much time has passed, her wounds are scabbed over. 'I pushed him into the river,' she says, taking her daughter by the shoulders. 'We can both go to the well, if you like.' Lata Bai looks directly into her daughter's eyes, offering her the opportunity to announce her presence in Gopalpur.

Suddenly Mamta is unsure. 'No, the well can wait.'

'Let me make you something nice,' Lata Bai continues to avoid the obvious. She intends to keep the talk simple, frothy with familiar jocularity, just like in the old days.

The two women bend over the fire, her mother blows into its heart, the smoke flies up into Mamta's face. Lata Bai laughs loudly, Mamta smiles. She looks around, expecting to see her sturdy horse-shaped stick still lying in a corner somewhere.

'You look well. More meat on your bones. Yet, you look different. What's happened?'

The question possesses all the stealth of a stalking cat. What's happened? Everything! Her life has happened. So many words are crowded on the tip of her tongue, in exactly the place where one's tastebuds for sugar lie. It has been more than five years since she's

seen her mother. What can she tell her? Shall she say something about Lokend, about Manno . . . about the city? 'Amma, look at this, it is salt and this is sugar,' she says, opening the paper bags. 'You can't tell from their colour, can you? So white and . . . and . . . pure.' She pinches the salt and sugar into the breeze, letting both powders float away like memories.

'Yes, Saraswati Stores has the same,' says Lata Bai. Saraswati Stores has the same. Why say that? Mamta is surprised by the strength of her disappointment. It is a bad omen. It is not time to talk about her illegitimate son and her lover now. 'Your husband came looking for you, but that seems like years ago. Since then, there has been no news of him. You are with him, no?' asks the mother, determined to hear the explanation from her daughter's lips. 'No, of course I know you're not. So, when is he coming to get you?'

'Coming to get me? Never! He is never coming to get me! He will never *get* me.'

'Well, you will have to go when he comes.' Not *if*, but *when* he comes. The under-the-banyan-tree rules have become instructions for Lata Bai's life.

'I'll never go back to him. Never! What did Bapu call me? "Someone else's garden" – wasn't that it? Someone else's garden.'

'Oho, what are you so upset about? Girls leave their homes when they get married . . .' Lata Bai manages to keep the conversation disapproving but soft, negotiable. 'That's all he meant,' she defends her dead husband.

'Why are you saying these things? I thought you understood. Understood how I hated my life.'

'Of course I understood. Why you ran away is your own business. But you earned money, so who am I to fault you? Many women leave their husbands to earn in the city, there is no crime in that. But you are back now, and here in Gopalpur you are a married woman, and you must go when he comes looking for you. I don't say send him news immediately . . .' she is willing to compromise '. . . but you have to understand, news of your arrival in Gopalpur will reach him anyway. And when he comes, you must go. You are his . . .'

330

'His property . . . his garden. I know,' says Mamta bitterly. 'We aren't investments, Amma, we are human beings. I'll not be staying here,' she adds petulantly. She hasn't come this far to have to swallow her mother's condemnation. She has been with people like Lokend and Eyebrows, she cannot go back to the old ways, she cannot now tolerate the smallest suspicion of being anything less than a whole human being in anyone's eyes. Lokend's words, *Let no one tell you who you must be,* hold her close.

'Where then?' It is unthinkable to the mother that her daughter might have another place to stay.

'With the bandit wives.' Mamta will not tell her mother about Lokend.

'Go then. Leave me.' As a mother she must be sometimes soft, sometimes hard, sometimes bitter, and sometimes sweet. 'One by one you all left me. It was only he who remained, but I pushed him in the river. Cruelty is the most lasting memory. Isn't that the truth?'

It is a new world that Mamta has walked into. By virtue of being Lokend's chosen partner, she is accepted by the bandit wives, and yet, she lives in apologetic distress, never arguing, always taking the lead from others whom she thinks have more right to their wretchedness than she ever did. In her eyes, she is on a lower rung than the women whose husbands looted and murdered for their livelihood. Her deference somehow heals the wounded hearts of many bandit wives, left virtual widows because their husbands languish forgotten in jail.

Though she finds her place amongst the embroiderers, it is Asmara Didi who makes her feel truly welcome. Like a fallen flower that brings colour to the bush it lands on, Asmara Didi brings a lot of pink into her life. Lokend was right, Asmara Didi is grateful to her for bringing her son home. In return, the older woman treats Mamta like a new bride.

'Here, I saved this in the hope that some day he would . . .' Asmara Didi offers her a crushed rosette of silk bearing a toe ring, the conclusive sign of marriage.

She never had a wedding with Lokend. 'But . . . but . . . we aren't . . .'

'In my eyes you are,' says Asmara Didi. 'You are more than a wife to him. You know we never thought he would get married, always living for others, but somehow . . . somehow he feels he can do both with you. That is a miracle. Go on . . . put it on. For my sake.' She draws Mamta towards her and kisses her on her forehead right above her bindi. Mamta closes her eyes in the shelter of the older woman's embrace, so authoritative, so charged with motherly love, enough to shut out all the world.

As long as she stays with the bandit wives she is safe, but the village is closed to her. On her first day she tried to buy some provisions at Saraswati Stores only to be chased by village children pelting her with dung at the say-so of Nathu's daughter. That's when she heard the word for the first time – Rakhale, mistress! Just like Sharma's wife, raped and shit-smeared, rakhale! Kept woman!

This is the first time Lokend is taking them to the Big House. In fact it is the first time he is meeting Ram Singh since his return. They are going for dinner at Ram Singh's specific invitation. She has waited long for this.

She has dressed carefully in an elegant grey sari embellished with tiny specks of gold. It belonged to Lokend's mother, and was given to her by Asmara Didi. 'Bibiji chose her clothes well. In this sari you will be perfect,' said the old woman, pinning flowers in her hair.

Mamta has primed Manno with her interpretation of high manners, hoping they will pass muster with the Big House: touch your uncle's feet and don't rise till you feel his hand on your head, walk slowly and silently behind the grown-ups, don't take seconds unless asked at least three times, don't show the soles of your feet to those sitting opposite you.

Manno is rocking on his toes and heels like a boxer ready to lunge at his uncle's feet at his mother's command.

'Not this rakhale or her bastard.' Mamta and Manno are stopped at the door by Babulal.

The boy stops rocking.

'You go. You go in. You should not have to choose,' she says to

Lokend, and it is with a heavy heart that she sees him do her bidding and disappear into the mansion's cavernous belly.

'Bapu?' the boy asks.

'He'll be back soon,' she says, tossing the flowers, one by one, from her hair into the darkness. 'See that? That's Dhruv Tara, the constant star. He used to be a boy, a boy just like you –' *wronged too, just like you* '– the god Vishnu put him in the sky away from jealousy and evil to show all wanderers their way. You are like that star, steadfast and good.' Perhaps that's the use of mythology, she thinks, to make sense of all injustice, so that the wronged don't grow up to become criminals and murderers, but instead become holy beings filled with wisdom, permanent and inspiring. She is in a murderous mood, *rakhale, bastard, rakhale . . . shit-smeared and raped . . .*

'You walk so slowly!' Lokend grabs her by the waist from behind, surprising her. 'You didn't stay for dinner then?' She is delighted by his choice.

'No, I said my hellos and just as quickly my goodbyes. Ram Bhaia is running the Big House even more efficiently than Bapu. Look, I got us all a parcel of food. I still have my friends in the kitchen. They gave me these too, for Asmara Didi.' He hands her a bouquet of pink roses, after picking one to place gently in her hair. 'Manmohan planted them for her.' The boy, hearing his name, lifts his head. 'Yes, you are named after a great friend of mine, Manno.' He kneels to hug his son.

'They must have really wanted her to have these roses for them to cut them after sundown. Now, Manno, you must never pick flowers after sunset. That's when they sleep.' How often do mothers drop innocuous bits of information that collectively form the blueprint of their child's life?

She hasn't ventured out since her rejection at the Big House's front door, and she is surprised her mother hasn't come to see her. It has been two weeks. She has planned to tell Lata Bai everything. Better her mother hear the details of her life from her lips than through village gossip.

But Nathu's daughter has got to Lata Bai first.

Finally, duty drags Mamta back to her mother's hut. 'Amma?' Lata Bai winces, sending more creases through her upper lip, hers isn't the voice her mother wishes to hear.

'So you've come back to see me. My, my, how did you find the time?'

'I tried to come back several times before, but I had so much to do at home.' Mamta bites down on the word *home,* but too late.

'Yes . . .' Lata Bai plans to ensnare her with her affirmations. A net of yeses, all of them disapproving. 'You must have had a lot to do at *home.*'

'So how is it with you, Amma?' Mamta piles the sticks between the hearth stones as she talks.

'Leave it. There hasn't been tea in this house for at least a year.'

'Not any more, I brought some with me.'

The mother looks into her daughter's eyes. *You'll not take the joy out of my unhappiness.* 'I've heard.'

'It's no secret.'

'It's no secret . . . did you think of me, of your family?'

No! No I didn't. For the first time, I thought only of me. 'I'll not let anyone tell me how to live again,' she says, more in Lokend's words than her own.

'What has he done to you?'

'Why do you say "he"? Can't it be because of me, because I have finally found my life and am trying to live it? Can't you see, for the first time I am happy. I have dignity.'

'Dignity?'

Mamta turns away, not wanting to hear the word from her own mother's lips. Rakhale. She moves towards the door, still rickety on its hinges. A gentle wind rocks it back and forth adding a kind of annoying creaky music to their conversation.

Her first meeting had given her a false sense of security. But Lata Bai is the quintessential rural woman. As an individual she may be able to stand behind her daughter, but as a member of her ilk she can't. She finds she cannot bend the ilk's rules, for then her own existence would become a waste, a sham, worse than death.

334

'Why do you care? Why does anyone care?' Lata Bai turns her back to her, visibly unlistening like the rest of the village. Rakhale. That's what she is to her mother: a kept woman, an unclean thing.

'You've been away too long. I have to live in this village,' says Lata Bai. The under-the-banyan-tree rules have made a solid home for themselves in her hut.

Her mouth is so bitter she has a longing to spit. Mamta never imagined it would be so judgemental. She'd provided her reasons to the world at large and had come to Gopalpur, her last place of refuge, to be accepted as the pure and laughing Mamta of her child-hood, a girl who had done well for herself. But now, now she is being chastised for her love. Not for the fact of it, but that it is requited. Her mother would have had nothing to say to her had she been a lovesick married woman hankering after a man who had shown her some respect, but as a married woman with a lover, her mother has the rule book to beat against her head. 'You wouldn't think this if you knew what he did to me.'

'Who? What? Who did what to you?' Her mother attacks her for thinking herself vainly deserving of self-pity. 'Whatever your reasons, I can't listen. You were married in front of Devi. There is no way out for you.'

'Say it – just like Sharma's wife . . . raped . . . shit-smeared – say it.' She can recall the sensation of her mother's fingers rubbing oil into her hair. *Then why tell me all those stories of pearly halos round women's heads and great and glorious females breaking out of social limbo, becoming one with something higher than themselves, living in history, when you believe this. This? This!*

'You ruined Sneha's life too. Did you think someone would marry her after her elder sister showed her *exactly* how to behave as a dutiful wife?' Her mother's voice is nasal with meanness.

'She is doing wonderfully well in the city; she has a job, she has a home, perhaps she will even find herself a husband. She has a life. Better to have love from strangers than nothing from one's own,' she is shouting her defence.

'Love from strangers, is it? Look at my daughters. Fit only for the Red Bazaar.'

'That's where Bapu would have sent her, had Prem not brought her to me.' She squats. 'Oh, Amma, stop it, please, stop it.' How has it come to this? This intransigence. She wants to say, Do you remember the story you told me about . . . But she won't pursue it, won't let her mother spoil it. 'I have to go.'

'To him?'

'To my home.'

'Where did you get the money for this fancy home of yours?'

'I told you before, I am with the bandit wives.'

'Other thieving women,' says Lata Bai with an air of satisfaction.

'You can come too, you know. You don't have to stay here with the darkness. It's just on the other side of town. It's a small place . . .' But full of love, she thinks spitefully.

'I thought you would have moved into the Big House by now.'

'Amma, don't,' she says without a fight. 'Don't you think I would get married if I could?'

'Who would have thought you would have more than one offer of marriage in this life.' Her mother's words cut far more sharply than her father's ever could.

'I have to go. Come with me . . .' Now she is pleading.

Lata Bai turns her back on her daughter and the door.

She runs from her mother's hut, tripping as she struggles to get away. The winds failed this year. Such an odd thing to say: failed. The winds only brought disaster, but they were a dependable clock hand, heralding the changing seasons. The seasons have changed all right, just without the destruction. Only Mamta sees the miracle in the absence of the winds. She's back in Gopalpur with the man she loves. No winds. Devi approves, so why can't her mother? She runs, gathering speed. Her feet, in sturdy sandals, eat away at the dust as they did once before.

'Amma, Amma,' her voice cries out to the arid land dragged along upon the unsteady notes of an inexperienced flute. It creeps under the soil, and bounces off the Red Ruins. Her childhood is blowing round her like searing chaff. She thought her mother would grasp her with arms of steel, support her with an indomitable will that

would require nothing of her own bones. There is safety in imagining, reality is a big risk. Shall she live in her imagination forever?

What has she been taught? Never laugh too much, never cry too much, never feel too much. Never let your emotions set the price of your existence.

The flute begins catching steadier notes.

Mamta has gone through all the stages – disbelief, hurt, anger – and has eventually steeped herself in scripture so she can regain her equilibrium. But even the *Bhagvat Gita* is no guarantee of peace. She sees duplicity in every sacred word: *Surrender all actions to me, with your thoughts residing in the supreme self, from hope and egoism freed.* Hope and egoism . . . are these the driving forces of her pain?

Master first the senses . . . it is said that the senses are great, but greater than the senses is the mind; and greater than the mind is reason; but what is greater than reason is the Higher Self. Where is this Higher Self?

Lokend, Mamta and Manno sit together in prayer. They recite the Gayatri Mantra: '*Ohm Bhoor Bhuwah Swaha, Tat Savitur Varenyum, Bhargo Dewas Dhimahi, Dhiyo Yo Naha Prachodaya,*' and Lokend explains its significance: 'The Gayatri Manta inspires wisdom, it is a prayer to the Higher Self to bless us with enlightenment. The rhythm of the words will melt in your soul and cure you of your heartache, just like one of those fancy city antibiotics.' He smiles as he says this. And thus, Mamta eventually learns the meanings of all those esoteric words she has recited with her family through her life, at every birth, at every death, at every festival.

Perhaps the Higher Self has heard her plea, or is pleased with her devotion, for Mamta's situation is about to change.

'Arey-oh, Lata Bai, still eating once a week, are you?' Only Kamla can be rude to her without stinging. The two women know each other in a deep and final way, bound by the secret of Seeta Ram's final resting place downriver.

'So what's it to you?' Lata Bai has been in bad humour since Mamta's last visit.

'I have terrible news for you. I too am moving in with your married/unmarried daughter.' Kamla cocks her head to one side, the coquettish gesture looks obscene on the old, balding woman. Her words put Lata Bai in worse humour.

'Why does the world come to my door? What could I possibly want with it?' In truth it is a great disappointment to her that she lacks the courage to go to Mamta, and she doesn't need to be reminded of that by Kamla.

'Start living your life like you promised you would after that bloody Seeta Ram left you in peace. Why do you insist on eating alum every day? Tell me, do you really begrudge her her life? How can you? I thought you of all people would understand. You were the only one who managed to accept Lucky Sister, so why not your own daughter?' asks Kamla, knowing full well that it's often easier to accept dissension in other people than it is in one's nearest and dearest. 'Doesn't she deserve better? Go to her, Lata Bai, and see for yourself how she has bloomed. It is enough to crumble the oldest custom, the toughest social mores, the hardest heart.' She places the greatest emphasis on *the hardest heart,* leaving no room for doubt to whom that belongs.

'Tch, tch. I see you have been watching too many Hindi movies.' Yes, that's right, a TV set has come to Gopalpur, where else but at Lala Ram's doorstep. Kamla is a regular on Wednesdays when *Chitrahaar* is on. 'For once in your life leave the theatrics alone and let me be.'

'Let you be! Since you changed out of your coloured sari into this widow's cloth you have lost your senses. Let you be, indeed! To what? Your cough and bent back? At least before you had hate to keep you going, now it's not even that, it's . . . it's . . . What is it for? For God's sake, no one else in the village cares as much as you.'

'What about the vows they took in the name of Devi? And now she has a child. What's its name, by the way?'

'Oh no you don't. If you want to know *its* name you will have to ask her. I am not doing you any favours.'

'A marriage is a marriage, whatever you say,' says Lata Bai, as immovable as the Red Ruins.

'A marriage is a marriage! Maybe for my enemies!'

'Kamla, you were born with words in your mouth, it's a wonder you have room for any teeth.'

'So what should she do? Go back to that husband of hers?' Kamla is shouting now. 'Where was Devi when he cut out her side and sold it like a piece of meat?' Yes, Kamla knows all about that through none other than Asmara Didi, that wise old woman, who gave away only as much information as would be vital to better Mamta's future. Kamla visibly bites her tongue. She'd promised Asmara Didi her discretion, but there is discretion and then there is downright justice, she rationalises. 'You should know that part too,' she says smugly, setting her secret free in the name of justice.

'What are you talking about?'

'You know nothing! Because you bore the cruelty, the beatings, you expect her to do the same. It is your arrogance that keeps you from accepting her. By rejecting her you think you can pay him back for all the things he did to you. You want to crush him . . . for his freedom and your bondage . . . for his power and your weakness . . . for his apathy and your anxiety . . . for his voice and your silence. The only way you know how is to tolerate without accepting. You judge every-one through your life, confusing it with fate. If you give up this fate business, what will you do with yourself? Isn't that what you are thinking? You are thinking: then my life will have no meaning. All this, after I helped you push that man into the river. How dare you judge her? The only thing dependable in her life has been that goddamned birthmark. Go to her, Lata Bai, while there is still time. It is beyond time for fairytales and nursery rhymes, beyond time for childish toys. Now is the time to give her something tangible – your approval.'

Lata Bai looks desperately round her, but there is nowhere to escape. She grips her ears, and falls to the floor. A piece of her daughter's flesh, was she to die like an animal then? 'It is a terrible curse to live in a time and place where you don't have any dreams for your children. I couldn't even give her a respectable birth . . .' For the first time, Lata Bai acknowledges to another that Mamta could be illegitimate. 'She was always someone else's garden. I served weevils on her wedding. Oh, Kamla, what have I done?'

'Nothing yet, my sister, nothing is ruined yet. Come, let's go.' She takes her friend's hand, forgiving her just as quickly as she had censured her only moments ago.

Once they leave the hut behind, things are back to normal. 'Shall we stop by the bank to get ourselves a loan? They won't say no if you tell them you are Mamta's mother. She's a good risk. Brought more than five thousand rupees with her from the city, said she'd saved it through the Post Office Deposit Plan. That Lokend of hers opened the account for her at the bank. So what do you say? A loan first?'

Lata Bai can't share in her friend's joke, in her laughter rising, unexpected, unwanted. She gulps down her guilt. 'This is no time for jokes, Kamla, let's get to the bandit wives as soon as possible. I have wasted enough time on foolishness.'

Then and there, Lata Bai resolves never to look back over her shoulder at her old life again.

Mamta sends Manno to greet his grandmother, she has to, to spare Lata Bai the humiliation of a formal reconciliation. The toddler, newly walking, wandering like a blind thing, finally blunders into his grandmother's arms as she moves from side to side like a goalie waiting to grab the ball, suddenly agile for her age.

The little creature, innocent as fluffed cotton, used to having a hundred hands help him up, isn't shy of strangers and grabs her dirt-encrusted sari.

She clings to the tiny body as if he is the only branch in a flood. The past recedes. 'My boy,' she whispers, visibly shrinking into herself like cheesecloth left to dry in the sun, 'my poor boy, with no grandma to look after you. But now I am here. I am here, you see –' she offers her arms as proof '– I am here.'

'Amma.'

It is a whispered meeting between mother and daughter but with all the energy of a dam holding back a deluge.

'Amma!' The man holds out his arms. Though his hair is shock white, Lata Bai knows who he is. There is no precedence for an intercaste union in her life. She is afraid of the man who is approaching her swiftly. How did her daughter muster the courage

for a relationship with him? A zamindar's son, no less. Suddenly she is afraid to cross the caste and status sea. He does it for her and touches her feet. It isn't the zamindar's son's hands she feels on her toes, but her son-in-law's. 'Amma, come. I'm so glad you've come home at last,' he says.

Mamta is still struggling with the whys, streaming towards her like bats at sunset: Why did she reject her, why didn't she see her, why did she put the whole village before her?

'Aren't you glad, Manno, that your grandma has come to live with us?' she says, giving her son's name away as accidentally as possible. She has learned a lot from her husband.

Thankfully at last, there is nowhere for Lata Bai to go.

'How are you?' the mother makes it a point to ask her daughter each day.

'I am well, Amma,' replies Mamta, still on the defensive, unforgiving. But more often there are days when she watches her son and mother come closer out of the corner of her eye. She smiles, her mother's presence has brought her more satisfaction, something she mistakes for peace, than all Lokend's scripture could.

'Here you are. You two, talking mother–daughter things,' says Kamla, still the lubricant between them. 'Not disturbing, am I?' Her eyebrows dance above the bridge of her nose. Both Mamta and Lata Bai know the signs of Kamla's face well.

'Is everything all right?' they ask together. The daughter uses the exact same intonation as her mother, feeling immediately betrayed.

'No, nothing is all right. We have to move,' says Kamla without preamble.

'Oho, Kamla, stop scaring the girls, will you,' Lokend shouts from the edge of the garden. 'I said we'd find some place to go.' Her husband's face has changed considerably from living in constant pain. His side never did heal properly.

'How is it possible?'

'Temporary lease, Amma –' from the day she arrived, he has referred to Lata Bai as Amma '– a temporary lease, and we've been here four years already.'

341

'Yes, four years to the day. My husband would have been out tomorrow,' says Daku Manmohan's widow, starting to crumble, a sandcastle succumbing to rain. Her son looks on with detachment.

'Come, come, my daughter, what's past is past.' Lata Bai places her arms round the collapsing woman. Mamta feels a twinge of envy.

'Yes, what's past is past,' says Mamta, dragging her mother's conscience over the gravel of guilt.

'We must look for a new place quickly.' Kamla was always the practical one.

'Where?'

'Where?' All the women face Lokend, asking him to solve the problem.

'My place.' It is hardly a whisper. 'My place?' Another whisper. 'How about my land?'

'Arey, Lata Bai, your land. That dry, hard, dust pit, filled with snakes and demons? That bitter piece of land that only gave you tears. That foolish piece of land that never gave you any pleasure. Yes, why not? Why not that scraggy piece of land not fit to grow one vegetable? It will be perfect for us. Just perfect,' says Kamla without sarcasm. 'Why *not* your land? What a wonderful idea.'

'Thank you, Kamla. Thank you,' Lata Bai says to her friend for her second chance.

'Your land, that's a wonderful idea. We could buy the adjacent plot and then we'd really have something,' says Lokend, always dreaming big dreams.

Mamta is the only one not convinced. Where was her mother when she needed her? Why is she becoming their saviour now?

'Let the past be the past, meri jaan.' He pulls her back to the past, her bedside vigil, lifting her far above all those present, forcing her to acknowledge the greatness in others' actions and therefore in herself. 'Mamta and I will personally look at the land tomorrow. After all, no one knows it better than her.'

Things change when you look at them differently. That's what Mamta finds when she goes back to her mother's abandoned hut.

It is standing untouched, shunned even by the poorest of the poor who can find no use in its crumbling mud walls, rusting tin door and shredded roof.

They walk up to her former home. It looks unbelievably small to her.

'I lived here!' It is surprising how soon human beings get used to a higher standard of living and that too in such a conclusive way that their older, harsher life seems like a dream. However unreal, Mamta doesn't know it but she walked away with something very tangible from her harsh dream, an energy that is impossible to switch off. Her past has made her into one of those who will forever strive to improve their lot, someone who will always believe in the sacredness of the struggle.

She turns to face him. That's the part he likes best, to look into her eyes and sometimes discipline a stray strand of hair. His affection will always take her by surprise. 'Well, this is my home. I mean, was my home.' Lokend puts his arm around her, trying to protect her from her own emotions. She doesn't want to think about the future, she doesn't dare think about the past.

He sits in the shade of the Babul to give her a moment. She walks inside. Disturbed from its long sleep, the rusty door releases a metallic screech. The sound sends her on her journey as avidly as a gunshot might the most seasoned sprinter.

'That's where he used to tie me when I did something bad, ate too much, laughed too much, didn't bring in enough hay. I'm glad he's dead and I'm glad she's with us. I can say this to you.'

He holds her confessions safe.

'He gave me to that man, right there in front of this hut. Amma pushed me out of this door . . .' She laughs bitterly at her memory game. 'It's good that we've come back here, so there is no chance to forget. Not just for me, but for all women like me. There were so many of us, at least twenty by our well alone.'

'I want to give you every chance to forget, Mamta, to live again, unfettered.'

'I'll never forget, that would be a sin. Look at what Devi gave me –' she reaches for him '– you. What did I ever do in my life to

deserve you? How many didn't get someone like you? We can all be saved only by a Lokend of our very own.'

He says nothing. Someone else might have been embarrassed by such absolute admiration, but not Lokend. He only feels the bedrock of sincerity in her being, and her pain.

Her husband is the child of a legendary love. Perhaps he carried its intensity in his veins like a genetic seed, which sprouted when nourished in exactly the right way by the perfect person. Intercaste unions are dangerous and illicit in places like Gopalpur. It is always up to the man to wrench his mate to a higher rung where she is to sit until she is accepted by his family, his peers and finally society. There was no such wrenching in Mamta's and Lokend's case. They simply came together, mingled into a single stream and flowed on, leaving an eddy of confused, bent and broken rules behind them. It had to be black magic. Plain and marked Mamta must have enticed Lokend with everything in her power to capture his heart. Her punishment for such impudence would have been the purifying ritual of gang rape. Luckily there were no such reprisals against her in Gopalpur. Here they are protected by those who will gladly give their lives for Lokend. They will survive, and in time, their love too will become legendary because it was conceived against such incredible odds.

He loves her from the deepest part of his being. She brings meaning to his life.

Mamta of the birthmark, born to love and be loved.

She walks into the hut again. The door does nothing this time, disabled on its broken hinges. She wraps her sari pallav round her hands and pulls at it. The mirror is the first thing to fall off the back of the door. The mirror, still cracked from side to side. She picks it up and blows on its surface. There is no sound from the outside, even the birds are quiet. She can see her face, sliced exactly as before. She cleans the mirror with her sari and sets it just outside the hut.

She pulls at the door again leaning all the way back. Almost falling, she staggers away with the piece of tin in her hands. It is a

weapon, a bludgeon of wrath, a club of anger. She smashes it against the walls, pokes at the ceiling with it, tearing down the last walls of her childhood.

She bashes on. Today she will be satisfied. The clay walls have all but crumbled, providing little resistance to her perseverance. By the time Lokend comes to look inside, she has demolished two walls, and kicked the hearth stones out of sight to lie on their blackened sides, denying any responsibility towards the fire that sustained her family for years.

'I got you this,' he says, handing her a good stick shaped like a horse. Of course it is just a trick of her imagination, the frolicking of her mind that sees this stick in another time, but in the same place. 'Let's mark out our new home.'

Hours later they have their home marked out, a square, built round a courtyard with five rooms to one side and an outside veranda. The latrines are off to one end, and there is the place for the well, their own.

'What will we call it?'

'Let's leave that to your mother.'

The women gather at Lata Bai's farm. It is a special time for them, coming together to create something in exactly the image they would like. Never has such abundance of possibility been available to them.

'Mahila Sangat! That'll be its new name.'

'It's a good name,' they agree, 'Mahila Sangat: the place for women. It's about time we had our own place.'

The building goes up in a babble of banging and hoisting, and lots of laughter. Lata Bai's field, crowded with bricks and cement, drainpipes and electric cables, usurps the lives, loves and hopes of each of those who will call it home. It is a glorious time, filled with joy and kinship. Nothing can break that rejoicing collective spirit that grows, first filling the field, then the patch between the river and the growing building, continuing to extend all the way out to other fields on either side, spreading across Gopalpur to encompass the Red Ruins, the Big House, the hills beyond, and finally the whole world.

Many new faces join them in their labour: Lala Ram provides free tea, Lucky Sister sends bags of cement, Ragini a truck of bricks, and then there is the most surprising contribution of all: doors and windows from Nirmala Devi, who never forgot Lokend, her former political opponent. Each one has a job, and they follow the rules set out by the building contractor as only women who have had to obey someone or other each day of their lives can, to the finest detail.

The building is nothing short of a miracle, erected by unskilled hands on a hostile terrain. But to them, their hands are strong, and the land yielding, a willing accomplice. Help seems to arrive at the very moment they need it. Rajiv from the *Times of India* brings architects from the city. They are twins fresh out of Architecture College who attack the project with gusto, hoping to leave behind a permanent reminder of their mastery. They are assisted by Gope and mute Kanno, who have joined the bandit wives just to be close to Lokend Bhai their saviour.

Brick by brick, the building rises, brick by brick the women have their hopes returned to them.

And their new home is finished two months before the lease on their old one expires.

The whitewash is the always the best part of building. Almost as much goes on the women's clothes as does on the new walls. When it's over, lime-burnt palms are painted with henna and the swings are erected in the Babul.

'I knew there was a reason I didn't let your father cut down that tree. To see this before I died . . .' Lata Bai's eyes are streaming with unabashed tears. Mamta knows just how much her mother needs her now. She moves a step closer, but cannot fold her in her arms.

The women take turns on the swings. Their pallavs fly upwards in the draught to cradle the sun. Coloured patches of light move amongst them like long-lost friends, and many eyes that have witnessed much too much tragedy for tears experience the joy of weeping for the first time.

The procession makes the journey in all modes of transport – in trucks, on cycles, in bullock carts, on foot – to begin life at the Mahila Sangat, the place for women.

It is a triumph of survival.

Lokend cuts the ribbon. It is an affectation that all those who have visited the city insist upon. The others are simply awed by the ceremony. The Gopalpur band plays the same songs it does at every marriage, and the hijras dance together with the definite sexes.

'Come,' Mamta pulls Lokend and Manno into the fray. Gope beats the goatskin drum, faster and faster, a smile carved into his face. Lokend rushes up to Lata Bai and brings her into the circle. It is a perfect day, where each element taken individually may have flowered to its precise potential. He leaves mother and daughter dancing and hugging. This is the real miracle. This change in Mamta and every other woman who has laid even one brick of the building. The act of building has allowed her to cross many barriers, including making a tentative peace with her mother.

For Lata Bai, Mahila Sangat is more than just their collective dream, it is the concrete realisation of her spirit, her atonement for rejecting Mamta, her karmic absolution. Her belief in Devi, the female energy that she felt obliged to pray to for the sake of tradition, for the sake of history, for the sake of that's-the-only-way-she-knew-to-live is at last alive for itself, without the life-support of the times.

Mamta looks in the mirror. She sees faint wrinkles just like her mother's appearing at the corners of her eyes. She finds herself twisting her hair back on her hand and knotting it tight at the base of her neck without pins. It is the same style her mother carries.

She's starting to admit that she may be more like her mother than she knows.

19

THE FLAT ROOFS OF MAHILA SANGAT gaze into the distance, attracting many life-weary travellers to its doors. There is a constant ring of women round the building, some who have walked for miles to find shelter here.

Mahila Sangat has changed the fate of so many that Lata Bai knows it is time to do the same for her daughter. She will use every power she can muster to discover the fate of Mamta's husband, and it will be through a curious, crookedly linked chain that she will find the exact location of the place her daughter moved to after her marriage.

The first name that came to mind was Lucky Sister's, the most worldly, connected person in her family.

It hasn't been easy coming to Lucky Sister for help. She's taken a tonga to her brothel.

Lucky Sister greets her from the top of the stairs with a mixture of ecstatic surprise and gratitude. Lata Bai has never come to meet her at the brothel before. It has always been the other way round, with her making a clandestine trip to Lata Bai's farm or sending her a gift through one of her customers.

'You came,' she says, clasping her hands to her heart. Lata Bai can't believe that the plump woman with the dimpled hands, bright red hennaed hair and nose ring that dangles halfway down her chin is really her sister.

'Come, Lata, come. Arey-oh, Revti, we have a guest. Arey-oh, Revti, my younger sister is here.'

A young novice brings a bowl of warm water with floating rose petals into her employer's graceful presence. She coaxes Lata Bai's ungainly feet towards the bowl. Lata Bai stretches her toes into the water, concentrating on not tipping its contents on to the tufted carpet, as soft as winter cat fur. The foot-washing complete, the novice hands her a precisely rolled cold towel, signalling to her to wipe her face and hands with it. Lata Bai uses it with trepidation, unwilling to spoil its white wholeness with her facial grime.

'I came to ask . . .'

Lucky Sister places three scented fingers across her lips as soon as she starts talking, offering her a plate of evenly sliced fruit, sweetmeats and nuts.

'Later, after you have eaten. All crises can be put off till one has eaten,' she says, stilling her younger sister's mounting outburst. Lucky Sister hasn't come to terms with the prostitution business, giving up all hope of joining the respectable masses, for nothing. She's earned the right to be well-fed and satisfied.

Though the huge meal and Lucky Sister's display of largesse leave Lata Bai at a grave disadvantage, she eventually musters the strength to ask her question. 'It's Mamta. Well, not really Mamta. It's her husband. The one she married. Do you have news of him?'

Lucky Sister offers Lata Bai a sweet betel-leaf wrapped in edible silver foil. 'In the old days these paans were wrapped in gold foil. The sweepers would collect the rich shit for all the gold in it.' Lucky Sister giggles like a little girl, showing two gold canines.

All Lata Bai has brought with her is her respectability. In front of that flood of food and her sister's grateful pleasure, it seems like a very meagre gift. She swallows. 'I didn't ask for his address. They were married and then they left.' She can still recall the sense of relief she felt at having got Mamta, Mamta of the birthmark, married.

'She's the one with the birthmark, no? I liked her best of all your children. I know she's living with that man now,' she says, leaning into Lata Bai slyly. 'I've heard. It's quite the news. It would be. In

your village what else is there to talk about anyway?' She suddenly straightens up and declares loudly into the room, 'Hypocrites! How many of them use my facility? But let a girl live in peace, n . . . o that's just too much.'

Lata Bai looks at her toes. 'I should've asked about the family, their ancestors, their village. I knew nothing of him. Nothing. And yet I let her go. And go to what? A hell . . .' She checks herself, unsure of whether she should give her successful, recently perfumed sister more ammunition to judge her. 'I need news of him now.'

'I find it odd how families are willing to lose complete touch with their daughters once they get married to become productive gardens for someone else.'

'Yes, her father used to say that feeding her was like watering someone else's garden.' She drops her defences, *judge me if you will.* 'It's all my fault. I should never have let it happen. I was weak. Give me news, my sister. Please, I beg you.'

'It's not your fault.' Lucky Sister has become partial to philosophy, and in her position, she is apt to share it. 'It's the world, Lata, it's the world. It extracts its price, weight for weight.'

Lata Bai's impatience boils over. 'Do you have news? I must know where to find him.'

'As a matter of fact, I do know where to find him. Her bastard husband used to love the gambling tents and one particular prostitute. He thought they'd get married one day, he thought he'd make a respectable creature out of her – probably his one and only noble thought – she didn't want it, but she strung him along all the same. She was one of mine, well trained. So she drummed him like a tabla, and got many gifts from him, with which she repaid her loan to me. That's how I got these back,' Lucky Sister holds out the pair of gold earrings Lata Bai had given Mamta before her wedding. 'So of course I got to know the whole story. She was so proud, said he had no backbone, she could make him dance! I told her to treat him extra badly and to make him tremble, but I didn't tell her he was married to my niece. He lives in Barigaon on the farm next to the milkman's, the one who has thirty cows. You'll find news of him there. Here, take these –' She presses the earrings and the remaining

betel-leaves, all damp and silvery, into her sister's reluctant hands. Lata Bai leaves more indebted than ever.

Lucky Sister sends Revti with Lata Bai to the bus stand with enough money for the to and fro journeys. The widow in white draws no attention, but a barrage of catcalls greets the prostitute, who wiggles her hips at prospective customers. Lata Bai hides her head in her pallav, distancing herself from the silent transactions of the prostitute, and gets on the bus unaided.

This time only mother and daughter make their way to the Red Ruins. Neither wants to dwell on that other journey they made to the ruins the day of her first marriage. Mamta declined the ceremonial henna, and her mother understood it was because she wanted to keep the wedding simple.

They leave at sunrise. The women are already out, putting their washing on trees. In her time, the women would have been just returning home from the well. But not any more. Now they use the newly installed tube wells, dotted round the terrain, minutes walk from their homes, constantly gushing water, seven in all. The new wells, dug because of Lokend, her son-in-law, her grandson's father. She should have been proud, instead . . . 'Mamta, I am so sorry.'

'Ssh,' says the daughter, embarrassed by her mother's confession even more than by her apology. 'Amma, don't . . .' She looks at the older woman and feels a pang of guilt. *All this time I had a mother, while . . .* She has to know. 'Tell me . . .' she must ask about that one thing that has been a stone on her heart for years '. . . tell me, was there any news of a girl?'

'A girl?'

'When you went to my old house . . .' She shudders at the word house; more like my dungeon, she thinks. 'You know, when you went to find him, and . . . found him dead –' She is startled by the word, dead. She repeats: '– dead, when you found him dead, did you get news of a girl? She would be almost as old as Sneha by now.'

'I didn't have to go to your old home. There was a woman who knew all about you, just four fields from the bus stop.'

'By the big mango tree?'

'Yes, that's the one.'

'That would be Geeta, I sometimes met her at the well.'

'Said he became very ill and died and then his land got taken over by his creditors.'

'And the girl?'

'Oh yes, she did say something about a girl. She ran away too. I wish I had gone to find him sooner. You didn't have to wait this long to get married after all. Oh, how fate torments us!' She cracks her knuckles against her temples and runs them along Mamta's aura. 'Live long, my daughter, live long and well.'

She ran away too . . . To what? Where could she be now? Mamta is with her stepdaughter, and it is a while before she notices that the Red Ruins have changed. There are holes appearing in them where the stones have been stolen for the new road.

It is perhaps for the loss of the girl, or for leaving her behind, or just that she has come far enough to be concerned with preserving her personal heritage that the holes in the Red Ruins affect her deeply. 'Oh no, not the Red Ruins. Not our ruins.'

'Yes, that's the price of progress. You have to pay one way or the other, but on balance I think it is a good thing. I'll take the holes any day if that means a new road.'

Mamta doesn't have the energy to challenge her mother's practicality. Why did she leave her stepdaughter behind? She changes the subject, but the pathos of the ruins resounds in her words. 'Amma, see, there are hardly any offerings here now.' Her voice seems to be coming from a lost place, from inside a cave. *Why did I leave her behind?*

'Now the girls make their offerings at the place where your man jailed Daku Manmohan. People will make gods of anything and anyone. That tells you just what state this country is in,' Lata Bai drones on, as confident as an untrained voice in a singalong.

Perhaps that's why my man is dying. Because I left her behind. He has taken my karma on to his own head. A life paid with a life. It is my turn to be lonely now, just as she must have been all these years. Mamta's heart is shuddering, suddenly she has to squat.

'Are you all right?' Lata Bai attributes it to nerves. The mother

smiles, she finds Mamta's nervousness like a shy new bride very endearing.

The marriage ceremony is just that, a ceremony; conducted to paralyse wagging tongues. No one was invited, but they've all turned up. This time Lata Bai has more to offer them than weevils: Asmara Didi's famous samosas and Kamla's halwa. Nirmala Devi personally dances for them and blesses the couple from her position as the region's model mayor and leading eunuch. Her clan dances with her, and all those present remark on how graceful and refined their moves seem. Rajiv of the *Times of India* jokingly says he'll put their pictures in the paper, which has Lokend embarrassed and Mamta excited.

This is Gopalpur's first widow remarriage. Mamta's marriage will change things in the village just slightly. For a while widows won't have to shave their heads quite so close. After a while, the people of Gopalpur will realise how different their traditions are from neighbouring villages, and they will say it is because a great love was born here.

20

TODAY SHE IS DRESSING TO MEET her mother at the Mahila Sangat. Now the journey takes only forty minutes and costs six rupees.

Lokend has organised the motor rickshaw. She can see the smoke curling out of the plastic window. Satya, the driver, is smoking a bidi. He was the first one to get a motor rickshaw. They all said he was making a mistake; after all, where was there to go to in Gopalpur? But no, he could see the future quite clearly, and he'd got his loan and his rickshaw, and for six months all of Gopalpur's travel business.

'Mamta. Ready?' she can hear the sound of domestic words. They thrill her each time. She gets Manno ready to meet his nani, combing his fine hair, parting it just right. Looking at the swirl of hair on the back of her son's head, she realises that her life has vanished into the little things she hopes to give her child: kites in the sky, the sourest mangoes, light on a butterfly's wing, long stories making short nights.

'Yes, one minute,' she shouts, giving Manno's hair one last brush. She has the bloated feeling of pregnancy. Her second. She rushes to the bathroom, lifts her sari to squat. Her pee tinkles into the drain. She dries her hands on her pallav. 'Ready,' she says, taking the cup and saucer out of his hand and placing it in the kitchen sink, raised above the floor just like Mrs D'Souza's.

'Here, take this to Satya –' She tucks a sweetened betel-leaf

wrapped in newspaper into her son's hand. 'Go, run along, we'll be right behind you.' She waits for her son to disappear down the stairwell before she leads Lokend to the stairs, shutting the front door carefully behind her. He has difficulty with the stairs. He has difficulty with most things, but she doesn't think about that. The stairwell smells of ammonia. She mopped it herself this morning. She is proud of it. No writing on these walls, clean as blue-white, they are.

'Will you tell . . .' he breathes in, holding his side; she ignores his pain, that's how he wants it '. . . Amma today?'

'Maybe,' she says slowly, giving him time to be distracted. 'What do you think? I am four months past now. Why, when Amma used to get pregnant she never told Bapu, he'd just notice one day that she was big. I don't think Amma even remembers the year of our births. Only their colours.'

'Colours?'

'Did I never tell you? All our births were colourful. Mine was green, could have been new mustard or young wheat; and my baby sister who died, she was yellow, definitely mustard flower. And the others . . . the others . . . I don't remember.'

Satya is already chewing his betel-leaf when they get into his rickshaw. She grabs Manno by the arm and sets his bottom down firmly between her and Lokend. The motor rickshaw still frightens her with its wide open sides and gaping hole in the back.

'One more month, Lokend Bhai, that's all. They said I would never be able to do it.'

'Yes, better than the loans of the zamindars.' She looks sharply at her husband, but relaxes with the crinkles round his eyes. They all laugh.

'Yes, much better, Lokend Bhai, much better. My wife has taken one too. Bibiji, she is going to join your amma.' They drive away from Saraswati Stores, the new centre of Gopalpur, along the river and past a tall straight single row of electric poles, connecting to the very spot that Mamta reached the night she ran away. The road smells of fresh tar and looks wet enough to masquerade as water reflecting a shaky heat. The newly prosperous Gopalpur has begun

attracting its own labour force from villages further away than the last electric pole. There are men and women working on the road that Mamta doesn't recognise. The women are dressed in the backless blouses of gypsies. Their mirrorwork skirts reflect diamonds of light, competing with the quiet river making its placid way behind them, shattering into a million suns in each gentle ripple. The women break the rocks, cruelly torn from the hillocks round the Red Ruins, into tiny pieces, their fingers wrapped in protective rags like lepers. Mamta turns away. She has reached that point in her life where the destitution of others sends a pinching current through her being. In Begumpet there were hundreds of such unfortunates, the ditchside latrine people, the tin and cardboard people, but she never once felt empathy for them, because she was one of them. This concern for others is a new feeling, a privilege she can at last afford.

'Where are they from?'

'Out there –' Satya points with his finger to the west. Satya can still comfortably ignore them, he doesn't feel drawn into or connected with their life cycle. 'Bibiji, you know what they say, the ghost is back at the ruins again. I know we need a road, but we must respect the home of the dead also.'

'Where do they live?' She can't leave them alone. That is her penance for this life of luxury with a man who loves her. This mad caring, even guilt, for anyone less fortunate.

'By the gambling tents.'

'The women and children too?'

'Yes, they will sell themselves for less than nothing, Bibiji. Our little Gopalpur is becoming quite the place for . . .' He gives his head a you-know-what flick. Never before would anyone have been this coy with her, but Satya considers her respectable, pure even, much too respectable to be told about the rapidly growing prostitution. Other peoples' attitudes towards her, an officially married woman, are the biggest surprise. 'These gypsy people . . .' says Satya, shaking his head, putting his kind ahead of the rock-breakers with his judgement.

* * *

356

It is no longer an impersonal land. Mamta can predict exactly how close they are to Mahila Sangat by the newly dyed chunnis left drying by the side of the road, some indigo, others red. Now that water has come to the village, all of Gopalpur is on the move, at any time of day. Even as the motor rickshaw bumps its way along the dusty road, having left the tarred section behind, women wave to them carrying pots on their heads in the middle of the day! When was that ever the case? Her son sees nothing extraordinary in the afternoon's waterline.

Thanks to the water, the women have time on their hands, with which they have set a new standard for decoration of their homes. There are stamps of ownership everywhere, in the mud houses studded with shrines, wall niches for oil lamps and paintings as elaborate on the outside as the inside; and vines, not just those belonging to vegetables, but flower vines as well, scampering up the walls.

At Mahila Sangat the writing starts at the far end of the retaining wall, slightly obscured by flowering bougainvillea, and repeats itself all the way to the gate: Mahila Sangat, Mahila Sangat, Mahila Sangat . . . The motor rickshaw stops with a lurch.

'Shall I wait?'

'Yes, Satya, if you can.' Lokend always says 'if you can', as if Satya has customers lining up to drive off in his rickshaw. 'Go. Go on,' he says to Manno, urging his son to run free.

Manno's eyes seek her approval and she feels her heart bump. He doesn't like to be hugged by her. Even at this young age, he has become such a little man, a miniature version of Lokend, whom he adores and from whom he sometimes tolerates a hug, which makes her both jealous and proud.

She has relived Manno's birth so many times: Eyebrows and Lokend urging her to push only at the right time, saying, 'One more push and you'll have a baby.' He had lingered while Eyebrows cleaned the baby and cut the cord. He'd had that precious time with her baby, his son, their creation, and he couldn't have loved him more. Washed with a father's tears, what better way to come into the world?

Manno jumps out of the rickshaw and across the ditch, landing

with both feet on the other side, seeking a precarious balance. She finds herself reaching out to him, she knows if he falls he can get no help from her at this distance. She worries excessively, her concern isn't commensurate with the depth of the ditch. Lokend is nonchalant. He gives Manno the space to explore his limits, letting his son trust in himself.

The Mahila Sangat smells of new rain as the women water the verandas every day to keep the dust down, just like in the Big House. She takes a deep breath. The warm wet air cocoons her in its arms like a mother's love. She is only just discovering that this is the true smell of her life: wet, productive earth.

She feels pregnancy tears rise in her eyes and her husband's hand on her shoulder. He says, 'Go on,' and her husband and son are off, scattering like flies before a swat, loping in graceful strides towards the flower garden, trailing laughter like a bright ribbon. He keeps his energy for this time, to run with his son. Each step costs him, she knows, but he does it, making it into a game. He has collapsed kneeling, pretending a hurt, but it isn't a pretence. She knows she won't have Lokend with her for long.

Her son looks back, laughs at his father's antics and runs even faster. She follows, also running as fast as she can. Soft buttery clouds fill the sky, their burned-sugar centres look more solid than the ground under her feet. She catches up with Manno and takes her son's hand as she runs without a care in the world, believing that if she misses her footing, she will land on a place as reliable as earth and soft as cotton wool.

She can see Asmara Didi beckoning to her from the roof of the building with a kitchen towel as if she has been waiting impatiently for her. The white cloth floats in the sky in slow motion, perhaps because the breeze is soft or because her thoughts run slowly, almost lazily, keeping pace with the stillness of Mahila Sangat. She stops running, and waves back.

When the two women meet, they hug big and deep. 'How are you?' she asks, slightly straightening Asmara Didi. Asmara Didi is one of those women who will never grow older slowly or visibly. She will stay white-haired and unwrinkled as she has done for the

past decade and then suddenly die. Anyone who saw her in the time of the zamindar is amazed by how time literally seems to have stood still for her.

'Good, good. We had some new ones come in this morning. Your amma is with them now.' Asmara Didi turns, offering Mahila Sangat's expansive veranda for observation. Mamta remembers the day when she marked out the buildings around the courtyard with a horse-shaped stick. The hut in which she lived as a child is now the open pickling room with a steadfast wood-fired stove in the middle. The girls have grown useful plants, henna, indigo, tulsi, sisal . . . in every inch of soil. The industry of Mahila Sangat is astounding.

'What's on the boil today?' Mamta points to the smoke. A girl stirs the mixture with a big stick.

'Sticky toffee. She's new, came to us with a small piece and gave it to your amma, saying it was her mother's recipe. Taste it. It's good,' says Asmara Didi, handing her a square in a professionally printed wrapper.

Tiny, intricately patterned hennaed palms, the emblem of Mahila Sangat, offer themselves up for scrutiny. 'Asmara Didi, did you ever think we would be selling sticky toffee in the stores of New Delhi?' she asks, opening the wrapper. The paper crackles noisily.

'Come, come, there is someone very special here to see you,' says the old woman, pulling Mamta towards the building.

'Mamta!'

She knows the voice instantly. She turns sharply, not to waste a moment, towards her past. 'Didi! . . . And Prem! Arey-oh, Manno's father, see who has come to visit from the city. See, Asmara Didi, you did the right thing by sweetening my mouth! This is such an auspicious day!' She presses bits of sticky toffee into Eyebrows, Prem and Asmara Didi's mouths, popping a final piece into her own.

Eyebrows takes Mamta in her arms. The strength of her embrace squeezes the breath out of her friend's lungs. 'It was never the same after you left,' she says, fighting the wetness in her eyes. 'I forced him to come,' says Eyebrows, looking to Prem. 'I told him, stay a few days. He works so hard, never comes to see me. He's a machinist now, with a good job.' Prem basks in her praise like a cat in sunlight.

'Yes, Didi, I work two jobs. You should see my room, and my new bicycle. Here, Didi –' he hands her an elaborate silver toe ring. News of her marriage must have reached him. 'Amma sent word,' he says, closely regarding his sister's new countenance, trying to unlock the secrets of her heart. He hugs her.

'Oh but, Mamta, I want to stay. Do you need a dispensary here? A school? Anything? I've already made arrangements for the city dispensary.' Eyebrows knew she wouldn't go back. She's left the dispensary in the hands of four wives who had once been her patients, all cured and stronger for it, not just in health, but in the core of themselves. The women will do a good job, having at one point been there themselves; they know what is at stake.

'You don't need a reason to stay, Didi, and yes, we need all those things here and more. And what about you, Prem? We need a machinist here too, you know. Are you and Raja staying too?'

'No, we came just to see you,' says Prem in a grown man's voice, but with a boy's impish smile on his face.

'Oh, look at my little brother,' says Mamta with happiness. 'Just look at him, what a man he's become!' They walk towards Lokend, sparing him the effort of catching up with them.

Prem touches Lokend's feet. Raja scampers from his shoulder up the older man's arm. 'I have a good job in the city, Lokend Bhai. Sneha is well. She might get married soon. The way they are, so much in love,' he says, letting Lokend know that he and his sister have done well for themselves.

'Here's our machinist,' says Asmara Didi, taking Prem by the arm. 'Get him to fix all those broken-down contraptions in the back shed.'

'I'll fix all your broken machines in no time. Lead on,' Prem waves to his sister, 'lead on.' The boy walks slowly, keeping pace with his brother-in-law; Raja bounces comfortably on his shoulder.

'Now, about that school. You can put it right there, under the Babul,' says Mamta to her friend. 'And as for your dispensary, you have to discuss that with Asmara Didi. What do you think, Asmara Didi? Are you up for some competition?'

Asmara Didi laughs. 'Oho, look at me, I have one foot in the grave now. Of course we need a youngster like your friend.' She looks at

Eyebrows and adds, 'I'll help you, if you want. This hair wasn't bleached by the sun, you know –' she holds the tip of her plait at arm's length '– it's wisdom that's sucked the black out of it.'

'I want you to meet my amma,' says Mamta.

Four girls are squatting outside, waiting to see Lata Bai.

'Namaste,' says Eyebrows cheerfully to them. They just stare at her with big eyes, the whites nearly yellow with jaundice. 'Where have you all come from?'

The girls look at each other, trying to decide who will speak first. Finally they shrug. They have walked miles to get here, they are exhausted, and plan to reserve their energies for the one person they have to impress. Lata Bai.

From the doorway Mamta can see her mother talking to a child no older than Manno. She feels that motherly love take over. The roles are once again reversed. She is the protector, Lata Bai the protected.

'Amma,' she calls from the doorway.

Lata Bai looks up. She now wears white with pride, starched and crisp, brightly clean. She is finally content to be a widow with Seeta Ram dead and gone more than three years. 'I will come to you,' she says to Mamta. 'I must finish here.' Lata Bai has become consistently busy in the way of a city entrepreneur. There is a frenetic energy to her now, a sense that time is too short.

Mamta's eyes soften with love. 'Sometimes I think it is her breath alone that keeps this place running. She never tires,' she says to Eyebrows. 'Amma has found her place at last. Jai ho Devi,' says Mamta. It is close to one year since Lata Bai took a loan from the manageress of the Bank of India to establish a pickling shed at Mahila Sangat. 'Let's talk to her later. Come, I'll show you the rest of the buildings.' They start walking through the vegetable garden toward the rose bushes. Just above the flowers, Mamta can see two heads, one belonging to Kanno and the other, a new girl.

How can she describe the feeling of being with these women plucked from their miserable existences and planted caringly in this colourful flowerbed full of fragrance and love? Like the flowers, she too is nourished every time she comes here with exactly what

she needs: hope and acceptance everywhere, each minute of every day.

The girls emerge from behind the bushes into fenugreek plants lapping at their ankles. Kanno puts her arm round Bela, the glassy-eyed new girl who arrived last week. Even from the distance Mamta can see the ligature marks on Bela's ankles just above the fenugreek.

'Her ankles? Those marks?'

'Slow.' Asmara Didi circles her finger round and round by her temple. 'Her father drugged her and tied her to the doorpost to prevent her from smearing her own shit on the walls. God, what is one to do? If her mother hadn't come to Lata Bai in tears, the girl would still be there. You should see her hips: sores the size of lotus flowers. She couldn't straighten up, but Kanno fixed that, put a board up her back as she slept.'

A board up her back? Mamta winces, Eyebrows marvels, Asmara Didi laughs. They all acknowledge the averting of tragedy in their own ways.

'Now you can't get her to let go of Kanno's hand!' Asmara Didi says. 'Bela talks, and Kanno listens. She says everything into her ear. There . . . there, look, there she goes again.' Bela's mouth is close to Kanno's ear. Kanno has both her hands over her mouth, to stifle a giggle or a scream?

'I wonder what they talk about.'

'Gope.'

'Gope?'

'Wants to marry Kanno, silence and all.'

'Marry her?'

'Why, Mamta, yes, a love marriage.'

'Devi jai ho,' they say together.

Mamta notices the jeep resting in the sun, its paint peeled so thoroughly that no one can tell what colour it once was.

She twitches. She dreads her brother-in-law's rare visits, which leave her feeling unclean, vulnerable and frightened. Ram Singh taunts her by never speaking to her directly and still refuses to acknowledge Manno, continuing to refer to him as his brother's bastard in spite of their marriage. The older woman takes her hand.

'Oho, you're not over that still. How long have you been married? I keep telling her that that man cannot do anything to her, still she is afraid,' Asmara Didi says to Eyebrows.

'In his eyes I can never be one of them. I am not even worthy of being Manno's father's rakhale, let alone his wife.'

'He doesn't matter. He doesn't hold up the sky for you, Lokend Bhai does. Remember, don't let people tell you who you must be,' says Eyebrows.

'I've left Prem with those machines. What a gem he is, that brother of yours, he's in his element amongst all that twisted metal! Now what have you girls been plotting all this time?' asks Lokend, joining his wife. His breath is short and he sucks wind into his belly through his teeth.

Mamta restrains the urge to hold out her hand to him and forgets to breathe herself.

'I was just telling her not to let your brother bother her so. He does it because he can get away with it. Isn't that the truth? You tell her.'

Lokend looks to the jeep. 'My brother can be a hard man, don't let him upset you,' he says, putting his arm round her. 'These are the things of the body, the habit of the mind. Mamta, you are something else,' he whispers in her ear.

She releases her breath; Lokend's words bring her great solace. Even a little of his knowledge protects from great fear. That perhaps is his biggest gift to her.

Now that there is time to take a good look at the two of them, Eyebrows can see that Lokend is infinitely weaker than when they lived at her dispensary. She can also see that Mamta is infinitely stronger.

Ram Singh is lounging on the veranda in the shade drinking tea from a cup balanced in a saucer.

'Bhaia. What brings you here?'

Ram Singh looks up, shading his eyes to see who addresses him, even though he knows the voice well. Mamta closes her eyes for long enough for it to become a mixture of a blink and a ponder.

Ram Singh looks into his brother's face. There is a debate going on in his head, anyone watching can see that. He is afraid to say anything, to give himself away. Suddenly he thrusts a piece of paper folded in three into Lokend's hands. The paper is thick and stiff, stained brown in several places, official. Mamta can see the sturdy three-headed lion embossed on the very top. 'For you. Of course, he left it to you.'

'Left what to whom?'

Ram Singh turns around to give Mamta the eye. He will not tolerate such an interruption from a wife, any wife, let alone a once-kept woman.

'For you,' he talks exclusively to Lokend. 'Read it.'

'Oho, it's so official. Just tell me what's in it.'

'He left it to you.' Since his father's death, Ram Singh has held on to the deed. If there was any other way, he would not have brought it to his brother's attention today, but he has come up against an infuriatingly incorruptible government servant who will soon mail an official letter to Lokend informing him that as the owner of the Big House he is liable for all government back taxes.

'The Big House, Bapu left it to you.' Inwardly and outwardly Ram Singh retreats into himself, gathering strength to attack. His shoulders hunch over his chest as if preparing to swallow his heart. His eyes narrow. Then he has to look away. The poison possesses him.

Lokend gives his brother the dignity of an oblique look, then he folds that precious piece of paper over and over to just the right thickness and places it in his pocket. 'No one needs to know. It's big enough for all of us. Let bygones be bygones.'

21

LOKEND PASSES AWAY IN THE BLUE room beneath the picture of Ganesha painted by his mother. Mamta clings to her husband's hand as it grows cold. As she guides Lokend's soul out of the Big House, just as she might an honoured dinner guest, she becomes acutely aware of her own mortality. In that instant she has her first taste of how her husband lived his life, in inspired splendour, each and every moment of it. She is able to shed her sorrow like an old skin, and it is she who comforts the inconsolable Asmara Didi, Gope and Eyebrows.

Asmara Didi bathes the body, Manno lights the pyre, Ram Singh cracks the skull. This time the funeral is different from the last funeral conducted in the courtyard of the Big House. There are hundreds of mourners present, many of whom Mamta doesn't know. People Lokend unknowingly helped, people he unconditionally loved. The number of policemen attending the last rites is astounding.

Two weeks later a baby girl is born to the widow Mamta.

Kamla provides her expert services to the mother, who delivers her baby quietly and quickly.

There was a time when Love seemed like the biggest word to fill, but not any more. She stopped asking 'Why me?' long ago. She is certain that the lines etched in her palms include one, the thickest,

most visible one, for him. She continues to grasp his memory as firmly as her destiny.

She knew it would happen, had prepared herself for it the day their hands touched over his hospital bed, him just alive enough to feel everything the more intensely. In fact she was so prepared that she'd never wished the end closer or farther, just accepted with an equanimity he would have approved of.

And now she is a widow, his widow, in widow-white for the rest of her life. All other trappings of marriage are put away – her hair is washed and oiled, the red dust in her centre parting scrubbed out with ash from her husband's funeral pyre, her toe ring resting neatly in a tied-up napkin, her bangles smashed at the Red Ruins like other widows' before her . . . But what of her memories, more lasting than any dust, toe ring or bangle? Where will she put her memories?

She will at first be a miser, hoarding her memories, never speaking of their union, using them only to return to her potential self. Later, much later, because there will be no service of tears, no absolution through grieving, she will understand that life isn't exclusively about loss, that you don't start dying from the day you were born, that longevity isn't dictated by the time of your death but on how you lived your life; and she will realise that she is healed, that she was always whole, and that once and for all we *can* transform the past, not in how it happened, but in how well we learned from it. After all, it is in the lessons that the healing begins.

In the minds of others, for a long time the widow Mamta will remain the appendage of her man, a thing without the right to exist on its own. But many long days after his death, they will one day seek her out for advice; she will have somehow become her own person without ceremony.

And so, in the dusty little village of Gopalpur, where rigid social customs govern not only the actions of its people, but some say the ripening of the grain itself, Mamta will inject an element of un-certainty, a tiny seed of perhaps-things-can-change, which will allow other women to dream their own astonishing dreams.

The Smell of Wet Earth

22

'SHANTI, YOU HAVE TO BLOCK ME.' He thrusts the lid into her hands and jumps back on split feet with a stick in both hands, ready to strike. His little sister is unconvinced. The lid clatters to the floor.

'Mam . . . Mammo,' she calls him Mammo, the 'n's still out of her reach. She puts her arms out to him to be carried. Shanti is devoted to her brother.

'Where's your amma?' Eyebrows enters the Big House with a flourish.

She takes Shanti on her knee. Shanti likes the smell of her aunt; clean, like tooth powder. 'This is for you –' Eyebrows hands her a sweet and a toy stethoscope whose tubes you can break but not bend. 'Tell your amma there's someone to see her.' She talks to the boy as if he were her own.

'What's for me?'

'A hug first, then go tell your amma, and then I'll show you.' He won't hug her. He won't hug anyone. He misses Lokend even more than his mother does.

Eyebrows holds up a water pistol. He puts out his hand for the toy. She quickly snatches it away. 'Go call your mother. You'll need this to drench your sister,' she teases him, revealing the muzzle from under her arm. The boy stands his ground, then finally calls out, 'Amma, Amma.'

'No, I don't mean like that, go call her nicely.'

'Amma, Amma,' he repeats.

'Uffo, what's the rush? Hell isn't going anywhere,' says Mamta, running down the stairs. For the first few months Mamta tiptoed around the Big House as if she didn't belong. But now, having planted both her children's umbilical cords under the mango tree to make sure they would return lifetime after lifetime, at last she accepts it as her rightful home.

'Neither is heaven,' Eyebrows informs her friend. 'There's someone to see you. Rani,' says Eyebrows, virtually pushing the woman into the room.

'Hello, Rani.' This one is silent. Usually they start talking fast the minute they walk in the door.

'Amma.' The woman looks quickly to her face and then to the floor.

Mamta peers into the glaring light outside, expecting to see the woman's mother. 'Yes, Rani.'

'Amma.'

'This is Rani. Rani. Remember her? Rani? Your daughter,' says Eyebrows.

'Shanti?'

'No, the other one. Your stepdaughter. The one you left behind.'

Mamta sits on the edge of Bibiji's chairs. 'Rani?' The smell of saffron, a dangling nose ring, the money, flapping slippers, mile after mile of dust, and finally the electric poles.

'Amma.' It is a woman's voice. There is nothing familiar in the voice, the sound, or the image. It should have been a young girl with snot running into her teeth. Rani may have changed, but Mamta has hardly changed. To Rani there is everything familiar in the woman standing before her with a toddler swinging off the lower pleats of her sari. 'Amma.'

The child squeezes herself behind her mother and starts kicking her back. 'Amma,' she chants, kick, 'Amma', kick, 'Amma.' Mamta doesn't want to hear that word in the presence of Rani, the daughter she left behind.

Eyebrows takes the girl's arm, and sets her down in a chair.

Then she scoops Shanti into her arms from behind Mamta's back. Holding her face forward like a soiled cat, she takes her to the kitchen, where she will entertain both children with the help of Kamla.

'I didn't know where to find you,' says Mamta.

'It's all right,' replies Rani in that voice of the downtrodden who cannot accept anything good in their fate.

'No, no, it's not. I tried. We both tried, Manno's father and I.'

'They said they would beat him to death if he didn't pay them soon. He said he'd sell one of mine so he could pay them off, but he fell sick and died.'

'And you?'

'Me, I ran away.'

'Where?' The question out in the open, Mamta puts her hand to her mouth and shakes her head, she doesn't want any answers, doesn't want to delve too deep. The guilt is making her sick. 'Forgive me.'

'There is nothing to forgive,' says the girl with everything to forgive.

'So how did my friend find you?'

'I found her. I've known about you for a long time. I should have told you about his death, so you could have got married. Yes, we heard about that. There isn't a soul in Gopalpur who doesn't know about that.' There is some acid in her tone, a need to hurt. 'I should have told you, you could have been married sooner.' Mamta feels the knife twist.

She deserves it; for sure she deserves it. She is back in her husband's hut, with her foot poised in the door of maturity, holding on to Rani for companionship. *Tell no one, we will run away together and be safe forever.* She'd said those words. Yes, she deserves it.

'Are you well? You can stay here. You will stay here with me. You must meet my mother. Oh, Rani, you will be so happy here. Come, you will sleep in the blue room tonight. Upstairs. Next to me. My mother-in-law decorated the walls of it herself. It is beautiful. Oh, Rani, we will be so happy here together. Forgive me. I should have come back, but I can't even begin to tell you how

it was. No direction, no hope, no safety till Manno's father came along. Forgive me,' she says, her exuberance lye soap for lifelong guilt.

Dinner is a solemn affair. There is seriousness to their happiness, an acknowledgement of Devi's divine hand in bringing them together.

'You two have much to talk about,' says Eyebrows, stretching after an unusually heavy meal. 'I must get back to the Sangat. Good thing I brought the bicycle. Three were brought in today, they will all sleep in my room.' Mamta knows Eyebrows is talking about the babies rescued from the dumpster. Some mothers pretend their babies are born dead so they can throw them in the garbage. Mamta shudders with guilt. The babies rescued from the rubbish have more of a chance than she gave Rani.

'Tell Amma I will come to the Sangat tomorrow.' It is Mamta's job to make sure the cement is mixed properly. Her shoulders ache from carrying Shanti at the mixer all day, but she never complains. What do they say? A mother's arms are never tired. She pushes back her chair and stands up. Rani, following her stepmother's actions closely, also stands up.

'Who's this?' Ram Singh always appears at this time for his meal, just before she leaves the public downstairs to go to bed.

In deference to her husband's unspoken wishes, Mamta is civil with her brother-in-law. They haven't fought since Lokend's death, and have managed to somehow carve out their own separate orbits at the Big House. 'This is my friend. My friend Rani.' The women look at each other. It isn't a lie, but it is so far from the truth that it could be one.

He nods without looking up from his thali. He has made a tacit agreement with himself to be dispassionately satisfied with his loneliness. He will never have a legal heir, because the Big House is lost to him forever.

'We are going upstairs. Rani is staying.' She could never have dared say those words to him before. No explanation, just three words: Rani is staying.

* * *

The true dawn reveals an old cracked photo of herself as a young girl and Lata Bai lying next to a steaming cup of tea. She'd never forgotten that photo, the one from her memory box. The one she'd left behind in the dip of Rani's bed when she ran away, the one that Rani carried with her all these years.

Some time while she slept, Rani slipped back into the night, disappeared from sight.

Mamta looks into her cup. Her face still, even thoughtful, resigned, like her stepdaughter's heart must have been last night. Help me, she thinks, and turns around, seeking his eyes. The feeling of being watched over is strongly with her, but before she can grasp it fully, it is gone like a shiver on a warm day, leaving behind the reality of her loneliness.

Rani must have known all through dinner that she wouldn't be here in the morning. Why did she leave?

Don't fault her for her decision. There are so many Ranis in this world. They come in all guises, all lacking any sort of encouragement from their circumstances. Had Rani experienced a great drought she might have had the courage to stay, had there been less acceptance in her father's prostitute she might have had the fortitude to ask for what she'd lost, had there been just something a little different about one of her patrons she might have accused her stepmother of cowardice . . . But there hadn't, and so her life played out in an altogether other way.

In the end, this is not Rani's story but Mamta's, so all we can do is wish Rani an obstacle-free journey and the kindness of destiny.

'Amma?'

She jumps with surprise.

'Shanti!' her two-year-old crawls into her lap. She puts down her cup, the tea still hot enough to burn.

As she takes this daughter in her arms, she realises she will never see her other daughter again. Rani will once again lose herself in that great faceless, nameless mass of unloved humanity that flits from here to there trying to make sense of this world. Every once in a while, Mamta will catch a glimpse of her in a crowd, will run

to her, but won't be able to catch up. Until one day. One day she will be by her side, will tap her on the shoulder, only to come face to face with a stranger's eyes as befuddled as her own.

Mamta's name means mother's love. It is a good and fitting name. In her own mother's love, she had more than most. It was a practical kind of love, never frivolous, always conferred with discretion, much like a limited resource. In that she is different.

> 'Make a chapatti, bake a chapatti,
> Give one to your father, give one to your mother,
> One for your sister and one for your brother,
> Then what's left? One burned and dry,
> Give it to the little girl to make her cry.'

Each phrase of her nursery rhyme is punctuated with kisses on her daughter's palms. She sings the words not to toughen up Shanti but to remind her of where she came from. Finally, she burrows her face in her daughter's hair.

What is it they say about innocence? It is being harmless and unharmed at the same time.

Glossary

Abba: see Bapu.

Aindri Mata: a manifestation of Devi. All perception is a manifestation of her energy.

Amma: mother; Mummy.

Apsara: these young women, with supernatural powers and complete mastery over the performing arts, are the handmaidens of Indra, ruler of Heaven; intoxicatingly beautiful, divine entertainers, they may be considered to be the equivalent of the muses, naiads, and nymphs.

Arey-oh/Arey: a call to attract someone's attention, as in 'Hey there . . .'

Ashram: place of sanctuary or refuge, usually associated with a particular temple or religious group.

Atal Bihari Vajpayee: Indian statesman who served as Prime Minister of India, heading a coalition government from March 1998 until May 2004.

Avatars: manifestation of Hindu gods in human or animal form on earth. Avatars possess the same attributes and powers as the gods they represent.

Babuji: a respectful way of addressing a man from a higher caste.

Babul: type of tree also called the Acacia Arabica.

Bakelite: kind of hard plastic used for making toilet seats.

Bapu: father; Daddy.

375

Barfi: sweet made from reduced milk solids and sugar.

Betel-leaf: also known as paan is a leaf from the pepper family. It is chewed with slaked lime and betel-nut, and turns the saliva red. Red betel-juice paan stains are commonly seen on Indian streets and in buildings.

Betel-nuts: Areca nut chewed by Indians wrapped in betel-leaf.

Bhagvat/Bhagavad Gita: literally 'the Lord's Song', the holy book of Hindus. The content is the divine learning imparted by Lord Krishna to his disciple Arjuna on the eve of the great Kurukshetra war mentioned in the Mahabharata epic. The *Bhagvat Gita*, rendered in verse, is the oldest spiritual text known to mankind. The English translation referenced in this book is by Annie Besant.

Bhai/ Bhaia: elder brother.

Bhajans: hymns; devotional songs.

Bhajiwala: man who sells bhaji, a vegetarian preparation.

Bibiji: a respectful way of addressing a woman from a higher caste.

Bidi: hand rolled tobacco-leaf 'cigarette'.

Bindi: dot between the eyebrows of a woman placed for adornment.

Brahmi Mata: a manifestation of Devi. She is divine speech, her energy represents the immutable sound.

Brooke Bond: brand name of a bestselling Indian tea.

Chacha: literally 'father's younger brother'; respectful way of addressing a man belonging to one's father's generation.

Chai: sweet spiced brewed tea.

Chaiwalas: chai seller.

Chakra: literally 'wheel'; chakras in the body are focal points for receiving and transmitting cosmic energy.

Chitrahaar: literally 'garland of pictures'; this popular thirty-minute television programme features the latest songs from Hindi films.

Charpoy: literally 'four legs'; Indian rope bed.

Choli: short blouse that may be worn with a ghaghra or sari, leaving the midriff exposed.

Chunni: long scarf (2.5 metres) worn with a ghaghra or salwar-kamiz.

Congress Party: complete name The Indian National Congress; a major political party in India.

Daal: soupy lentil stew, a staple throughout India.

Daku: dacoit; bandit.

Devi: the Hindu divine mother, embodiment of all expressions of female energy. Devi has many manifestations propitiated on specific days for specific purposes.

Dhobi: washerman who does the laundry off-site.

Dhobi-ghat: the place, usually by the banks of a river or stream, where a dhobi does the laundry.

Dhoti: four-metre-long loincloth commonly worn by Indian men.

Dhruv Tara: the constant North Star.

Didi: elder sister; respectful way of addressing a woman your own age.

Diwali: festival of lights; the start of the new year for Indians.

Eve-teasing: euphemism for groping/sexual harassment of women in public.

Fenugreek: a bitter leafy vegetable whose seeds are used as a spice.

Ficus: a type of tree with aerial roots.

Ganga: another name for the Ganges river.

Gautam Buddha/Buddha: literally 'Awoken One'; spiritual teacher and founder of the Buddhist faith.

Gayatri Mantra – *Ohm Bhoor Bhuwah Swaha, Tat Savitur Varenyum, Bhargo Dewas Dhimahi, Dhiyo Yo Naha Prachodaya:* Highly revered mantra recorded in the *Rig Veda*, requests the blessing of enlightenment.

Ghaghra: skirt made with 8.25 metres of material.

Ghazal: poetic song that celebrates the pain of loss and the beauty of the struggle.

Gnostic: of or having mystical knowledge.

Gopal: another name for Krishna, the blue Hindu god of love.

Gulab jamun: deep-fried dumpling made from reduced milk soaked in sugar syrup.

Gundas: gangs of men and boys who indulge in Eve-teasing and unruly and destructive behaviour.

Gurdwara: holy temple for the Sikh community.

Guru Dutt: Indian film actor, director and producer. He ushered in the golden age of Indian cinema, always tackling social issues head-on.

Guru Nanak: the first of the ten divine teachers of the Sikh faith.

Hai: long sigh.

Halwa: any preparation that is made with a combination of carbo-hydrate, clarified butter, sugar and spices. Halwa can be made from semolina, flour, carrots, lentils etc.

Henna: a flowering plant. The dye made from its leaves is used to decorate palms during marriage ceremonies;.

Hijras: members of a third gender, neither men nor women. They refer to themselves linguistically as female and usually dress as women, though they never attempt to pass for women. Some hijras are eunuchs, and many consider only castrated men to be true hijras.

Hir-Ranja: tragic Muslim Jat couple who died for love.

Indigo: plant used for producing blue-black dye.

Ishvari Mata: a manifestation of Devi. She is pure reflection, she represents absolute freedom.

Jaggery: blocks of unrefined sugar.

Jai ho/Jai ho Devi, Devi jai ho: Hail/Hail to the Divine Mother, Divine Mother hail.

Jalebi: deep-fried sweet pastry doodle soaked in sugar syrup.

Kabari-man: the man who collects a household's recyclable rubbish.

Kali/Kali Mata: a manifestation of Devi. Her energy represents cosmic destructive power.

Kalidas: one of the greatest and most enlightened Indian literary personalities of all time.

Karma/Karmic: the Hindu law of cause and effect that governs the universe.

Kaurav: the hundred sons of the Kuru clan; in the epic tale of the *Mahabharata* they fought the five brothers from the Pandava clan.

Khadi: Indian hand-spun and hand-woven cotton cloth.

Koyal: bird from the cuckoo family, famous for its sweet song.

Kshatriyas: warrior caste, ranked just below the priest caste.

Kumari Mata: a manifestation of Devi. She represents valour. Harmony of thoughts, actions and feelings are guided by her energy.

Kurta/Kurta pyjama: long tunic worn with baggy pants.

Laddoo: sweets made with lentils, nuts and clarified butter.

Ladli: beloved.

Laila–Majnu: tragic Persian love story in which Majnu goes mad when he discovers that his beloved Laila is to be married to another man. The story appealed to the Indian psyche so much that it developed a local Indian 'twist'. The graves of the lovers are believed to be in Rajasthan and their gravesite has become a place for pilgrim for other desperate lovers.

Lakshmi/Lakshmi Mata: Indian goddess of wealth; a manifestation of Devi.

Lassi: a shake made with yogurt, water and spices or sugar.

Maharashtran: person from Maharashtra.

Mahavir: Indian sage and ascetic, contemporary of Buddha, who is the founder of the Jain faith.

Maheshvari Mata: a manifestation of Devi. She is the compassionate supreme ruler.

Mangalsutra: a necklace of black beads worn by brides as a visible sign of marriage.

Mantra: a sacred verbal arrangement repeated in prayer, meditation, or incantation to bring one closer to achieving enlightenment.

Masi: literally 'mother's sister', a respectful way of addressing a woman older than you.

Masterji: a respectful way of addressing a wise or knowledgeable man.

Mata/Mataji: literally 'mother', a respectful way of addressing a woman who could be your mother's age.

Mauwa fruit: almond-sized fruit of a large deciduous tree.

Maya: literally 'illusion'; the principal concept which manifests and governs the play of duality on the stage of the phenomenal universe.

Mela: fair.

Memsahib: mistress of the house.

Meri jaan: literally 'my life', a strong term of endearment.

Milkcake: solid block of reduced milk and sugar.

Mirrorwork: kind of embellishment created with fragments of mica or mirrors and embroidery.

Motor rickshaw: three-wheeled motor scooter that can carry two or
 three passengers.
Murdabad: literally 'death to'.
Namaste: Indian salutation, often accompanied by folded hands,
 acknowledging the divinity within the person being greeted.
Nani: maternal grandmother.
Neem: large tree of the mahogany family.
Netaji: leader, role-model.
Nizammudin Chisti: a famous Sufi saint of the Chisti order.
Ohm: the first divine cosmic sound, a very sacred symbol for Hindus.
Paan: see betel-leaf.
Pallav: loose end of the sari which is slung over the shoulder and
 often used to cover the head.
Panchayat: assembly of wise and respected village elders.
Parandis: hair extensions made of silk.
Paraya: literally 'the other'; outsider; not of the family.
Parryware: brand name of a leading commode manufacturer.
Petromax: brand of kerosene lamp.
Phenol: a strong-smelling cleaning fluid, also known as carbolic.
Policewalas: another term for police force.
Pooja: prayer.
Postmanji: a respectful way of addressing the postman.
Pukka: strong, made of brick.
Pundit: priest.
Puris/Puri bhaji: fried unleavened wholewheat bread served with a
 spicy vegetable preparation.
Pyaasa: 1957 blockbuster Indian film starring Guru Dutt.
Rajasthan nuclear weapon tests: in May 1998, India conducted five
 controversial underground nuclear tests in Rajasthan.
Rakhale: kept woman; whore.
Rangoli: literally 'coloured rows'; auspicious painting done with
 coloured powders especially on festival days.
Ravana: king of Lanka and chief villain of the Ramayana epic.
Red Bazaar: red-light district.
Rickshaw: three-wheeled bicycle taxi.
Rudali: literally 'crier'; professional mourner.

Sadhus: holy men committed to austerity and seclusion.

Sahib/Sahibji: respectful way of addressing a man of station.

Salwar-kurta: Punjabi dress consisting of pants and a tunic worn by both men and women.

Samsara: bondage to the endless cycle of life and death.

Sardar: head; chief; chieftain.

Shakuntala: the most beautiful of all apsaras.

Shiva: Hindu god of the holy trinity; god of dance, destruction and creation.

Sikh/Sikhanni: man/woman of the Sikh faith.

Sindhoor: red dust worn in parted hair as a visible sign of marriage.

Sudama: childhood friend of Krishna.

Sudras: the lowest caste, given undesirable tasks such as cleaning toilets.

Swaha: the offering of a gift or sacrifice to a deity, usually uttered when feeding the ritual fire with sacred offerings.

Swastika: meaning pure, auspicious. It is a sacred symbol of an equilateral, usually right-facing, cross with its arms bent at right angles.

Tamarind: sticky, extremely sour fruit from a tree of the same name. Widely used in Indian cooking.

Thali: tin plate.

Three-headed lion: The Indian national emblem adapted from the capital of iron pillars erected by pacifist Emperor Ashok (269–232 BC). The national emblem is an adaptation from the Lion Capital seal of Ashoka. In the original there are four lions, standing back to back, mounted on lotus, carrying reliefs of an elephant, a galloping horse, a bull and a lion separated by intervening wheels of Dharma Chakras. In the state emblem, adopted by the Government of India in 1950, only three lions are visible, the fourth being hidden from view.

Tilak: dot between the eyebrows of a man, placed as a blessing.

Tonga: horse-drawn cart.

Tongawala: driver of a horse-drawn cart.

Tulsi: sacred basil.

Turmeric: yellow rhizome commonly used as a spice in Indian cooking.

Uffo: mildly chiding as a mother might a young child. Somewhat equivalent to 'Come on now, don't be that way.'

Vaishnavi Mata: a manifestation of Devi. Her energy is that of sustenance, preservation, perfection and performance.

Varahi Mata: a manifestation of Devi. She is all consuming. Creation is digested by her to make the universe play in harmony.

Veda Asi: literally 'containing the Vedas'; vessel of all cosmic knowledge.

Vedas: Literally 'wisdom'; sacred Hindu texts written in ancient Sanskrit, the Vedas consist of four canonical sacred texts composed four thousand years ago, which contain sacred hymns and can be considered the technical manuals of Hindu philosophy. They cover diverse subjects including ritual, spirituality, mantras, warfare, performing arts and medicine. The Vedas were preserved and passed down through faithful recitation.

Vishnu: one of the three gods in the Hindu Trinity; Vishnu is the Preserver, the supreme being who pervades all time and space.

Vrindavan: a town in the Mathura district of Uttar Pradesh, North India. It is the site of an ancient forest where Lord Krishna spent his childhood.

Vyasia: working class; the second level in the Indian caste system.

Yamraj: collector of the dead, commonly depicted riding a bull.

Yogi: someone who practices a disciplined spiritual doctrine.

Zamindar/zamindari: land owner/land ownership.

Zindabad: literally 'Long live'.

Sources:
Bhagavad Gita text and translation by Annie Besant
Facets of Chandi-Nava Durga by Chaman Lal Raina

Acknowledgements

I owe special thanks to Nome Obermeyer, Katharine Houghton, Raj Sisodia, Indira Rai, and Barbara Johnson for their encouragement and advice, and to Douglas Peckham for his meticulous correction of grammatical lapses.

I also thank my early readers Hinke Zeick, Kiki Sandin, Teresa Segadelli, Denise Abe, Mariella Pilato, Sherri Dean, Michele Hollingsworth and Patricia Widayat for their wonderful support throughout the project, and Vikram Phillip for his wise and patient counsel.

Thanks, too, are due to everyone at Redink Agency who believed in the project and helped bring it to fruition, my wonderful and compassionate UK agent Diane Banks, and to all the folks at HarperCollins, in particular Clare Smith and Jeanette Perez. I could not have done it without you.

Finally, to Shaan and Tara, who kept life real, and Moti for being cheerfully present each morning.

'Good books, like good friends, are few and chosen; the more select, the more enjoyable.'

LOUISA MAY ALCOTT

'SOMETHING SPLENDID'

A Word from the Author

'LEARN THE TRUTH'

Things to Think About

'OPENED WITH EXPECTATION'

What to Read Next

BEHIND THE SCENES

'SOMETHING SPLENDID'

'I want to do something splendid . . . Something heroic or wonderful that won't be forgotten after I'm dead . . . I think I shall write books.' So said Louisa May Alcott on why she wanted to write. And yet the precise nature of the creative process is a mysterious one. What is it that inspires authors to put pen to paper: curiosity, sympathy, passion, obsession? In her own words, Dipika Rai reveals what inspired her to write *Someone Else's Garden* . . .

As children we travelled with my parents all through India in a trusty Ambassador car with a bedroll on the roof and boiled water in a sturdy steel thermos. Each time we reached our destination I collected a story. As I grew older, I realised that I was born into an extraordinary country where hundreds of inspiring and interesting things, worthy of recounting, took place on a daily basis. The eternal stories of the milkman, the ayah, the dhobi, of the neighbour, the landlord and the dacoit were all vignettes that kept me company throughout my life. I knew a time would come when I would have to explain to my children why India is the way it is. So, armed with enough material for several books, I started out to tell a good story and record my impressions of India.

On a deeper level, I also used *Someone Else's Garden* as a vehicle to examine Indian philosophy and values without compromising the authenticity of the day-to-day cruelty and hardship of living in the country. I chose to write a redemptive love story, because I could thoroughly explore the tension between all pairs of opposites – good and evil, love and hate, tradition and modernity, deification and rejection – in this context. I wanted to write a story that would impart a message of social conscious-ness and the need for people to change their attitudes regarding girls and women in India and elsewhere in the world, because I believe that cultures who do not honour their women are doomed to perish a slow and indi-gent death.

By the time *Someone Else's Garden* was completed, I realised something extraordinary: sharing Mamta's journey all these years had led to my own

emotional and spiritual awakening. I had somehow changed in the telling of her story. And I wished the same for my readers.

It is my hope that *Someone Else's Garden* will inspire a few people, question a few rules, and change a few beliefs.

'LEARN THE TRUTH'

..

'Do the things you know, and you shall learn the truth you need
to know.'
<div align="right">LOUISA MAY ALCOTT</div>

From Socrates to the salons of pre-Revolutionary France, the great minds
of every age have debated the merits of literary offerings alongside ques-
tions of politics, social order and morality. Whether you love a book or
loathe it, one of the pleasures of reading is the discussion books regu-
larly inspire. Below are a few suggestions for topics of discussion about
Someone Else's Garden . . .

▶ *Someone Else's Garden* is an epic Indian novel. Which genres do
you think it falls under and why?

▶ How has Lokend's character contributed to your understanding of
Indian philosophy?

▶ Lata Bai and Mamta: two generations of Indian women. What did
you know about the position of women in rural Indian society
before reading *Someone Else's Garden?* In what ways has this book
shaped your understanding of their experience?

▶ In chapter two, Singh Sahib muses to his late wife: 'One of our
sons gives away our lands while the other never tires of acquiring
more. And they both do it in the name of honour!' What is your
view on the relationship between the two brothers? And what do
you think about the wider conflict alluded to here, between love
and land?

▶ 'The slap damages her eardrum and sends her spinning to the
other end of the hut. The blow takes her by complete surprise . . .
Mamta runs her tongue along the inside of her mouth, and spits
out a piece of broken tooth. Her eyelid is torn.' After she marries,
Mamta is treated savagely by her husband. How successfully do
you think the author portrays Mamta's abuse, and her reaction
to it?

► 'Her first meeting had given her a false sense of security. But Lata Bai is the quintessential rural woman. As an individual she may be able to stand behind her daughter, but as a member of her ilk she can't.' Does the author successfully explain the cycle of violence against women that is sometimes sustained and reinforced by their own mothers, through Lata Bai's rejection of Mamta and her lover Lokend?

► Love, relationships, identity and redemption are all central themes of *Someone Else's Garden*. In what ways do you think these are tested as the novel progresses? Are there any other themes that in your view lie at the heart of this book?

► How significant is the character of Prem? What do you think he brings to the novel?

► What do you think the future holds for Rani?

► The phrase 'someone else's garden' appears throughout the book. What, for you, does this title symbolise and do you think it is a powerful one?

► *Someone Else's Garden* is divided into four parts – The Sky is for Dreaming, Monsoon Darkness, Love is a River, The Smell of Wet Earth. What do you think the author has achieved by structuring the novel in this way? Is this an effective technique?

'OPENED WITH EXPECTATION'

'That is a good book, it seems to me, which is opened with expectation and closed with profit.' LOUISA MAY ALCOTT

If you enjoyed *Someone Else's Garden* you might be interested in these other titles from Harper Press . . .

The Swimmer by ROMA TEARNE

Forty-three year old Ria is used to being alone. As a child, her life changed forever with the death of her beloved father and since then, she has struggled to find love. That is, until she discovers the swimmer. Ben is a young illegal immigrant from Sri Lanka who has arrived in Norfolk via Moscow. Awaiting a decision from the Home Office on his asylum application, he is discovered by Ria as he takes a daily swim in the river close to her house. He is twenty years her junior and theirs is an unconventional but deeply moving romance, defying both boundaries and cultures – and the xenophobic residents of Orford. That is, until tragedy occurs.

October 2010

The Lotus Eaters by TATJANA SOLI

As the fall of Saigon begins in 1975, two lovers make their way through the streets, desperately trying to catch one of the last planes out. Helen Adams, a photojournalist, must leave behind a war she has become addicted to and a devastated country she loves. Linh, her lover, must grapple with his own conflicting loyalties to the woman from whom he can't bear to be parted, and his country. Betrayal and self-sacrifice follows, echoing the pattern of their relationship over the war-torn years, beginning in the splendour of Angkor Wat, with jaded, cynical, larger-than-life war correspondent Sam Darrow, Helen's greatest love and fiercest competitor, driven by demons she can only hope to vanquish. Spurred on by the moral imperative of documenting the horror of war, of getting the truth out to an international audience, and the immense personal cost this carries, Sam and Helen's passionate and all-consuming love is tested to the limit. *January 2011*

Close Your Eyes by AMANDA EYRE WARD

The savage murder of eight-year-old Lauren's mother, and the sentencing of her father Izaan to life imprisonment for the murder, tears her world apart. As an adult, she can't understand why she has panic attacks, is unable to accept her boyfriend's marriage proposal, or listen to her brother Alex attempt to convince her of their father's innocence and wrongful imprisonment. Meanwhile, Sylvia Hall is running away from her loser boyfriend, determined to keep the baby he doesn't want. She knows that her best friend since childhood, Victoria, will help her – but Victoria has her own problems that threaten to consume her. All three women are connected by tragedy and betrayal: *Close Your Eyes* is a heart-breaking page-turner about what happens when a family is destroyed.

March 2011

Plague Child by PETER RANSLEY

September 1625: Plague cart driver, Matthew Kneave, is sent to pick up the corpse of a baby. Yet, on the way to the plague pit, he hears a cry – the baby is alive. A plague child himself, and now immune from the disease, Matthew decides to raise it as his own. Fifteen years on, Matthew's son Tom is apprenticed to a printer in the City. Somebody is interested in him and is keen to turn him into a gentleman. He is even given an education. But Tom is unaware that he has a benefactor and soon he discovers that someone else is determined to kill him.

The Civil War divides families, yet Tom is divided in himself. Devil or saint? Royalist or radicalist? He is at the bottom of the social ladder, yet soon finds himself within reach of a great estate – one which he must give up to be with the girl he loves. Set against the fervent political climate of the period, *Plague Child* is a remarkable story of discovery, identity and an England of the past.

April 2011

Visit www.harpercollins.co.uk for more information.